MADE TO LAST FOREVER

A Family. A House. A Nation.

Sharmin Fairbanks McKenny

This book was inspired by actual people, locations, and major events in the 17th century. Historical references, including those from the Dedham Town Records and other sources from the 1600s, have been used to inform the narrative. Any physical attributes, personalities, characteristics, thoughts, dialogue, or actions of individuals, and their relationship with the Fairbanks family, as well as many details of the events depicted, are fictional and the product of the author's imagination.

Copyright © 2025 Sharmin Fairbanks McKenny

Three Hearths LLC

Library of Congress Cataloging-in-Publication Data has been applied for.

ISBN 979-8-9988978-0-1
ISBN 979-8-9988978-1-8 (ebook)

Cover Art: Lance Jonathan Fairbanks. Made specifically for the cover of *Made to Last Forever: A Family. A House. A Nation.*

Cover Design: Tamian Wood, www.BeyondDesignBooks.com

Interior Design: Claudia Volkman, Creative Editorial Solutions

Dedication

In memory of Jonathan and Grace Fairbanks and their family, who built the oldest frame house still standing in this nation and whose lives, legacy, and enduring spirit—together with their descendants, friends, and townsmen—have shaped our lives and our nation. Their contributions are woven into the tapestry of our shared history. May this book serve as a lasting tribute to their remarkable impact and timeless influence.

"If history were taught in the form of stories, it would never be forgotten."

RUDYARD KIPLING

The Families
Some given names were changed slightly to avoid confusion.
Names are included only if relevant in this book.

Fairbanks Family of England to Massachusetts Bay Colony
Jonathan Fairbanks m., 1617 Grace Smith
John m., 1641 Sarah Fiske
George m., 1646 Mary Adams
Mary [Eliz.] m., 1644 1. Michael Metcalf Jr.
m., 1654 2. Christopher Smith
Jonas m., 1658 Lydia Prescott
Susan m., 1647 Ralph Daye
Jonathan [Jr.] m., 1649 Debra Shepard
Martha Pidge taken into the family c. 1646, m., 1659 Benjamin
Bullard
Samuel Bullen—indentured servant
Admitted into Dedham (1640)
Richard Wheeler—friend and in-law of Jonas
Admitted into Dedham (1646)
James Fales (Vales)—apprentice to George
Admitted into Dedham (1654)

Richard and Elizabeth Fairbanks
unknown relationship, Boston (1633)
Constance
Zacchaeus

Prescott Family of England to Massachusetts Bay Colony
John Prescott m., 1629 Mary Gawkroger Platts
Mary [Marie] m., 1648 Thomas Sawyer
Martha m., 1654 John Rugg
John m., 1668 Sarah Hayward
Sarah m., 1658 Richard Wheeler
Hannah m., 1660 John Rugg (after Martha's death)
Lydia m., 1658 Jonas Fairbanks
Jonathan m., 1670 DorothyHeald
Jonas m., 1672 Mary Loker

Cast of other characters found in back of book

PART I

1625–1633

TURMOIL IN ENGLAND 1625

Jonathan Fairbanks led his packtrain past a small family that had stepped off the narrowed section of the Great North Road out of London to let him pass. The father cradled a limp child in his arms. *She's about the age of my Mary Elizabeth,* thought Jonathan. Jonathan stared at the small girl with sunken eyes, a purplish-black welt on her neck and a scattered rash—she coughed weakly.

Jonathan instinctively raised his arm over his mouth and nose as he hurried the lead horse past the family. He plucked lavender and juniper out of his pocket and breathed in their protective essence. *Blessed be Grace for sending the herbs.* Jonathan shuddered as he looked back over his shoulder and scratched under his hat.

He squinted ahead to focus on the oncoming crowd filling the narrow trail as more travelers came north out of London on the chilly March day. What were they doing on the road? Didn't they know packtrains take precedence?

Jonathan, traveling two hundred miles to London's Blackwell Hall from Halifax, West Yorkshire, had stepped lightly on this trip. It was the first time the clothier had sent him to sell the West Yorkshire kersey, the thick wool cloth for heavy coats and military uniforms, at the most prestigious cloth market in England.

Jonathan grabbed the lead packhorse's tinkling bell and rang it, demanding deference from the unusual travelers ahead. They weren't the expected courtiers of the king or merchants. The approaching throng wearily pushed their handbarrows with small children sitting on bulging cloth bags to the side of the road. With desperation in their eyes, they called to the mangy, flea-bitten dogs that followed.

London

In London, the cobbled street should have been bustling, but only the sound of the constable's boot-steps echoed along the narrow alley between the hovels. In one hand he carried a rope-handled firkin filled with red paint, and in the other, a brush.

The constable winced as he watched the searcher rap sharply and persistently on the door five houses ahead. Her white staff denoted the danger of her task. The door opened a slit, letting the wails and screams from inside shatter the quiet of the street.

He hesitated until the searcher disappeared inside, then he wearily continued. His pail jostled in his trembling hand, and red paint splashed on the cobblestones like a trail of blood.

A rat scurried along the gutter between the houses and the street, the recess ripe with refuse and food scraps. At a sound from above, the constable, holding his hat, turned and ducked just in time to escape slop thrown from the second story. He shook his fist at the window.

The rodent kept pace with him until it disappeared into a hole under a wall. The constable paused and listened as it scratched a trail up the lime plaster, stopping at the thatched roof.

At the next door, he shook his head. *Another sign*. He set the bucket down and brushed a large red cross on the door and scrawled, "Lord Have Mercy on Us." He unfastened a lock from his belt and affixed it to the door latch. With white knuckles, he picked up the pail, shielding his nose and mouth from the reek of death and warding off fearsome evils coming from behind the door. He moved down the cobbles sadly.

Clopping hooves and rattling cartwheels drew near as the constable examined the next door. The cadence ceased. A horse and cart loaded with dead bodies had stopped at the door he had just painted, and the carriers entered the house.

The constable's shoulders sagged, but he continued his rounds. The hoofbeats fell more quickly. *By Gaw, the cart seems to be after me.* He shuddered, looking both ways. Where could he go? He stepped into the seething gutter as the cart passed.

Its pile of bodies would be deposited on the mounds of decaying corpses awaiting mass graves in the nearby churchyard.

Wayside Inn

Jonathan's steps slowed as he trudged toward an inn for the night, adjusting his tall black hat as the sun fell toward the horizon. Pulling his kersey cloak tighter against the cool dampness of the fading day, he looked back at his pack of short, stout Galway horses carrying panniers of kersey wool.

He followed the dim light to the wayside inn as the road became too dark to navigate. Before turning his horses over to the inn's stable hand, he glanced in the direction of the people pushing northward. "With all the travelers, is there a space to sleep?" he asked.

"The tavern keeper instructed me to turn them away." The attendant led another horse to the tie line.

Jonathan's train and their burden settled, he removed his hat and shrugged off his cloak as he ducked into the low doorway of the tavern, then scanned the dim room with piercing dark eyes. Train masters, no travelers. Running his fingers through his mound of dark hair, Jonathan recognized where each train master came from by the wool fabric of his clothes. Jonathan Fairbanks's kersey cloak designated him as a Yorkshireman, and his prominent nose and his clothes hanging gracefully on his medium frame gave him the distinguished look of a yeoman or gentry, though he hadn't achieved that status.

He motioned for an ale and sat with the men at a dark stained table. "Tell me, goodmen," said Jonathan, "are the lanes always clogged with people in this part of England?"

"Have you not heard? You're not from around here," jested a man.

"Nay, from the North, Halifax Parish of West Yorkshire," said Jonathan, looking around.

"We can tell by your brogue," one said, and the whole group laughed. Jonathan laughed with them.

"It was just announced that London is gripped with the plague," said one. "You have a place on the floor tonight only because this tavern keeper has turned away anyone coming from London. A mandate will be issued allowing no one to leave London and no one to take in those who have."

Jonathan cringed. *That's it. The child by the path.* He sat up suddenly and brought the herbs from his pocket to his nose. *It's happening again.* He rested his elbow on the table and propped his brow in his hand. He couldn't continue to Blackwell Hall in London. *I can't put my family in danger.*

Despite nightfall and the distance back to Sowerby, he had to leave. He placed both hands on the table and began to rise.

A town crier burst through the tavern door. Standing in the frame, he shouted, "King James is dead!"

Jonathan stopped, his body hovering over the bench, then stood abruptly, spilling his ale. "Has the king succumbed to the plague?"

"Nay," replied the crier. "Earlier, he left London for one of his summer palaces in Hertfordshire. He died of the flux."

"What will happen now?" called another fellow to an empty doorway. The crier had left to spread the news.

Phygill Croft

After four days of hard travel with his packtrain, Jonathan arrived home. Grande, a fawn-colored mastiff, bounded to the stone wall enclosing the yard of Jonathan's small gritstone house in Sowerby. The house was nestled on the face of one of the Pennine Hills near the confluence of the Rivers Calder and Ryburn. Jonathan turned aside as he opened the gate, so the massive dog couldn't jump up on his shoulders with its pancake paws. Jonathan squatted to pet the huge head of the drooling dog and scratched both ears. Looking at the tenter frames beside the house where wool cloth dried, Jonathan murmured into Grande's fur. "Ta. You've kept my family safe and guarded the kersey for me."

Grande shook her head, sending slobbers over Jonathan's woolen breeches. Woofing her greeting, she bounded for the door to let everyone know their master had returned.

Jonathan pushed violently on the heavy, oaken door, suddenly worrying he'd find the whole family stricken with the plague. His two oldest sons, John and George, sat at the trestle table, the Bible open between them. Three-year-old Mary Elizabeth sat on the floor with Champ, their brown-and-white-spotted English setter, who wriggled away from Mary Elizabeth's grasp to greet her master.

Grace, in a soiled apron, had turned with one-year-old Jonas on her hip. She wiped her furrowed forehead with the back of her hand, her wooden spoon dripping pottage on the baby. She dropped the spoon in the kettle hanging over the open coal fire and crossed the rug-covered stone floor, pushing at a stray light brown hair that escaped from her white cap.

"I would have your meal ready, if I had known you were coming," Grace said, not asking the question that was clear in her expression. Jonathan noted that her gray-green eyes were ringed with dark circles.

"Aye," said Jonathan, embracing his wife and enfolding Jonas. "I have news."

Grace started to turn away to finish preparing the meal, but Jonathan put his hand on her shoulder.

"Ne'er mind it, Grace. I'm home early to tell you the news. It will quell the hunger."

"Pray tell," Grace said, looking expectant. "What news do you bring?"

"King James is dead."

Grace recoiled. "Dead?" she gasped.

"The packtrain drivers are carrying the news. He was ill with flux and died since the last Lord's day."

"Will there be trouble?" Grace glanced nervously at the door. "Will the throne be contested? We haven't yet forgotten the Wars of the Roses."

"Nay, the traders say Parliament has called to Scotland for his son, Prince Charles, as successor. They named a Spanish bride for the new king to ease relations between England and Spain."

"King James was no friend of the godly. Wasn't it he who dubbed us Puritans?" Grace plopped Jonas down by Mary Elizabeth, and Champ licked the pottage from his face. "Will his son be any better? I can ask that, now that he's dead, can't I?"

Jonathan took her hands, "You can say it to me." He looked back at his older sons, paused, and looked intently at Grace's eyes, hoping she sensed his caution.

"King Charles will have to proclaim his favor for the Catholics or the Puritans, just as each monarch since King Henry VIII has before him."

As Grace turned toward the hearth, Jonathan took her shoulders, again turning her back toward him. "There's more."

Grace froze. The fear in Jonathan's face reflected in her eyes.

"There's a plague in London. People are leaving there and heading this way."

Grace buried her head in Jonathan's shoulder.

St. John the Baptist Church, Halifax

Jonathan and Grace plodded three tedious miles from Sowerby to push their way through the throng at Halifax's St. John the Baptist where they had been married eight years before. The crowd was so dense, they had to stand on their toes and strain to hear the parish's ceremonial pageantry of King James's funeral.

A well-dressed man looked furtively around the crowd as if avoiding someone. As the gentry filed out of the church, a small group gathered around him. He spoke in a low voice, so Jonathan and Grace edged to the outside of the circle to hear. "King Charles has brought Henrietta Maria, a Catholic bride of his own choosing, from France."

A collective, muted gasp emanated from the group.

"What does this mean, Jonathan?" Grace whispered.

"Hush, Grace." Jonathan had spotted a man in dark clothes, not from their region, edging toward the group, so he pulled her away abruptly and whispered, "We'll discuss this at home."

As they climbed the steep Pennine Hills toward home, Grace, nearly out of breath from the climb, scowled, asking, "How can King Charles rid the Anglican Church of Papist ways if he chose a Catholic bride?"

Jonathan remained quiet until they had trudged all the way back up the path to their small, rented house at Phygill Croft.

"The train masters say King Charles professes support for the Anglican Church," Jonathan explained once they were safely alone. "He holds himself divinely appointed and only second to God in governing the church and the country." Jonathan shook his head. "He can't be a Papist with that idea."

"What will we do if King Charles turns against the Puritans? Leave like the Separatists at Plymouth?" Grace pulled herself into Jonathan's arms and buried her head in his shoulder, then pulled away. "We vowed to live by the Bible, not the pomp and ceremony of the Papists," demanded Grace.

"Aye. We shall," Jonathan straightened. "We are far from London. For now, Halifax remains mostly Puritan."

Ring a Ring O'Rosies

John Fairbanks, the oldest son of Jonathan and Grace, twirled his brother Jonas around the room, barely missing the table board. He chanted:

Ring a ring o'rosies
A pocket full of posies
Atishoo! Atishoo!
We all fall down.

Then John plopped to the floor with the baby.

"John, stop that right now and put Jonas down!" Grace growled, then she was sorry, as she could see the hurt in John's eyes. At seven, he didn't often play with his little brother. But she continued her warning: "Do you want to bring evil to this family? Where did you hear that chant?"

"At school—the lads."

John's six-year-old brother, George, with a tousled head of brown hair and wide moss-green eyes, moved to John's side.

Grace's voice rose sharply, as it did on the rare occasions she talked to her children in anger or fear. "You are both forbidden to sing that song—not at home, not anywhere." Her jade eyes went gray.

The boys stood at attention, downcast.

Grace, to still herself from wringing her hands, picked up Jonas and bounced him on her hip.

"But why, Mother?" John looked up into her eyes. George slipped his hand into his brother's and moved closer to his side.

Grace paused and took a deep breath, releasing it slowly. "That is the song of the plague. The ring of roses are the circles that are found on the skin of those who suffer. Atishoo is for the sneezes of the sickness." She reached into her pocket and brought out some sprigs. "You know the herbs you carry in your pocket when you go to school? Those are the posies. They sweeten the air and dispel the smells that might cause ill humours." Grace jostled baby Jonas to calm herself, then added quietly, "Falling down means they are dying."

The boys gasped, looking at each other with welling eyes.

"The pestilence is in London, not here." she said soothingly, ruffling wide-eyed George's hair, trying to reassure him, as heat crawled up her neck and into her cheeks.

A pause of silence sealed the words.

"Posies, posies," chanted three-year-old Mary Elizabeth.

"See what you've done?" Grace stamped her foot, glaring at the boys.

Pestilence

Jonathan returned home from the sheep shearing in Northern Yorkshire one late afternoon in July. He brought the finer northern wool to the Halifax market for women of the parish to card, comb, and spin into threads. Then men wove it into the dense kersey cloth of West Yorkshire.

Grace was pulling a loaf of bread from the mound oven behind the house and carrying it on a long-handled wooden paddle when she spied Jonathan leading the horse up the lane, laden with wool for her to spin. His head hung low.

"Jonathan, you're home," she said. Her greeting startled him from his reveries.

"What's the matter?" she asked.

"The news continues to be troubling."

"King Charles?"

Jonathan took the paddle and bread from Grace and led her through the door, taking in the aroma of the freshly baked bread. "King Charles needs money to wage his nautical battles with Spain. Parliament doesn't like his high church, papist ways any more than we. They gave him only one year of funds—through ship tax—to support the wars.

"What's wrong with that? He got his funding." Grace had planted her hands on her hips.

"He expected a lifetime grant like former kings received. When Parliament openly challenged his papist tendencies, King Charles dismissed them." Jonathan put down the bread and threw up his hands. "Parliament is our only voice. Many in the House of Commons are Puritans."

"Can't they meet again later?"

"The outspoken members were sent to their areas to be sheriffs, so they can't sit in Parliament when it's recalled. Sir Richard Saltonstall, our representative, is now our sheriff of Wakefield. But that's not it, Grace." Jonathan shook his head.

"Pray tell, why are you so melancholy?"

"The plague. It has spread. It's expanded to many parishes across England."

Grace put her hands over her mouth, then looked back at the children sleeping on a ticking by the hearth. "Are we in danger?" she whispered.

"They don't know how it spreads. I return home from many places. I could be carrying it now." Jonathan shook his head. "This could be God's wrath for England's move toward papist ways."

"Certainly, we will be spared?" Grace looked to the sky. "We must pray."

The next morning Mary Elizabeth squirmed and kicked at the covers, her whining waking her brothers lying beside her on the straw mattress.

John, rubbing his eyes, got up and stumbled to his parents. "Come see, Mother. Mary Elizabeth's not well." His eyes welled with tears. "Does she have roses? Did I bring evil into our house?"

Grace and Jonathan shared a wary glance, and she hurried to the pallet. Jonathan threw his arm over his eyes and prayed before joining his family hovering over Mary Elizabeth.

Grace warned the boys away as she searched for the rings and rash of the plague. She found none but prepared infusions and plasters of ginger and cloves to draw out evils, in case.

Messenger

Heat rose from the earth in early August when a persistent rapping came from the open door of the Fairbankses' cottage. Grande lifted her massive tawny head from a shaded corner of the house, her tongue lolling out, and Champ stood bravely and yapped. Mary Elizabeth, still ill after days of fever, moaned a little and turned on the pallet in the kitchen.

The older boys came from their studies and crowded the doorframe, leaving little room for their father to talk with the stranger. The messenger handed a folded, sealed dispatch to Jonathan, who read the front: *Haste, post, haste. Deliver into the hands of Jonathan Fairbanks of Sowerby.* The seal was that of his family.

The messenger waited. The boys stood on tiptoes and craned their necks to peer at the folded paper.

"He waits," said Grace, looking toward the door as she held a spouted vessel to Mary's lips.

Jonathan looked up to see the messenger standing

expectantly. Jonathan reached for coins in his pocket and placed them in the man's palm. As the man turned away, Jonathan's gaze returned to the paper. As the courier started down the path, Jonathan raised his hand and called, "Ta."

Jonathan turned from the doorway and went to the small table by the ladder-back chair near the hearth. He sat and reached for his spectacles that lay beside the Bible and his clay pipe.

Grace motioned for the boys to go outside, but they lingered in the open doorway, frequently glancing toward their father.

Jonathan carefully slipped his knife under the seal. He hadn't heard from his family in Thornton-in-Craven in a long while, though it was only thirty miles away. He adjusted the spectacles halfway down his prominent nose and read the salutation first. It was from his elder half-brother, George, his father's second son by the first marriage.

My Dear Loving Cusen,
Our father has suddenly taken ill and is preparing to make his will. Father has called all his remaining sons to his bedside. You must come in haste.

Jonathan glanced at Mary Elizabeth, pale and limp on the pallet, then up at Grace. "It's my father. He's dying."

"He waited 'til he's dying?" Grace snapped and narrowed her eyes. "*Now* he wants to see you?"

Jonathan bent down to touch the burning hand of his only daughter. "It's nine hours to ride to Thornton-in-Craven," he murmured, afraid to say what they were both thinking. *How can I put my family at such a risk?* "I hate to leave, but my father has finally called for me."

"Must you go?" questioned Grace. She looked at Jonathan with hard eyes, then glanced at the other children. "What if your father has the plague?"

"I must go." Jonathan set his jaw and looked at the door. "Now."

In the inky night, Jonathan searched for George's house. He knew it set among those on the land their father and Jonathan's two older half-brothers had bought in the Hague of Thornton-in-Craven Parish.

A dim light seeped through the shuttered windows of a large gritstone house up the long path. Jonathan tied his horse and then tapped gently on the door, hoping not to disturb the whole household. Inside, dogs yapped as a male voice scolded them into silence.

When the door opened, the light coming from inside blinded Jonathan. A young man twice Jonathan's girth stood before him, disheveled from sleep. He smiled as he opened the door wider and said, "Jonathan! I have waited for you several nights."

Jonathan stepped closer, but the two did not embrace. "I only received the message this afternoon," he explained. "I came straight away."

"Aye, Father wrote his will yesterday. He was failing, and he passed away at sunset today."

Jonathan stepped into the house and removed his hat running his fingers through his hair. "Was he very ill or in pain?"

"Aye, but it went quickly," said George. "He had company at the Great Hague House"—he nodded toward the next hill up the road. "Father's wife's relatives from London brought their belongings and a dog to escape the plague. A few days later, Father fell ill."

"He made his will so shortly before he died?"

"His mind was clear. I was with him before he had it written.

Ellen wouldn't allow anyone with him when he professed, except witnesses and herself as executor."

Jonathan searched George's face. "Did he speak of me? Do you know of his last thoughts or wishes?" Jonathan's father had sent him away after his mother, the second wife, died, never to call him back after he remarried.

"Nay, he spoke only of the land he gave me. I'm sure he left land and such to John, the eldest son, he is not expected to come to the reading of the will. After I met with Father, he called in Michael and Jeremy, Ellen's boys. They did not take me into their confidence."

Jonathan, still standing at the entrance, looked down at the hat in his hands. He hardly remembered his own mother, Isabella, who died when he was very young.

"You know that both Father and John have had many land dealings, as have I. Many lands, Jonathan. Perhaps Father left you land in his will, even though you didn't arrive in time to speak with him."

Jonathan nodded and turned to leave.

"Nay, brother, you'll stay until daylight. There are too many thieves in the valleys, and the witches still practice rituals near here. Joyce will make up a bed for you . . . we have no children."

"Aye, I'll stay only the night," said Jonathan. "I'll need to see to my horse."

In the morning, as Jonathan fed the horse and prepared to leave, George asked, "Won't you see the widow? Or at least stay for the burial? It will be at St. Mary the Virgin in Thornton."

Jonathan spat his words: "Nay, Ellen has never welcomed me since Father married her. And Father had little interest in me once they wed. I was sent away to learn to make spinning wheels." Jonathan glared at his brother and tightened the girth strap. "I must go to my *family*. My daughter is ailing."

George backed away quickly.

As Jonathan started down the path, George called to his back, "Jonathan, your name was on the summons for the reading of Father's will in November." Jonathan didn't turn around. "You must come," George added. "Perhaps he left you land."

Father's Will

Jonathan removed his hat as he opened one side of the heavy double doors into the lawyer's office and held it open for Grace. The dignified man sat behind his desk reading papers. He acknowledged them with a nod.

At thirty-one, Jonathan resembled his late father. His jet-black hair was receding at the crown as his father's did at his age, and his dark piercing eyes and prominent stately nose were also traits of the Fairbanks family. Jonathan's mourning clothes were the fine quality befitting the clothier business. John Fairbanks, his father, was a yeoman, a man of land, but Jonathan's uncle, George Fairbanks of Sowerby, was a clothier like many in the family before him.

Jonathan led Grace into the room, cold this November morning, and gestured to the third of four empty benches facing the lawyer's heavily carved desk. The widow and current family of Jonathan's father would sit on the front rows, so the third must be theirs.

The lawyer lifted his head. "Ahem!" When Jonathan looked up, the man shooed them with his hand to the last row. Obediently and quietly, they slipped onto the back bench near the door.

Grace whispered, "If you get land, will you build the house you promised?"

"We must remember, Grace, I am not the oldest son," he answered. "John and George have already received land—before Father died. We can only hope the lands are vast enough that I will be endowed as well."

Grace nodded and smiled. Since they were away from the

children who always distracted them from serious conversation, Jonathan tried to explain more fully.

"My father has two more sons by his third wife, Ellen, and Father spoke with them before he died. Of course, they are younger than I . . ."

He reached for Grace's hands that were clasped quietly on her lap and gave them a squeeze. "I should have arrived at my father's bedside earlier. Then perhaps I'd know his mind, why he abandoned me."

Jonathan rubbed his chin as they waited. He nodded toward his younger half-brothers, Michael and Jeremy, as they entered. He whispered to Grace and took her hands, "There are the young sons." They passed without acknowledging him and took seats in the second row. George followed a few moments later and paused by Jonathan for a few quiet words before he took his seat with the younger men.

The lawyer looked at the door several times, reshuffling the papers, then finally tamped the papers into a neat pile and tapped his fingers on his desk. He rose, walked to the entry and opened the doors. "Ah, the Mistresses Fairbanks."

Ellen and her three handsome daughters made their entrance, and the lawyer led them to the front bench. Ellen passed Jonathan and Grace without looking their way. She stopped briefly at the second row to touch the hands of her sons and nod to George. The lawyer stopped at the first bench, opening his hand toward it. After filing in, Ellen looked straight ahead, but the youngest daughter's head twisted and bobbed as she looked around at those attending.

Jonathan glared at the empty bench between their last row and the family in the first two. *Father, though naming me in the will, has done nothing to shrink the distance between my family and me.*

"Ahem." The lawyer looked over the assembled family to see

if he had everyone's attention. "This is the reading of the last requests of Yeoman John Fairbanks of the Hague of Thornton-in-Craven, who wrote this will the fourth day of August, 1625, while of sound mind. He died and was buried at the church of St. Mary the Virgin in this town on the seventh." The lawyer waited to ensure there was no contest.

"Represented here today are the three families of John Fairbanks. Two children from his late wives and five from the dowager Ellen Parker Fairbanks," he nodded at widow Fairbanks. "John Fairbanks addressed each of these families in his will, which is to be read without dispute."

The room was a silent tomb, except for the shuffling of the youngest daughter's toes on the stone floor.

"One third of the estate is left to Ellen, the widow, as customary in the country of England under King James…uh, Charles." The lawyer reddened at his slip. The family members nodded as the widow looked around for approval.

The man regained his composure and stated the conditions of the widow's bequest, then shuffled the papers to a second grouping. "The sons George, Michael, and Jeremy have already been counseled. As their father instructed, they have been preferred lands prior to his death. They shall make no other claims against the estate."

The half-brothers in the second row nodded in acknowledgment of their inheritance.

Jonathan held his breath and waited.

Thoughts circled in his mind. *Was his deathbed my only chance to receive land?* He had not been named among the other sons. Land was the hallmark of a son's inheritance, the only way for a man like him to get land in England. It would elevate his station in life and in the eyes of God. He released Grace's hands and clenched his fists on his knees.

The lawyer paused and scanned the papers, then looked

straight at Jonathan as if something were amiss. In the pause, the younger brothers glanced back at Jonathan, then quickly away, before he could read their expressions. Dowager Fairbanks faced forward and waited.

"The next third portion of the estate John Fairbanks claims for use at his own discretion. From these monies, he wishes his granddaughter, Sarah Crook, of his late daughter, Anne, to be cared for. He also wills his wife, Ellen, to see to the upbringing and education of his young daughters, Marie, Susan, and Abigail. These three daughters are to receive £40 each when they reach twenty-one years." Ellen put her arms around her daughters and gave them a squeeze.

"The remaining third of the estate: the young daughters, Marie, Susan, and Abigail are to divide equally, amongst themselves"—he paused—"and Fairbanks's son Jonathan, by his second wife, Isabella Staincliffe Fairbanks."

Pressure built behind Jonathan's eyes, his jaw firmed, and his face heated up. He stared icily at the lawyer, who fidgeted with the last set of papers. *I have been treated as a young daughter, not as a grown son. I haven't even been given the forty pounds they were given.*

The younger half-brothers glanced back at Jonathan without meeting his eyes. The lawyer stacked and tamped the edges of the papers hard on the desk and placed them down firmly, indicating the finality of the reading.

Jonathan reached over and squeezed Grace's hand until her fingertips turned white, holding her hand as he held his seething emotions. *My father called me to the reading of his will to humiliate me in front of my family.*

The lawyer stood and walked to the front row. He helped the widow to her feet. She collected her daughters and moved toward the doors. The half-brothers followed, hats in hands, still avoiding eye contact with Jonathan.

Grace and Jonathan sat in the empty room. Grace nudged

him, but he didn't seem to notice. She nudged him again. Slowly Jonathan stood, taking Grace's hand as she rose, directing her to exit before him. When she was out of the way, he turned and kicked the support of the bench, sending it careening into the bench in front of it. Hat in hand, he passed the esquire standing at the door without as much as a nod.

Challenges

Jonathan and Grace bade their goodbyes to his half-brother, George, and his wife, Joyce, who had welcomed them in their travels. George hesitated at the awkward parting, finally saying, "W-wait a minute, Jonathan. Why don't you move your family to Thornton-in-Craven? I need help with all this land and buildings. You could move into a cottage. Rent free."

Jonathan strained to keep himself composed. "This is my concession for getting no land?" he hissed through his clenched teeth. "I can work the land I didn't receive?" He raised his chin and said, "I work for a clothier. I am away often on wool business. I have little time to work land or make improvements such as you would expect."

"You have growing sons—I have none. How old are John and George?"

"Seven and six."

"They're old enough to learn farmwork or be apprenticed."

Grace and Jonathan looked at each other. Jonathan's jaw set. "Grace and I want our sons to get a good education, not be sent to other families."

"The Earby Grammar School in the Parish of Thornton teaches Latin. The boys can attend school and work on the farms as well. You can help with improvements when you aren't traveling. Joyce will enjoy Grace's company, especially with the garden harvest."

"Thank you for your hospitality." Jonathan's nails dug into

his palms. "But this is just an indenture without a covenant." He turned away, as did Grace, and the door closed behind them.

Jonathan pushed his hat low on his head in disgust. Outside the dooryard, his stout horse awaited. Jonathan lifted Grace onto the horse as it stamped the ground. With white knuckles, Grace grabbed hold of the coarse mane, and the animal craned its head around, studying Grace with a large liquid black eye.

"You may ride until the path gets steep," said Jonathan, then turned away in seething silence.

After a distance, Grace broke the quiet between them. "Must you move the family again? This will be four times in eight years."

"The family grows. We need more space and money. Our lease in Sowerby will be up soon. You heard the will. I received no land and little more." There was a long pause. "If we pay no rent and the boys and I work for George, perhaps we can save money to buy land and build a house." Even as he said it, Jonathan knew those chances were slim.

"But Jonathan, what about the Pendle witches here? Even King James was afraid of them. Witches still hold rituals near your family's houses.

"The Pendle witches were hanged before we were married." Jonathan said dismissively.

Grace cowered as she searched the shadowy forbidding woods along the trail, looking for signs of evil.

Life or Death 1627

A weak cry broke the silence in Thornton-in-Craven in the late fall of 1627. The babe was not soft and pudgy like the rest of Grace's babes—translucent skin stretched over her delicate bones. Grace scrutinized every inch of the baby for witches' marks and looked out the glazed window toward the woods where the witches were known to gather. She shook the fear from her head and thought back over the months. Yes, this one came too early.

Grace's breasts grew large, hard, and painful. Fear clung to her because the baby would not suck. She gently coaxed its mouth to her nipple, but no cajoling made the tiny bow of a mouth latch on. "If you won't suck, my wee one, I cannot save you," Grace murmured, rolling her eyes up hard to keep the tears from flowing in front of the other children. *My breasts are sore and fevered, and only you can save me.* She thought to the babe in her arms. If Grace died, what would happen to the infant and to her brothers and sister? *Our family depends on you.* Grace pleaded silently followed by a prayer.

Grace harbored other fears. If she lost the child, she would be vulnerable to another pregnancy, and she had seen too many women succumb during childbirth when the babies came too close together.

In this new community, Jonathan might not be able to remarry quickly. Their children would be placed in other homes. Grace pounded her fist against her thigh. *We vowed we wouldn't let that happen.*

Desperate, Grace made a sugar teat from a small piece of cloth twisted and dipped in honey, then pushed it into the wee lass's mouth. The babe sucked at last. Grace resolved to express a bit of breast milk onto the sweetened teat for each feeding.

The next day, she left three-year-old Jonas in Mary Elizabeth's care and hustled the older boys to the Earby School while the baby slept in a cradle by the hearth. Despite her declining humours and strength, Grace methodically went through her daily tasks. While sweeping, she winced as her shin bumped the cradle. Not a squeak came from the bundle inside.

Suddenly, Grace was jolted from her weary fog. The babe's lips were blue, her limbs limp, her chest not rising. Grace tore at her apron strings and unwrapped the listless infant, tucking the delicate flesh under her shift against her own skin. She held the baby tight, as if her own heartbeat and warmth would be enough to bring the child to life, as they had sustained the child in her womb. Grace nudged the tiny head closer to her own heart and against her painful throbbing breast. She willed life to return. Grace croaked and crooned and prayed, "Don't go, don't go. Save yourself. Save me. Save the family."

Mary Elizabeth rushed to her mother's side, dragging little Jonas along. Grace hurriedly gave Mary another task further away in the room, but she drew Jonas to her to suck his thumb while he clung to her skirts. She wept quietly.

An almost imperceptible flutter moved across Grace's breast. A lightning bolt of pain grasped her nipple and clung to it with powerful suction. The painful hardness Grace had endured immediately released as both breasts flowed, one to the wee girl and the other over Grace's entire shift and down her skirt. The physical relief coursed deep into Grace's soul. She had never lost a child, nor faced her own death. This time both had shadowed her with every step.

Grace swaddled the infant in the cradle by the warm hearth and frequently fed her until the babe's cheeks were chubby, and she beamed with a toothless smile when Grace coddled her to the breast. She would live—they would call her Susan.

The country hadn't recovered from the plague—church services were still banned. Justices of the peace still closed taverns and forbade gatherings for feasts, wakes, games, and dancing.

After Jonathan lost his father, he did not attain any peace from his past. But Mary Elizabeth regained her health, after the threat of the plague.

Thankful the baby would live, the Fairbankses scheduled a private baptism at St. Mary the Virgin in Thornton on December 27.

Blacksmith for Sowerby

Jonathan led his horse over steep hills and desolate moors on the way home to the Hague in Thornton. Monotony overtook him on the long journey. Leading the bell-tinkling front horse, he mulled over what he had heard at the taverns. To ease his mind of the constant troubles of England and the new colony, he hummed the tunes of the traditional long sword dance of Yorkshire. In his mind he heard the cadence of the swords clashing and boots stomping, with the dancers connected with sword hilts and tips.

His heart thumped with exhilaration as he hopped over and turned under the lead rope of his horse, mimicking the dance.

Then his thoughts darkened. If the dancers were to part from the tradition of the steps, they would risk the cut of a sword. *Is this what I would be asking?* Would he change the flow of tradition, at the risk of peril? Would he not miss the comfort of the known, even if his homeland caused him anguish? *Dare I break tradition and take my family into the unknown?* Like in the dance, a misstep might bring forth perilous consequences.

The altitude and its weather, along with his dark musings, made Jonathan pull his cloak around him.

"Jonathan Fairbanks."

He heard a voice calling in the distance and his head jerked up. He recognized the Sowerby brogue and tipped his tall hat to the wayfarer, who stepped to the side to allow the packtrain to pass. He was glad he had stopped his solitary dance.

Then Jonathan recognized his old friend and slowed for the man to join him.

"I have been waiting for you to return," said the man.

"What is the trouble? You have come a long way."

"Aye," said the Sowerby man. "I am on other business, but I will go with you a while on this. I believe the Sowerby blacksmith was your friend."

"Aye, he is still. Is he well?"

"Nay, he was seriously injured when he was kicked when shoeing a horse. He won't be able to work for a long time. But we'll soon need to repair our harvest tools."

"Will you find a new blacksmith?"

"His family is an old family of Sowerby, like yours. They have beseeched the village not to entertain another blacksmith until they know how this fellow fares. The town can't wait."

"Aye, that is a dilemma," said Jonathan, rubbing his stubbly chin.

"You know our village, and you travel," said the man. "We are asking you to find a young, apprenticed blacksmith to come to Sowerby. We would entertain him and use him well until our own smith returns to work—or relinquishes his shop."

"What you ask requires a special man." Jonathan removed his hat and ran his fingers over his head. "Do you have anyone in mind?"

"We heard, by the traders, of a young man, John Prescott, apprenticing with his uncle in Wigan of Lancashire County. He is nearing his majority and the end of his apprenticeship. But the traders couldn't speak for the young man's intentions or character."

"I don't go to Lancashire often, for they deal in light wool and flax. This is shearing season in the north, and thus I go there to barter for wool."

"You must use blacksmiths on your travels, to shoe the packhorses."

"Aye. I will ask as I journey, but Wigan isn't on my circuit. I won't be near there until late summer. Can the town wait until then?"

"Sowerby can get by until harvest. Then we'll have to seek someone permanent if our blacksmith hasn't recovered. The townsfolk respect you, Fairbanks, and will rely on your judgement. Sowerby is depending on you."

Massachusetts Bay Company 1628

Weary from traveling in the autumn heat, Jonathan sat at a table under the low beams of the dim tavern, as far away from the hearth as possible. He leaned back in his chair, sipping his ale and mulling over his day's wool transactions.

A conversation droned among men at the other end of the table with their heads bent close together. Jonathan picked up bits and pieces with little interest.

"It is called the Massachusetts Bay Company. What kind of name is that?"

The spirited leader of the group continued. "They've named it after the Indians."

"The Indians? Why's that?" asked another.

The leader disregarded the comment. "Half of the stockholders and the board of the company are Puritans."

Jonathan sat up and placed his ale on the table. He recognized names mentioned. Mr. John Winthrop, a Puritan lawyer, was spokesman for the company. Jonathan had attended a conference at St. John the Baptist in Halifax where Mr. Francis Higginson, a Puritan minister, had preached. Jonathan pushed his mug toward the group and leaned forward into the discussion when they spoke of Sir Richard Saltonstall.

"A West Yorkshireman," Jonathan said, pounding his fist on the table in frustration. "His family is in Warley across the Calder River from Sowerby." The men looked at him and he continued. "He sat in Parliament until King Charles appointed him Justice of the Peace of West Yorkshire, so he couldn't return to Parliament when it reconvened."

"We all know Sir Saltonstall," said another. "He's the nephew of the Lord Mayor of London . . . active in the Merchant Adventurers, trading our wool to other countries. That's important."

Putting their heads closer together and lowering their

voices, the conversation turned to whether the Massachusetts Bay Company would be a means of escaping the new King's religious practices—out of sight and out of reach of the king and bishops in England.

Jonathan placed his elbow on the table and rubbed his forehead until a red welt appeared. *Can I afford to invest in a stock company and still have money to move and build in the new land?* Even if land were free, dared he risk his family on the sea for an uncertain opportunity? Grace would go if he demanded it, but she'd never been out of the parish. She'd be leaving family.

He rubbed his hands together restlessly. When he lifted his head to clear his thoughts, he saw a man in dark clothes watching them from the bar.

Prescott

In early fall, Jonathan Fairbanks arrived at Heptonstall's Cloth Hall on the border of West Yorkshire and Lancashire Counties, he realized he was as close as he would get to Wigan. *I must go there now,* he thought, *or let Sowerby down.*

Every breath was a puff of mist as Jonathan started early over the rough, craggy rocks and desolate moors of the Pennine Hills. Jonathan noticed his lead packhorse, who had a slightly deformed hind leg, limped as she climbed the Pennines. He examined her shoe and cleaned around the frog of her hoof.

"Steady, Lucky—the terrain will get easier. We'll soon be in the rolling land of Lancashire County." *I hope this blacksmith lad is good. I need this horse reshod before I return over those hills.* It took special skill to make a shoe to compensate for Lucky's crooked leg.

Jonathan approached the open door of the soot-covered blacksmith shop. Only a shard of daylight remained, but the forge blazed, illuminating a young man.

With long tongs, the smith carried a scythe from the shimmering coals of the forge and placed the glowing iron on the anvil. He looked up at his visitor, and Jonathan saw the young man's bronzed muscular body complimented his brown wavy hair tied back with a leather string. His sleeves were rolled up, and the front of his shirt gaped under his apron, showing a broad chest and a sheen of sweat.

When Jonathan didn't enter, the apprentice continued his work within a circle of flying sparks and the repeated ear-piercing ring of the blacksmith's hammer. The smith took a couple of precise blows. The iron hissed as he dunked the scythe in black water. He ran his thumb over the edge of the scythe before engaging Jonathan.

"Can I help you, good man?" He looked up with confident, ice blue eyes.

"Are you John Prescott, the apprentice?

"Aye—do I know you?"

"Nay, but I have a horse that needs a shoe tonight. I will travel over the Pennines on the morrow."

"It's late," said Prescott, tipping his head back to indicate the low sun outside.

Jonathan handed him the damaged horseshoe, and Prescott raised his brows as he examined it. "Aye, a special shoe. I must see the horse."

Jonathan smiled to himself that Prescott had accepted the task so late in the day. He left Lucky with the blacksmith.

When he returned, shadows of night were creeping out of the corners of the smithy, and Prescott had already nailed the shoe to the hoof. Lucky rubbed her forehead gently against Prescott's shoulder.

Jonathan scrutinized the shop in the dim forge light. The table Prescott worked from was neat and organized compared to what must be the master's portion of the shop. After Jonathan handed him an acceptable fee for the special work and extra for working late, Prescott meticulously entered the entire amount in a ledger.

Jonathan's eyebrows raised as Prescott recorded the extra money to the fee instead of pocketing it.

"Won't you come to the tavern with me, young man? My name is Jonathan Fairbanks."

"Pleased to meet you—call me John."

The locals at the tavern greeted the young blacksmith with friendly taunting. "You find any more burning wells, Prescott?"

John volleyed back, "Cooked a rabbit over one just this afternoon. I was too hungry for only a baked egg." The locals roared, then eyed the stranger who accompanied him.

As the two sat with their ale at a well-worn table away from others, Jonathan said, "Burning well?"

"There are wells you can set afire around Lancashire's coal fields, but I haven't baked a rabbit." He paused and smiled beneath his mustache that had enough curl to keep it neatly above his lip. "Yet."

"Are you from the Prescott family of Shevington, just north of here?"

"Aye, until my father died when I was about five. Then they sent me to apprentice with my uncle here in Wigan. I don't see my family much." Prescott looked down at his mug as if to find answers in the ale.

"I talked to the townsmen while you worked on that horseshoe. They say you have an education—and an exemplary reputation at field exercises on training days."

"I suppose I like to compete," replied John.

Jonathan found Prescott personable, witty, and skilled— not boasting. He seemed well-liked by the locals. With more conversation, Jonathan deduced the young man was an independent thinker who readily saw an opportunity for advancement and was willing to take risks. Jonathan admired that, considering his own apprehension about voyaging to New England. Satisfied with all of this, Jonathan made John Prescott an offer on behalf of Sowerby.

Prescott hesitated. "I can't give you an answer now. Can I send a message with the linen and wool traders? Or with the cattle herders going to the Halifax faire this fall?"

Fairbanks's brow knit against his will. "Nay, I must leave early in the morrow. After that, the job isn't assured. They need a man soon."

Before dawn the next morning, as Jonathan readied for his journey, he saw Prescott enter the stables at the inn. The smith went right to Lucky, presumably to inspect his work. When he looked up, he saw Jonathan and smiled.

"I hope you find the shoe to your satisfaction," he said.

"Aye," said Jonathan. "'Tis a fine job." Jonathan raised his eyebrows in anticipation of what he would say next.

"I appreciate your offer, Goodman Fairbanks, but I cannot accept."

Jonathan's brow furrowed. He remained silent.

"If your local smith recovers, I won't have a job ongoing. Even if he does not recover, I don't have the means to buy his business. Taking the job without any sure opportunity would delay my chance in another village."

Jonathan pinched his chin between his forefinger and thumb. He had told Grace he was saving money to buy land and build a house. Or it could be for passage to the New World. *But I like this young man. Is it God's will that I help him and Sowerby?* With some hesitation, he replied, "Perhaps I could covenant with you to buy the shop if it becomes available, then share your profits."

"That is more than I could ask, sir. I have no assurance I could repay you."

"I do this for Sowerby. They need a blacksmith now."

John Prescott bowed slightly, and Jonathan nodded. The deal was sealed. John would come later in the fall, before the Halifax faire.

What have I done? thought Jonathan a thousand times on the journey home. *I have herded myself into a narrow lane.*

Strained Relationships

Jonathan's wrath exploded on his return to Thornton when he discovered his half-brother George had pulled John and George from school several times to help with farm work while he was away. This strained to the breaking point the tenuous bond between the men.

"Your expectations are too taxing. My sons must have a good education. You knew I must travel for my work and took advantage." Jonathan stepped forward, closing the distance between them. "No amount of work we do will make up for lacking land such as you hold. But you have no sons—you couldn't understand."

Jonathan braced for a rebuttal, but when George remained stoically silent, he continued. "I must make my own opportunities to better myself and my family. I need to live a life which is worthy of the grace of my God."

"You Puritans . . . what's wrong with the Anglican Church as it is?" complained George. "You go every Sunday with us to St. Mary le Ghyll. Your daughter was christened in St. Mary The Virgin at Thornton. You come from a long line of ministers and church wardens in the Halifax Parish. Father was Church Warden of Sowerby back in 1601. What makes *you* so different?"

"We have discussed religion," Jonathan snarled, "We don't agree. Grace and I are considering going to New England to be amongst those who believe as we do." Jonathan looked around to see if Grace was nearby, for he had not shared this plan with her. "Every change in king or queen determines whether the Catholic or the Puritan will be persecuted. You know that—you have a priest's hole in your house!"

"That's not of my making," George interjected, afraid of its implications if anyone found out.

"With King Charles, we fear for our Puritan beliefs," Jonathan explained. "A corrupt practice of the faith is being imposed upon us. Even far from London, we are no longer immune to religious scrutiny."

"How can you go to a wilderness where no fields have been opened, just for religion? Religion won't feed your children. There are no markets, schools, or taverns there, you know. By Gaw, not even a wool trade." George raised his voice and wagged his finger. "You have only worked in the wool trade. You know nothing about farming, as you have shown here." He scoffed at his brother.

Jonathan stood firm, jaw and fists clenched, eyes dark and piercing.

"I've tried to help you," George raged on. "You live here rent free. But I can't help you if you leave, whether from Thornton or from England altogether. If you aren't staying, go now, so I can lease the cottage and get real help working the land."

Mary Gawkroger Platts

Jonathan walked past the small Brigg Chapel on the east end of Sowerby Bridge, where the River Calder and the Ryburn flowed together. To the west lay Briggbotham, whose name resounded in his mind. It was Uncle George's land, and his cousins would inherit it. *My Father had much more land,* he grumbled to himself, *and I received none.* Jonathan rubbed his brow. He had forfeited what he could have made working for George in Thornton, and he would soon have to pay for his sons to start their own apprenticeships. *I could easily become a beggar, like many others.* He trudged ahead west with his eyes cast down.

I won't let my family down. He raised his head and scanned the horizon. He had been apprenticed to a wheelwright before his work in wool, and he could make spinning wheels when not traveling for the clothier. This valley was ripe for that business. *Every cottage spins.*

Jonathan trudged up the hill to his uncle's one-acre lot and rental house—Phygill Croft. He shifted his stride to ease the blisters he was rubbing inside his new shoes.

Grace rose from her spinning as Jonathan entered, straightening her cap and wiping her brow with the tail of her apron. She greeted Jonathan with a sidling hug around her swollen belly.

Jonathan sank into a chair and eased off his shoes. Grace examined his new blisters and calluses, wrapping them in plasters and cool rags.

"We will soon have six children, my good husband," Grace said as she smoothed her skirts and apron over her bulging belly. Jonathan looked up from rubbing his feet and saw Grace's eyes were settled deep into dark circles with bags underneath. "Joyce helped me at Thornton, you know. She enjoyed our children . . ."

Jonathan stood gingerly and held Grace at arm's length, looking deep into her gray-green eyes. "Help for you would draw on our savings," he said.

Grace rarely asked for anything, but now she was standing firm. "Aye, but I have a cousin in the Platts who might help for a *small* wage."

"You have many cousins." Jonathan sat again and ministered to his blisters.

"Mary, Mary Gawkroger. She's of the Gawkroger family in the Platts."

"That's not far from the Fairbankses' Brockwell Estate."

Grace's face lit up, and she didn't even notice the bickering of the older boys who had just tumbled in the door.

"Aye," she said with a smile. "She's sixteen and not in service with anyone. I have always been fond of her."

Jonathan toyed with his clay pipe, trying to light it with an ember from the hearth. Grace returned to her stool at the spinning wheel, wiping her forearm over her brow.

Jonathan puffed some smoke from the pipe and said, "When will we eat?" After a few moments, he added, "You may inquire about Mary Gawkroger Platts."

Grace beamed over at him. He wondered, *What will I do to cover this new debt?* Grace did not know about his covenant with Prescott.

Two More for Dinner 1629

John Prescott's arrival as the blacksmith of Sowerby met the town's need and Jonathan's own. Both men had lost a parent when they were young, been apprenticed, and lost touch with their families.

Since he had encouraged Prescott to relocate to Sowerby, Jonathan felt responsible for him, though Prescott had reached his majority. So, Prescott became the younger brother Jonathan never had, despite his many half-brothers.

Jonathan invited the young man to dinners and family activities, never forgetting nor regretting his covenant to help him buy the blacksmith shop. Grace asked her cousin Mary to help with the chores on the days John came for dinner so that Mary might join them.

Prescott was laboring over glowing coals late one evening when he saw a figure in the doorway and recognized Jonathan's silhouette by his tall black hat. Prescott didn't pause, but carried the hot iron in long tongs, placed it in the exact center of the anvil, then motioned Jonathan into the shop.

"Prescott, I've heard more about the Massachusetts Bay Company. The traders say the Puritans bought out the commercial half of the Company. John Winthrop is heading it and has attained a charter from the king. A part of the charter was left out and as governor, Winthrop will be allowed more freedom than ever before to rule a colony," Jonathan blurted, even before exchanging greetings. "They are sending one of their board members, Mr. Francis Higginson, to New England on the first several ships. Sir Richard Saltonstall, one of the most respected men in West Yorkshire, will accompany Winthrop later."

Prescott began to hammer out the edge of the badly bent tool. Sparks flew with each beat. Prescott listened but kept his eyes on the glowing metal as he pummeled it with the sledgehammer. Jonathan had confided with him his interest in New England and the Massachusetts Bay Company.

Prescott didn't have strong religious reasons for leaving England, but his sense of adventure and the pamphlet Jonathan had given him, telling of ores found in the New World, intrigued him.

Jonathan brushed a few sparks off his doublet and said, "Mr. Higginson is looking for three hundred fifty Puritans to make the first voyage."

"Can they get that number?" asked Prescott, incredulous.

"Aye. They are so sure, they have set a departure for May. He is taking two men to assess the minerals and metals in their chartered area. Men are already working to produce iron in the Virginia Colony, John."

"What's your interest in iron, Jonathan?" Prescott dropped the hot blade into the water tub and steam filled the space between them. Prescott looked at his friend with narrowed eyes. "You don't seem to be an adventurous sort, but you always bring these stories of possibilities to me."

"You are a single man, interested in iron. There may be opportunities for you in the colonies."

"Aye, but I have only begun here and am gaining the town's trust." Then, with a playful cock of his head, he said, "Are you trying to get out of our covenant?"

"Never," Jonathan said, with his hand raised in assurance.

Prescott said quietly, "I may have found someone to take as my wife."

"Would it be Mary Gawkroger of the Platts?" Jonathan asked with a knowing smile.

The glow of the embers couldn't rival the burning redness of Prescott's ears, but he didn't divulge his secret. He changed the topic quickly. "Why aren't *you* going to the colony, Jonathan?"

"I must honor my covenant with you, and you can plainly see Grace's condition. I won't put her and the babe at risk on a voyage, especially on one of the first ships. What would I do with the other children there if I lost Grace?" Jonathan rubbed the back of his neck. "'Tis so dangerous, a man isn't even to take bred ewes or mares on the voyage."

Five-year-old Jonas panted as he ran to the open door of his home. Grande, the mastiff, loped behind him, nearly knocking him down. Between gasps, Jonas called, "Mary of the Platts is bringing treats for Prescott at the blacksmith shop. She says he doesn't have enough to eat with the crop failures this year."

Earlier that morning, Mary Gawkroger Platts ducked in the doorway of the blacksmith shop with a basket. "Oh, Jonas," she said when she saw him, "I would have brought you something if I had known you were here."

"Are you coming for supper in the morrow?" ask Jonas, as he ardently turned the grindstone for Prescott to press a blade against. Jonas delighted in the sparks flying like little shards of lightning scattering from the blade. "Mother said Goodman

Prescott is coming." Jonas had noticed that each time John Prescott came to dinner, Mary seemed to be there, too.

"Well, I don't know, Jonas. I *will* be helping your mother in the morrow." She looked at John while she ruffled Jonas's dark hair.

As Mary left the shop, Jonas stopped turning the grindstone and whispered to John, "She likes you."

Prescott smiled and said in an authoritarian voice, "Turn that grindstone, lad. We have work to do."

The Faire 1630

A cool breeze ushered in another fall, the sun lighting the earth from an angle. An early frost had abated a resurgence of the plague that had again haunted Halifax all summer. After a poor harvest, anticipation of the upcoming faire in Halifax lifted everyone's spirits.

Grace and Mary, who recently married Prescott, sang and told stories about the upcoming faire, the third largest in all of Yorkshire. In the spring, St. John the Baptist's Feast Day faire had been sullied with the looming plague, and they had attended only the local stalls for necessities, avoiding crowds. Grace had noticed from a distance a ceramic jug and had pined for it since. She hoped the vendor from Asia would return.

Jonathan called to Grace, "John and I are starting early. We'll meet John Rugg on the way. We're going to buy and share out a beef on the hoof from Lancashire."

Grace ran to catch his arm. "Do you have the lavender and sage in your pocket?" she asked anxiously. Jonathan pulled them out and waved them.

The women lagged behind, telling stories, singing, and managing the children, who herded the geese to be sold for the late September Michaelmas holiday.

They traveled the steep Pennine Hills, whose grasses were brown with an underlay of green moss and protected shoots.

Cushions of heather that had been flush with purples and pinks in summer, were bitten by frost and losing their luster. Only the Michaelmas daisies' tresses hung onto their colorful splendor and the green of life before the chill and dimming light starved them. Soon they would turn brown, followed by the nakedness of their yearly death.

The women talked about their Michaelmas preparations. The newlywed Mary Prescott was baking the bread and Grace, the blackberry tart.

"I hate to see the blackberry season end," she said.

Young Mary Elizabeth overheard and slowed, letting the geese waddle ahead. "Why can't we have blackberries after Michaelmas?"

Using this moment to rest, Mary Prescott put her hand in the small of her back and stretched, adjusting to her changing body as she expected their first babe, "St. Michael," she explained, "the Chief Archangel of the Divine Army, defeated the devil. When Satan fell out of heaven into a blackberry bush on Michaelmas Day, he cursed the fruit and spat on them."

"Bleh!" Mary Elizabeth screwed up her face and ran ahead to keep the geese out of the ditches as Grace and Mary laughed behind her.

The Farrar brothers caught up with the husbands ahead. They chatted about their work with Abraham Shaw's coal mining in Sowerby and Hipperholme.

Waves of bawdy laughter breezed back to the women as the men jostled each other. Grace pointed and smiled. "You can hardly tell the younger from the older men from behind." she observed.

The Gibbet

As Jonathan and the men approached Halifax along the higher ground from the west, he could see St. John the Baptist

Church presiding over the gritstone buildings enhanced with timber frame and plaster. Before turning down to Market Street, the men came to the gibbet with five worn stone steps to the platform. Jonathan winced as he looked at the edifice, imagining the blade raised in the tall frame, ready to lop off a wool thief's head.

Grace, Mary, and the children caught up with Jonathan and the men. They all paused at the gibbet before entering the main town before the men left to tag a steer.

Never failing, Jonathan cautioned his sons as he always did: "Remember Hell, Hull, and Halifax. May God deliver us from the three." He stood for a moment looking at the gibbet, letting the admonishment sink in. "Watch what you do, sons. Punishment is harsh."

John and George took off mimicking the run for Hebble Brook, a mile away. Everyone laughed, and Jonathan shared the story of one lucky wool thief who was reprieved from execution by crossing Hebble Brook to asylum outside Halifax Parish boundary.

Jonas, now six-and-a-half, hesitated just long enough for Prescott to teasingly snatch his knitted mons cap off his head. Jonas reached up to grab his hat, but his legs had carried him too far to retrieve it without going back. He kept running to catch his older brothers.

"Remember the head that landed in the old lady's basket as she went to market!" called Prescott with a smirk. "Can't you hear the bagpipes droning the dirge?" Prescott continued, loudly enough for the running boys to hear.

"The year before Jonas was born," Jonathan said, "a George Fairbanks—not my brother—this one was called Scroggin, he and his illegitimate daughter were beheaded. I didn't know him. The family motto is *Finem Respice*, live your life for the end. But I suppose that isn't enough to keep every Fairbanks honest."

They neared the village Market Crosse after securing the beef on hoof, glad to arrive at the faire after the strenuous walk, trying not to think of the greater uphill challenge going home. The Crosse Pub beckoned just across the lane.

"Let's get to market while we have the pick of the stalls," said Jonathan as he saw John Rugg eyeing the tavern.

Despite the summer's plague, throngs of people milled around. The vendors were calling out their wares; foreign merchants wore their distinctive, exotic clothes; and jugglers were tossing objects into the air as music played around them.

The boys had returned and ran to their father with outstretched hands. Silently, Jonathan pulled a few coins from his pocket and doled them out with a measure of warning about pickpockets. "John, you and George watch over Jonas." Jonas frowned and followed a few steps behind George.

Jonathan called after them, "Stay away from crowds." He pulled his herbs out of his pocket and put them to his nose. The men separated with plans to meet at the Market Crosse before going to the Crosse Pub, their last stop.

Black Lacquered Jug

The women set up their stall with the geese and wares. "I'll tend first, Grace," said Mary. "You leave Mary Elizabeth and Susan with me to watch the geese." She smiled and added, "Now get on with you."

Grace smiled and eyed her girls as a reminder to behave.

Unburdened by children, except for baby Jonathan Junior on her hip, she headed straight to the canopy where a proprietor stood in a silk embroidered shirt and trousers with a black braid, long mustache, and small goatee. He held his hands as if he were praying and bowed low. Unconsciously, Grace bowed forward with Junior. She remembered this man from the spring faire.

She sat Junior on the packed ground by her feet and gestured with her hands. She pretended to pour, then used her hands to indicate a height and diameter. The man smiled, bowed, and turned around. Almost disappearing as he bent into a tall basket in the back of his stall, he returned displaying a small black lacquer-coated clay jug adorned with flowers.

"Oh, they remind me of the Michaelmas daisies on the way to the faire," Grace chirped, taking the black-lacquered jug and holding it to her bosom. She tilted her face to the sky. *I've worked and saved all year for this.*

Grace didn't notice the lady standing next to her until she remarked, "You know those flowers are a sign of farewell, a coming to an end."

Grace eyed the stranger with suspicion. She bit the right side of her bottom lip and looked at the jug.

"But they are also protectors from darkness and evil," the lady continued.

Grace discreetly shook her shoulders with a slight chill, then looked down to assure Junior was all right. She nodded and watched the woman disappear into the crowd.

Handing the jug to the merchant, she tapped her hands together gently in front of her chest. This elicited a plea from Junior to be picked up. She bent to tussle his hair, reminding him he wasn't forgotten. Handing coins to the vendor, Grace beamed and bent over to lift Junior back to her hip. They both bowed to the small man as he dipped low to show his appreciation and respect, then handed her the jug.

Book Stall

Jonathan, drawn to the book stall, caressed the bindings and ran his thumb gently along the edges of the rag pages. Smelling the new print and the rubbed leather, he opened each carefully, not to crease the spine.

The seller finished with another well-dressed customer, then looked expectantly at him. Jonathan nodded and smiled, set the book down, turned, and walked away. A few steps later, he hesitated. Putting his hand in his pocket, he looked back longingly. He took off his tall hat and scratched a spot on his dark head. *I must save, but I might not have another chance to get one.* He glanced back again but continued walking away.

Jonathan stopped to admire the finely finished mazer bowls on display at the wood turner's stall. He was drawn to one in the center. He picked it up, admiring the rich walnut wood turned with a disk foot. It was decorated with a silver pattern around the sides and rim of the bowl. His great-great grandfather's brother had passed down to his family a mazer bowl made of walnut with a silver inlay—much like this one. He turned the bowl in his hands. Grace would cherish this. *We could pass it down in our family,* he mused. Unconsciously, Jonathan held the adorned bowl as if it were filled with ale, ready to offer it to his family.

Grace doesn't know I'm thinking of leaving, he thought with a pang. *She won't get to take her things.* This could be a token of their England home.

He felt the money in his pocket, then closed his fist around it, contemplating. A woman approached the bowl. Jonathan's hand shot out to it before he knew what he did, then peered at her. The woman reddened and veered to another piece.

Jonathan Fairbanks finished the transaction, thinking, *I'll keep this a secret and give it to Grace when the time is right.*

Omens

On her way home, Grace peeked into the basket on her arm. *Yes, my little jug will remind me of the Michaelmas daisies.*

Then her smile became tense. *What did that woman say?* Grace tried to erase it, but it kept creeping across her mind. *Farewell. Coming to an end.*

She straightened her back and looked ahead. *Very well, farewell to fall.* The tension melted a bit. The woman had also said the daisy meant protection from darkness and evil. Grace nodded resolutely.

The Crosse Pub

The men met at the Market Crosse, where the cacophony of the pub drew them in. Men from all over the parish and beyond had settled in for a mug of ale, despite the earlier plague.

Prescott, a towering man, led the others, his broad shoulders furrowing a clear pathway. The Farrar brothers left the group to greet Abraham Shaw from Northowram among the younger townsfolk. Jonathan tipped his hat to Abraham, now a friend since the Fairbanks family had spent two years in Shelf. He also nodded to the young Bearstow brothers from Beacon Hill in Halifax.

Minister Richard Denton sat on a bench at a long table, and Jonathan led Prescott and Rugg to the clergyman, who made room for two on the bench and pointed at a stool for Jonathan.

Prescott's mass dwarfed the small minister he sat beside, but Pastor Denton's presence could not be overshadowed. "Reverend Denton grew up in Warley, across the Calder River from Sowerby," Jonathan explained.

Jonathan asked the minister about the liturgical situation, and Denton's good eye shifted around the room before he spoke. They all knew faires brought all varieties, though Halifax Parish was mainly Puritan. He tilted his head toward the men.

"It appears Bishop Laud will become Archbishop of Canterbury soon. Archbishop Abbot's health continues to fail, possibly with remorse after that terrible death"—the archbishop had accidentally shot a fellow hunter with a crossbow. "Abbot has been the only deterrent to King Charles's moving toward a church of more ritual and ceremony. The king is waiting for Archbishop Abbot to die so he can elevate William Laud. He's already put Bishop Laud on the Privy Council in Abbot's place, an unprecedented move." Mr. Denton scowled. "It's rumored that when Laud becomes Archbishop, he will reinstitute the *Book of Common Prayer*, the reading of the *Book of Sports* during worship, and audits of all churches for upkeep and grandeur."

"If he requires that reading, will our Puritan ministers comply?" asked Fairbanks.

"Nay, as I will not. There's no place for sports on the Sabbath. He'll use that to root out Puritan ministers for persecution." Denton looked around again. "If Laud is appointed Archbishop of Canterbury, I must leave."

Fairbanks focused on the dregs of his ale. *Saltonstall is leaving, and now Denton.*

"Have you heard about Minister Francis Higginson from Leicester?" Denton continued. "Anyone thinking about going to Massachusetts Bay Colony should heed the letters he wrote home to his village. It won't be easy. Peace comes at a price, with personal toil and sacrifice."

He looked straight at Jonathan and said, "You know Higginson died in the colony just this August. Sir Richard Saltonstall returned with his daughters after founding Watertown. He said the climate was unbearable. However, his sons remained in New England."

"Things must get better," said Jonathan. "No matter the weather in New England, it is unbearable here—these two years of poor crops and the plagues after the arrival of King Charles and his elevation of Laud . . ."

Denton looked up as he watched a man in dark clothes enter the pub. With a nod toward the man, he began discussing the weather.

Jonathan added up in his mind what he needed for the

voyage to the New World and to provide for his family until he harvested a crop, built a house, and set up a business. *How can I tell Grace?* She wouldn't want to leave.

Jonathan stood abruptly, sending his stool screeching across the floor. He picked up his hat, excused himself, and hastened out the door.

Book Vendor

Jonathan glared at the Market Crosse as he hurried through the faire, wondering when they'd remove that papist symbol from their Puritan town. The faire vendors were closing shutters along the permanent Market Street, and some of the entertainers were enjoying a beer with their clown faces on and stilts by their sides. They merrily asked Jonathan to join them, but he raised his hand in a friendly, dismissive gesture and hurried on.

As he turned the corner, the bookseller was carefully packing the last of his books into a large basket.

"Goodman, might I trouble you at this late hour?" Jonathan called out.

The merchant turned with a frown, then recognized the man who had mulled over a purchase and now returned. He halted his packing and stood, putting his hand on his lower back to stretch.

"I believe I saw in your stall a pamphlet written by a Mr. Francis Higginson," Jonathan said.

"Ah, you are perceptive. That was indeed at the back of the stall where it would not attract attention." He stopped to study Jonathan. "You know such things don't please everyone. West Yorkshire is one of the few places I display it."

"No need to worry, good man. I would like to purchase a copy if I could."

"Let's see," the man said, pulling a couple of books from the basket. "It may be at the bottom." Then he grumbled, "It's too late to be taking all these books out again."

Jonathan shifted his eyes from basket to basket, hoping he'd find it soon. The merchant rummaged through a few and found a small, folded brochure.

"New World—sounds like a troubled place," he said as he smacked the folder down on the counter.

Jonathan took out coins and displayed them on his open palm for the bookseller to pick out the appropriate amount. Then Jonathan handed the seller an extra ha'penny for his trouble. He tipped his hat, turned, slapped the pamphlet against the palm of his hand, and strode off.

Before he reached the crowd of entertainers, he slid the brochure into his breast pocket. Now, the clown faces seemed sinister, for the dark-clothed man from the tavern had joined them. Jonathan hurried past.

Mr. Higginson's Pamphlet

Leaving the Crosse Pub, the men retrieved their steer and headed home. Jonathan patted his doublet pocket to feel the folded paper.

Though the fall evening was chill and full of shadows, Jonathan warmed from the climb to his house. He patted the pocket of his doublet again and glanced around to see that no one was watching, took it out, and opened it in the moonlight. His eyes couldn't focus in the dim light without his spectacles, so he stuck it back in his pocket, and quickened his pace.

As he climbed the last steps to his dooryard, Grande bound toward him, folds of skin flying around her great body with every leap. She jumped at Jonathan, but he stepped out of the way, and she thudded down on her huge paws.

Grande shook her massive head, flinging happy slobbers

over Jonathan's stockings and shoes. He scratched behind her right ear, and she followed him to the house, dutifully remaining outside.

Champ, the English setter, whined from the other side of the door. When Jonathan opened it, Champ wriggled around his legs, and he responded with a scratch at the root of her tail. Then she returned to her evening spot by the hearth.

Jonathan pulled his hat off to duck through the threshold, calling to Grace as he reached into his doublet. As he put his hand on the papers, he saw his wife and abruptly moved his hand as if to adjust his buttons.

The coal fire had dwindled to a pile of glowing embers, the children were now sleeping in the garret after their long day at the faire. Grace said she had saved some pottage and white bread from the faire for Jonathan. She stared at him, her eyes bright and her eyebrows raised, with her fists on her hips. She turned her head and let her eyes rove around the room. *What is this about?* he wondered.

"Jonathan, you must look more carefully at your castle."

He huffed at the thought of this small, rented hovel being his castle. But he took her meaning and looked high and low in a quick scan—he knew he had missed something.

"Aye, but the candles are low," he said, "and I did arrive late." He tilted his head by way of apology. *What have I done wrong? What am I missing?*

Grace stood planted before him.

He scanned the room again. "You must help me," he said.

Grace lifted the black lacquered jug from the mantel with both hands as if it would shatter at her mere touch. She handed it to Jonathan to examine.

"Isn't it exquisite?" She reached out to take it, lest Jonathan not treat it with the respect it deserved. "I used the money I saved from the eggs, eider feathers, and geese. Look at the painted flowers. They remind me of the Michaelmas daisies on the moor." She paused, then said, "They mean farewell."

Jonathan flinched imperceptibly. *Does she suspect I have thoughts of going to New England?*

She looked at her husband and added, "But they bring good luck in the coming darkness of the cold season."

The candles had burned to nubs, casting wavering shadows over the ceiling and walls. Grace looked tired.

"Go to bed, Grace," he said, without mentioning the jug. "I'll settle the fire and join you shortly."

"Don't forget to keep a few live coals for the morrow," she said as she replaced the jug on the mantel. "I don't want to have to borrow fire from the neighbors."

As soon as Grace's even wisps of breath indicated she was asleep, Jonathan settled his weary body by the fire, pulled a couple of candles close, and propped his spectacles partway down his nose. He pulled the pamphlet from the pocket of his doublet. It felt heavier now, as if it held an omen instead of an opportunity. A shiver quaked his shoulders. Mr. Denton had said that Higginson wrote this in 1629, now he was dead just a year later, leaving a wife and eight children in the Massachusetts Bay Colony.

This title read, *New England's Plantation, or a Short and True Description of the Commodities and Discommodities of that Country.*

Jonathan's fingers fumbled as he opened the brochure, eager to read about the voyage. *It's not here.* Jonathan turned over the close-printed page. *I need to find it.* What would he be asking of his family, putting them on a ship? *None of us swim.* He huffed at his own grim joke.

Fairbanks thumbed through the brochure. The exhaustion of the faire day was stealing his attention quickly as his body warmed and the light dimmed.

He found a page entitled "A Catalogue of Such Needful Things as Every Planter Doth or Ought to Provide to Go to New England." He tilted the brochure toward the waning candlelight.

The pamphlet read, "One set of armor complete." Why would he need armor? The Indians made a siege on Jamestown in 1622, but he'd heard of no problems recently. *I can't take Grace and the children into trouble. We're leaving trouble.*

Higginson said a man should bring to the new land tools for building and farming. *But I know nothing of building or farming.* But Prescott worked on farm tools, and his father and grandfather were farmers. Would he go?

A learned man, Higginson didn't mention books until an afterthought, listed amongst nets, hooks, lines, and cheese. *Those seem important. I can't go without books.*

Jonathan caught a glimpse of another section, where Higginson wrote, "There are no markets, fayres, pharmacies, butchers, or grocers. No taverns."

Jonathan rubbed his brow with regret. He looked up at the mantel where Grace's new lacquered jug sat. Suddenly he panicked. *Where's the mazer bowl?* He ran his splayed fingers through his hair, then sighed with relief. *I left it with my boys to bring home.*

The pamphlet dropped into his lap as he nodded off. When his head fell to the side, he awakened. He glanced back through the brochure and looked around the room until his eyes settled on the Bible. He went to it and thumbed to the Book of Exodus. He slipped the brochure in there, carefully slid the Bible back into its place of honor and turned to go to bed. He stopped, realizing the boys would study from it on the morrow. He removed the small pamphlet and looked at the other books. His eyes settled on Shakespeare's *The Tempest*.

Yes, that's where it belongs, with a play as foreboding as his feelings.

Night after night, Jonathan slipped the pamphlet out and read while the candles burned low. Removing his spectacles, pinching the bridge of his nose, and closing his eyes, he weighed his desires against his fears. One of those nights, he noticed a pile of candle nubs to be melted into new candles. Grace had said nothing about so many candles that he had burned. *I must share my plans soon.*

Jonathan wanted to be certain of his own mind and to have details planned out, to allay Grace's fears. But he couldn't quiet them all. The same fears traveled his spine, up behind his neck, and prickled at the crown of his head.

Jonathan read over and again what Higginson wrote—that one of the main reasons to go to the New World was to teach the Gospel to the Indians. That would create a bulwark against the Papists. *I'll leave that to the ministers*, Jonathan thought. But what could he tell Grace about the Indians?

"We starve in England," continued Mr. Higginson.

We spend so much labor and cost to acquire an acre or two of land. In New England, a man can have hundreds of acres. The earth is the Lord's Garden to be tilled and improved.…What warrant have we to take the land which hath been long possessed by other sons of Adam? That which is common to all is proper to none. The Indians have much land, they don't enclose it, raise cattle, nor stay in one place in a house. We should be able to live among them on their waste lands and woods. We should leave them their corn fields.

Jonathan put the pamphlet in his lap, tipped his head back, and smiled. *This is my answer. My Heavenly Father has given me land in New England. I can pass it down to my sons.*

Jonathan read on and winced at Higginson's next words.

"It's dangerous to go. Are we willing to see our wives and children through this?"

Am I doing this in the best interest of my family? Jonathan's fingers fidgeted with the corner of the pamphlet. He put his hand on his brow. At the end of each night's reading, he reflected on Higginson's first message. "We must trust in God."

Jonathan sighed and said very quietly, "Amen."

Another pair of candles guttered into their candlesticks. Jonathan folded the pamphlet, now falling apart in places. He placed it on his knee with his right hand over it and looked to the heavens. He was ready to talk with Grace.

The next morning, Jonathan woke before daylight. Grace slept in quiet such as she never knew in her busy days. Several times he reached to awaken her but restrained his eager hand. *We need to prepare*, he whispered in his thoughts as he willed her to awaken.

When breakfast was over, the older boys off to school, the younger children still asleep, Mary Elizabeth was sent to pick up walnuts. Jonathan came to Grace at the hearth. "I bought you something at the faire," he said.

Grace, startled, turned wide-eyed to find Jonathan behind her instead of preparing for his wool route.

Jonathan held a cloth-wrapped object.

"You don't buy me presents," Grace said, her hands folded on her chest.

He unwrapped it carefully, laying the wrapping on the partially cleared table, then ceremoniously held out the elegant mazer bowl.

"Oh, Jonathan, this is beautiful," Grace said as she took it in both hands. "Why did you buy this for me? It has seemed you have been more frugal of late."

"This bowl symbolizes trust and fidelity." Jonathan

recounted the story about the lairds and military leaders using the bowl as a symbol between them and their vassals—their fighting men. "If the men took a sip from the bowl after their laird, they pledged fidelity, and the laird in turn pledged that he would make decisions in the interest of his men and their land."

"But you know I trust you and will always be true to you." Grace searched Jonathan's face. "Our marriage is based on our trust and fidelity." She looked down at the finely finished walnut bowl, rubbing her fingertip gently around the silvered rim.

"My family, long ago, had mazer bowls they handed down through generations," said Jonathan.

"Is this . . . ?" Grace took in a deep breath, and her eyes brightened to a deep green.

"No, but this one will be special." Jonathan took Grace's forearms in his hands. "I am going to ask you to do something we'll both find difficult." Her face darkened in confusion as he said gently, "Pull the pot off the fire and come sit with me."

Grace's hands trembled as she moved the pot higher above the fire and followed him to their bed.

"You and I agree that we're desirous to worship according to the Bible and not like the Papists. King Charles is using Bishop William Laud to dictate how we practice our faith." He waited for Grace's assent, knowing it prudent to start with an agreement. Although it was his decision to make, it would be easier if she agreed.

"After we married, we have moved from place to place within Halifax Parish. We have always wanted a house of our own."

Grace nodded a little sadly.

"I can provide that now," he said, and Grace's face lit up; she took a deep breath but remained silent. "If we build here,

Grace, we will never leave. Should we not go where our lives and our beliefs can prosper?"

"Where? Away from family?" Grace began to stand, but Jonathan gently pulled her down beside him.

"Grace, George has no use for me if I am not helping him with the land I didn't inherit. If I use our money to buy a bit of land and build a house here, I will only have enough for our first son's inheritance. The others would live beholden to him, as I am beholden to George." Jonathan's eyes hardened; his jaw clenched. "In New England there is land to be had."

Seven-year-old Jonas sneaked down the ladder from the garret where he had hidden when the older boys left for school. He took a bite from the porridge still on Grace's spoon, then slipped into a dark corner when Grace's voice rose.

"But Jonathan, what about the girls? What about Mary Elizabeth? Who will she wed?"

"Don't you think it's a bit early to worry about marriage? Mary is only nine. By the time she learns to run a household, there will be many worthy men in New England."

"But what quality of families will go there, Jonathan?"

"The same as ours. The poor cannot afford to go, except those who indenture for the fare to cross the sea. I hear it is good to bring indentured servants to help settle." He hoped Grace would pick up on the last thought. He wondered if Prescott might be interested in going with them.

"But the rich won't go, either—they are too comfortable." Grace pulled a face of disdain.

"Do you think our Mary Elizabeth will marry a prince here? I have no dowry for that."

Jonas raced from his corner to grab a crust of bread from the table and then scurried to the door. He flung his arms up in exasperation. "Let her marry an Indian Chief like Pocahontas married an Englishman." Then he escaped out the door as Jonathan jumped up from the bed.

Jonathan stopped short, realizing the conversation with Grace outweighed discipline at this moment. "I'll deal with him later."

"Oh, Jonathan, what about the Indians?"

Jonathan wasn't ready for this discussion but realized there was no delaying it. He would have to include the children. "Where did Jonas hear about Pocahontas?"

"The older boys learned about the Indian people of the colonies in the Earby school." Grace looked at her fidgeting hands. "Poor young thing, Pocahontas was going back to her people when she died on our soil. Is that what will happen to our children?" Grace looked up into her husband's dark eyes. "Jonathan, is that what you would have us do?"

Preparations

"John," Jonathan said to the blacksmith as they walked along the moor out of earshot of others on the path. "I can't quiet my convictions any longer." He plucked at the taller weeds as they brushed against his hand.

"Aye, Jonathan. Even though you have said nothing, I suspected as much after the conversation with Minister Denton."

Jonathan cast a nervous glance around. "Last week in the southern part of Yorkshire, a Puritan minister was giving a sermon when Bishop Laud's men pulled him out of church and jailed him. Laud isn't even *officially* Archbishop of Canterbury." His ears and the nape of his neck burned with indignation. "With his *Book of Prayers*, soon we'll have no right to speak to our God in our own words."

"I know how important your religious beliefs are. You have good reasons to leave."

"Come with us? I know you have land and family in Lancashire, but we feel like you are family."

"My situation is different." Prescott shortened his strides and looked silently forward.

"You're right," said Jonathan. "My boys are of an age to help start in the new land. I need to move before they go out on their own. I want to get our feet on dry land and our plows in the dirt while grant land is offered.

"Another plague has vexed us. Heptonstall lost 107 people, all their clergy, and almost the whole village. I go to their Cloth Hall regularly on my circuit, and thus I put my family at risk. God has forsaken this place."

Prescott nodded but remained silent.

"John, I have one more problem." Jonathan stopped and looked directly at Prescott. "I won't be able to help buy the smithy if I go," He looked at his friend for a reaction. "I need what I have to start again."

Jonathan took off his tall hat and ran his fingers through his hair. "But what I could do is take you, Mary, and the wee one as indentured servants. I will make sure I can do that with my funds."

"I am beholden to you for your help here in Sowerby and this offer, but I won't enter a covenant of indenture or apprenticeship ever again. You could speak well of me to the neighbors before you leave, so my worth is not pinned to your presence. If I find it becomes unbearable here, perhaps I will come."

"But the land grants go to the ones who settle early. They need blacksmiths even more there."

"Fairbanks, I cannot go with you," Prescott replied bluntly.

Jonathan stopped at Prescott's emphatic response, for he had expected him to at least consider the offer.

"My wife is with child," Prescott explained. "My family left me at an early age, and I will not leave my family of my own desire to go with you, nor will I put them in danger while she is in this condition. You made the same decision when you considered going with Mr. Higginson."

"Then would you help me prepare tools and teach me what you know about farming?" Jonathan asked. "We live on rocky, barren hills. I know only wool and spinning wheels, not farming. I am going into a different world."

"I left the farm when I was little more than five. But I can help you with your tools."

"You are like a brother to me, John," Jonathan said. "Are you sure you won't come?"

Haunted, Grace prepared for the voyage, a two-month suspension above a watery grave just to arrive in a wilderness. She threw another garment into the trunk in agony that she couldn't talk to Jonathan, for he counted on her support. She needed to confide in another woman.

Grace threw another garment into the trunk when a knock came at the door. Mary Prescott stood holding a bundle of knitting, with two-year-old Marie straddling her hip, one leg upon Mary's well-rounded belly.

"Oh! I was just praying for someone to talk with!" Grace exclaimed and pulled Mary into the house. She plucked the toddler from her friend's arms, kissing the wee one's head and handing her to Mary Elizabeth. Grace poured Mary a cup of small ale before she emptied her heart.

"Jonathan brings Higginson's booklet out nightly. The boys like to pretend they are hunting in woods teeming with game, shooting into air blackened with birds, and fishing where it looks as if you can walk over the water on their backs. They giggle when Jonathan describes the Indians' clothing or lack of.

It's disgusting. The Indians are no better than the Scots. Maybe worse. They don't wear as many clothes."

"That's unsettling," said Mary. "Will you live amongst them?"

"Oh, Mary," said Grace, "I don't know. Jonathan won't talk about Indians to me. The pictures of Pocahontas dressed as a wealthy Englishwoman look exotic, but she was not so different from us. She embraced the faith."

"It sounds as if you will live near the natives."

Grace ignored this as she turned her back to Mary and made her shaking hands stir a pot. "The boys are looking at the voyage as an adventure. I'm already seasick."

"It can't be worse than the first months of pregnancy," quipped Mary, rubbing her belly.

"We need to take food and clothes for a year or more, they say. And Jonathan is talking of an indentured servant. Oh, Mary, won't you and John come?" Grace pleaded.

Mary rubbed her swollen belly. "New World—the very words are daunting,"

"I'm o'ertaken." Grace wiped the moisture off her hands with the hem of her apron and dabbed at the corners of her eyes. "I tell myself it's a chance to start anew. Aye, there will be problems, but these will be new problems. The troubles in England are insurmountable, or we wouldn't go. It has to be better, doesn't it?"

Mary held up the knitted items that Grace had barely noticed when she entered. "I know you don't have much room, but clothes are expensive. I knitted these mons caps for the boys."

"Oh, ta, Mary," said Grace as she reached for the colorful, woolen skull caps and held them to her cheek. "It sounds like the men will need them in the cold months."

"What will you do for other clothes?"

"As I do here," said Grace. "I'll take extra for Jonathan and myself. I'll make tucks and pleats to fit the children, then let them out as needed. The little ones will get hand-me-downs. I'll keep baby Jonathan in gowns. He'll get breeches when I have the cloth or old clothes to make them. Will you send me word of the latest fashions, even if I can't hope to keep up with the trends?"

Grace folded another pair of breeches and stuffed it into her cloth bag to take on the ship. How could they leave England as it awakened from winter slumber and the colors returned to the moors? But Jonathan was determined to go.

What kind of house can I expect there? She was determined not to live in a dome house as many described in their letters. *We had better have a house.* Grace stood and picked up one of Jonathan's books.

These books. So heavy and taking so much space. *What about my chests and my good dishes?* She threw another garment into the travel chest and *The Tempest* on top of it.

Grace assessed the space left. She would take her lacquered jug and mazer bowl, to be sure. *They'll remind me of home. I won't leave them behind.*

The words of the woman at the faire echoed in Grace's memory. It looked like their lives in England were coming to an end. Grace quaked with a sudden chill. Maybe she shouldn't take the jug. "But the daisies are protective from darkness and evil," she reminded herself aloud. *Oh, what are we doing?*

Grace looked down at Jonathan's books nestled in the corner of the travel chest, then at her jug and bowl. *These are staying with me.*

She filled the jug with grains to make it stronger against pressure and wound strips of cloth around it. She could use these for bandages and compresses.

Grace settled the jug into a nest of soft clothes in the mazer bowl, then put both in a cloth sack and stuffed that into her large canvas bag with the clothes for the family for after the voyage. *Other than my family, this will be the part of England I'll take with me.*

The Voyage

The Fairbanks lodged at the port inn during the last hot summer days preparing for their voyage. They had all undergone health examinations for the licenses to permit them to sail, and now Jonathan and the older boys had built the family's berth in the middle hold of the ship.

Nine-year-old Jonas burst through the inn door and shouted to his parents, "The ship with all the colors and the lion's head—is that ours?" Father raised his hand in affirmation, and John and George left Jonas behind as they scrambled out of the inn and plowed through the crowd to be the first to reach the ship. Jonathan followed calling them back, but they disappeared in the throng.

As the family caught up, John and George pointed at the boom swinging crates and barrels over the side onto the ship. Jonas arrived out of breath and was immediately mesmerized by the mechanics of loading, so he lost sight of the family. The ship was smaller than he expected, considering all the people waiting to board.

The crew hung from ropes to swab the rough sides of the ship with fresh tar, and Jonas's nose tingled with the acrid smell. The ship's company shouted at one another as they loaded supplies for the Massachusetts Bay Colony.

The crew ignored Jonas's incessant questions, but they eagerly called out to Jonas, telling him the consequences if the ship leaked despite the tar, if a tempest shredded their sails, or if pirates boarded the ship with knives to slit his throat.

A young man holding a bundle and guarding another at his feet searched the faces of the men boarding with their families. Jonathan saw him from a distance and called out, "Would you be Samuel Bullen?" He surmised the boy was about seventeen or eighteen years old, about two years older than his own John. But in the din of activity, the young man didn't seem to hear Jonathan's question.

Nearing the ship, Jonathan called out again, "Would you be Samuel Bullen?"

"Aye," replied the lad. "You must be Goodman Fairbanks from Sowerby."

"Do you have the papers?" asked Jonathan.

"Aye," the young man nodded, holding a paper for Jonathan to scrutinize.

"Then, young man, you have agreed to indenture for seven years in return for passage to the New World, lodging, food, and a suit of clothes at the end of our covenant."

"Aye. I figure the transaction will be complete in 1640."

Fairbanks was pleased with the deportment of this Samuel, for he would be responsible for the boy's actions as long as he was his indentured servant.

The men climbed the steep, swaying plank while water smacked the side of the ship. The boys carried their bundles at their chests to steady themselves and rushed up the incline while firing questions at the new boy.

As the men arrived on board, each was drawn to different curiosities and responsibilities. Jonas left the group to touch the white canvas sails rolled around long wooden poles, attached to an array of thick ropes. He pointed and looked back at the others when he spied another ship alongside being towed further down the river by a rowboat. Its sails were being hoisted up the stately masts as if she were a great bird unfurling her wings. The giant white squares caught the wind, flapping and billowing. Jonas's fingers glided along the heavy fabric on his own ship.

His mouth hung agape as he looked up at sailors monkeying up the masts to untangle ropes and set the sails. Others sang a cadence while tugging ropes through pulleys.

A young boy, a little older than Jonas, was dressed like the other seamen, working with the sailors on the ship. Jonas caught the young sailor's eye and smiled just as the young lad was ordered up the mast to untangle a twisted rope.

Mary Elizabeth carried the precious canvas bags as Grace balanced three-year-old Junior on her hip and held Susan's tiny hand. At the ship, they fell several paces behind the men. Grace occasionally glanced down at the bags to ensure Mary Elizabeth wasn't bumping them against the pilings. Grace lifted Susan's hand as she staggered on the gangway with every slap of a wave against the bulwark.

Old fish, ocean debris, briny air, and scared livestock assaulted their nostrils. As the waves licked against the ship, the calls of orders, creaking booms, screeching winches, and frenzy of goodbyes yelled to friends and family rattled about their heads.

The vessel lurched about, challenging the newcomers. Susan paled even before she stepped aboard. Grace rushed her to the rail, wondering if they were up to this journey.

Passengers looked at Susan, then at Grace, murmuring behind their palms, "How did that sickly little girl pass the health examinations?" They gave the Fairbanks women a wide berth as they passed. It could be the plague, dreaded pox, scarlet fever, or even dysentery.

The evening's late-summer breeze held freshness from the ocean, and the spray soon dampened their clothes and hair.

When Susan could move, they went below, hoping for more tolerable accommodations.

Jonathan overheard the captain say he was looking for a favorable wind to sail. Jonathan calculated again when they might arrive. *Perhaps we can plant a late garden*, he thought.

A sailor herded all the travelers down the ladder like livestock to the gun deck amidst the cannons, ever a symbol of another peril of the sea.

The next morning a cock crowed in its crate. Word came down into the hold that they would soon sail, and everyone gathered in prayer. They didn't pray in excitement for their departure but that they would arrive at the New World safely with good winds, no storms, and safe passage from pirates.

Grace gathered their perishable food, eggs, and fresh pork for breakfast and stood in line for her turn at the brazier nestled in sand on the 'tween deck. As long as the ship was stable, Grace could cook over the small burner.

The chickens that had not been secured the day before were taken to the top deck in their crates and settled in a shallop, a small one-sailed boat. Frightened chickens wouldn't lay and took up too much space in the family's stall. Yet they were necessary for survival in New England.

Susan hadn't slept during the night and refused to eat. On the rolling sea, everyone seemed to be stricken by an oceanic epidemic that swept through the hold. One by one they took turns supporting one another's heads over a chamber pot. Access to the top deck was strictly forbidden.

As soon as small groups of passengers were allowed on deck, Jonathan took Samuel and the boys to the top deck, where they held the rails in the aft to steady themselves. Jonathan pointed out the receding land on the horizon. "This may be your last glimpse of the Old Country." Jonathan's past blurred behind him as the boys turned and exclaimed over the deep blue expanse leading them to their future.

The children in the hold became restless. The Fairbanks boys brought out a rope to swing around near the floor for other children to jump over, but there wasn't enough room between the stalls and the chests to keep the rope circling smoothly.

John, George, and Samuel, the new servant, resorted to flipping small, sharp knives at each other's boots when Grace was not looking. Jonas was banned from the game after his first shot pegged George's boot.

Jonas sneaked off followed by Grande, his dog. He went to the hammocks at the aft of the hold where the sailors took turns sleeping when not on duty. The young sailor he had watched before was braiding a hemp rope. Jonas tried to imitate the boy's action with stray strands of hemp.

"Want to learn the ropes?" asked the young sailor. "I started sailing when I was about your age. I'm Thomas."

"I'm Jonas."

Other seamen took an interest in the inquisitive, energetic Fairbanks boy. Few passengers were allowed on top deck when the ship was in full sail, but occasionally, the sailors endeavored to sneak Jonas up to view the sea.

The white sheets billowed with the breezes, straining against the mast and ropes, snapping and shuddering in the winds. The fresh briny sea spray chafed Jonas's skin. *I will be a sailor someday,* he decided.

The sailors wouldn't let Jonas near the roped sides of the ship. They explained that since he was kept down in the hold most of the time, Jonas wouldn't have gotten his sea legs. One lurch would put him overboard. He had to hide when a passenger brought the bucket of chamber slop to heave overboard. The excrement and spew rode the salty breeze and found Jonas in his hidey hole. He pinched his nose and hoped he wouldn't be noticed.

There were no clerics aboard the ship, so in the evenings, Jonathan unwrapped the Fairbanks family Bible from its protective oilcloth. He was an eloquent reader, so the whole ship, even some sailors, gathered round.

The nights at sea weren't peaceful, with the sounds of the deckhands' calling orders and heavy footfalls close overhead interrupting the steady rhythm of the waves. On this vast sea, the passengers had little to do to occupy their time or their minds in the dark when they couldn't sleep.

The four boys tussled for their bit of space, cramping their legs between crates and lopping their limbs over each other like puppies in a pack. Mary and Susan slept with Grace on the hard cot that was softened only with a thin ticking. No one saw Jonathan sleep, for he put them to bed and then woke before they rose.

Tempest

On day twenty, the ship went still. No breeze wafted into the hold, and it was hard to breathe in the suffocating damp. The captain shouted orders to the crew to mend ropes and clean rigging.

A calm meant they would use precious food reserves while making no progress toward their new homes. They began rationing. Their anxiety was harder to endure than the rolling seasickness.

The lull was a sign of a tempest brewing in the distance. A chilling draft, rips of lightning, and cannons of thunder affirmed that a storm was rolling toward them on dark clouds.

Then the mountainous waves came. The ship was pushed high in the air, just to slide back into a trough as the flat hand of a wave slapped the deck. A flood of seawater rushed through the hatch before it was slammed shut and locked. But rushes of water still cascaded through the cracks in the ceiling and into the portholes. Grace grabbed her essential bags and gave them precious space on the cots.

The passengers were trapped in the 'tween deck with no light and just the thick, fetid air, unaware of what was happening above and unable to do anything about it. They had little time to think about their fate, though, as crates and boxes skidded across the floor and slammed into their feet and shins.

The travelers were bereft, uncertain, and ill-tempered. They couldn't escape the fulminating smells of sickness, excrement, and the restless livestock below. They couldn't escape the swearing sailors and men, the bickering youths, whining petulant children, and crying babies, nor the tuts and off-key croons of the mothers. They were locked in with troubling thoughts of what they had left behind, of the treacherous sea, and of their unpredictable future, amplified by their superstitions.

No one could sleep on the floor, though anyone not strapped into their cot was tossed to the floor. Fear and fatigue fueled arguments and accusations. With one mighty wave, the ship spun and skidded sideways off the heaving precipice, leaving them wondering if they would be permanently off course or plummeted into the depths of the sea, locked into a watery death. Prayers and goodbyes were issued across the hold.

Suddenly, another lull quieted the ship. They retrieved their belongings and took account of their families. Just as quickly, the boat heaved up and crashed down as if it were determined to smash itself into wreckage.

That night they called upon one sure thing—God. Jonathan Fairbanks opened the Bible and chose the appropriate passage. The words jumped riotously across the pages in the dim light, so he recited Psalm 46:1–3 by memory and called back the voyagers' will and fortitude to sail toward the godly life that was unattainable in England.

The next morning the sun shone through cracks in the wood. The boat swayed as gently as if nothing had happened. But everything was wet and disheveled. Grace turned all her thoughts to Susan. The frail lass continued to refuse food, and Grace made a sweet teat as she had when Susan was a fragile newborn. Now at five and half years old, this was the only sustenance Susan could keep down.

As Susan gained strength, Grace searched for something she could use to administer more liquids to the child. She rummaged through her large canvas bag, shuffling past the essentials and the precious items. Her eyes fell on the daisy jug with its small neck and spout.

Grace emptied the grain in the jug into a cloth and tied it securely, then poured the sweetened liquid into the small jug. Then she paused as the words of the woman at the faire echoed in her mind. The Michaelmas flowers symbolized farewell or a coming to an end. Grace held the jug away. She looked at Susan and then at the jug. But it also meant protection from darkness and evil. *What else can I do?*

Jonas's new friend was fond of Grande. One bright morning, for fun, they sneaked the burly mastiff to the top deck and hid from the captain's view behind the shallop. The busy crew didn't notice Grande until a beam knocked over a chicken crate that tumbled and unlatched its door.

Grande chased a hen to the side of the ship, where it took flight, and the dog's bear-sized paws skidded across the wet deck. As her hindquarters went over, her big, black, watery eyes pleaded for help as her foreclaws scratched deeply into the deck.

A nimble seaman caught her leash, but the dog was as big as he and pulled him toward their watery fate. Others ran to his aid and at last they were able to pull Grande on deck, grabbing her loose, tawny fur to ease the noose around her neck.

Grande lay still with her blank, watery eyes staring and her tongue lolling out. The sailors surrounded her, and Jonas, afraid of their wrath, hung back, wiping tears on his sleeve. When he couldn't wait any longer, he crept forward with the young sailor, Thomas.

In one swift movement, Grande rose to her feet and shook her heavy coat. Everyone laughed, even when Jonas slipped between their legs to hug his mastiff. At the first sign of abating gaiety, Jonas and Thomas hurried Grande down to the 'tween deck, keeping their heads down. No one questioned or reprimanded them, and Jonas was relieved that no one seemed to know what had transpired.

Jonas hugged Grande tight that night as they slept together on the floor under the hammock. For the first time, he began to think of what was to come and wondered what the New World held for him.

Land Ho!

Sunlight sifted through the cracks in the hull and around the covered portholes. The ceiling pounded with the footsteps of seamen rushing to hoist or furl sails in time to catch the best winds. The women folded the blankets they had draped around their shoulders during the cool damp morning, for the hold was now sweltering hot.

After eight weeks, the endless rocking and pitching had left the passengers disoriented. Fatigue and boredom had dulled their senses so they lost track of time and season. They knew only hot or cold, light or dark, or an exceptional change in weather.

One morning, the hatch banged open, and a piercing ray of sunlight blinded anyone in its beam. An almost inaudible cry of "Land Ho!" trickled into the hold from high on a mast. A thunderous roll rumbled across the upper deck as the seamen made the ship's preparations.

The boys in the hold heard the call first and bolted up the ladder to the bright opening, but the captain stood, arms akimbo, barring the exit. He called several hands to manage the exodus of the curious passengers who were hoping to get a glimpse of the thin green tinge that stretched across the horizon.

The men were allowed up first. As they stepped onto the open top deck, they reeled, grabbing hold of each other or of any steady object, their legs wobbling from disuse. The pitch of the top deck seemed different, somehow, and the ship's hands shoved them in various directions to safeguard the balance of the ship.

John, George, Jonas, and Samuel rushed out of the hold to join Jonathan as soon as they were allowed, excited to see the new land. The arduous voyage was forgotten, and they stretched their cramped legs that had grown longer during their eight weeks at sea. This was the adventure they had awaited. Out of a bank of clouds on the horizon, blue hills emerged from greening waters.

The women waited patiently, then a few brave souls popped their heads out of the hatch. An air of jubilation rushed down into the hold with the land breeze. Soon smells of grass, trees, and fish would waft down to Grace and Mary Elizabeth.

Pale, limp Susan didn't care where they were. "Just let me off this boat," she croaked.

Junior played with an iron ring attached to the hull next to the initials the older boys had carved there. Grace urged Mary Elizabeth to take her turn at the open hatch and bring back news of what she saw.

Mary Elizabeth bobbed her head out. Her nose twitched with the fresh air. She blinked as if she were a new pup just seeing the light of day. A hand clamped on her shoulder from behind, and Mary Elizabeth shrugged it off as she enjoyed her first sensations of their New World. Then she backed down the ladder to make room for the next woman.

The top deck was packed with male passengers, laughing and yelling congratulations. Dogs barked and the seamen brushed brusquely past in a well-choreographed dance of arrival.

Thomas ran to Jonas's side at the rail, proud to point out the dark green revealed by the parting mist. "See, where that looks like islands rising out of the water? Those are pine trees."

Before Jonas could respond, the young shipmate was called away. Jonas looked after him wistfully, then watched the islands of green grow through the mist. *This is where I belong*, he thought.

"Don't ye see we're busy bringing this ship in?" a seaman shouted at Jonas. "Ye don't want us to blow off course like yer Mayflower, do ya? There's plenty of rocks to get dashed on. Get ye down that ladder!"

The Fairbanks were the last to leave the prow. After weeks of only occasionally seeing the ocean, a great fish, sea turtle, or bird, now flocks of birds flew in the distance and schools of fish churned the waters. White sails dotted the water near the coast, lots of white sails.

Jonathan reached the hatch to find Grace standing by the ladder looking into the sky past the descending men. A rare tear trickled down her cheek.

Before Jonathan could reach Grace to see what caused her tear, the first mate approached and beaconed the men who had proven themselves leaders of the passengers. He spoke to them in a hush. The men pushed in to hear over the din of excitement and clattering on the 'tween deck.

"The harbor is *full* of ships," said the first mate. We won't be able to dock. Start rationing food and water as we are already low.

One man gasped, and Jonathan put his hand on the man's shoulder to warn him against alarming the rest of the passengers.

"Docking will be delayed," said the seaman.

The stillness of the ship was as treacherous as the rocking and rolling of the great waves in rough seas. Though their destination was in view, they could not move toward it. The stagnant air and sunbaked boards made the 'tween deck an oven.

Men complained about their ship duties. Women bickered over rations and their turns at the brazier. Babies fussed, and all the children, now like brothers and sisters, wrestled and fought.

To escape the strife, Jonathan went to the top deck to help the captain and seamen assemble the shallop to go ashore in Boston. They winched the boat into the green water that slapped the side of the ship. When they were almost ready to depart, the captain said, "Fairbanks, will you join us?" They would go ashore and bargain for a place to moor nearer the dock.

Once on the smaller vessel, he watched every move of the

seamen as they prepared to row and sail across the remaining expanse. *I'm a man of wool and land, not water.* Was this yet another skill he must learn? He cared not to see the sea again.

As Grace prepared to disembark with their meager belongings in the hold, she steadied herself on the 'tween deck after being moored for so long. She heard a commotion above as jubilant sailors answered orders from the wharf and dock workers greeted the sailors and shouted commands. A crowd beyond them murmured, anticipating the newcomers.

Grace envisioned people waiting excitedly for friends and relatives to arrive, hoping to receive letters from home, or expecting to retrieve long-awaited supplies, as Mary Prescott had promised.

Would someone from Sowerby, Halifax, or Heptonstall be waiting to greet them? Would Richard and Elizabeth Fairbanks be there? Grace slapped the fabric of her soiled travel skirt, thinking she would be disgraced to meet friends or family in her foul-smelling clothes. She looked around at the squalor. Getting fresh clothes out of the cloth bags seemed futile.

As the sounds of a crowd grew, Grace smiled at the memory back over the ocean, at the faire in Halifax. Everyone came. Everyone was happy.

Then she looked down at Susan's sunken eyes in her pale, gaunt face. Her thin translucent skin stretched over her bones. *Will there be a place for Susan to rest tonight?* The shouts of excitement on the top deck seemed to change to arguments and tussles.

A tear glided off Grace's nose onto Susan. Junior stood on the edge of the cot and patted his mother's cheek, then cupped her chin in his tiny hands and looked into her grey-green eyes.

The passengers stirred with excitement as they prepared to disembark, exchanging farewells with new friends who would go separate ways. Jonas looked around for his new friend Thomas. Susan just lay listless on the cot. Jonathan relayed his plans to his family in a quiet, stern, and precise voice. "George and Jonas, you see to the women." Handing John the master checklist of the family's cargo, he said, "John, you and Samuel watch the crates, barrels, and implements as they're unloaded. "I'll go ahead and find Cousin Richard to see if he can keep us for the night."

"I hope he and Elizabeth have room for us." Grace said. "Surely, they have arrived."

"It won't be easy to find a place to stay the night with so many from our ship and others seeking refuge," said Jonathan.

"What will we do if they don't?" asked Grace.

Jonathan ignored the question. "Where's my tall hat?" he asked. "I'm not going into town without it. There are men other than Yorkshiremen there."

Looking up and down at Jonathan's clothes, Grace said nothing, but she went to the trunk. Its lid, swollen from sea air, scratched and creaked as she pried it open. She removed Jonathan's carefully packed hat and ran her fingers around the brim to remove lint, then handed it to him.

On the dock in his hat, Jonathan asked local men if they knew Richard Fairbanks.

"Sure, everyone knows him," one man answered. "I think he came over on the *Griffin* with the ministers—John Cotton, Thomas Hooker, and Samuel Stone. Go down the road"—he waved his arm towards where most of the houses stood. "Ask anyone. He goes to the church."

Just a few minutes later, Jonathan knocked at the door of a small house near the commons of Boston. Richard came to the door when he saw his cousin. "Well, Jonathan. I didn't know you were coming." He looked behind him into the house and then said, "Did you come alone or bring your family?"

"Aye, the family. I have come to find a place for them for the night."

Many voices mingled within, and three weary travelers squeezed past the two men. "I have barely arrived and found a place to stay myself," said Richard.

"Do you know of other lodging?" asked Jonathan.

"Check with Samuel Cole. He just opened his inn."

"Ta," said Jonathan. "I'll see you when we settle."

"Fare thee well, Cousin."

It was late when Jonathan reached Samuel Cole's new inn. He found the house welcoming yet brimming with newly landed travelers. Cole welcomed him when he learned he was a Fairbanks. But finding Jonathan had eight more and one ill, he turned him away for want of floor space and fear of pestilence.

"Please direct me to a place for my family tonight," Jonathan pleaded, with his hat in hand.

"You'd best sail to Watertown up the Charles River," said Cole. This late, after so many ships have arrived, it'll be difficult to find quarters here. "Hire a shallop and sail the tide. You could reach Watertown tonight and might find lodging there."

"Ta," said Jonathan, tipping his hat as he wheeled on his heel toward another wharf. With great strides, he covered the distance to the private boats where he found a farmer ready to take his new shipment of English grain upriver. Jonathan told the boatman his intentions, not mentioning that Susan was ill.

The farmer had just enough room for the Fairbanks family, if some sat upon the cargo and the stronger boys helped sweep and pole the shallop through the narrows.

"I will wait only as long as the tide and winds are favorable," warned the farmer. "If you can't get them here before it turns, you will be left on the docks."

Fairbanks nodded, touched the brim of his hat, and made haste for the dock. *I must trust the Lord to find my family safe harbor tonight. Amen.*

Jonathan reached the main wharf as the crane lifted the last crates off. The ship bobbed and weaved on its ropes. He searched through the welcomers and passengers on the dock, gangway, and deck, looking for his family.

He went aboard the ship and caught a glimpse of John and Samuel among the crowd back on the wharf, so he hurried to find that John had warehoused their belongings after inventorying them. Jonathan beamed with pride, mingled with worry, for what could this firstborn inherit from a father who had nothing yet? Jonathan patted him on the back and completed the transaction with the dockhand. "John, you and Samuel find the family. Take them to the docks for the small boats and call out for Farmer Parker. We'll sail on his shallop to Watertown tonight, but we cannot miss the tide."

The two young men headed for the crowd that had disembarked. When they saw an opening, they pushed through to find George carrying Susan. She clung limply to his neck, her legs dangling over his arm.

When Grace saw John, her eyes implored him for good news from his father. John didn't reveal the plan but hurried them to the private boats to find Jonathan had just arrived.

Mary Elizabeth sighed at the sight of the shallop and looked at her father. "Another boat?"

Jonathan waved her toward the vessel. On wobbly legs, Mary Elizabeth stumbled into the arms of the boatman as she tried to board.

The farmer eyed the limp girl in George's arms and stared hard at Jonathan.

"Take Susan to the front of the boat, George," commanded Jonathan.

The farmer stepped back while George and Jonathan carried Susan aboard, staying as far away from them as possible.

The trip up the Charles River was peaceful and steady as they glided along with the tide. They used sweeps to row when the tide or wind wasn't enough, and they pushed the boat away from banks with poles.

Their route was lined with forests and periodic clearings where deer grazed, and fields where dark tree stumps smoldered. Small, private farm docks jutted out along the banks.

The Charles River flowed narrower and shallower as they arrived at Watertown. The banks were steep, but walkways and piers had been built to facilitate going ashore.

"Would you have room at your house for us tonight, Goodman Parker?" asked Jonathan.

Farmer Parker looked at George holding Susan and shook his head vigorously.

The light was dimming. Fairbanks looked around at the windows glowing atop the banks. "Is there an ordinary where we can stay?"

"Not yet. You'd think with this many people, someone would build one. But there is a young bachelor here that built a fine house. It's not big, but it's only him. That house is up this path. You can tell it by the long bench in front. Perhaps for some news from the Motherland and a few coins, he could be enticed to take visitors."

Grace looked between Jonathan and Goodman Parker. The farmer was already helping the older boys unload their meager belongings. He was eager to have them leave.

The family stood on the dock staring at the boatman as he

maneuvered the shallop away from the pier and up the river to his own home. The remaining daylight followed him.

PART II

1633–1637

WATERTOWN TO DEDHAM 1633

Awaking in the garret of the small Watertown house. Jonathan shook the shadows of night from his shoulders. *Praise the Lord.* Solid ground—no rocking, no slapping waves. No foul smells or coarse sailor talk.

Then he felt the onus of the unknown. *I have nothing.* No way to provide for his family, no one to give direction. Only a thatched roof over their heads, and that wasn't assured past morning. Jonathan looked over at little Susan. The brave front he had projected during the last eight weeks melted into mist in his eyes. His frail daughter was breathing quietly beside her mother. One thing was right.

Jonathan's whole body swayed when he stood, everything rose and fell after the months on the ocean waves. He pulled his breeches over his hose and shirt, put on the doublet he had wadded for a pillow, and smoothed his clothes with his hands. Picking up his shoes, he stepped gingerly over the bodies strewn over the rough board floor of the garret and climbed down a ladder to the main room. Young John Vahan was tugging on his doublet to do early chores. He pointed out a crock of lard, a sack of corn, a hand grinder, and a small array of utensils on his bachelor's hearth. "I am glad for a woman in the house this day," he said with a grin. "Your wife may use those to make our breakfast."

Jonathan climbed back into the garret to rouse Grace, who started until she remembered where she was. She pulled on her skirts and apron and pushed her light brown hair into her cap before climbing down. Jonathan pointed to the sacks and various vessels.

Grace ducked her head into the hearth made of rough-hewn logs covered with clay. She stirred the coals banked under a green backlog, then added kindling and small wood from beside the hearth to stoke a fast flame. She searched the rafters and fetched down a few scraggly dried herbs, onions, withered root vegetables, and found dried salt fish in a small barrel. Even this ill-equipped kitchen was better than cooking on a small, swaying brazier on the ship.

Jonathan took eight unsteady strides across the dirt floor of the only room and grabbed the bed frame to stabilize himself before he reached for the heavy oaken door. Outside, he lifted his hat and waved as neighbor men passed, already feeling a camaraderie with those who had also risked leaving England for this strange country. The men greeted him coolly with brief nods, though they greeted one another with enthusiasm. Jonathan scratched under his hat band.

A huge, strange bird with a white head and tail flew overhead. Jonathan watched in awe as it soared gracefully until it disappeared behind a thick copse. The Charles River was to one side of the road, and the huddled, steep thatched roofs of the village on the other. Wood smoke, not coal, curled from the chimneys. The solid houses comforted him as another wave of sea unsteadiness gripped him. Chimney sparks might start fires. The gritstone and slate roofs of West Yorkshire were safer. What other perils lurked here?

He took a deep breath. The fall fresh air tingled his throat as it inflated his stagnant lungs. He became aware of a foul odor and sniffed at his doublet neckline, then pulled it away with a grimace. He had been numbed by the stench on the ship and now awakened to his own foulness. He hastened to the well to wash.

As Jonathan finished his ablutions, a couple of swine with crude yokes around their necks waggled up the rutted dirt footpath. They rooted at the tender weeds under Vahan's split rail fence that protected the corn and squash. Jonathan pulled at an ear of corn and stripped down the husks. This must be Indian corn. He had much to learn.

A pig snuffled at the garden under the fence. Jonathon smacked it away, then grabbed a clod of dirt and hurled it, hitting the other pig on the rump. They ran a short distance, grunting in protest, then waddled aimlessly. One had a ring in his nose. They did not seem to be Vahan's, and protecting Vahan's property was the least he could do for the lodging. *May his hospitality hold 'til I find a place.*

"Goodman Fairbanks, thank you for moving those swine along," called out Vahan as he came in from chores. "Ears notched?"

"Lower left ear, two notches."

"Goodman Dudley's." Vahan grabbed a clod himself and hurled it in the direction of the pigs. "They travel the roads causing considerable havoc. Dudley will be called to court if the hog reeves catch them destroying gardens this year. We can't afford to feed his swine. Better the wolves get them."

"Why the yokes?"

"The yokes catch on the underbrush, so they don't wander into the woods where the wolves can kill them. Yokes also keep them out of properly fenced gardens." Vahan grasped the fence post and pushed it, showing it was secure.

Jonathan helped Goodman Vahan carry the long bench and two large log stools inside to add to the two chairs and trestle table. The young children would stand, but Grace, Mary, and the older boys needed to sit.

Various trenchers, spoons, knives, and mugs were laid on the table board to be shared. Grace ladled out a steaming pottage of ground corn with the herbs and fish she had found, filling the shallow wooden bowls. After the severely rationed fare on the extended voyage, this was a feast, even if unfamiliar to their palates. Jonathan offered to say the prayer as the children squirmed with hunger and excitement.

Grace tutted the children into submission as the men conversed about England.

Vahan drank in news from the homeland, saying Jonathan's report would be fare for community talk later. "I'll be able to hold Timothy Hawkins's ear for hours."

When Vahan's need for news was sated, Jonathan started his own inquisition, and Vahan, a talker, was happy to oblige. "The whole colony rejoices that we have found the English grains will produce crops," the young man beamed. "The tradesmen have ordered English farming implements, which will be dear until we have more smiths to produce and repair tools."

All the more need for John Prescott here. Jonathan thought.

"We can support more stock and these hordes of people if we produce more grain," said Vahan.

"Aye, we heard the English grains had proven viable here, so we brought what we could." Jonathan leaned back on two legs of his chair. "What we can't use, we'll sell and trade for things we need."

Jonathan saw Grace turn away from the conversation with a grimace. He suspected she regretted leaving her things behind to bring the grains, but they would assure the family's well-being for a while.

Vahan's eyes glimmered with opportunity. "By Gaw, Watertown is straited with settlers."

Jonathan could feel Grace cringe when Vahan took God's name in vain.

"We are the largest of the plantations, with a hundred families," Vahan said with disdain. "Like you, they keep coming steadily. All the plantations are complaining. Newtowne has approached the General Court about getting relief from new settlers."

No wonder Jonathan had been given such a cool reception. He had brought yet another family to the overcrowded plantation.

"At this rate, there'll be no land for the heirs," Vahan continued. "The early settlers received enough land to give to second and third sons."

Jonathan slumped back in his chair. "I have four sons, and I'm already disdained as a new settler."

"I wasn't a first son in England," Vahan said, waving his hand dismissively. "No land there for me. But no matter. I have no wife." His gaze slid toward eleven-year-old Mary Elizabeth. Grace glared at the man, and Jonathan determined to remove his family as soon as possible.

"Some say they laid out the plantations too close together," Vahan continued. "The land grants aren't large enough to provide for our growing herds of cattle, so Watertown is sending herdsmen with their cattle northwest of here. They're calling it Sudbury."

John, the eldest, listened intently while the other boys squirmed at the table. Mary Elizabeth snapped Junior's ear to quiet him as he sat on her lap. When he squealed, she put her hand over his mouth. Grace fed Susan small bits of watered-down pottage.

"Who builds your houses?" Jonathan asked, changing the subject as he looked around the room.

"We do. We help each other. Most of the craftsmen stay in Boston where there's money."

Jonathan nodded. *I'll have to find someone to build a big, sturdy house for my family.*

"You're almost too late. There are already rumors of closing Watertown to new settlers. Townsmen are talking of leaving to start new plantations, even without the General Court's permission. The governor warns against leaving. He thinks if we spread out it will encourage Indian attacks."

Jonathan caught Grace glaring at him, so he changed the subject.

Trucking House

After the meal, Jonathan walked the dusty path over clumps of grass vying for strongholds where feet had not often trodden. He kicked at chickens that continued to peck the ground even after he was upon them. He tipped his tall hat to women and children working in the fenced gardens and fought back some anxiety. They had few supplies after the extended voyage, and it was too late to put in a fall garden. Settlers had died of starvation their first year in the colonies. He rubbed his fingers under his hat band.

Jonathan passed a common pasture of grazing cattle. *Ah well, I didn't bring cattle.* Vahan had said there was no fresh milk in winter, that the stored cheese and butter must last until the wet cattle freshened after calving. He wondered where he could buy cheese and butter.

An older man sat on a stump outside a house sharpening a hoe with a rusty file.

Jonathan doffed his hat. "Good morrow, my good man. Could you please direct me to the trading house?"

The man grinned, showing only a few teeth. "You must be new. We call it a trucking house."

"Ta. Just arrived last night."

The old one pushed himself up with his arms and hobbled headfirst, shoulders stooped, to the fence. "You heard of Trader Oldham, have you?"

"No, just looking for the tra...trucking house."

"Oldham seems a good man around here, but they booted

him from Plymouth. They called him 'Mad Jack." The old man put a foot on the lower rail of the fence.

Jonathan nodded, patiently waiting for his answer.

"No one sees the trader much outside the trucking house. He and his wife live by the river. He has two young nephews that visit. They come into church regular." The old man leaned on the fence. "They say if it wasn't for his trucking house, the Indians would go to every door—with their strawberries in spring, corn in fall, and venison in winter. The women folk don't like that much. Heh-heh."

"Could you tell me where to find the trucking house? I need to stock up for my family."

The old man's face clouded. "We already have too many people here." He started tottering back to his stump. "It's on the west edge of town. Keeps the Indians out."

At the trucking house, Jonathan found a young assistant with a thin, ruddy, pock-marked face tending the goods. The boy, about the age of Jonas, talked fast, as if he had not talked with anyone in a long time.

"My uncle is the trader for Watertown," the boy said, pointing at the painted sign outside the door that read John Oldham, Trader. "He's pretty good with the Indians. He's out west with Minister Hooker and a few others. He followed the Indian trail all the way to the Great River Valley." The boy pulled some products off a crude shelf and straightened to his full height. "Uncle says I can go help trade with the Indians one day."

Fairbanks gave up on getting information there and gathered his few supplies. Passing through town, he had seen no empty houses. *Where are we to live? The colony won't let people leave, and the settlers don't want newcomers to stay.*

Returning to the house, Jonathan found Vahan talking amiably with Grace. *I'll speak with him now*, he thought, *before he tires of the children and dogs.*

After a few minutes of conversation, Jonathan guaranteed that Grace and the girls would do the housekeeping, washing, mending, garden harvest, preserving, and planting. Likewise, the older boys and Samuel, the servant, would help with chores, clearing land, and tillage. Jonathan would help when not on family business.

"It'll be mighty nice having women around." Vahan smiled, with a nod toward Grace and Mary Elizabeth stirring a couple of pots and checking the bread baking under an overturned kettle near the fire. "I'm often out with my friend, Timothy Hawkins. You and the goodwife can use my bed. I'll use a straw ticking on the floor by the hearth with Samuel when I'm here."

The next morning, frost nipped the air, warning of an early freeze. Grace warmed leftovers for breakfast. Everyone already knew their place at the trestle table.

"What would you say if we finished the wattle and daub behind the clapboards before the hard freeze?" Jonathan asked Vahan. "It will keep us all warmer this winter."

"Sounds like work for the ladies and your young men," Vahan said with a smile as he finished and pulled on his doublet to leave.

"Grace, you manage the work of Samuel and the children," said Jonathan. "Since we will be here a while, John and I will hire a boat to Boston to get necessities from storage."

The few trees in town and the dense copse on the hills were turning gold, red, and brown. The morning air was crisp, and the sun dropped behind the hills earlier in the evening. John Vahan's garden was bare, except for the bent and trampled brown plants that had provided the season's bounty, now covered by a skiff of snow.

Inside John Vahan's house, Grace presided over a meal of bread and pottage. Vahan surprised them with his arrival. He smacked his lips and sniffed at the aroma of bread baking. Then he sat with a grin in the chair next to Jonathan.

"Any luck finding a place?" Vahan asked Jonathan around a big wad of bread he'd ripped off his portion. "Hope not—I enjoy having women here." He looked up at Grace, winked at Mary Elizabeth, then dived into the trencher before him.

Jonathan cleared his throat loudly with a stern stare at Vahan and said, "No luck. The men who will stay in the Great River Valley over winter left their wives in Watertown. Seems the General Court's rule about leaving is keeping them here."

"You know you can stay here this winter," said Vahan, hesitating as he looked up at Jonathan.

"Aye, we have a covenant," Jonathan continued eating.

Vahan looked at Grace, then quickly at Jonathan. "I sold my house to my friend Timothy Hawkins. He wants it this spring."

Jonathan dropped his spoon, all eyes turned to him, all eating stopped. He coughed on his last bite of bread and bore his hard dark gaze at Vahan. "We have a covenant."

Jonathan glanced at Grace. Her face was stone.

Vahan continued, with a smile, half-chewed bread showing in his mouth. "Word in town—Oldham will take Minister Hooker and his congregation to the Great River Valley—in the spring. Wives, too. You can find a place then."

Letters

Grace and the girls cleared the evening meal. The older boys tutored Jonas and Junior using the Bible and a stick in the dirt floor to form letters and numbers. Jonathan took out a quill, ink, and paper he'd brought from the warehouse and set about to write to Prescott.

My Dearest Friend John,

I implore you to come to the New World with haste. The land is filling, and additional grants in the coastal towns are being meted out to only the early comers. We are in Watertown, founded by Sir Richard Saltonstall. We're in a rented house but must find another by spring. I promised Grace we'd settle somewhere we will never have to leave. Watertown is overcrowded. They change rules frequently and aren't solicitous to latecomers. I am three years late for the best allotments. I am considering three other groups looking for other land to settle. No one will explore before spring because the ice that forms on the Charles River is treacherous. We won't go west away from the protection of the coastal towns.

The air is fresh. Susan is recovered after a long sickness on the voyage. We have no plague here, yet smallpox swept the colonies this year. Thanks be to God our family was spared. Only two of this colony died. Plymouth was hit harder. Not as hard as the Indians.

News of the Natives comes from the Watertown trader, John Oldham. He says whole tribes were wiped out. The pox goes deep into the west where the Dutchies spread it. Some Indians are dissatisfied with the English using the land, but now they won't need it. Some say it's the work of God to provide more land for us. I can only tell you what I hear. We don't see them often.

The Governor is denying new settlements beyond the coast to assure we have large numbers if there's a conflict. However, Trader Oldham with Minister Hooker and ten families, went west without consent. They're the first English to go that far west. Oldham says the Natives want settlers to build there. They need protection from bigger predator tribes. The larger tribes dictate whom the smaller tribes can trade with and ask for tributes for protection.

People are coming fast. More are risking the voyage, since Governor Winthrop brought the charter with him. The colony is already well-governed with freedom to worship as Puritans.

This new colony severely needs craftsmen. The supplies of iron goods from England can't keep up. The arduous work of opening the land calls for repairs. There is even consideration that metals and minerals may be plentiful here for mining and exporting. Think on joining us. They would make land concessions for a blacksmith.

Love remembered to you and yours,

I rest your Loving friend Jonathan Fairbanks

The hard winter passed without much opportunity to make friends in Watertown. The meetinghouse was cold, so no one tarried to talk after services, and the sharp weather kept everyone inside.

Few ships sailed during the winter months, but in the spring of 1634, a letter arrived. The whole family gathered around Jonathan when they found it was from their friends in England.

My Dearest Friend Jonathan,

The delay of your letter gave us much anguish. Your account of the colonies is more pleasing than others.

King Charles is continuing to prejudice our country, trying to raise funds for his Royal Navy. He demands ship taxes even from inland towns. Sowerby defies the inland ship taxes; claiming our part is fulfilled by training soldiers. Taxes weigh heavy, even on my shoulders. We are being fined for cutting wood or hunting in the king's woods. It's enviable that you can do both.

In August after you left, Bishop William Laud was elevated to Archbishop of Canterbury. He says, "The Puritans are the most dangerous enemies of the State. By their prayers and sermons, they are awakening the people's disaffection and therefore must be suppressed." He wants rid of us. Anyone deemed to speak against the king is hunted. I regret that you are no longer here to hold my confidence. I choose carefully with whom I share my words. I'm ever in your debt for this position in Sowerby.

Laud's men enter churches on the pretense of inspecting for repairs, but they come to ferret out the Puritan ministers. Clerics must flee England in disguise. I pray you are far enough from the reaches of the bishops and have a strong Puritan society.

Send more about the opportunities for a smith, mining, and minerals. Mary misses Grace and the children.

Remaining Your Steadfast Friend from Afar,
John Prescott

Another Move

Tender shoots of grass forced their blades through the crusted earth, defying the winter to last a minute longer. The spring breezes stirred Jonathan's blood. He felt as if he were awakening from hibernation, and there surged in him a hunger for a new start in life.

He pushed in the heavy door of Vahan's house and saw Grace standing by the hearth at a boiling pot, her woolen skirt-tail swaying inches from the outlying embers. Mary Elizabeth was in the garden breaking clods of dirt preparing for spring planting. In the meantime, supplies were growing scant. No one knew when they would find a new home or be pushed out of this one.

"I have found another place," Jonathan proclaimed, forgetting to remove his hat. He headed straight for Grace and gave her a twirl. "The families are leaving for the Great River Valley, the women, too."

"But Jonathan, I heard the Natives from the west came into the General Court asking for protection from other tribes. Now these men are taking their wives and children there?" Grace wrung her hands under her apron skirt to hide her worry. "Over the winter you said you were dissatisfied with this town." She grabbed Jonathan's arm and looked up at him, her eyes welling. "But I feel safe in Watertown."

"Grace, I feel more resentment from the early proprietors of Watertown than I sense danger from distant Indians. We aren't wanted here. Watertown land was taken by early settlers. Didn't we leave England as Puritans because we weren't wanted? Didn't we leave because we couldn't get land? I have no employment. As soon as our stores run out, I'll no longer be a middling man—I'll be a pauper. There's still opportunity, but we must find it amongst people who think as we do. The only way we can assure land for our family is to move to a new plantation."

"We can't go west," moaned Grace, drawing back from Jonathan. "What good is land if we're dead?"

"I'm not taking you to the Great River Valley. There are other men in Watertown looking for land to settle nearby."

Grace leaned her forehead into Jonathan's chest, so he couldn't see her tears. "I feel safe here."

With one arm around Grace, Jonathan ran his fingers over his head. "We are here for now, but many in town are frustrated, not just me." He laid his hands on Grace's shoulders and held her at arm's length. He peered into her deep grey-green eyes. "God is our protector. He'll provide for us."

Jonathan released Grace and began to pace. "It's God's grace to be patient with our lot." To himself he thought, *How can I be patient when my family toils to further the settlement of others, because I cannot provide a home of our own?*

Munnings Tavern 1634

Jonathan watched with interest as the clapboards went up on the frame for a large building in Watertown. Unlike most structures, it was being built by craftsmen. A plump fellow stood there with his hands on his hips, eyeing the progress.

"Good morrow," said Jonathan.

The man turned, lifting his hat in a pudgy hand. "How fare ye, good man?"

"I'm admiring your work. It looks like it could be a tavern and ordinary."

"Aye. That it is. I'm George, George Munnings. I'm building a tavern for you fine men of Watertown. Nothing like a place to sit and share a mug of ale and news of here and home," said Munnings, smiling. "Then I'll start the ordinary."

"That is a right good purpose," said Jonathan, thinking of their first night in Watertown when an ordinary would have been sorely welcome.

"The tavern will soon be ready," said Munnings, "so I can invite you fine men in."

"Where are you from?" asked Jonathan.

"Suffolk. Was a cordwainer," said Munnings, wagging the toe of his shoe. "I made fine shoes but always liked the taverns and people. Where is your home?"

Jonathan lifted his hat, raised his hand to his forehead, then settled the hat firmly back on his head. "I suppose I'm from here now, but I'm considering to plant in a new village, if one fits my mind and humours. I *was* from West Yorkshire. I plan not to return. Do you bring a family?"

"Aye, a wife and two girls. It's difficult for a man to start a farm without sons. But women are good for a tavern and an ordinary. I'll take care of the spirits. The women will take care of the food and board." Munnings chuckled. "Speaking of spirits, the Great and General Court banned the sale of strong water to the Indians."

Only here a short while, Munnings already knew what was happening in the colony.

Munnings held up a finger and said, "Come see what I've been working on while the craftsman builds?"

Jonathan followed the man, examining the workmanship of the workers as they walked.

"Firkins." Munnings handed one to Jonathan. "I make these containers myself. They'll have a bail and wooden lid. When a man leaves after a few mugs, he can take beer home for the family. Makes coming home late more acceptable," said Munnings, with a wink. "Then it can be brought back for a refill. I'll be able to get wine and rum soon. Trader Oldham is arranging that."

"Right wise," said Jonathan. "I miss the evening company of men. It is unlike the noon break on the Sabbath or at home with the goodwife."

Before the ordinary was built, George Munnings and his wife invited locals for evening discussions in the tavern. Each time Jonathan entered the new place, he admired the progress. Where would he find a builder, and where should he build? He was as anxious to get out of Watertown as they were to get rid of the Fairbanks family. *Yet, there won't be a tavern in a new plantation.*

Becoming a Man

As winter gathered, Jonathan called to his sons in the garret early one morning. "Let's go, boys. Jonas, come along. You'll learn the work of a real man."

Ten-year-old Jonas stretched into his leather working breeches and then pulled on his wooden-heeled boots over his knit hose. He shrugged on a heavy kersey coat that was a bit too large and pulled on his old, knitted mons cap, ready long before the others.

"This is one thing we're doing for ourselves," said Jonathan with a determined nod. "Get your axes." Jonathan ran his thumb along the fine sharpened edge of his axe, appreciating Prescott's work. "We'll have to fell a big pine to make a canoe. It won't be a sapling like you're used to, Jonas."

"How big, Father?"

"Big enough," Father said dismissively, never having built a canoe. "You will work with me. George and Samuel can help John Dwight, since he has no grown sons. Your older brother will spell each of us as needed."

Jonathan took the long gun, and John took an axe in each hand. George and Samuel carried theirs in one hand, but Jonas needed both hands to carry his. As Jonas stepped through the doorway into the early morning darkness, he turned back to his mother inside and smiled.

Their second fall in Watertown was showing omens of another harsh winter. It would be prudent to drop the tree and clean off the branches before the snow. Once the snow fell, a friend's oxen could pull the thirty-foot log over packed snow more easily than over hard ground.

"Where's our pine, Father?" asked Jonas.

"We don't have our own lot, so the town granted us a pine in the commons. I put my mark on it. You'll see trees with the king's mark, too. We can't touch those. They'll go to England for ship masts."

The Fairbankses met other men at the meetinghouse. John Dwight, Edward Alleyn, and John Gaye were there. Young and old shared excitement and enthusiasm as the work became a competition. The winners who felled their large pine first would receive rounds of ale at the end of the day.

Jonathan laid his hand on the trunk of a tall, straight pine with his mark and looked up its full length. Jonas imitated his father.

Fairbanks looked around at the lay of the forest. "Jonas, the tree must fall with a clear path to the ground. It can't catch on another tree. It also must be oriented for removal from the timber." With gloved steady hands, Jonathan took the first reverberating bite in the trunk with his axe, bringing the blade down from above. He followed with a bite from below. Jonathan worked the spot until a big chunk fell to the ground.

Jonas caught his axe handle between his knees and clapped with delight. His father looked at him with a wry smile, knowing this son's childish muscles would soon learn the agony of a man's job. *Jonas is about to become a man.*

Jonathan assigned Jonas the side of the tree that he had started. The tree would fall the father's way, he being the hardier woodsman. The townsmen's axes reported on the resonant trunks, the cadence ringing through the timber and out of the forest as the lumbermen established a rhythm of work.

By late afternoon, excitement and warning cries interrupted the throb of the axes. Cracking, crunching, and thumping was followed by a loud "Huzzah!" from the men of Edward Alleyn's team as they felled their tree first. They would hold Munnings's pewter mugs for others to fill tonight.

Jonathan allowed Jonas to take the last few hacks at their tree on the fall side. The tree moaned and swayed in Jonas's direction. Mesmerized, Jonas stared up at the tree as it cracked, creaked, and groaned as it listed, and finally snapped. Jonathan pulled Jonas out of the way. The whole earth shook around them. "You are a regular beaver, son," Jonathan said.

John, George, and Samuel laughed and pounded Jonas on the back. He winced at each congratulatory blow.

Jonas, tired but proud, tried to keep up with his father's strides on the way to Munnings's. On this evening, Jonas had strong ale for the first time. He smiled with froth on his upper lip. "I'm a man now," he said to no one in particular.

As they walked home late, Jonas chatted incessantly. "You said I'd be sore all over, but I'm fine." He puffed his chest and ran ahead to show he still had strength and energy to spare.

But when Jonas rolled over in the morning, he realized how painful it was to become a man. Biting his lower lip, he refused to show his agony, but it was evident to his brothers. Jonas lagged behind as the others prepared for another day's work. Jonas knew he could no longer stay home with his mother. Like a man, he would go chop, too.

That day Jonas's axe felt four times heavier, and his father found odd jobs and errands to take him away from work on the tree. When he returned, he was assigned to clear the smaller limbs.

When Jonas fetched the dinner their mother had packed, John worked on his younger brother's side of the tree. Jonas returned to find a nearly cleared trunk. He said nothing, but his grateful smile shone through the remaining branches.

The next day, the Fairbanks's log was raised on supports so the center could be hollowed out. A length was cut along the center of the log. With long-handled adzes, the men and boys chopped into the wood until a fire could be built within. The char was then scraped out over and over until they had hollowed out a place to sit. There was plenty of work for everyone, until dark clouds threatened a winter storm.

Toward dusk, big, fluffy flakes danced and swirled through the air as the men headed home. The women came out of the houses to witness the strange beauty with them. Young girls twirled in the wonderland of white confetti. Boys frisked like yearling colts, kicking up their heels and knocking each other over into the drifts of white on the ground.

"How can something so beautiful be so cruel? asked Grace. "The women tell of harsh, dangerous winters, worse than the one we ever knew at home." She looked up at their chimney as the smoke mingled with the flakes. As Jonathan joined her, she added, "I'm grateful for the fire in the hearth that will keep this a moment of peace and joy."

Jonathan put his arm around his wife to keep her warm. "Tomorrow, we men will go out again. Regardless of what the night brings."

The Fairbankses awoke to a six-inch carpet of white over the ground, along tree limbs, fence posts, and rail tops. It would melt quickly from the thatched roof as Grace started a larger fire in the hearth.

The new snowfall was already crusted as Jonas led the men back to the canoes, crunching with every step. He rushed ahead to make the first path, sinking knee deep into the drifts.

They finished their canoe with a flat bottom to keep it from tipping in the water.

As the men of the village finished their canoes, the talk turned from worries about a foreboding winter to hopeful plans for spring.

John Gaye, a wealthy, portly man posed a question to the men working near his dugout: "Are you thinking of going west?"

"Not me," said John Dwight. "I'm building this canoe to go up the Charles River. I think we can find land much closer." He turned to Jonathan and asked, "What about you, Fairbanks?"

Jonathan busied himself by smoothing the bottom of their vessel, pretending not to hear.

In Jonathan's silence, Jonas spouted out, "I'll go up the Charles River with you. I can't wait to put our canoe in the water!" When he looked up, his father was glaring at him.

Every man and boy felling and cleaning logs was grateful when the Sabbath came. Jonas's sweet respite was sitting for four hours for church service in the morning. When they stood to exit for noon break, Jonas knew just which of his bones were stiff. His muscles screamed nearly as loud as the trees had when they fell. Four more hours sitting for the afternoon service felt like a blessing, but staying awake during the later sermon was agony.

John and George put Jonas between them during the afternoon. They remembered their heads nearly splitting when the tithing man had brought his six-foot staff with the heavy knob down on them when they had dozed in church. They poked and prodded Jonas when he nodded off. He jumped, glaring defiantly at one brother then the other, denying silently that he had been sleeping.

Finding Tiot 1635

The unrest of the people crowded in the coastal towns of the Massachusetts Bay Colony became greater trouble for the General Court than were the Natives. Under pressure from the huddled towns, the General Court ruled that people could move inland, but they'd remain under the governance of the colony.

Jonathan Fairbanks hurried to Munnings's tavern the evening the Watertown men returned from their canoe expedition up the Charles River to look for land. Six men had returned, including John Gaye, John Dwight, and Edward Alleyn. They would speak on the matter.

As Jonathan arrived from another meeting, he took off his hat as he entered the tavern and found a seat. Edward Alleyn, a distinguished educated man, began speaking even before the growing audience was seated.

"We came to the first falls. It wasn't large, but the canoes couldn't traverse it, so we portaged around. The second falls was so close, we didn't bother putting the canoes back in the water. There were more rapids further down, but we were able to navigate them."

"The falls were easy to portage around," chimed in Gaye, "but the canoes are heavy." He rubbed his arms. "The Charles River is narrow south of there, choked with roots and trees, but it remains deep. We were thankful there was little current to paddle against." Gaye lifted his mug to Munnings for a refill.

Alleyn took the floor again. "We came to thick forests, and when we came out, it was a new world. There was a great bend in the Charles and wide-open meadows."

John Dwight piped up, "That river snakes about, twisting and turning after the falls. It turned back on itself, making several islands. I couldn't keep my directions straight. There's another swifter river nearby. Further up on land, there are low rocky hills forested with a good supply of wood for building and fuel."

Gaye added, "You should have seen the fowl. The sky blackened in a flutter when we disturbed quail and grouse from the chest-high grasses. Those meadows are lush with coarse grass for hay. We could have stock even before we started clearing trees."

Alleyn, who had taken the lead, looked off as if he were in his own thoughts. Then he said, "I think we've found our new home."

I hear the Indians call the place Tiot," Dwight interjected. "They named it right, if it means 'land surrounded by water.'"

Alleyn peered around the room to see if Dwight's comment alarmed anyone. He quickly added, "We didn't see any Natives the whole time."

"What did you learn at the meeting you attended today, about the other proposed plantation, Goodman Fairbanks?" asked Gaye.

Jonathan replied, "Two pastors with a trader named Simon

Willard from Newtowne are the leaders for that one. Willard is on good terms with the Indians. He speaks some Algonquian, is a military man, and he appears to be a shrewd businessman. He has both education and a military background to start a plantation right. They're calling theirs 'Concord.'" He looked around as he paused. "But the Indians call it Musketaquid or 'grassy plains.' They say it has low-lying meadows and kettle holes, but it also has sharp embankments."

"I think we should call our land 'Contentment,'" said Alleyn. "That's what I want after England and Watertown. What we found is rich meadows surrounded by water, and only a neck of land to access it, so it looks plenty safe."

Gaye looked around the room, "Has anyone heard more about Watertown's cattle commons?"

"The one the cattle herders call Sudbury?" replied Dwight. "It's about fifteen miles away. The General Court considers that a favorable distance for a new plantation."

"That would just be an extension of this troubled town," complained Alleyn. "You're not going to get away from this town's governance unless Watertown approves the separation. Who knows how long that may take?" he said with a huff.

"Another town at Sudbury would mean more men close enough to help protect Watertown if the Indians attack," said Dwight.

"But," Alleyn cautioned, "Sudbury would be attacked first and act as a buffer for Watertown."

Gaye shook his head, "Our only other option, Wethersfield in the Great River Valley, is out of the question for me."

"If we start anew," reasoned Alleyn, "we could grow a plantation where people would be more content. We could gather people that think the same as we do."

Fairbanks sat quietly taking in the conversation. Many men left, but he stayed in case there was more information to be garnered.

"Well, Fairbanks, are you with us for Tiot?" questioned Dwight.

"That I cannot say. You have encouraged me with your accounts. But I still have many considerations."

One Hundred Yorkshiremen

"Jonathan, do you know Abraham Shaw from Halifax Parish?" asked Munnings, handing him a firkin of ale. "They say he was a clothier and miner there. He and his family arrived in town."

Jonathan brightened hearing of his old friend, neighbor, and trade colleague. "Aye, he was from Northowram in West Yorkshire. We lived near him when we were in Shelf. He runs mines there and at Sowerby." Jonathan smiled to himself. Having Abraham and Bridget with their children here would make Grace more content.

Jonathan donned his hat and took his firkin, his steps were quick despite the muddy path that sucked at his shoes. He didn't even notice the chickens or the stray pigs impeding his path home. *Perhaps Abraham and Bridget will have news about our friends,* he thought. *Maybe even about the Prescotts.*

Before Jonathan opened the door wide enough to step in, Grace ran to meet him and took the firkin. "Guess who I saw in town?"

Jonathan opened his mouth to speak, but she burst in with "Bridget Shaw!"

Jonathan wouldn't tell her he already knew, lest he spoil her merriment. Besides, some women's gossip held more information than the men's.

"Oh, Jonathan, Abraham has sold his tailor business and mines, and they're staying here. They're using one of the empty houses near the commons and have started a late garden."

"I shall walk over to speak with them," Jonathan said, and turned to walk directly over to the Shaws' lot. As Jonathan came upon Shaw working on the fence, he greeted him with, "Abraham, my good man. You have come to join us."

Abraham turned quickly, surprised by the familiar voice. "Aye, it was shortly after you left when I realized I must leave, too. I spoke with Sir Saltonstall, who told me of Watertown."

"Are you building here?" Fairbanks looked around the property. He knew Abraham would want a finer house than this.

"We aren't staying in this house, but we may stay in Watertown. Are you planting here or moving like many others? I hope not, for Bridget would like to be close to Grace."

Jonathan told him about the three options—Contentment, Concord, and Sudbury—and of his own inclinations. But he stopped short of divulging his plan.

In August, fishermen and merchant shallops brought the rumor of a ship carrying one hundred Yorkshire passengers, coming toward the bay. The *St. James* was accompanied by lighter, faster ships that had also left Bristol, England. Those vessels ported at Newfoundland. Another large ship, the *Angel Gabriel*, sailed on with the *St. James*.

Excitement rushed through the Fairbanks family with gale force. Everyone except Susan wanted to sail down the Charles River to Boston to meet the ship, to greet those from home, and to hear news of England. But for her, the thought of a boat ride brought only nausea.

Grace understood that the women wouldn't want to be seen in the clothes they had worn throughout the arduous voyage, but the thought of seeing someone they might know from home won out.

Mary Elizabeth wished aloud for girls her age. Eleven-year-old Jonas wished for boys his age, since John, George, and

Samuel usually left him out of their activities. But even more than finding friends, he wanted to get close to the big ships. Jonathan promised the family a trip to Boston, and seeing his family filled with excitement gave him satisfaction—like faire days in Halifax.

A wind blew hard from the south-southwest for about a week, and the skies seemed to grow heavier in that direction. Jonathan hesitated to take the family. However, he couldn't resist meeting the ship himself, even with bad weather coming.

Before they arrived at the Watertown dock, a drizzle had turned to rain. The shift Grace had sewn for Mary Elizabeth stuck to her daughter's thirteen-year-old body. Jonathan blushed, seeing how Mary Elizabeth had become a young lady. Susan whined to go home, and Grace's eyes turned darker than the storm clouds at the thought of continuing to Boston.

The boys urged their father on. "We can bring news home to Mother." It was decided, Junior would be sent home with Mother and the girls.

Jonathan promised the shallop handler extra to take him and the boys down the river with the current and wind challenging all the way. The boys took turns with the sweeps when the sail failed the small craft, and Jonathan stared at the landscape with the pole in his hand to keep the boat from the riverbank. It seemed they were at a standstill. *Are we getting nowhere or am I just anxious to get to Boston before the ship arrives?*

The wind and waves tossed the small boat, so it was difficult to stand. They finally moored at the first dock they reached near Boston, even though it was far from the larger ship wharves. The boat owner cursed at them and ordered, "Leave! I'll go no further in this storm. If this craft is dashed against the pilings, you are responsible for it, Fairbanks."

Jonathan tipped his tall hat slightly. The water guttered down his hand into his doublet sleeve. Midday was becoming dark as the blinding rain drove sideways. Jonathan squinted, in search of anything familiar to get his bearings. He hoped they were headed toward Cousin Richard's house. He watched the waves breaking over wharves, hoping the house would be far enough away from the swells. In the strong wind, Jonathan took off his hat and led the boys in prayer for their safety as they pushed against the rain, wiping water from their eyes and grabbing each other's clothes to stay together.

After they arrived at Richard's, their prayers turned toward the passengers aboard the *St. James*, remembering the nights of treacherous tempests that they had endured in their crossing. A ship this near land could be dashed upon the rocks.

After a brief calm at midnight, the winds changed, now coming violently and relentlessly from the northwest and making projectiles of the rain. Though they felt safe at Richard's shuttered house, the wind coming in between the daub and cracks around the door guttered the candles. "Mother says candles protect against darkness and storms," whispered Jonas to George with a quaver in his voice.

Sparks flew from the hearth as wind rushed down the chimney. Each spark searched for a piece of cloth or wood to extend its life. Everyone rushed to pull everything away from the hearth, then huddled together with blankets to keep warm. They covered their ears against the howling, remaining in silent prayer.

Morning brought an eerie quiet after the din of the storm. The hot August day before had turned humid and chilly. Jonathan crept out of the house to find the town littered with wreckage, roofs blown off, houses demolished. At the edge of town, large trees were uprooted, tall pines were snapped in half, and new oaks twisted.

When Jonathan ascertained that all was safe, the men sloshed to the nearby meetinghouse where others gathered to share news. One man told of Indians saving themselves by clinging to trees. No one had news of the *St. James*. Everyone told their own stories of surviving turbulent waters when they crossed the sea. It did not seem possible that the passengers of this ship could have survived.

Two days later, the ship limped toward Boston's harbor, and the crew of the *St. James* informed the ferry boats that they had lost three anchors at the Isle of Shoals, trying to ride out the storm. Her sails were tattered and near useless, and the harbor men wouldn't risk a sunken ship blocking the wharves for incoming merchants.

The passengers of the *St. James* arrived at the docks in small boats, they clutched for the boards and pilings of the wharf, reaching for safety. The passengers came on shore and told bits of the story with fear still bright in their eyes.

Jonathan was surprised and delighted to see Mr. Denton, the Yorkshire minister, among the many others, remembering the day they met at the faire in Halifax. When Denton saw him, he grabbed Jonathan's shoulders and looked into his eyes, saying with deep emotion, "We had given up all hope. It looked as if we would be dashed against the rocks. Then God sent his mercy in the winds from the opposite direction—saving us from a watery death."

Denton wanted to wait for Mr. Matthew Mitchell and his wife, the respected Yorkshire merchant. Then Jonathan guided the minister and Mr. Mitchell's family to Richard's large house, warning his boys to hold their tongues and questions until the voyagers regained their warmth and composure.

"What will you do here, Mr. Mitchell?" Jonathan asked.

"I must find a place nearby until I complete the business I was assigned in England. I need a house for a brief time, but we are hoping to settle on the Musketaquid River soon. I want to get in on the first land grants."

"Concord!" exclaimed Jonathan. "I just talked to the trader, Simon Willard, about that new plantation. I hear Michael

Bearstow has a house in Newtowne he is selling." William and George Bearstow from Halifax are coming over on the ship *Truelove* in September. I don't know their plans"

"Where have you planted, Fairbanks?"

"Perhaps you have heard of Tiot? They are ready to petition the General Court for that land about the same time as the others will petition for Concord. I'm deciding between the two."

"I must follow the trade of beaver pelts to send back to England," said Mr. Mitchell. "I will go to Concord."

"How about you, Mr. Denton?"

"To Watertown, but then my congregation and I will journey to the Great River Valley as soon as possible." Jonathan didn't share his knowledge of Wethersfield as the only plantation yet settled in the Great River Valley.

Jonathan left the newcomers to rest in his cousins' home, and he went out to help clear paths in the storm-littered streets.

I wonder if I'm making the right decision, he wondered. Two men he respected were going separate ways, while he followed new, less familiar friends to Tiot. *It's not too late to change my mind. Nothing binds me.*

John Dwight found Jonathan at Munnings's getting a firkin of ale for Grace. "Jonathan," he said, "there's going to be a meeting tonight. A dozen men are gathering to write a petition to the General Court for the land we found this spring. Have you made your decision?"

Jonathan lifted his hat and scratched the balding spot on his head.

"Fairbanks," he said with a little impatience, "I admire how you methodically decide your intentions, but if you wait too long, you'll find yourself out of our group."

Jonathan listened.

"Edward Alleyn is drafting the petition for the land in Tiot. He is educated and wise about our undertaking. We'll go over the document tonight." Dwight put his hand on Jonathan's shoulder. "I know how much you value peace, faith, and education. We are a group of successful men who think the same. Why don't you come along?"

"Dwight, they just lifted the ban for moving from the coastal towns this spring. My family moved so much in England; I promised Grace we would settle when we arrived. I just moved my family again after John Vahan sold his house. The next place I settle, I'm going to stay. I don't know if it's even safe to move yet, so I'll keep my mind open to options."

Tiot Land Grant

"Huzzah! Huzzah! Huzzah!"

After securing a grant at the General Court at Newtowne on a cool September morning, the twelve men arrived back at Munnings's tavern. Jonathan Fairbanks and several other Watertown men joined them.

"You should have heard John Rogers present our petition," said Dwight as he winked at his friend, who had come with him from Dedham, England.

"We were granted two hundred square miles of wilderness," said Edward Alleyn, "but really it's more than a wilderness— marshy meadows with hills, trees, and rocks. The General Court deeded the land from Sachem Chickataubutt, leader of the Massachusett, and Sachem John of Mystik.

"We have plenty of planters. Now we must prepare a covenant to assure the General Court that we can govern ourselves. We have several potential ministers, and we are prepared to ask Mr. Thomas Cakebread to come as our military leader to meet the other requirements."

"The General Court said Tiot is only two miles above the Newtowne falls at the Great Bend of the Charles River," John Gaye said with a smirk. "That seems little distance to them, because they didn't have to paddle those miles or portage the falls." He rubbed his arms as if he'd just put down a paddle. "They'll find out differently when they send men to survey."

"What about Samuel Willard's plantation?" asked Jonathan. "I heard they petitioned the same day."

"Yes, that land was granted," said Alleyn. "They call it Concord."

"Are you straddling the fence, Fairbanks?" asked Dwight. "When are you going to stop considering and come with us?"

"I must listen to my own heart, not follow the convictions of others," said Jonathan still holding his decision close to his chest, like a Yorkshireman. "It's late to be going anywhere this year. But I'll drink to getting out of Watertown."

They all raised their mugs. "Huzzah!"

"I say we go out and start felling trees and make a good landing place for our canoes," said Gaye, "then prepare for common crops and houses. I want to be able to move out of Watertown by early next year."

"I'm going out as soon as I can," Dwight replied, rolling up his sleeves as if he were ready to work. "Fairbanks, can I count on you and the boys to help?"

"Aye, we'd rather help there than in Watertown."

In late fall, the Fairbanks men helped the twelve founders of Tiot turn the tangled grass roots clutching the earth so the clods would soften with the winter freezes and snow. They started building a fence around a common night pasture for the cattle of the new village.

The winter was long and hard, unwilling to release its stronghold on the land. A delayed thaw rotted the seeds in the ground, threatening the food supply for the following winter.

The Fairbanks men planted a garden in Watertown and helped plant in Tiot, but they had to do both over and over during the cold spring.

The ice finally broke enough on the Charles River in March that the General Court sent a survey team to set the bounds of Tiot. By April, the boundaries were laid, and the men of Tiot started planning their town and home lots.

It was Jonas's turn to accompany his father on an expedition of canoes to Tiot, and Jonathan asked, "Are you sure you want to go? Trader Oldham's nephews are in town. You always spend time with them when they visit."

Jonas hesitated. "But I want to go on the water to the new land. John and Thomas get to sail with their uncle on the river."

In the canoe, twelve-year-old Jonas pretended to be a sailor who had just found land. He pointed out birds, rabbits, raccoons, and animals he hadn't seen in England. Jonathan repeatedly commanded him to sit down. Abraham Shaw, who was accompanying them, helped balance the canoe when Jonas's antics threatened disaster.

Jonas's arms burned from rowing when they reached Newtowne falls, and he stumbled over rocks as he stretched his arms to help support the canoe when they portaged around the falls.

"Are you helping us finish the night pasture fence, lad?" called Ezekiel Holliman to Jonas as they boarded their boats in less turbulent waters.

"Won't the wolves get the cattle if you leave them in a night pasture?" Jonas called back.

"Nay, for some reason the wolves won't cross a fence," he responded.

"We can make you herdsman, boy," boomed Abraham, "You can stay out there with the cattle."

The men laughed, and again Jonas jumped up, rocking

the canoe precipitously and yelling, "Look, Father! There's the landing place."

Jonathan glared at Jonas as the boat steadied. "They are calling it the Keye." Jonas sat back down and kept the rest of his discoveries to himself.

After landing in the tree clogged water of the Keye, they picked their way up the gentle slope. Jonathan ran his fingers along both sides of a new green blade of grass that would grow chest deep by summer. "Look at this fine meadow of grass. This will support a wet cow for your mother. I can have a yoke of oxen for plowing."

He pulled a blade of grass, holding it between his upright thumbs, and with a firm, steady puff of air, he showed Jonas how to whistle with the grass. Men appeared over the rise, walking down toward them.

Jonathan strode toward them, turning to see if Jonas followed. He smiled at the lagging boy inspecting every oddity.

Jonathan looked past the meadows to the upland in the distance, where the massive oaks shivered in the gentle spring winds. *Plenty of wood for a fine sturdy house for Grace.* They would not be pushing poles into the hillsides for a place to live as would be necessary in Concord.

"Do you think there are wolves in those swamps?" asked Jonas.

"I'd rather the howl of the wolves in the swamp purgatory than the constant bickering of Watertown," said Jonathan.

John Dwight reached them and said, "Yes, that's a good name for a swamp, 'Purgatory.'"

War, Peace, and Fire 1636

Jonas hustled up the bank from the river in Watertown, a fishing pole in one hand and a stringer of bass in the other. His gait was between a sprint and a waddle as he slowed occasionally to catch his breath. His father was heading home, and he had to reach him now. Once they arrived at the house, he would be forbidden to tell his father what he had heard. Father didn't allow talk about Indians in the house. It disturbed Mother and raised her resistance against leaving Watertown to settle in one of the new plantations.

"Father!" Jonas panted as he caught up to him. Jonathan put his hand on his son's shoulder and took the pole and stringer from him.

Jonas put his hands on his knees, trying to catch his breath. "The boys I was fishing with say the Indians are attacking!" Twelve-year-old Jonas was trying to be brave, like a man, and hold back his tears.

"Jonas, there are many kinds of Indians in this new country, just like there are many kinds of men in the old: Spanish, French, Scots, Dutch. Even here, the men are from many places. They don't always get along. Seems that England is always at war with someone."

"But, Father, the Indians aren't fighting each other—they are going to fight *us*. Madman Oldham—"

"Now, Jonas," Jonathan interrupted, his eyes hard, "we give Goodman Oldham our respect. He knows a lot about the Indians—about the Pequot tribe in the south that are trying to stir up trouble with other tribes, like the Narragansetts. But Oldham thinks the Indians here are our friends and trading partners. They will stand with us if something happens. Were his nephews fishing with you?"

Jonas, still panting, shook his head vigorously but remained silent. He knew better than to interrupt his father.

"Besides, the Indians have few guns and little powder. If it weren't for greedy traders, they wouldn't even have those. The General Court told the traders they aren't to sell firearms to them."

"But Father, Goodman Oldham is dead on his boat! The Indians did it."

"Jonas." Jonathan grabbed the boy's arm hard. "Catch your breath and tell me what you heard."

"On Sunday, John and Thomas said their uncle was taking them to Block Island to trade with the Indians this week," Jonas searched his father's face to see if he shared his anxiety, but Jonathan's face remained impassive. "Someone saw the Indians on Oldham's boat before they took off in their canoes. When the captain boarded Oldham's shallop, they found him dead—beaten. They said the Indians did it."

"Son, don't let yourself be stirred until we know the whole story."

"But what about John and Thomas? They're my friends— my age. They were with their uncle. Do you think they're all right? Do you think the Indians will attack *us*?"

"I think Block Island is eighty-six miles south, and I know God is looking after us." Jonathan handed the fishing pole and stringer back to Jonas. "Go clean these fish for your mother. Don't bother her with the news. I'll find out about your friends."

Jonathan ruffled the black hair on his son's head and said no more. The conversation was over.

Watching Jonas leave, Jonathan looked over his shoulder, peering far to the southeast, toward Block Island. His gut twisted even as he had comforted his son. He had been seriously considering settling in Tiot, but might he be trading his family's safety for land? Major Willard would work to protect the people of Concord, but Tiot had no military leader.

Jonathan headed for Munnings's. Grace would find out soon enough from the women's gossip, and he wanted the details before he confronted her questions. The tavern hummed like a giant wasp's nest, but no one seemed to know what had happened to the boys.

"I feel bad for Goodman Oldham," he said to the general company, "but I understand he strayed from the narrow path of God in dealing with the Indians."

"Was Oldham selling them guns?" asked another man.

Yet another declared, "If the Indians of this area remain our allies, we should be safe, but if the Narragansetts don't support us, we will be outnumbered even with our superior weapons. We are only safe in numbers here." Men around the tavern nodded.

Abraham Shaw entered the tavern and announced, "I am just back from Boston. There it's rumored that young Governor Vane is confirming the Narragansetts' fidelity. He's calling ninety men under Captain Endicott to go to Block Island to find the murderers."

Contentment

As the sun shed its glow over the land in early August, the twelve men who had received the grant for Tiot met in one of their Watertown homes. Edward Alleyn let a gavel fall on the trestle table where the leaders of the first petition sat.

"I call this meeting to order," he announced. Alleyn held a stack of papers high enough for everyone to see. "This will be the covenant for Contentment. We're founding our town on everlasting love, mutual comfort for all, and the good of the community to bring true peace." He smacked the papers down on the table. "Every man who wishes to settle amongst us must hold these words in his heart and sign that he, his heirs, and servants will uphold this promise forever."

We have twelve men who were granted the land, but we need more," said Dwight. "If we have enough interest, we can petition the General Court for more land this September, at their quarterly session. But anyone who doesn't believe as we do must settle elsewhere."

Random discussions broke out around the room until Alleyn's gavel pummeled the table twice.

When they settled down, Dwight continued. "We need men of the right sort, who are like-minded with the founding body. We also need men to develop the community through skills and trades. And lastly, we need manpower for the safety of the village. The unrest of the Indians, though miles away, is close in mind."

Once again, animated conversations broke out.

Alleyn plied the gavel and furthered the business at hand. He ended with, "Each man who commits to the covenant of Contentment is charged with finding suitable candidates and bringing them to the next meeting. It will be a public gathering on August 18 at Edward Alleyn's."

As John Dwight walked past Abraham Shaw's rented house, he hesitated, then knocked on the door.

"Abraham, my good man," said Dwight. "May I have a word?"

"Aye, come in,"

"Nay, I'm on my way home. I just came from a meeting of men who hold the grant for Tiot."

"Aye?"

"We are looking for men of like mind and good skills to settle in our new plantation. What do you think about settling?"

"We *are* looking for a permanent dwelling. We are open to opportunities."

"I would like you to come to our next meeting about Tiot. The founders are calling the plantation Contentment now. Do you think you might bring Jonathan Fairbanks?

"Aye, I know he likes the men settling Tiot. He speaks of you, too. I think he'll come."

Two weeks later, Jonathan announced to Grace, "I'm going to a meeting tonight to hear about Contentment, one of the new plantations."

"What? Another new plantation? You've already talked about three." Grace, pursing her lips into a hard pucker, pulled out one of Susan's braids and jerked a comb through her hair. Susan's hand flew to the side of her head as she yelped.

"This is the first public meeting for settlers of Tiot, as you've heard about. They call it Contentment now, and they're asking the General Court for more land."

"Will you take us out of Watertown during Indian trouble?" Grace demanded, yanking Susan's head back with the comb. Susan quietly whimpered.

At least these men seem to welcome us and care about us. They think as we do in religion, education, and morality."

"Or do they just want our nearly grown boys to marry their daughters?" snapped Grace.

"Even their covenant talks of a loving community that thinks alike." Jonathan didn't have time for another discussion. He raised a hand to quiet her and turned his back and went out into the warm August evening, past the commons, to meet Abraham Shaw at Edward Alleyn's house.

The door to the Alleyn one-room house was open when they arrived, six men were seated at the table. Alleyn was at the head with a quill, inkwell, and paper. A half-dozen men were standing around inside. A few looked up as Jonathan entered. One greeted him jovially—"We wondered when you would show your face among us."

The house was warm and soon filled with men sitting on the bed, the rungs of the ladder to the garret, and the low stool by the hearth. Others leaned against the walls. Alleyn had banked the fire to ease the summer heat.

Crowding in with the other men, Jonathan thought it would be nice to have a house large enough to have a proper meeting.

More men arrived, cramming at least eighteen to twenty in the house by the time Alleyn pounded the gavel on the table. "This opens the meeting, August 18, 1636, of Contentment. We have the following men attending that have been involved in ordering this town." Edward Alleyn was listed first, Abraham Shaw, second, and after two others, John Dwight, fifth. Eighteen in all were named.

Abraham Shaw? Jonathan turned to look at him with a shrug of surprise. He'd decided? The men seemed to be listed in the order of importance. Shaw as second was a valued member.

Abraham faced forward, not reacting to Jonathan's stare.

"This town shall be of men with like minds. We will have no idlers, unprofitable planters, fowlers, coasters, or tobacco takers," said Alleyn. "The first petitioners are already seeking men we'd like to settle amongst us."

Fairbanks saw Dwight looking in his direction. *So, he has been pursuing us, then?*

"We'll now appoint a committee to examine the characters of those who wish to plant with us," Alleyn continued. "All persons planning to sign our covenant must declare their name and explain their motives for joining the membership. All other proprietors are responsible for telling anything they know about the prospective member's character or actions that may be of detriment to the village."

Aye, that is why John Dwight and Hannah visited us. He had been insistent on Jonathan deciding which plantation he would join.

"Ahem!" Alleyn cleared his throat loudly. "We received our boundaries in April. The twelve early petitioners who have already signed the covenant have received their lots. Some are already working at Contentment for the good of the community."

"To conclude this meeting, I'll announce the men who will receive their lots today," said Dwight, wisely saving the lot assignments for last. After that announcement, order would not be easily regained.

"The men granted lots today are these: Sam Morse, Philemon Dalton, Daniel Morse, Joseph Morse, Ralph Shepard, Lambert Genere, Nicholas Phillips, Abraham Shaw, and Edward Alleyn. We have only thirty lots on this grant."

When Fairbanks heard Abraham Shaw's name read, a lightning bolt coursed through him, sweat dotted his forehead, and his hands grew clammy. He rubbed them together and then on his breeches. *Am I too late for these allotments?*

Dwight pulled Abraham aside after the meeting. "How well do you know Fairbanks?"

"We knew each other in Halifax Parish. He and his family are of good stock. They are clothiers and yeomen."

"I like the man," said Dwight, "but he's stubborn. He is interested in Contentment and the men who are founding it. But I haven't been able to persuade him to join us."

"You have read him correctly. He's a Yorkshireman. He's stubborn. Some of his stubbornness comes from the county we hail from," said Shaw. "He's educated and resourceful. He has near-grown boys who would benefit the village."

"You're from West Yorkshire. Do you think you might speak with him?"

"Aye, but I know better than to push a Yorkshireman before he has made up his own mind."

Jonathan hurried to the late-August meeting at wealthy, influential John Gaye's Watertown house. He hesitated at the door. Several men hovered around the table. He recognized each as an original petitioner or someone who was later allotted land. There were a few others around the room, talking intently.

Am I late? Have I lost my chance? Jonathan looked behind him. Groups of men were coming into the dooryard, and others were coming down the lane. Fairbanks stepped in the door and went straight to the table.

He greeted them hastily and then said, "I've read the covenant. I would like to sign and be allotted land."

John Dwight furrowed his brow and looked at Edward Alleyn. "I'm sorry, Jonathan—all our first thirty allotments are taken. The best we can do is put you on our waiting list for our next allotments, if we get more land in a new petition."

Jonathan's heart sank, and he looked behind him. Thomas Carter, John Eaton, and Ralph Wheelock stood in the line, and others followed. Jonathan pulled on the waiting list as Edward Alleyn pushed it his way and handed him the quill.

At least I'm first on the waiting list, he thought.

After Jonathan signed, he turned and greeted the men in line with a smile. As he passed the last, he let out a long, silent sigh.

As the room settled, the men discussed the second petition to the General Court. There were an ample number of settlers, particularly freemen. More land was needed for those expected to come. In these times of unrest, they thought it wise to ask for land to include more ground for a larger training field. Captain Thomas Cakebread had signed the covenant and would speak to the need for a training field and military concerns on their behalf.

The moderator explained the covenant was meticulously prepared to ask the General Court to incorporate their land as a village instead of a plantation; villages had more freedom to order their own town business. They had several potential clerics, relatives of men who were already committed to the village. Mr. Feke, a prominent man in Watertown and in-law of Governor Winthrop, also promised to be a petitioner for their grant. He added influence to their request. The petitioners were optimistic. As the session ended, the moderator announced, "The men who wish to participate in the petition for more land shall meet September 5."

Dedham

With petition and covenant in hand, the Tiot contingency arrived at Boston September 6, 1636, at 6:00 a.m., they waited their turn before the magistrates, Edward Alleyn holding the documents.

Abraham Shaw whispered to him, "We must have twenty men assembled here to support our petition."

Alleyn looked around, "I see the original twelve and maybe seven more."

Dwight said with a shrug, "I thought with both Abraham and the Bearstow brothers from West Yorkshire, Fairbanks would be here too."

"Will the men from Tiot approach the table?" announced the clerk of the court.

The men stood before the magistrates and addressed their main issues: additional land on the other side of the Charles River for military exercises, four years free from country charges, and four years of no responsibility for military exercises outside of their own village, unless there was an emergency. The owners of the land would be free to allot the land and govern themselves under the blanket rules of the colony. Finally, they asked their village to be named Contentment.

Just before the petition was handed to the magistrates, Robert Feke, Thomas Hasting, and John Huggins rushed to the desk to add their names to the nineteen on the petition. That made twenty-two signatures, more than enough proprietors and freemen to be given privileges of a village rather than a plantation.

The magistrates spoke briefly amongst themselves in hushed voices as the Tiot men watched every move. Finally, one of the magistrates addressed the men, saying, "The men of Tiot must return on September 10 for the final decision."

There would be no celebration that night.

Four days later, a handful of men stood before the General Court magistrates again to receive their decision. First, they would have only three years immunity from taxes and concessions for military responsibilities. Though the men were disappointed, they knew that meant the land was granted. They shuffled their feet and held their jubilation, because the magistrate hadn't finished. He announced, "The new village shall be called Dedham, instead of the proposed 'Contentment.'"

The Contentment men looked at each other with disappointment, but having been granted all other requests, they stepped out of the magistrates' chamber and erupted in "Huzzah! Huzzah! Huzzah!"

Fire in October

"Fire!" yelled Jonas as he ran into the house. "Father, there's a fire down the way."

Jonathan looked up, smelling smoke, but he remained calm, knowing the Natives burned the underbrush every fall to make hunting easier during winter. Some of the settlers had started doing the same, and the smell of fire could float on the air for long distances.

"It's a house fire, Father!" cried Jonas, and Jonathan's chair careened back, almost toppling as he rose. Grabbing his cloak, he rushed out into the chill October night. Near the meetinghouse, dark clouds rose in the distance, orange flames emanating from underneath. Sending sparks toward the stars.

"Boys," he called to his sons who had gathered, "grab shovels and buckets. Come as fast as you can!"

Jonathan knew it must be Abraham Shaw's rented house before he got there. Flames engulfed only the one building, but the weather had been dry and the breeze stiff. Any fire endangered every thatched and wood-shingled house in Watertown as the wind tossed the glowing embers about. Every man who could see or smell the fire ran to assist the family and the town.

Bridget Shaw, their girls, and young John were outside wrapped in blankets. Abraham called orders to his son Joseph and various neighbors who had already arrived. The Bearstow brothers passed buckets from hand to hand in a line of men between the town water barrels and the burning house.

Flames licked the roof near the chimney. "We need a ladder over here!" yelled Jonathan over the roar of the fire and men.

"I'll get mine!" called another man, and several took off running.

The fire covered the thatch and was sending tall tongues of orange and red into the night sky. The glow of the flames in the dark illuminated all the surrounding homes as if the fire were deciding where it would wreak havoc next. The energy of the pyre warmed the surroundings, but a chill still coursed through Jonathan's bones from the threat of the flaming invader moving across town, perhaps even to his own house. It was too late to save anything for the Shaws, but the men worked late into the night to save the rest of Watertown.

As the full moon lit the bones of charred wood and glowing embers, there was nothing left to do but stare at the wreckage.

Abraham sadly bade the townsmen "Ta and good night" and turned to Jonathan. "The big hearth and chimney of this house kept us warm. I didn't know the daub around the wood in the chimney could burn through. It took flame and spread quickly to the thatch. There was naught we could do to contain it. If only I could have reached the chimney, I could have salvaged something. Alas, everything is gone." He was silent for a moment, then added, "I'll never be without a tall ladder again."

"Perhaps God has other plans for you, Abraham. You must give it into his hands. He has given you a place to build in Dedham and me as your friend. You and your family can stay with us until you find a place or build."

"You're a good man. A warm place for the night is welcome. It's difficult to think past that."

Fairbanks put his hand on Abraham's shoulder, "In the morrow, early, we must return with buckets. You, the boys, and even the girls, will sift through the char for nails as soon as it cools. Perhaps we can find an iron pot or pewter, some spoons. We'll look for whatever we can find. The nails can start a new house. I'll soon go to Boston for more supplies."

Jonathan looked forward to getting away from the house bulging with people. With so many more, the Fairbankses' reserves would be taxed, but Jonathan couldn't think about that now.

In Boston early, he stopped at his Cousin Richard's place on the way to the warehouse, noticing the fine quality of the workmanship of the ordinary and tavern. He entered the nearly empty establishment and found Richard leaning on the post by the bar, looking at his ledger.

"Good morrow, cousin." called Richard, stepping around the bar to greet Jonathan.

"How fare ye?" asked Jonathan

Richard nodded politely and said, "Can I offer you a beer? If

Elizabeth were here, she could offer some food. I am hoping for a license to add wine and strong liquor within the next year."

Jonathan looked around and saw that only one small table in a far corner was occupied. Taking off his tall hat, he ran his fingers over his increasing bald spot. "No beer, thank ye kindly," said Jonathan, pausing. Then he began, more formally. "As your cousin, Richard, I feel compelled to speak with you."

Richard brow furrowed in question.

"I hear you are supporting the Goodwife Anne Hutchinson and her kin, Reverend Wheelwright, in their altered religious views," said Jonathan.

"Aye, Jonathan," Richard said with a smile, "of all the ministers in the Colony, only they are preaching the Covenant of Grace for salvation. All others espouse the Covenant of Works."

"We all know, cousin, that salvation is by grace, and that the works follow on in testimony of God's work in a heart. But even in Watertown, we hear of the concern over their teachings and rumors of government action against them. Do you think it wise to follow them?"

"Well, I do believe in what they say," Richard said, rubbing the back of his neck. "But do ye think it could harm my petition for licenses? I suppose I must consider what effect controversy might have on getting permits. And if they are worried as far away as your place . . ."

Richard was not a close enough relative for Jonathan to press the matter, so when Richard started talking of the latest news from England, Jonathan relaxed.

After accepting another offer of beer and chatting about the news, Jonathan took his leave, saying, "I pray you well on getting your licenses." As he passed Richard's fine adjoining garden, he considered how their own food would be stretched with the Shaws in their home.

The Boston meetinghouse was just south of Richard's,

within earshot, and Jonathan knew his cousin had joined the church when they arrived in Boston. Jonathan stood on Great Street at the crossroads of the main thoroughfare in town and wondered at it: *Richard can hear the sermons from his doorstep, yet he follows Mr. Wheelwright.*

As Jonathan headed toward the wharf to see Coggan, the trader, he passed the din of the busy market that reminded him of England's markets, of home. He was enticed to stop. But he had urgent business.

Jonathan walked into the trading store on the wharf and found a strange young man running the business. Could he trust this fellow's counsel? Fortunately, a mason was discussing a shipment of bricks from England with the young man.

Approaching the mason, Jonathan said, "I am in need of a large fireplace, three hearths."

"Sorry, my good man. I'm currently on a job; I won't finish until spring. That's if we find enough mortar to finish the job."

"I found good clay in the bed of the Charles River in Dedham, the new village. My boys and I could dig the clay for bricks before winter if you know of a brickmaker. I think you must let it texturize in the cold, so then it's ready to mold and bake into bricks in the spring." Jonathan wouldn't tell the mason he didn't have land yet, that he was only on a waiting list for a lot in Dedham.

"That will take too long. I'll have to start another job before you're ready. I have shiploads of bricks coming by spring. We could use those when my current work is done."

Jonathan silently calculated the extra cost.

"You know that bricks from England will be rose bricks," said the mason. "They are soft and won't withstand the harsh winters here."

"Aye, but the chimney I desire will be completely enclosed in the house except for the small bit at the center of my roof."

"That will do," the mason nodded.

"My boys and I can dig clay from the river for mortar."

"It's Fairbanks from Dedham," he called to the mason as he left.

Acceptance 1637

Jonathan trudged to the monthly meeting in Watertown through the mud covered by newly fallen snow at the end of 1636. He had left his house early to avoid a fine for arriving late, knowing some of the men working on houses in Dedham wouldn't make it back.

After the reading of the minutes, a man in the crowd addressed the group. "Nicholas Phillips and Ezekiel Holliman are felling trees in the Dedham common areas and putting clapboards on the houses. We voted against that for our village."

The moderator responded, "Appropriate fines will be issued."

Jonathan hesitated, hoping one of the early proprietors would speak to the benefit of clapboards. No one rose. With his hat in both hands, he stood. "I've been helping in Dedham," he said. "It's mighty cold with few houses in place, and there is no lime for insulating the wood framing as in England. The wattle-and-daub—just clay and straw—won't hold up to this weather if they aren't covered by clapboards."

"But what if Indians stick their fire brands between the boards?" asked another man. When the word "Indians" was mentioned, the usual ripple coursed through the meeting.

"Indians can't do much harm if you've frozen to death," said Jonathan, bringing a roar of laughter and a release of tension.

One of the landholders said, "I move we allow clapboards until spring for the early settlers building this winter. These are not the king's woods. Trees are plentiful."

"But trees were once plentiful in England . . ." Abraham Shaw, nodding resolutely, making his point.

The motion passed.

During the dead of the winter, Jonathan attended another meeting in hopes of a place. The second allotments had not been assigned, and he had a mason coming to work in the spring. He mulled over his predicament while the meeting droned on about a wet cow commons at the border of the Little River. *Grace sorely desires a milk cow,* thought Jonathan, *but this does me no good until I'm a proprietor.*

Then John Dwight made an announcement that caught Jonathan's attention. "The men on the waiting list for the second grant of lots may buy into this common pasture."

It's coming, it's finally coming! thought Jonathan. They would get land, and Grace could have her cow, even if they didn't have a house. *I'll write to Prescott to send two.*

The next month, February, Jonathan trudged to the meeting in icy wind, shards pelting his face. He held his great cloak around his neck and pushed his head into the bitter gale. The tails of his cloak flapped around his legs. He had left his tall hat at home, when it was swept off at the door. He pulled the mons cap that Mary Prescott had knitted over his ears.

The smoke blew toward him in a downdraft, and he coughed and spat phlegm until he pulled his cloak to cover all but his watering eyes. Someone tending the door let Jonathan in before he knocked. Then the man slammed the door against the gusts, grazing Jonathan's shoulder. Proprietors and men on the waiting list were restless from winter inactivity, and waiting to work their land was as bitter as the weather.

Ezekiel Holliman stood next to Jonathan and confided, "I came in from Dedham. I'm not going to be talked about in my absence when I can't defend myself."

The meeting moderator started. "Our town will be too far to travel to Watertown to get flour from their mill. Thomas Cakebread, a millwright and petitioner, has attended meetings only sporadically. He seems uninterested in talking about a mill for Dedham, so we can't count on him for our mill. Until we have our own mill, our women must grind by hand."

"Can we count on him to lead our military, at least?" called someone. "We are still at war with the Indians, you know."

Without waiting for an answer to that question, Abraham Shaw stood up. "With the right help"—he looked at Jonathan—"I could build your corn mill."

"The town would grant you sixty acres if it's a water-driven gristmill." said Alleyn. Shaw nodded, and the room erupted in a resounding "Huzzah!"

Abraham turned to Jonathan and said, "Every Yorkshireman knows a bit about putting water to work—we harnessed ours by directing it off the Pennine Hills to run mills. Might you come with me to look for a place? It looks as if you'll get your land soon."

"Aye," assured Jonathan.

"Without you, I wouldn't undertake such a task."

After the meeting, Jonathan stopped Abraham and said, "You're one of the most respected members of the new village. Your name is called only second or third on any roll. Will you present me to the townsmen at the meeting when they vote whether I will become a proprietor?"

"I'd be honored, Jonathan, but I believe it wiser if you're sponsored by someone who isn't a Yorkshireman. I suggest John Dwight. After your time in Watertown, he knows you, your family, and your servant well. He's also respected."

"Ta, I will talk with him."

"You know I'll support you should questions arise regarding your character or motives here or in England."

Warmed by thoughts of finally joining Dedham and receiving land, Jonathan passed the landing place called the Keye and rowed to Little River on March 23, 1637, just two days before the new year. This would be the first meeting of Dedham proprietors on their own soil.

As the sun melted the remaining sparkling crystals of frozen snow and ice, and the brisk wind still held a chill in the early morning, Jonathan worried he might not be accepted into the society of Dedham, even after all he had done with and for them here.

Past the arm that stretched off the Charles River to become the Little River, there sat a fine starter house on the east side of the small stream. Jonathan knew it well as the home of John Dwight.

Jonathan trudged, boots squishing, up the slippery, muddy slope of yellow tangled grass. He waited for the other settlers to converge to join him on the way to Dwight's house. The men bantered congratulations and jovial conversation as they approached. They were feeling their freedom from the ever-changing rules and wary proprietors of Watertown.

As Fairbanks removed his tall hat to enter, Dwight nodded at him but remained at the table in deep conversation with Edward Alleyn. When it was announced that the second grant of lots was being laid, Dwight told Jonathan that he expected to present him as the town voted on his proprietorship, even before Jonathan asked.

Jonathan recognized each of the sixteen proprietors huddled into Dwight's house. *I feel at peace with these men and trust the land to provide for and keep my family safe, but will I be allowed to sign the covenant today?* Would his name be written in the book as a proprietor or as someone who was turned away? If he was not accepted unanimously, what other settlement would take his family? *Where would we go?*

The gavel startled Jonathan, and he watched as Edward Alleyn began to meticulously scribe the attendance and begin the new minutes. As educated men, they realized the importance of preserving their proceedings for future reference.

Jonathan's knee jumped in quick cadence as he waited for the minutes to be read. He put his hand on his thigh to wipe the sweat from his palm and still his leg, but it resisted all restraint. Jonathan knew he would be scrutinized. He had to state his name and motive for planting in Dedham. Then the proprietors could ask questions about any actions in England or the colony that might incriminate him. Jonathan looked around at the men in the room.

Dwight had wooed and screened him for fitness. If he was not accepted, it might taint Dwight's reputation.

Jonathan's gaze lit on Abraham Shaw. *He will stand up for me*, he thought. If this town knew his own father thought him unworthy of a proper legacy, they might think so, too. But no one knew Jonathan had been slighted with only a daughter's inheritance.

Then Jonathan's eyes narrowed upon William Bearstow. A chill coursed from his crown to his toes. *He's from Halifax. He could know about my father's will. He's young and unpredictable.* Jonathan put both hands on his knees to settle his nerves and jumping legs.

But that didn't vex him as much as did his cousin Richard's support of Minister John Wheelwright and Ann Hutchinson. The trial for Wheelwright's sermon promoting the Covenant of Grace and denouncing the Massachusetts Bay Colony's ministers and magistrates with their Covenant of Works had been held earlier that month. Everyone knew about that. All the colonial ministers attended the public hearing, and Jonathan hoped the men of Dedham didn't know Richard had signed the petition in support of Wheelwright. If the man were convicted, Richard's weapons would be confiscated like those of the other signers. If anyone brought up the family connection, they could use it against Jonathan, even though none of it was his doing.

Jonathan wouldn't lie about his relationship with Richard or any other aspect of his life. If anyone found him in a lie, it was grounds for immediate expulsion. Not only he, but his presenter and anyone who stood up for him would suffer from such an act.

Time warped as the minutes were read. First, it slowed, then it raced to an end as Jonathan strained to keep his mind on what was being said.

"The second order of business..." announced the moderator.

John Dwight stood and said, "Who here knows Jonathan Fairbanks?"

Jonathan looked around to unanimous nods.

Dwight continued, "He has attended our public meetings, not as a proprietor, but as a staunch supporter. I spoke with him and his wife after our first petition. I think they are the right sort to live amongst us. He has a good education, strong common sense, and sound judgment. He has moderate principles like the rest of us."

He makes me sound good. Jonathan's knees still jumped.

"Fairbanks probably has more means than many of us for settling. He brings materials from England in preparation for a fine house. Jonathan and his near-grown sons will be firm assets to our plantation. He came early with his boys, before being accepted into town, to help work on common lands and buildings. I would like to have him as my neighbor. He narrowly missed the first allotments because of his indecision, but he has firmly made up his mind now. In fact, he is first on the list for our second allotments."

"He has a servant," someone in the crowd said. "We must know that he is of an amenable character. Fairbanks must know he can't be allotted land."

"He has one indentured servant, Samuel Bullen, who has not reached majority, nor served out his covenant. Under Fairbanks's directions, he, too, has been of value to our community and brings meekness of character."

"Now, Fairbanks, you must speak for yourself," commanded Alleyn. "Give us your name and why you wish to join Dedham."

Jonathan's tongue stuck to the top of his mouth. He rose deliberately and stood tall. "I am Jonathan Fairbanks, from Sowerby, Halifax Parish, West Yorkshire, England. I work in wool and make spinning wheels. After studying the possible plantations for my family to permanently reside, I found the men of Dedham hold the ideals and morals most like ours." He nodded and sat down.

"Do any members have questions or comments about Goodman Fairbanks, before we vote?"

Jonathan watched while the men looked back and forth around the room. His knee resumed jumping under his firm hand.

One man smirked and said, "Some clothiers of West Yorkshire who make kersey uniforms for the king's army are accused of deception, using cheap and inferior materials to increase their profits. They say if it rains the uniforms shrink to the size of a lad."

The whole meeting erupted in laughter at this old joke. But Jonathan knew he was not immune to the judgment people made of his peers in the trade.

Abraham Shaw stood and said, "I knew the Fairbanks families in Halifax Parish. I suppose all here know of Sir Richard Saltonstall from there. The Fairbanks and Saltonstall families have intermarried in the past. Sir Saltonstall, the Fairbanks families, and I all worked in the clothier business in Halifax Parish. The Fairbankses are respected there. He will be an asset to the community. He makes a fine variety and quality of spinning wheels. We need him in this town. He helped my family after our fire in Watertown, and I'd be pleased to have him as a neighbor."

A murmur swirled about the room. No one raised a question.

After a long pause, another man asked, "What relation is Richard Fairbanks to you, Goodman Fairbanks?

Moisture beaded on Jonathan's forehead. He paused. "Why, I believe he is a cousin. Do you need to know the exact lineage?"

"No, I hear he's asking for a license to sell wine and strong waters at his tavern in Boston. I thought we all might enjoy his hospitality when we are there." Several sniggered and nodded. Whispers floated about the room.

Alleyn waited a few moments. No more questions were presented. "Have you read the covenant, Fairbanks?"

Jonathan nodded.

"Are you willing to sign it, abide by it, and see that your family, heirs, and servant subscribe to it?"

Jonathan raised a forefinger with a slight nod.

"Let's vote. Hand me your hat, Fairbanks. No one needs to show their vote. One grain of wheat, yes, one grain of corn, no." Samuel Morse, the collector, passed the hat for the men to drop their grains. After Morse circuited the room, he looked in the hat and hesitated. When he looked up at the men anticipating the tally, he said with a smile, "The vote is unanimous. Welcome, Fairbanks."

Alleyn stood and applied his gavel to the top of the table, saying, "As proprietors of Dedham, we're happy to have you amongst us." A general shuffle of congratulations and welcome came from around the room, then the gavel came down again to restore order.

"You may come forward and sign as our thirty-first proprietor of Dedham."

Jonathan quietly approached, signed the document, and shook the hands of Edward Alleyn, and the other men at the table.

"Huzzah! Huzzah! Huzzah!" came from the crowd.

"It's about time," someone said in the back of the room.

Jonathan sat down. The gavel cracked again, and Alleyn said, "Fairbanks, you'll be expected to pay all common fees of the town to Samuel Morse, our collector. As a married man, you'll receive a twelve-acre home lot with four acres of swamp land and meadows. Looks like your land will abut John Rogers's on the north, Wigwam Swamp on the east, and Little River on the west. Philemon Dalton is on the south."

Jonathan was pleased. This was a good lot for a second survey, between those of two early petitioners.

"If you accept that lot, you can start clearing and share in all future divisions of land. You and your boys must clear one fourth of the extra swamp land each year. If you do not, the land will be forfeit."

A man whispered from behind Jonathan, "You're fortunate to have manly sons to help. We all have lots of work to do."

"Speaking of work," continued Alleyn, "we are now building a hog pound on the Big Island. Lambert Genery oversees the actual building. Fairbanks, you and your fellow Yorkshireman, William Bearstow, along with Samuel Morse, will be responsible for getting wood for Genery."

The discussion moved to Abraham Shaw's corn mill. "Every lot owner will help bring the millstones from the Watertown Mill by land to the boating place and get them to Dedham."

As the final gavel cracked, the men congratulated Jonathan for becoming a settler among them. Jonathan thanked Dwight and bade him goodbye.

Dwight leaned close to Jonathan's ear. "You are fortunate you made your move. We are discussing closing the proprietorships at forty-six. There are others on the waiting list and some lots will be held for proprietors with trades we need for our village, like a blacksmith and a wheelwright."

Somewhat relieved, Jonathan walked to his canoe, his legs shaky.

Shaw overtook him. "Are you going to see your land?"

"Aye," said Jonathan as he untied the canoe, still partially hidden by the early morning vapor off the river. "We were given a fine lot to build a house—I know the place. But as contented as these men feel this place, I feel no contentment."

"Why not?" asked Shaw. "Haven't you been longing for this?"

"I've been given a town job, as you heard. Town orders stipulate I must have clapboards up to protect my house by the first of May, only a bit more than a month away." Jonathan started pushing the canoe into the water—he didn't have time to tarry. "The lot must be cleared and timber gathered to build. We must occupy the house by November, and I don't yet have a builder. The swamp land will be forfeit if parts of it aren't cleared within the year. I am fortunate to have near grown boys and a servant. Even with them, I don't see any way to get this all done. And still we must eat!"

PART III

1637–1650

INDIANS

"It's not safe to be in Dedham." Grace said in a quavering voice as she grasped Jonathan's arm. "What if the Indians attack? There are few men there, and you're taking our sons."

"That's where I've chosen for our family, Grace," said Jonathan. "We must work there every minute we can—we have twelve acres to clear, a house to build and occupy by November, a garden and crops to plant, and village obligations. I must be ready for a mason and craftsman to build as soon as I can find them." He clawed his fingers over his head, then turned to his sons.

"Boys, get ready. Prepare to spend several nights. We'll beat the sunup and defy it to set."

The older boys and Samuel gathered their things by the door, and six-year-old Junior rushed down the ladder with a bundle of clothes.

"Junior," said Jonathan, "Mother needs a man here, so I need you to chop wood and do chores. I'll see if your young friend, John Dwight, can come back with us from Dedham to stay a few days."

Junior dropped his bundle and balled his fists at his sides.

The Fairbanks men pulled their canoes onto the east bank of the Little River near their grant, and Jonathan checked the dole rods that marked their property. "We'll cut all trees in the dooryard area first. Stack the poorer pieces there for firewood. Leave anything straight and about five feet long in a separate pile for fence posts. Jonathan clapped his hand twice on a large white oak. "Leave this one until I return. We'll use it for a summer beam."

"What's that?" asked Jonas, patting the tree as his father had done.

"The biggest beam in the house. It will hold up the second story above the hall."

"What about the stumps, Father?" asked John, who would act as foreman in his father's absence. Though Samuel Bullen, the servant, was two years older than John.

"This knoll where the house will sit must be clean and level. Hack the centers out of the stumps, and we'll set them afire to level them to the ground," Jonathan looked up at the sun, shielding his eyes with his hands. He paced off a rough rectangle in the lot that lay close to the Native path that passed their land. As he coursed the perimeter, he marked the area. "This will be the Fairbanks house."

At his Boston tavern, Richard Fairbanks gave Jonathan a warm smile. "Good morrow. How fare ye, Jonathan? Have you decided where you'll dwell?"

"Aye, in Dedham, among the educated Puritans who bade me there. I signed the covenant in March. I'm in Boston to find a carpenter. Do you have any suggestions?"

"The wealthy in Boston keep our craftsmen busy. I know the carpenter for my place is already engaged. Go to Trader Coggan. He takes delivery of their supplies and may know someone available."

"How is Elizabeth, and your wee one—Constance?" Jonathan asked, and Richard smiled.

"Well, Jonathan, well. They've gone to market to get supplies for the tavern."

Jonathan looked around for listeners, still wary of discussing Richard's religious affiliations. "I hear rumors that you and many prestigious Boston men following Goodwife Hutchinson and Mr. Wheelwright—that you will be asked to relinquish your weapons."

"No, cousin, I have no need to relinquish mine, for I have denounced Mr. Wheelwright. He and his followers are being banished."

Jonathan left the tavern and passed through the din of the spacious marketplace where the two main thoroughfares of Boston met. The aromas enticed him, and he marveled at the bartering and the variety of wares. He caught sight of Elizabeth and greeted her and the growing little girl. He hesitated, then took Great Street east toward Boston Harbor.

Jonathan laughed at the coincidence that the very mason he had hired earlier at Trader Coggan's was signing for a load of bricks from England. "Are those for me?" he asked, startling the man.

"We shall see—I need to assess the place," said the mason, and they agreed to meet at Dedham to finalize details.

The hearth construction was secured, but Fairbanks was no closer to finding a carpenter. A hearth alone would not protect his family nor secure his land grant.

On April 23, alarms rang out across the Massachusetts Bay and Connecticut River colonies while Jonathan's boys cleared land and stacked the bricks from England. Mr. Thomas Carter arrived from Watertown and brought bits of news about an Indian attack to the west. Jonathan and the boys immediately headed back to be with the women during the alarm.

As the boys climbed out of their canoes, Jonathan warned, "Don't talk to your mother about the Indians. She'll know about them, anyway. I'm going to Munnings for details." Then he walked swiftly toward the tavern.

After a quick "How fare ye?" to the innkeeper, Jonathan waited for the details he knew would come.

Munnings didn't answer at first, then said with his head cocked to one side, "Fairbanks, have you not heard of the trouble with our brothers in Wethersfield?"

"Little information comes to Dedham." Jonathan moved closer.

"Things are bad." Munnings furiously wiped a horn cup. Young Governor Vale sent 160 men on an expedition to Wethersfield earlier this month. News just arrived that the Pequot have attacked the place."

Munnings set the horn mug down with a clack and threw the towel on the bar, drawing Fairbanks a draft. "Only a week ago, the savages killed six men and three women. This is the first I've heard of them killing women. Worst of all, they took two girls captive while they were working in the fields."

"Do you know who was struck?" asked Jonathan, leaning across the bar. "Reverend Denton and his family are there."

"Nay. Rumor says the new Connecticut governor, John Winthrop the Younger, will declare war. They are gathering Natives for support."

Jonathan sat quietly, his knee jumping.

"Do you know young Edward Culver?" asked Munnings.

"I do. Some say he'd be welcome in Dedham. He's a wheelwright."

"Culver came from England with John Winthrop the Younger and is involved in asking the Mohegan tribe for support. If an agreement is made, they'll fight together."

"Have you told any others from Dedham?" asked Jonathan.

"I talked with Robert Feke." Munnings wiped his hands with satisfaction. "Wethersfield is a hundred miles away, but those Pequot have gone all the way there from the mouth of the Connecticut River. What will keep them from coming back this way?"

"Robert Feke may have land in Dedham, but he hasn't shown interest in coming to us since the petition," Jonathan said with disgust and stood. "I must talk to Edward Alleyn about plans to protect our village."

"The General Court called for more training in every town." The tavern keeper looked hard at him. "Where will you and your boys train? Does Dedham have training?"

"If we have to come to Watertown for training, we'll never get our work done," called back Jonathan, halfway to the door.

Protection

Jonathan hurried to Dedham in time for the April 25 meeting at John Dwight's house. Edward Alleyn sat at the table working on the agenda. Jonathan spied Dwight and pulled him outdoors as men filed inside. When they reentered the house, Dwight spoke in a low, urgent tone, saying, "Edward, you had better listen to this. We may need to add to today's agenda."

Rumors churned as each newcomer related what he had heard of the news until Alleyn demanded order with his gavel. "The next man on the waiting list for the second round of lots is Mr. Thomas Carter, who now assists the church at Watertown."

Carter was put through the same scrutiny as the others had been and was readily accepted.

Jonathan was relieved he did not have to endure that again, but this time he worried about the Indians.

"Next issue." said Alleyn, "The Pequot have attacked Wethersfield."

The room exploded with chatter again. The gavel came down hard. It took a second rap to quiet the room.

The moderator took the floor. "We must choose someone to direct our militia and training."

A voice came from the corner of the room. "Where is Captain Thomas Cakebread, the military man?" He had helped petition for the grant and signed the covenant. The men looked around the room.

"Since he's not here," said Alleyn, "we must select a man among us." He searched the room for a candidate. The proprietors voted Daniel Morse as Sergeant of Arms and Abraham Shaw as clerk.

Daniel stood and said, "We can't wait to build a town to prepare for our protection. Sure, we are almost surrounded by water, but Wethersfield itself was on the Great River. The General Court has already ordered that all able-bodied men in every town train for the militia each Saturday."

"Aren't we exempt from duty for the colony?" A disgruntled voice asked.

"We're not exempt from protecting ourselves, and we aren't exempt in case of an emergency," responded Morse.

A rumble circled the room.

Alleyn plied the gavel.

Daniel spoke again. "The General Court has ordered a watch and ward held around the clock to alert the colony of suspicious activities. I believe our Neponset Natives near Fairbanks's lot have left Wigwam Swamp for the summer, but we still must be on guard."

"What about clearing our land and getting our houses built before winter?" came another voice. "When are we supposed to do that?"

"If we are not safe, there is no need for houses," interjected Jonathan, with nods around the room.

150

"Fairbanks," said Morse, "you have two sons and one servant—sixteen or over—that must train. Age aside, every able-bodied man will participate."

"Jonas will train, too," said Jonathan. "He's almost thirteen, and I won't be able to keep him away."

Laughter ensued. Jonas, with his energy and questions, had already established a reputation among the residents of Dedham.

Daniel Morse continued. "Since 1631, the General Court has required all men have weapons and powder. If anyone is without provisions, the town will provide them."

"Where are we going to get the money for that?" asked another voice.

Alleyn explained, "We'll arrange funds from the proprietors. Everyone must be able to protect the town. Now, we must complete today's business, so we can get back to our land and building." After a brief pause, Alleyn said, "Lambert Genery has been in bad humours all winter, though he has worked for the town's benefit. Now, he's unable to put clapboards on his house by the May deadline. He already has the boards drawn. I say that as a peaceful and loving society, we should extend the village's deadline until the first of June."

As the crowd voiced their approval, Jonathan watched a ray of sunshine cross the floor. He found it difficult to sit any longer. *Will they extend the deadline again?* he wondered. He wouldn't be ready for clapboards even by late fall.

But if the trouble with Indians continues, Grace won't bring the young ones here, anyway.

Devil's Oven

Jonathan gathered the boys to return to Watertown for the Sabbath. Before casting off, he cautioned them, "You heard a lot about the Pequot here. We were talking as men.

151

Don't bother the women about this. Men take care of these problems."

"You're back," Grace said, letting her spoon slip into the pot and held out her arms to give each son a hug, including Sam, who had become like family. "I heard about Wethersfield and the Pequot. Do you think Reverend Denton and his family are all right?"

Jonathan kept his back to her as he hung up his cloak. Instead of answering her question, he told her about the new plans for the security and fortification of Dedham.

"You and the boys are there all the time," Grace remarked. "What about Hannah Dwight? Is she staying there with her children?"

Jonas piped up with excitement, risking a reprimand from his father. "If the Indians come to Dedham, we can hide in Devil's Oven."

"Jonas!" gasped Grace. "What is a Devil's Oven?" Her face contorted in worry, and Mary Elizabeth and Susan giggled. Junior moved closer to hear.

"We found a cave at the bottom of some rosy-colored speckled boulders in the west. You'd find these rocks to your liking, Mother." Jonas nodded sagely. "There's a small opening at the bottom where you can squeeze in. It is kind of hot and steamy in the cave, but the Indians wouldn't find us there."

"Jonas . . ." his father growled, and Jonas fled up the ladder to the loft.

Relief and Refuge

A drum throbbed, announcing the July 14 meeting in Dedham. Cheerfully, the men gathered, talking and joking, for the crisis with the Natives seemed to be quelled.

John Dwight started the meeting with the announcement, "Ezekiel Holliman wishes to lay down his lot." Jonathan looked around. Holliman wasn't there, even after vowing he'd never miss a meeting after the fine for using clapboards.

Private discussions broke out. In a small town, it was difficult to keep one's thoughts to oneself. Word was getting around that Ezekiel followed Reverend Roger Williams and was wandering from the Puritan way. Jonathan shook the chill from his shoulders, knowing how close he had come being denied proprietorship because of his own cousin's beliefs.

Dwight continued. "Major Thomas Cakebread assisted Sgt. Morse during our fears of Pequot attack, but now he won't dwell amongst us, either. He's selling his land." Apprehension quaked through the room at the loss of military assistance. Jonathan shook his head.

John Dwight silenced the side discussions. "We do have twelve new men asking to settle, and they will be assets to our village. Several are clerics from England."

Someone grumbled, "The colony smarts with so many religious men leaving England—they've all come here to find a congregation."

"Have they received their certification from the General Court?" someone asked. "After Roger Williams, Wheelwright, and the Hutchinson woman, we can't be too careful."

Jonathan spoke almost to himself, "We'll need all the prayers we can get if we don't have a strong military leader."

"We're not discussing who should be our pastor—we're simply admitting godly men who wish to settle amongst us," continued Dwight, side-stepping the comments. "As a cleric, Mr. John Allin disguised himself to board a ship from England. John Morse and Ralph Wheelock were also clerics. Many know Mr. Timothy Dalton, brother of Philemon. Timothy will settle with us even if he doesn't become our minister. Mr. Thomas Carter is already among us, though detained in Watertown by the church there.

"Mr. Allin brings with him some of his congregation, the three Fisher brothers. Thomas Fisher is a master carpenter. We'd like to talk with you after the meeting, Thomas, about a meetinghouse . . ."

"As an educated society, we welcome Eleazur Lusher, who will help with our town's record keeping. Next, we have Michael Metcalf. He fled England's authorities after speaking out against the king. His wife hid him under straw in the garret of their house. He was a successful clothier but also has skills to educate our boys."

Words were dangerous in England, Jonathan mused, though they could be dangerous in the colony, too. *I tried to warn Grace to be careful.* When he had confided in Prescott, he made sure they weren't overheard. Even at the taverns and the faire, there seemed to be a watcher about.

As the acceptance process dragged on, Jonathan shifted his weight against the wall, knowing the work that needed to be done before nightfall. He hoped one of the new men had brought a team of oxen.

The Fairbanks House 1637

As Jonathan walked, heat shimmered over the surface of the only well-trodden path of Dedham. At a distance he saw Thomas Fisher approach. "Goodman Fisher," Jonathan called to the middle-aged man built like one who worked hard. "May I have a word with you?"

"Oh, aye. You must be Jonathan Fairbanks. You have a fine chimney nearly complete. I walked that way after the meeting last month just to see what you've done. Large indeed—must be eight by ten at the base, with three hearths. Quite impressive."

"Aye, forty thousand bricks. I understand *you're* a skilled craftsman," said Jonathan. "We're fortunate to have you in our village. Would you be interested in building a house around that chimney?"

"Goodman Fairbanks, I'd be proud to ply my trade to that edifice, but I have covenanted with the village to build the meetinghouse. I can't take on two large tasks at once. And the town is more demanding of my time."

"Thank you, Goodman Fisher. I'm sure you will build a fine meetinghouse. Will your brothers be helping you?

"The whole town will help."

Jonathan pressed his lips together in disappointment. *Not only no carpenter for me, but yet another task for the town!*

He continued on his way to meet Philemon Dalton, Abraham Shaw, and Samuel Morse to plan the causeway and bridge to be built over the Little River. Jonathan clenched his jaw. *The whole town needs the bridge, to be sure, but I need a house for my family.*

By mid-August, summer was dragging on for those who toiled in the oppressive heat. The Fairbanks chimney was finished with a fine plumb on both faces. The family had felled timber to be sawn at the pits for the house frame and clapboards, hoping those would still be allowed. The boys gathered saplings and made slats of wood to use for wattle, remembering John Vahan's frigid house before it was insulated with wattle and daub.

Jonathan visited with Joseph Kingsbury on the west side of town, knowing of his skills as a mechanic and woodworker. However, he was not the type of master craftsman to build Fairbanks's large house. As Jonathan left Kingsbury's house, he pounded his fist into the other palm. There would be others glad to take his grant if he couldn't settle by November. The thought galled him. *But God will direct our plans and our hands if this be His will. Our work won't be for naught. We'll have a house that will last forever.*

In August, along with a cooling zephyr through the meetinghouse came a breeze of optimism. John Roper Sr. and his twenty-six-year-old son, both carpenters from Norfolk, East Anglia, were admitted to the town. Were the Ropers God's answer to his prayers or just another disappointment?

Wood creaked as John Roper, Jr., followed his father down the steep steps at Munnings's ordinary in Watertown. The son carried a large carpenter's manual into the tavern.

"Greetings, Goodman Fairbanks," the father called out to Jonathan. "What type of house are you planning? We have started building a new style in England."

"I want the tried and true, an East Anglian timber frame style. I believe we have cut enough trees," Jonathan showed his calloused hands and smiled.

The son flipped through the pages of the book until he found one like Jonathan had described. "Aye," Roper Sr. said. "We have built plenty of these around London. After inspecting your fine chimney, I see you wish to have two rooms down and two up. Your house will stand above the others in Dedham, for most are building only one-story houses, most with just two rooms."

"Aye," Jonathan said as he looked over the well-worn plans. "This is close to what I have in mind. Grace wants the hall larger than the parlor." Jonathan ran his fingers over the lines of the house, indicating size differences. As you see, the house will face south, toward Wigwam Pond. Better to have the back against the northern blasts of winter. As you'll soon learn, these winters in New England are brutal." Jonathan shook his shoulders.

"On your lot," said Roper, "I think we can make a fine house, thirty-six feet by sixteen-and-a-half feet. We'll build it on a stone foundation. I assume you will want a main door in the middle, in front of the chimney bay, and windows in each room on either side of the door?"

"I have glass panes coming from England." Jonathan said with a nod. "Enough for four windows with four-inch hand-blown diamond panes that will be set in lead cames."

Roper put a finger above and right of the image of the doorway "Did you get a small window to light the chimney bay and another above it on the second floor? You may want light there if you put in a staircase later."

"Back to those winters," Roper continued. "With windows in every room, the house will get colder. But if we keep the ceilings low, it will hold the warmth down. I can put a little extra height in the parlor, to six feet at most."

"We'll start with a ship-like oak frame, held together with large trunnels—perhaps you call them wooden pegs or tree nails? They won't rust." Roper didn't wait for an answer but went on with his plans. "I've just come, but I hear there is no lime in this area. We'll have to go with clapboards for the exterior."

"Clapboards," Jonathan smiled to himself and nodded after all the agony over clapboards.

"You say the winters are harsh," Roper went on. "Daub will erode out of the walls if they aren't duly covered."

Jonathan nodded and smiled again, "The town approved them until next year, mid-June."

"Cedar is good for clapboards," said Roper, "and overlapping them should give your daub good coverage. We'll nail the clapboards directly to the studs, with no sheathing underneath, then back fill them with the wattle and daub from the inside. We can use swamp cedar for the narrow clapboards in the back and on the sides that are more exposed to the weather. Keeping them narrow helps keep out the wind. Then we'll use wide oak clapboards in the front for a finer finish."

"Any trees we can use out of our swamp will help us get our quota cleared for the year," said Jonathan, his shoulders relaxing. "I brought nails from England, thanks to a blacksmith friend. There will be no delay for want of them."

Jonathan's ease changed as he looked up at John Roper, Sr., and said, "We must occupy it by November.

"My son and I must provide for our own family first," said Roper curtly, "and we also must be in by November. Yours is a big house. I'm not sure we can finish it by then."

"What am I to do?" Jonathan put his hand to his forehead. "I have a lot, a chimney, and even timber. If the house is not livable by November, all my work will be in vain, and my lot will revert to town property."

The younger Roper started to close the manual while the elder said, "Perhaps I'm not the man for the job."

Jonathan shoved his hand between the pages as the book shut. He looked directly at Roper. "Then who? I've looked everywhere. I can't build it myself. I won't settle for a two-room house, for I already have a four-room chimney."

"You said you have several grown sons and a servant. My son here knows the trade." He looked at Junior, who nodded expectantly. "We can build the frame for your house and at least enclose the hall with clapboards. Your family can live there while you put in the wattle and daub for insulation, mixing it in a corner of the hall. Then we will *all* build a small house for *my* family before finishing yours."

"But Grace wants wooden floors," protested Fairbanks.

"We can put those in later. Since they won't be out in the elements, they can be pine, like all the trim work," said Roper.

"Can I bring the women and children out before November?"

"Aye, I think it possible, if you have the proper wood prepared. Do you have good oak for the frame and structure?"

"We have hewed several large oaks from our lot. We hope to use one particular white oak for the summer beam in the hall." Jonathan ran his finger across the page between the west wall and the fireplace in the middle of the kitchen. "But we won't have time to cure the wood before we start."

"That's not a problem. If the mortise and tenon joints are affixed while the wood is green, the joint will get firmer as it dries." Roper pointed to the top of the house. "We'll use pine for roof boarding. Or will you thatch?

"Which would you suggest?" Jonathan looked at Roper, hoping his deference would further bind the man to his cause.

"Thatch can be done quickly, and Dedham has lush, tall grasses in the meadow to use this fall. The garret will be steep, so the thatch will shed water and heavy snow. You can use wood sheaths or tile later."

"Can we put the back door at the west end of the north wall? Then we can enter the hall there. It will be the warmest room in the house and the busiest," said Jonathan.

"Sounds like a fine idea. Will you add a lean-to?"

"Let's just get the main building done now."

Roper agreed. "With our five young men and a team of oxen to move the wood—"

"I have no oxen!" interrupted Jonathan with panic in his eyes.

"I'm not sure we can get this done without them," Roper said, starting to close the book again.

"If I borrow a team, can we get this done?" Jonathan pleaded. "We both live on the east side of Little River. You are only ten lots from me."

"Pray for a late winter and no injuries. Then, I think we can at least be in our houses by November."

Fairbanks patted Roper on the back. Finally, he had a plan that might work. *Grace will be pleased.*

House and Home

Grace's eyes watered as she walked the paths of Watertown. The stench in the streets of the densely populated village had grown intense. Nowhere in the hills of Sowerby were the streets and ditches stagnant with the waste of animals and people alike. Here, the late August heat simmered the smells into the air. The flies feasted on the waste, then bit at any exposed skin.

Each time Jonathan and the boys returned from Dedham, they talked of the shade of dense trees, cool breezes off the fresh water, waving meadows, and progress on the house. Grace longed to be there in her new home.

She shook her head and groaned, "We must leave this place!" She decided she would abide the noise of building and abide living in an unfinished house. She could even abide the mournful wails of the wolves in the swamp. She'd stay in sweltering, stinking Watertown no longer.

Jonathan took Grace's hand as she stepped out of the canoe rocking against the muddy shoulder of Little River. He pointed up the hill with pride, where the large, framed Fairbanks House stood.

Grace's mouth dropped open. "Only the hall is enclosed!" she cried. "We will have less room than when we stayed at the Vahan house."

Jonathan dropped her hand and stared at what had become a monument to all his trials, the building of his hopes. "Wait until you see the hall hearth," he said. "It's large enough to build three fires for your cooking. There's room enough to step inside, hooks for curing meat. It's brick, so less risk of fire."

He waited for some approval, then added, "You survived a ship and a brazier for eight weeks. Find patience, and we'll soon have the home we've always wanted."

Grace pulled her skirts up and picked her way through the cracked, dried mud along the narrow path. The grasses grabbed at her hem as she charged up the hill to inspect her house.

Trees

"Jonathan, I don't know these people in Dedham," complained Grace. "We've now moved twice since we got to New England. You traveled about with wool, but I didn't set foot out of West Yorkshire before we left England. I miss my family and friends."

"You know Bridget Shaw and Hannah Dwight," said Jonathan. "They're here. Or do you want me to send you back to England on a ship?"

"I couldn't abide another voyage. Nor leave you." Grace's eyes glistened with tears as she turned away from the children exploring the unfinished house. "There's no meetinghouse here, Jonathan. That's where I met women at Watertown. But we can't go back there in the canoes every Sabbath. We must attend services." She looked deep into Jonathan's eyes. "Besides, we'll be fined if we don't."

"Nay, Grace. There are so many clerics here in Dedham, there is no reason to travel seventeen miles to Watertown. The Dedham clerics come from many parts of England, all here for the sake of piety, and they have asked us all to meet on a day besides the Sabbath to get to know one another. We are all working so diligently to settle that we have no time to get acquainted. The village can be of one mind, peaceable, and loving if we know one another."

"There's no meetinghouse," Grace, repeated.

"Not yet, though we are all asked to build it. For now, we're to meet the fifth day every week under a large shade tree on the west side of town near Mr. John Allin's lot. He seems to be taking the lead."

"Does that mean the meetinghouse will be built there?"

"Aye, many assume so."

"But how far is that? When you brought me to town, it seemed as if the homes on the west were quite far from here. How do we get there? Not by boat."

Jonathan let her have her speech, waiting for his chance to answer.

"What about winters with ice and snow?" she went on. "I'm not sure I can bear the heat of the summer, either." Grace threw her hands up and let them fall on her skirts.

"Aye, we must consider that, Grace. For now, we must abide some discomforts to keep you out of Watertown." Jonathan took his hat off the peg by the door and took his leave.

On the first meeting day, instead of crossing the Little River and the swampy land to walk to the Dedham gathering, the Fairbanks family paddled down the Charles River. Grace frowned as she juggled the food she had prepared while Susan and Junior rocked the canoe, twisting and turning to greet their young friend, John Dwight Jr., and to look for other children their age. Just before they reached Big Island, Jonathan pulled the canoe up on Joseph Kingsbury's landing.

Holding her skirts and grumbling, Grace trudged up the slope. As she approached the meeting tree, she saw goodwives gathered round a trestle table arranging an array of food. "There's Bridget Shaw and Hannah Dwight!" Grace said with delight, and her step quickened as she left Jonathan's side and dismissed her children to find new friends.

The summer sun bore down on Jonathan and the men on the east side of the Little River, which divided Dedham. They were planning a crossing over it.

"With more and more proprietors receiving grants on the east side, we should have some of our meetings under a tree in *east* Dedham," said Jonathan. "Grace is already complaining about the distance in a canoe and the long walks to Mr. Allin's."

"Aye, but we must have a plan before we propose a change," suggested Philemon Dalton.

"What about that giant white oak about four lots northwest of mine?" asked Jonathan. "I think it's on the lot Thomas Cakebread was granted. That oak is bigger than Mr. Allin's tree. It provides more shade." He wiped his brow and looked up at the glaring sun. "It's not far from the Little River, and there's a fine path beaten to it. Most of the other large trees nearby were felled for building."

At the next tree gathering, the town agreed to alternate meetings on the east and west side in loving consideration of the entire society.

Screams of Wolves

A strange young man pulled his canoe onto the Keye. Men gathering thatch in a meadow stopped and stretched, watching as he strode up the hill. From higher ground, John Ellis greeted the young man, and Jonathan overheard the greeting as he leaned on his pitchfork.

"Edward Culver," called Ellis. "They must have released you from military duty. Have you come to see me or Ann?"

Jonathan remembered the name. Munnings had talked about this man. Some men, including John Ellis, suggested him as a Dedham proprietor, given his military background. He was a wheelwright, too.

Culver and Ellis talked as they passed the common meadow, and Jonathan heard them mention the Pequot. Several dropped their tools and moved in closer. Soon, a crowd grew around Ellis and Culver.

Ellis scanned the area. "Let's stop under this shade tree, so everyone can listen. Otherwise, I'll spend all fall recounting your story to every man in the village."

The crowd grew as Culver related the struggle that led to the Pequot War and his friendship with Chief Uncas of the Mohegan.

Grace was on her way to barter for honey. She stopped when she saw the crowd and stood at a distance. She tucked her basket behind her skirt and looked around, trying to stay inconspicuous. Other goodwives were also gathered around at a distance, rarely welcome to men's discussions. Few men shared military talk with their wives, and Grace was sure Jonathan wouldn't.

"You remember John Oldham, the Watertown trader who was killed on Block Island?" Culver asked. The former Watertown residents nodded.

"What about the boys? What happened to his nephews?" someone interrupted.

"They were taken to Boston by the men who found them. They're all right."

Grace sighed with relief and resolved to tell Jonas as soon as she returned home.

Culver continued his account. "Governor Vale sent Captain Endicott with troops to Block Island in July to find the murderers. After a small skirmish, they found five or six Native villages abandoned. Endicott took it upon himself to destroy the villages, all their corn and supplies. Then troops were sent to Fort Saybrook to meet the Connecticut troops. We tried to find the murderers of Trader Stone there with no success, so our troops destroyed those Native villages.

"In autumn, the Pequot laid siege to Fort Saybrook in Connecticut. The Indians burned and destroyed all the storage and buildings outside the fort. Anyone leaving the fort was killed. The Natives blocked the Great River so no supplies could come by boat to the Fort nor to Wethersfield and Hartford farther west."

Someone in the audience offered, "Just like the Indians did to Jamestown in 1609." A rumble of discussion ensued until Culver started again.

"The Pequot tried to get the Narragansetts to join them, but they had entered a formal alliance with the colony. The siege at Fort Saybrook lasted until April, when the Pequot joined with a western tribe and went to Wethersfield."

A buzz rose from the crowd. The women silently stared at each other in the background.

"I guess you all knew some of those settlers," Culver continued as he looked around. "Six men and three women were killed while working in their fields. The Natives took two girls captive and killed all the cattle and horses they could."

Grace's hand flew to her mouth at the thought of Reverend Denton and Matthew Mitchell and their families.

"The first of May, John Winthrop, Jr., the new Governor of Connecticut, declared war. That's when Captain John Mason from the Great River Valley asked me to accompany him to the Mohegan Tribe where he asked his good friend, Sachem Uncas, for support. After our battles together, the chief and I became friends too. We sailed to Saybrook on the Great River and met up with the Narragansetts as our allies, thanks to Roger Williams having befriended them. The English outnumbered the Mohegan men, but the Narragansetts had twice as many as both of us. Three hundred forty set out on foot for a thirty-mile march to Mystic, Connecticut. Well"—he looked up with a wry grin—"the Natives don't really march."

The crowd laughed.

"It was hot, not like a typical May. The English were exhausted, but the Indians fared much better. We learned a lot about fighting tactics from our allied tribes. We camped overnight near a Pequot palisaded fort that enclosed their village. It was as well built as many of ours. We had received orders to attack only that fort."

The Dedham crowd hung on every word.

"At dawn, we quietly surrounded the Mystic fort. The English formed an inner ring and the Native allies an outer ring. Captain Mason and twenty Englishmen forced their way into one side of the structure, while Captain Underhill's men entered the other.

"The Pequot heard them breaching the entries and immediately retaliated. The English were ordered to battle with swords and to bring back plunder, but half of Captain Mason's men were killed immediately, leaving only ten to fight."

Culver paused as if replaying the scene in his head and shuffled his feet. No one interrupted.

"On the other side, Underhill met the same resistance. He realized the narrow lanes between the Indian wetus—their houses—made battle impossible."

The Dedham crowd cringed as a huge flock of crows suddenly flew up from the trees, cawing as they passed overhead.

"Underhill stepped into one wetu and brought out a stick of burning wood and set the thatch aflame. A stiff northeast breeze blew, spreading the fire through the village. Both troops retreated to surround the fort. The Natives couldn't escape the fire, and those who ran out of the flames were shot on sight."

Culver cast his eyes to the ground. "There *were* women and children." He shook his head, not making eye contact with the men in the crowd. "The sounds were like the mournful screams of wolves in a night swamp." Glassy eyed, Culver turned his gaze to the sky, and the men murmured to one another.

Large tears rolled down Grace's cheeks. The taste of salt curled into the corners of her mouth, bile rose from her gut.

She set her basket down and put her hands over her ears, trying to shake the cries of women and children from her mind. She'd heard those screams from mothers when she delivered stillborn babies and from anguished newborns as they were pulled from their mother's wombs. She knew the wails of mothers who had lost their daughters to childbirth.

One by one, the Dedham women slipped away like shadows. But Grace stood transfixed and let her hands fall to her sides.

Culver cleared his throat twice and looked away. "Now, if you'll excuse me, men, there is someone I mean to see." He looked at John Ellis, who nodded, and the two of them made their way through the crowd of men.

Everyone returned to his task in silence. As she watched him walk away, Grace wondered what they had done to anger God, to bring this wrath upon his people.

She headed to their unfinished house, knuckles white on the handle of her empty basket, avoiding everyone on the way. *This is* not *"a city upon a hill, as an example for the world to see" as Governor John Winthrop professed,* she thought. *Those poor women and children. Her own sons and husband could be called to fight. Maybe we should have stayed in England.*

The General Court ordered an observance of a day of thanksgiving in all churches in New England on October 12 to commemorate the end of the Pequot War. All the citizens of Dedham were obliged to gather under the west tree for a full day of sermons and prayers. The townsfolk shared a new sense of community spirit, but after Culver's story, they didn't find much joy in feasting as they had on other days of thanksgiving.

Gatherings

The earth shrugged off the heat of summer and the fear of impending doom. As the shade trees relinquished their leaves to the fading sun and chilling winds, small groups of Dedham settlers began meeting in established homes.

The Fairbanks house, though not completely finished, was spacious enough to make a suitable gathering place.

When hosting a meeting, each head of household acted as moderator to help the people to focus on acquainting themselves with one another's talents and spiritual temperaments. Each group discussed ways to conduct their town under the covenant of love as a congenial society.

The fifth day of the week, Jonathan walked into the parlor and looked over the fine linens that Grace was carefully spreading on the bed they'd gotten out storage in Boston. To provide for the guests, she clothed the trestle table in the hall and adorned it with her few pewter serving pieces and some simple treats, leaving room for the dishes their guests would bring to share. Jonathan smiled when he saw the mazer bowl and the lacquered jug amongst the settings.

"Ah, Grace, I have looked forward to this day since the meetings in those small Watertown houses to plan Dedham. I always envisioned a grand house to welcome guests."

Jonathan took one of her hands in both of his. "You have dressed yourself as fine as you have our new home. We can welcome our guests as they should be greeted."

Grace smiled to herself as she moved the lacquer jug a few inches and continued to work.

After the neighbors had gathered, Jonathan, as host, began the meeting with prayer. Then he asked designated questions related to the concept of a peaceable civil society and opened discussion about whether they had a heavenly right to establish a church. Everyone had an opportunity to comment. Only once did Jonathan have to remind someone that the guest who was speaking was allowed to continue without question or contradiction.

He wrapped up the meeting with another lengthy prayer. After the Amen, he remained silent, remembering when he had served as lecturer of the ship. God had answered his prayers and delivered his family safely to the New World, he marveled. *You, Lord, have shown the way to the peaceable and loving society of Dedham and provided the means to build this house.*

Northern winds blew the chaff of harvest, and an occasional flurry of snow passed over the fields. Chill seeped through every crack in Fairbanks house, showing where they would need better insulation. The children slept huddled together in their room next to the hearth in the parlor chamber on the second floor, privileged compared to other children.

Most late fall days were filled with husking corn, shelling nuts, quilting, and stripping birch in someone's barn. The raucous activity of many gathered people and the animals, surrounded by bales of newly harvested hay, kept everyone warm. All eyes were on Edward Culver, the new wheelwright, hoping he would find the red ear of corn during the husking. That was a sure sign the town would soon celebrate a wedding.

Jonas couldn't wait. Digging through the piles of corn, he found a red ear and secreted it into Culver's pile. Edward, talking to a neighbor blushed when he realized he had grabbed the special cob. The crowd urged him to kiss John Ellis's daughter, Ann. The public kiss was permitted without reprimand.

After the crops and vegetables were preserved and laid away, everyone in the Fairbanks family, except Jonathan, stomped the clay and straw mixture into a wet plaster to apply as daub to the wattle latticework. Soon, the house would be fully insulated against the sharp winter winds.

While farmwork was dormant, Jonathan climbed the ladder to the chamber over the hall where his tools awaited. He sometimes invited a son or Sam up to learn the spinning wheel crafts. Occasionally, he turned a wooden table leg to make a gate-legged table for Grace.

Grace and the girls spun the wool they received from England and the flax they grew and rotted in the river before beating it into fibers. They'd soon have enough threads to take to a weaver. And then they'd finally have some new clothes.

The Meetinghouse 1638

At the February proprietor meeting, the townsmen planned to build their meetinghouse for civic and spiritual events for the forty-six families. Holding meetings in various homes was dividing the families—they needed a place everyone could meet together.

It was decided that pines from Wigwam Plains and oaks from between Ralph Shepard's lot and the meadow west would be hauled to the land west of the Keye where the meetinghouse was to be erected. During the winter, all able-bodied men would work on the meetinghouse, directed by Thomas Fisher, until crops had to be planted. Jonathan was pleased that he already had his own house nearly built.

Winter opened its cavernous mouth, blowing sharp winds and drifts of snow, making it impossible for timber to be moved from distant places. So proprietors near the proposed meetinghouse were asked to donate timber from their home lots with due compensation. The Fairbanks lot, a mile away and across the Little River, was not called upon for lumber. Owners of central lots were asked to relinquish a portion of their land for homes for new proprietors, so everyone could remain within one mile of the meetinghouse and village center. Ultimately, they decided to move the meetinghouse to accommodate eastern Dedham, but it remained near the Keye and still about a mile from the Fairbanks House.

With a designated place for the building, the village had to build bridges to span the Charles and the Little River so villagers could reach the meetinghouse. Jonathan, Philemon Dalton, and John Dwight were charged with erecting the Little River Bridge, and Mr. Timothy Dalton was designated to cut four hundred boards to build the bridge. Fairbanks teased John Dwight, saying, "The convenience of having a bridge near means you will shovel snow for us all each winter."

Later, a special proprietor's meeting was held to encourage a blacksmith to settle in Dedham, the town supplying the coal. Jonathan had hoped Prescott would become Dedham's blacksmith, but he had not yet come to the colonies.

Anthony Fisher entered the meeting late, his hat in hand and his head bowed. All eyes turned his way. The room became unusually quiet, for all knew his brother Thomas had fallen while working on the roof of the meetinghouse. Anthony announced quietly, "Thomas has died."

A collective gasp and condolences filled the small house, and Jonathan solemnly said, "This is a great loss to our society."

Another man muffled his whisper behind his hand. "And the meetinghouse isn't finished. With spring planting coming soon, no one will be able to work on it."

John Roper spoke up. "I think Thomas Bayes, Joseph Kingsbury, and I can arrange for the completion."

Another weekly community meeting was held at the Fairbanks house. Everyone was gathered except Michael and Sarah Metcalf, who had become close friends of the Fairbankses and lived only two houses southeast.

Grace put a hand on Jonathan's arm and said quietly,

"Maybe someone is sick. You start the meeting. I'll go check on the Metcalfs."

"Nay, Grace. I will." Jonathan opened the door against a stiff northeasterly wind and looked in the direction of the Metcalf house, then north. Michael Metcalf alone walked toward him, clutching his cape and hat against the wind. Jonathan stepped out to escort him in and tugged the door closed behind him. Metcalf took his hat off and shook his bowed head as he approached a cleared place near the hearth and stood there. All conversations ceased.

"I just came from the Shaw house," Michael reported. "We were to accompany Bridget to the meeting, for Abraham has been in bad humours. . . . He has passed."

A groan filled the room.

"I left Sarah with Bridget," he added.

A commotion ensued as Grace and several other women grabbed their capes and hoods and headed for the door.

"Let us pray," said Jonathan. "The help of men will come later." Jonathan opened the Bible as a sign that the meeting would begin. "We'll start our prayers remembering the good friends we've lost—Thomas Fisher, the builder, and Abraham Shaw, millwright and a strong presence, a man who believed he could bring ore and minerals to our town. We must also pray for their wives and families."

After everyone left, Jonathan ran his fingers over his head and looked toward the ceiling. *These were good men and essential to our town. Why do you bring your wrath upon us?*

Conspirators

Fifteen-year-old Jonas rushed to his mother's side as they walked home through the colorful fall trees from a Sabbath celebration in the new meetinghouse, leaving Jonathan behind to talk to the other men.

"Lo! Goodwife Hinsdale just melted into her skirts!" Jonas blurted out. Grace looked around to see if the other women had heard.

"Did you see the look on Minister Allin's face?"

"Now, Jonas," Grace replied in a loud whisper to shush him, "she just swooned from shyness. That's enough about Goodwife Hinsdale."

Jonas turned back to watch for a new boy he'd seen who looked to be about his own age. *Maybe I can make a new friend,* he thought. John, George, and Sam always left him out as being too young.

"Who's the new boy with Joseph Kingsbury, Mother?"

"Kingsbury covenanted with an indentured servant to come apprentice with him. I suppose Kingsbury found him through a company in England that matches people who don't have enough money for the voyage to New England."

"How old is he?"

"Millicent says he's almost seventeen. Joseph contracted him until he reaches his majority."

"So, he'll be here at least five years." Jonas brightened.

"He'll get a good education in carpentry and mechanics from Master Kingsbury," Grace then quieted her voice, "but the man is hot tempered. I hope he doesn't teach the boy that, too. You should be careful of the company you keep."

The next Sunday at the meetinghouse, instead of pushing into the seat by his brothers, Jonas edged into the bench beside the new boy. As the service started, Jonas sat stiffly, carefully scanning the room, moving only his eyes, wary of the tithing man with his long staff.

When John Gaye's and John Roper's dogs at the feet of their owners curled their lips into guttural growls, Jonas felt a kick on his ankle. He turned to see the new boy smirking as he pointed to the dogs.

The lad whispered, "I bet the brown-spotted one can take the black one." For the next few minutes, they forgot about the sermon.

"I know Goodman Gaye's black dog," Jonas whispered out the side of his mouth, not turning his head. "He's mean. I'll wager on him."

"How long before there's a real fight?" asked the new boy.

Jonas's brothers turned to glare at the conspirators. Jonas bowed his head but soon started to snigger as the dogs faced off, challenging each other. The new boy reddened, and his cheeks puffed as he tried to quell his laughter. The tithing man eased in their direction with his six-foot staff with its wooden knob on the end. When he was within reach of the boys, both received a sharp rap on the skull. They resisted yelping but glared at the tithing man while rubbing their heads.

The dogs had caught the attention of other meeting attendees, also, saving the boys from admonishment by the whole church. But old Goodwife Genery still enjoyed her traditional sermon nap.

The tithing man approached Goodwife Genery, ready to tickle her nose with the feathered end of his staff. Jonas jabbed his co-conspirator in the ribs and nodded in her direction just as she woke from the commotion. Jonas made an "Aw shucks" motion with his fist over his chest. They missed seeing the woman swat the feathers like flies as she woke.

Jonas's stomach grumbled, and he fixed his eyes on the hourglass as the last bits of sand sifted down. When he glanced up, Minister Allin was looking straight at him, then started a lengthy noon prayer.

Mr. Allin dismissed the congregation after an admonishment to the owners of the unruly dogs to leave them outside for the afternoon session. Then the clergyman shot a piercing look at

Jonas again, followed by one to his father. Nothing more had to be said.

"I'm in trouble now," Jonas said with a wince.

But now he had a partner in crime. As they twisted and turned on their bench waiting for their time to leave, Jonas whispered, "What's your name?"

"I'm Robert. Robert Crossman."

"I hear you are apprenticing with Joseph Kingsbury. What's that like?"

"I'm yet to know, for I've only been there a short while." Robert looked around to see if it was their turn to leave. "But he has pretty daughters."

"What are you learning?"

"Carpentry, mechanics, and how to do his chores," grumbled Robert.

"How long will you stay?" whispered Jonas. "I hope it'll be a long time. I need a friend."

"The covenant is for five years. I hope I can last that long. Master Kingsbury is strict and has a hot temper, worse than your minister's."

They both chuckled behind their hands and looked for the tithing man.

"Can I come eat with you?" asked Jonas. "It'll be uncomfortable around my family. Maybe the Kingsburys will go easy on you since you're new."

"I doubt that. He's already told me he's responsible for my actions, but if you're there, maybe Goodman Kingsbury will hold his temper."

Jonas and Robert knew from that moment that this would be an iron-clad friendship.

As fall drifted in on the ocean breezes, the shivering leaves on the hills turned gold, bronze, and red. It would soon be cool enough to butcher what few animals the families were not saving to build their herds. Jonas and Robert went hunting to help feed the families and get out of chores. Robert took his musket, and Jonas took his birding gun.

"I want to get a deer," said Robert.

"Not many deer here. The bears and wolves get them or scare them away. We don't see many bears, but we do see wildcats."

"Have you seen a bear?"

"No, but old Abraham Shaw killed an eight-foot-tall one." Jonas rested his gun on his shoulder. "We don't see the wolves often, but sometimes you can see their yellow eyes at night when the moon is full or if you carry a torch. We know they're out there. The sounds coming out of Wigwam Swamp in front of our house are evil, like women wailing."

"We aren't going there, are we?" Robert looked hard at Jonas.

"No, we're going to the Big Island where they let the pigs run. By Gaw." Then Jonas looked quickly at Robert to see if he was offended by the curse. Not seeing signs of reprisal, he looked at the shoreline of the Keye. "Our canoe is gone again. I bet my brothers took it. They are hunting, too, and they don't let me go with them. Do you know which canoe is Goodman Kingsbury's?"

"No, he keeps me too busy. Can't we just take one of these? They all look alike."

"You can only tell yours if you know its particulars," said Jonas. "I guess we could take this one. I don't think anyone would need it before we get back."

Jonas let Robert climb in first because he was still afraid of the water like many of the colonists. Jonas lifted his brown-and-white-spotted English setter, Champ, into the boat, shoved it into the water, and ran after it.

"Get in before it gets too deep," warned Robert, holding the edges of the boat and looking around nervously.

Jonas ran a couple of paces more and jumped in. "It doesn't get deep at this place in the Charles River. The boys swim here in the summer. Our water is warm then. The women use it to rot their flax before threshing it for spinning."

Robert mastered paddling in tandem with Jonas, and they glided through the silky brown water, colored by fallen leaves.

"What will you do when it gets too cold to work outdoors?" asked Robert.

"My father takes me up to the hall chamber to learn to make spinning wheels as he does."

"Goodman Kingsbury is going to teach me how to repair guns and make drums." Robert tried to pull his oar in rhythm with Jonas. "Are you afraid of Indians?"

"When I was younger, they killed John Oldham, the trader, right in front of his nephews, my friends." Jonas hopped out of the canoe at Big Island and started tugging it ashore. "C'mon, get your feet wet. Help me get this on shore."

On land, Champ ran sniffing ahead until she was out of sight, then she bounded back for a moment before another scent enticed her away.

"So, you aren't scared anymore?"

"I'm more afraid of wolves. Young John Dwight, Jr., was killed by the wolves in late March . . ."

"I heard about it," said Crossman.

"He was about ten years old, my little brother's friend. He went into Wigwam Swamp by our house and never came out. The whole town looked for him for days. It was really sad."

"Maybe we can shoot a wolf?"

"Aye, and if we do, we'll hang its ears on the meetinghouse and get ten shillings." They grinned at each other with the prospect of a good hunt.

Jonas slung his knapsack over his shoulder to keep his ammunition close, then leaned his bird gun on his shoulder and led the way.

"Have you seen Indians?" asked Robert.

"The Indians go by our house when they come to town. They're mostly here in the winter. In summer, they disappear. They have a small village on the other side of Wigwam Pond and a burial ground not far from us."

Robert peered around, looking deep into the woods.

"One fall night," said Jonas, "when it turned cold early, a group of them came right into our house without knocking. They sat down on our hall floor by the hearth with their blankets around them and stayed the whole night. They didn't hurt anything, just ate all our pottage and messed around in Mother's crocks while we stayed out of the hall." Jonas shrugged. "I guess they're just curious."

"In your *house*?"

Jonas walked a bit taller. "Yup. Before they left, I asked one of them to teach me to shoot his bow and arrow. Dad said in the old country he used one. I tried, but the bows are wobbly and tough to pull back. My arrow got stuck in the thatch of the roof, and we never got it down."

"Indeed, I want to do that," said Crossman.

"Is making drums like making barrels?" asked Jonas. "My brother George is starting a cooper business, and Father wants me to work for him. But I want to be a sailor. If I can't do *that*, I want to mine like Abraham Shaw planned to do. He got the first grant from the General Court saying he could mine coal or iron."

"Do you know where he found the ore? That would be like finding a buried treasure."

"Goodman Shaw was going to erect a water-driven gristmill along the River Charles. The town gave him land there. Maybe that's where it is."

Champ stopped just in front of the boys and pointed. Jonas put his finger to his lips, looking over at Robert. He found a prop for his bird gun and flicked his hand at Champ, who disappeared into the tall grasses. A bouquet of pheasants took flight and Jonas shot into it. The flock was so dense, he was sure he'd gotten one. Both boys ran, following Champ.

Beaming, Jonas picked up the glossy brown bird with its green head and red around its eyes and handed it to Robert to examine. Then Jonas stuffed it into the hunting bag. "Or Shaw might have found ore close to my house. He bought a small island surrounded by swamp about three lots down, by Ferdinand Adams's lot. Why would anyone buy land like that? Maybe that's where the ore is?"

"Give *me* the bird gun this time," said Robert, nearly pulling it out of Jonas's hands.

"I like the sound of a buried treasure," Jonas mused. "Maybe I could be a miner instead of a sailor. My mother and father are against my going to sea. They say it's an ungodly profession and that sailors are coarse and foul. But I met a nice one on our voyage over—named Thomas.

Ditch

"Mary Elizabeth, can you turn the hand-mill any faster? asked Grace. We need more bread. I cannot keep up with the boys' appetites."

"Can't Susan take a turn?" Mary whined.

Susan sat on her small three-legged cricket by the hearth, turning the spit to roast a chicken. She made a face at Mary Elizabeth.

"You know she's never had your strength, Mary," said Grace. "The men haven't been to Watertown to get milled flour, and we need it today."

"When is Dedham going to get a gristmill?" Mary said with a pout.

"No one in town has wanted to build one since Goodman Shaw died."

Mary bit her lip and cast Susan an angry glance before bearing down hard on the mill handle.

Jonathan came in after an early morning session at the meetinghouse. "Good news, Grace. The town's going to dig a ditch. They already have the General Court's approval."

"What good is another ditch?" huffed Grace. "Everyone has one alongside the road, by their dooryard fence."

"This one will be big. We're going to connect the Charles and the Neponset Rivers. You know how each spring, during the thaw, the Charles River floods the meadows near the East Brook grazing area? Then we can't graze the cattle. A ditch will help drain it into the Neponset River."

"They should build a gristmill instead," retorted Mary. "So I don't have to do this anymore." She stood and slapped her hands together, sending flour flying.

"Sit down, Mary," demanded Grace.

"You're going to get a mill," said Jonathan. "This ditch will give us faster water to turn a waterwheel, and they're going to build a gristmill on the ditch."

"Now you have another job, Jonathan. When will you get all *our* work done? You keep taking land to open. John and Samuel have reached their majority, joined the village, and have their own share of the town work. And George is just a year behind them."

"Jonas and George can dig for us," said Jonathan, "and I can take our yoke of oxen. That will count for more than a man's work. John has only a bit of land, a bachelor's portion, so some of his work will count for our family. Every man in town must take part. With forty-six houses, there are a lot of men and boys. I'm sure they'll even find a job for Junior."

Jonas dragged a long stick on the ground until he arrived at the banks of the Charles River on the first day of the dig. "If you weren't so crooked, you wouldn't be so lazy!" he called out, shaking the stick at the river.

"You are calling me a crook, a penny shyster?" called Robert Crossman, loping up and slapping Jonas on the back.

"What are you doing here? Don't you have apprentice work to do?" asked Jonas.

"Kingsbury went to Lynn about a water mill for Dedham."

"Why can't Kingsbury build it?"

"He's smart, but he doesn't know about water mills. He sent me to do his work on the ditch," grumbled Crossman. "Does your father have you working for him?"

"Sure. He said I had to work off my part of the canoe fine by digging." Jonas twisted his face.

"What fine?"

Jonas gritted his teeth until he could hear them grinding and jabbed the stick into the hard ground with such force he heard it scrape a rock several inches down. "The fine for taking the canoe that didn't belong to us."

"Well, at least we get to do this together. How far do we have to dig?" asked Crossman.

"I don't know, but it's about three and a half miles from here to the Neponset River. I think it's only three-quarters of a mile to East Brook. Do you know anything about water mills?"

"Kingsbury is talking to a man named John Elderkin about building ours. I can't wait to watch him do it."

"Maybe we can help him and learn how they work," said Jonas.

Prescotts Arrive 1640

"Jonathan, this will be like when we went to the faire in Halifax," crooned Grace as she packed her soft bag. "We haven't been to Boston as a family since we arrived." She tapped her hands together in front of her chest. "I can't wait to see Mary and the little ones. Can we go to the market? I haven't been to a *proper* market since we left England."

Grace's excitement was contagious. "Father, where are we going to stay?" asked Mary Elizabeth.

"At Cousin Richard's ordinary in Boston. He is becoming an important man—he received another license last November, and he was named postmaster for the colonies. He tacks the letters going to and from England on a post in the tavern."

"Are we going to be there long?" grumbled John. "Sarah Fisk's family asked me for supper after Sabbath."

"We don't know when the ship will arrive. Remember how long we had to wait in the harbor?" asked Jonathan.

John stared longingly toward Sarah Fisk's house.

"Come in," called Richard Fairbanks to all the family at his threshold. "I've been waiting for you. We have plenty of room now, but whenever a ship comes in, we get busy."

Jonathan entered the tavern. "I hear the number of people coming from England is declining, since King Charles finally called Parliament to sit again."

Jonas went straight to the post where all the missives to and from England were tacked. He touched one and looked back at Richard, saying, "This one's opened. Can I read it?"

Richard stepped closer to Jonas. His voice took on an authoritarian tone. As he inspected the letter, he said, "Indeed, someone has already opened it. When I go into the back for supplies, the unscrupulously curious can't resist news from England. I am paid a pence a letter to see that each gets into the correct hands. This letter belongs to someone in particular, and you may not read it."

Jonas slapped the post and said, "Is this why they call this a post office?"

"I suppose that's why they name it thus."

Cousin Elizabeth, holding her year-old son, Zacchaeus, showed Grace and the girls upstairs to change out of their traveling clothes. Four-year-old Constance stayed close by her mother's side.

Grace knew the Prescotts would get off the boat wearing what they had worn for weeks, but she relished an occasion to dress up. She looked at her daughters and suggested, "Maybe Mary will bring dolls from England dressed in the latest fashion, so we can sew what's new."

At the wharf, Mary Elizabeth straightened her skirts and pinched her cheeks for color, looking around to see if any young men noticed. George talked with traders about buying barrels. Jonas moved closer to the ships at the wharf, and Junior tagged along. Susan stayed near her mother.

John paced, searching the horizon for the ship. He had just been given a lot at the east end of his father's land to build a house for himself and Mary Fiske. Samuel had finished his indenture and joined the village the same day as John, and he was marrying Samuel Morse's daughter. The two friends would help each other build.

"Ahoy!" exclaimed John as he saw the flag at the tip of a ship's mast.

Jonathan greeted Prescott as a brother, they reminisced on the way to the small boat wharf where a shallop waited to take them to Watertown. "The blacksmith shop in Dedham is in Edward Kemp's hands now—we wanted that for you."

"Aye, but only now it came time for us to leave England.," answered Prescott.

"But, my dear friend John," Jonathan said, "I have arranged an opportunity for you in Watertown. You can be nearby."

"You always come through for me. First Sowerby, now in New England, said Prescott.

"Daniel Pierce, the Watertown blacksmith, moved to Roxbury two years ago. His home stall and blacksmith shop remain available—just south of the meetinghouse commons."

"Let's see it then, soon as we arrive," said Prescott.

The family settled in at Munnings' ordinary, and Jonathan, satisfied that Prescott would buy the blacksmith in Watertown, took his leave. "We've missed you these past seven years. Now I must catch up with the family at the Watertown mill on the way home. Grace must have her fine flour. We're hoping to have our own mill soon. After all the ditch digging, I deserve some fine baked goods, not that trencher bread."

"The Ditch" 1641

The older men in town watched in anticipation as the younger men and boys hacked through the last dam of earth that separated the Charles River from the newly dug Ditch. They would mark this day, July 14, 1641, if the millwright, Elderkin, had enough flow to run a wheel for the gristmill.

Jonas and Robert scrambled up the bank just ahead of the spout of water and stood as close as they could to the wheelwright. At last, Elderkin announced, "The water flows well."

The boys threw their hats in the air, and the townspeople exclaimed, "Huzzah! Huzzah! Huzzah!" Startled birds in the nearby meadow flew up in dark clouds, the rapid flapping of their wings adding to the racket.

The women, ready for jubilation, set out a feast with breads and pies from the fine flour brought from the Watertown mill. Soon they'd have their own.

Later that day, Jonathan Fairbanks, Francis Chickering, and

John Dwight were ordered to plan a cartway and footpath to the mill.

More work, thought Jonathan. But a water-driven gristmill would ensure Dedham would grow and last for generations.

While hunting northeast of the village, Jonas and Robert were the first to greet John Elderkin as he came from Lynn as promised, after the fall harvest. They hurled questions at him about building the water mill. The boys lost his attention when Edward Alleyn met them and escorted Elderkin into his house. There he'd speak with the selectmen about the land the millwright would receive by the Ditch and Mill Pond to erect the mill. The boys, not included, slunk away.

"I can't build this mill myself," said Elderkin. "Nathaniel Whiting will be my partner on the project, but we need help from the whole community. There's a lot of work to be done when we are without rain and when the river is frozen. Then I must get back to Lynn before planting season."

The selectmen nodded. Alleyn said, "We've arranged for men to fell trees, bring them to your location, and build a saw pit. Joseph Kingsbury is sending Robert Crossman to help you. He's learned construction and mechanics and is nearing the end of his apprenticeship.

Jonas sneaked away from the farm after morning chores to visit Robert, who was helping build the gristmill. Jonas stood back, fascinated with the fitting and shaping of wood into a giant wheel.

"C'mon, Jonas, help with this," called Robert.

As Jonas trotted to Crossman's side, Elderkin eyed Jonas and strolled over. "Who do we have here? We can't let just anyone work on the wheel, Robert."

"Jonas Fairbanks. His father is directing the building of the cartway to the mill. Jonas knows as much about shaping wood as I do. His father taught him to make spinning wheels."

"They're smaller, but they're still wheels," explained Jonas.

"That's true," said Elderkin. "I could use more help if I'm to meet the deadline set by the village. Let's see what you can do."

"It sure would be better than working on the cartway. I did enough digging on the Ditch," grumbled Jonas.

Later that evening, he returned home just after dusk to find everyone sitting at the table. Jonathan stood, pulled his chest-size napkin away and threw it on the table. His face was stern. He opened his mouth to speak but stopped short when John Elderkin ducked under the low doorway behind Jonas.

"Father," Jonas said, "Goodman Elderkin would like to speak with you."

Jonathan's face softened. He nodded to Grace, who immediately started moving dishes on the table to make room for the guest.

"Ta, I can't stay," said Elderkin. "My wife and babe will be waiting for me."

Jonathan, still standing, invited the visitor into the parlor.

"May Jonas join us?" asked Elderkin.

Jonas smirked at his siblings around the table, knowing they wondered what trouble he had gotten himself into this time. Grace's hard glance quieted them.

"Goodman Fairbanks," Elderkin said, "you've taught your son well. He learns fast, knows his wood, and is skilled with his hands."

Jonas looked down at his open hands and stood quietly. Jonathan glanced at Jonas with a glint in his eye but kept a firm jaw.

"Could you spare him until we have the waterwheel finished?"

Jonathan looked to Jonas, whose head nodded like an angler's bobber when a fish tried to steal the bait.

Jonathan's hand went to his forehead and slid over the balding spot. "Since it's winter, we don't have as many chores, but he's supposed to help me with the cartway and my spinning wheels." Jonathan paused and looked hard at Jonas. "Perhaps he would learn more by helping you."

Jonas beamed but willed himself to remain quiet.

Elderkin took his leave with a smile, commenting. "Your fine Ditch may become a brook that will become the mother of much industry in your society." He winked at Jonas.

As Jonas sat down at the table, Grace reprimanded him— "You're late." But she ladled an extra helping of rabbit stew and placed a large piece of bread on his trencher.

Elderkin confided in Jonas and Robert that he would leave Dedham as soon as the gristmill was finished. "I have more requests for mills north of Boston by Lynn. With the passing of the Act of Encouraging Mines and John Winthrop Jr. starting an ironworks in Braintree, I could get busy. Lynn is a perfect place for an ironworks. It has flowing water, ore, and wood.

"Will you need help?" asked Jonas. Crossman nodded behind him.

"I believe I will. Are you prepared to come with me?"

Jonas and Robert looked at each other as if conspiring to escape with Elderkin.

Robert spoke first. "I have another year of apprenticeship with Goodman Kingsbury, and I don't want any hounds out sniffing for me."

"Jonas?" Elderkin looked his way.

"I'd have to run away from home. Along with the mill, cart path, and footpath work, Father just received a land grant in the Low Plains. The town is opening two hundred acres of common tillage next year." Jonas kicked hard at a clod of dirt. "He depends on me to help. He tries to keep me busy, so I won't run off to be a sailor."

Elderkin laughed. "Perhaps he won't mind if you work with me in a few years."

"If I could work with the great wheels and the water flowing through them," said Jonas, "I think I'd be satisfied on land. I feel the power when I see the water moving the heavy wheels. *Spinning* wheels are for women."

Elderkin announced, "You both have work with me when you're ready."

The lads exchanged a look of anticipation.

Lydia Prescott

The sun beat down on Grace and Jonathan as they plied their paddles through the brown water of the Charles River toward Watertown and the Prescotts. "Why do we have to be in such a hurry?" grumbled Jonathan.

"This is Mary's sixth baby, not counting the ones she lost. They come fast after five. Thanks be to God someone got us word quickly. I want to be there for her first born in the colony."

After they left the canoe at the docks, Jonathan walked with Grace to the Prescott house by the church commons and then headed for the blacksmith shop.

He removed his tall hat and ducked in the shop door as fading sunbeams came through the west window. He was reminded of when they had first met in Prescott's apprenticeship at Wigan. Everything was in its place, and Jonathan was pleased to see plenty of finely finished work done and more work waiting to keep his friend busy.

Prescott looked up from his ledger under a west window. He put his quill down and stood to greet his friend.

"I remember another time you came through my smith shop door, Jonathan Fairbanks. You made a significant change in my life. Now, because of all your letters, I'm come across the ocean to Watertown. As you promised, and as you can see, I have substantial business, even better than Sowerby." Prescott gestured to a stool for Jonathan to sit on. "You must have brought Grace for Mary. Maybe you've brought me a boy this time?" He cocked his head to the side and grinned.

Jonathan waved away the offer of a seat and asked, "Do you have time for an ale at the tavern before I leave for Dedham?"

"Stay the night, friend," said Prescott. "It will be too late to travel the dark river after we have a wee bit to drink. We'll stay in the upstairs room of the tavern while the women are busy." Prescott escorted Jonathan out of the shop and closed the front door to signal the end of the workday.

"How's the place since Munnings left?" Jonathan asked.

"See for yourself," answered Prescott.

The tavern was full and noisy. The new proprietor rushed to their table right away. "We'll both have a rum," said Jonathan. "We're celebrating Prescott here having another child—very soon." He handed the tavern keeper a coin for the box hanging on the wall—it was inscribed with TIPS—To Insure Prompt Service.

"You having a boy this time, Prescott, in that house full of girls?" the owner teased. He lifted his hand to acknowledge a customer waiting and returned to his other patrons.

"You heard the Act of Encouragement of Mines passed in June?" said Fairbanks. They say John Winthrop Jr. and Dr. Robert Childes are behind it.

"Indeed, your letters to England foretold this. The prospect was quite enticing." Prescott smiled. "But it was the dread of going to war in festering England that changed my mind about coming. Didn't they also enact an encouragement for wool, cotton, and linen spinning?"

"Aye, and my spinning wheel trade prospers. It takes four women spinning to keep one weaver at work."

They say bad times are coming for New England. The Bay Colony's financial welfare depends on new settlers coming, and they've been falling off," explained Prescott. "We won't get regular shipments, especially of ironware. So influential men are already in England getting financial support for an ironworks here."

The tavern door flew open and sixteen-year-old John Prescott, Jr., stood gasping for breath, sweating through his shirt. "She's here!" he called out, looking for his father.

The tavern erupted in a rousing "Huzzah!" and Prescott's friends called their condolences that it wasn't a son.

"Another bride for your sons," retorted Prescott with a lift of his mug.

"I see you've made friends here, as in Wigan and Sowerby," said Jonathan, as he pulled out a stool for John Jr. and ordered a beer for him.

"Mother is fine, says Goodwife Fairbanks," the boy said, "and I'm to tell you the baby's name is Lydia." He took a swig of beer and wiped the froth on his sleeve like the men did.

"Thanks be to God that Mary is well," said Prescott, with soft eyes for his son. "That makes you all the more precious, son." Then he shook off the sentiment and quipped, "Good thing I'm a blacksmith and not a farmer." He winked at Jonathan.

Sailor 1642

Fairbanks stamped the snow from his boots on the stone step in front of his door, then went in, hung his tall hat and heavy coat on a peg, stuffed his gloves in his greatcoat sleeves, and blew warm air into his curled hands as he walked to the hall hearth.

Jonas stood there, looking more a man than a boy of eighteen. He had his father's black hair, prominent nose, and dark eyes. He was cleaning his knife while Susan sat on her cricket turning the spitted rabbit Jonas had brought home from hunting.

"Robert Crossman has finished his apprenticeship with Joseph Kingsbury and was just admitted into town at the meeting today," Jonathan announced.

"Aye, he's been looking forward to that," said Jonas.

"You will join the village yourself in a couple of years," Jonathan remarked.

"You know I plan to be a sailor," said Jonas with a sharp look at his father. "That's what I've wanted to do ever since our voyage. I could sign on at any time. Remember Thomas, the boy on our ship? He was only a bit older than I was even then."

"Sailing is not a respectable occupation for a Fairbanks."

"But how would we have gotten here if it weren't for the ship and the men who sailed it, Father? Nothing could be brought over or taken back to England or anywhere else." He softened his tone a bit, "You like a bit of rum from the islands now and then, eh?"

Jonathan's jaw firmed; his eyes turned cold and dark. "Sailors are coarse and have no morals. I don't expect a son of mine to take such work. John will take over the farm, of course, but I plan to leave land to *all* my sons. Why do you think I came to New England?" Jonathan's stare pierced Jonas, who did not answer, and the rest of the family busied themselves to avoid the quarrel.

"To give you a better life," Jonathan answered himself. "Not to let you sink into the deep waters of debauchery."

Jonas stood tall and quiet. His eyes didn't waver from his father's, but he did not speak.

"You can't expect a part of the inheritance if that is your

direction, Jonas. You *earn* your inheritance. I will need all my sons as we get more grants." Jonathan stopped short and turned sharply away, glints of moisture gathered in his eyes.

As Jonathan headed to the parlor, he dug his fingers into his head as he ran his hand over his bald crown.

Jonas looked at his mother, who had just come downstairs. "His father slighted him in his will, Mother, but I never thought he'd do that to me."

Jonas slipped the knife back into its sheath and began taking his hat and cloak off the pegs. "Why should his misfortunes affect my life decision?" Jonas asked. "I cannot live his life."

Not waiting for her response, Jonas opened the door and disappeared in the gust of snow that blew in.

Free School 1643

Ralph Daye beat the drum in a rhythmic cadence to call all men to the annual January General Meeting. The wind blew cold and blustery as men trudged through the snow. The business at hand, as well as the weather, quickened their steps to the meetinghouse.

"We instituted seven selectmen to order the routine business of the town, back in '39," Jonathan commented through the scarf over his nose and mouth, to Michael Metcalf. "And that was a good idea. I don't relish these early morning meetings in the cold. Besides, it was a waste of time when everyone had to attend all meetings and be allowed to speak freely."

"John Gaye always made an oration," added Michael. They both laughed, sending puffs of steam through and around their scarves. "But annual meetings are important. I want my say in who will move into town, what grants will be made, and who will run the town the next year."

"I wouldn't miss today's vote," said Jonathan, "It's Satan's work to keep our youth ignorant. They must read and understand, or our town will be open to evil. I'm glad my older sons were educated in England. But Junior had to learn from Grace and the boys."

"Everyone should be able to read and understand the Bible and laws, even women," said Metcalf, an educator himself back in England.

"We've had public land set aside to produce income for years. The church, town, roads, and bridges have benefited, and now it's time it supports a school," huffed Jonathan.

The first order of business was discussion about how to subsidize a free education for proprietors and servants' sons, aged four to fourteen. Some of the public land money would pay a schoolmaster, and families sending sons to school would supply firewood. The funds that couldn't be raised from the lands would come from a school tax from every proprietor.

One man sitting beside Jonathan blurted, "Fairbanks, all your sons are past the age of schooling. Are you willing to support a free school when it'll be of no benefit to you?"

"Aye," Jonathan said as he stood for emphasis. "Fairbankses will be in this town for generations. I support the school for my grandsons and great-grandsons and the betterment of the community. We started this town with educated men, and we want this town in the hands of educated men when we are no longer the leaders."

"Huzzah!" erupted from the whole room. The moderator rapped his gavel on the front table and called for the collector to gather the votes. The men dug in their pockets for wheat or corn.

Jonathan held his wheat to vote. "I can't vote in colony affairs, since I haven't joined the church, but by Gaw, I can vote in town business." When the hat was passed, Jonathan dropped his wheat with a grand flourish.

The collector carried the hat solemnly to the front table, occasionally peering in. At the table, he tipped the hat upside down, raised it high, and let wheat rain onto the table and bounce to the floor. "The vote is unanimous. Dedham will have a free, tax-supported school for all our sons."

"Huzzah! Huzzah! Huzzah!" echoed around the bare walls of the meetinghouse and rang out into the commons.

Jonathan leaned toward Metcalf and asked, "When do you think we'll start educating the daughters?"

No More Waiting

"Jonathan, I have decided I will join the church," announced Grace. "Mr. Allin became our minister four years ago, many of the men are already members, and even some servants have joined. We came here so we could practice our faith, didn't we?" She put her fists on her hips.

Mary Elizabeth had joined almost three years before and took communion, and her parents had had many conversations about it.

"I don't feel like part of the church community, Jonathan, and I won't wait any longer for your decision. This I will do for myself."

"Aye, wife," said Fairbanks, "we do practice our faith already. And I have my scruples with how they are ordering the church and selecting members. I professed my fidelity as being of one heart with this Puritan society when I became a member of the town." A bead of sweat formed on his brow that was not caused by the July heat. "I don't feel I need to stand before the whole congregation and express my devotion to God. God knows my mind."

He paused and said more gently, "You go right ahead, Grace. Join."

"Do you think you might be a bit shy?" asked Grace, with a half-smile. "The church has courted you, several times. They'll accept you, to be sure."

"Bah! I have my scruples. They turned down Joseph

Kingsbury, and he gave land for the burial ground and was on the church founding committee." He looked away and mumbled, "I don't expect a woman to understand."

Grace's name was entered in the church books with only the reference, "Grace, July 1643." There were no other Graces in the book, and other women were entered with their first name followed by "wife of" and their husbands' names. Jonathan held out.

Burying a Friend 1644

A frantic knock disturbed Jonathan and Grace while they were taking a pipe by the fire. Jonathan jumped up and opened the door, still holding his pipe. His friend Michael Metcalf stood shivering without a coat and looked right past him.

"Grace!" Metcalf called across the room. "Come quick!"

"A moment, friend," said Jonathan and helped him inside.

Grace took one of the boys' cloaks from its peg and wrapped it around his shoulders. "We can't have you getting sick," Grace said,

"Sarah's been ailing for several days," Metcalf explained. "Dr. Deengain has left for Roxbury. She won't see Minister Allin, for she says he doesn't heal, just comforts. She wants you, Grace."

"I usually help with babies," Grace explained. "I know only common things about bad humours, but I'll gather my things." Grace shuddered while her back was turned, knowing she must be careful with her remedies, for she didn't want to be called a witch. *But these are our friends. I must help them.*

When Grace arrived at the Metcalfs' with the distraught husband, she found Mary Elizabeth cradling Michael Junior's head against her shoulder. The rest of the Metcalf children were milling around the hall. Grace proceeded to the parlor, where Sarah lay pale and feverish. Her bedding was wet from sweat, yet she shivered.

She looked up at Grace with wild eyes and cried, "Quick, get Michael up to the garret and cover him with straw!"

She is not thinking straight, Grace thought with despair. Clearly, Sarah was remembering when she hid her husband from persecution in England. She had told Grace the story many times.

Grace called to Mary Elizabeth, "Take wet rags outdoors to chill. We need to bring Sarah's temperature down quickly."

They worked for hours to break Sarah's fever, but she refused the cider vinegar tea. In a near lucid moment, she reached for Grace's hand and said, "Take care of my family. Michael won't know what to do with the little ones."

They were no longer little, but Grace said nothing. Then Sarah took Mary Elizabeth's hand and said, "You take care of my boy."

Grace called for Michael Sr. while Sarah was making some sense, but her energy soon waned. Michael sat on the bed and kissed Sarah on her damp forehead. She closed her eyes and slipped away.

The children came to their mother's side while Grace prepared the trestle board in the hall to shroud Sarah for burial. The thought of putting her good friend in the cold ground chilled Grace to her soul, and she demanded to sit the two-day vigil for the dead with her friend.

After the funeral, Jonathan and the boys were walking home from the Metcalf house and saw light flickering through the windows of their own house.

"Didn't we damper the fire?" he called to his sons and broke into a run, remembering the fire at Shaw's house in Watertown.

The boys overtook him, and he called as they passed, "Is our ladder up?"

Junior ran back toward him and pointed at the chimney. There was a steady stream of smoke floating into the chilly sky, no flames, but more smoke than from the dampered fire they had left when they went to the funeral.

"Somebody's in there!" called George, as they neared the house. Jonathan stopped them and put his finger to his lips. He motioned for Jonas to open the door carefully as he raised his gun and prepared to light the wick. Jonas lifted the latch as quietly as possible and plastered himself against the outside wall as the door swung open.

A tall man in a riding cape stood facing the fire warming his hands. The figure, shadowed by the light from the hearth, turned casually to face the men. "Whoa, Fairbanks," said Prescott. Jonathan let the barrel of the gun drop. "Where were you? I just got here and let myself in. I put the horse in the barn. I didn't think you'd mind."

Jonathan propped the long gun against the wall by the door and met Prescott in an embrace. "It's been some time," he said.

"Aye," said Prescott. The boys gathered to listen to what he might have to say.

"My three men have been working all fall to open the land out west for the Nashaway Company," he explained. "Since I'm directing them, I've been out there often."

"How fares it in Nashaway?" asked Jonathan.

"Quite well. Two houses are up for their quarters. The soil turns easily where the Indians had fields before, so we can start planting next spring. We fenced a night pasture for cattle."

The Fairbanks boys, having evening chores to attend to, left the men alone.

"That's progress for your settlement, it seems. When are you planning to go out permanently?"

"I'm taking the family next spring, for an early planting. I know your Grace disapproves of me taking Mary and the children to Nashaway."

"Women don't understand these things," said Jonathan. "Thanks be that Mary is willing to follow you with the children." Jonathan pulled out the two chairs and placed them by the hearth. "Sit. Grace would have you in the parlor, but the big fire is more comfortable in this weather." He reached into the cabinet for his clay pipe and tobacco. Prescott dug into his breeches pocket for his.

"What brings you here?" Jonathan asked.

"I'm herding cattle to Nashaway while the ground is firm and the Sudbury River is low. I thought your sons could help."

"Well, John is married and has his own responsibilities. George must make his barrels this time of year when there's no planting or harvesting. And Junior is too young—Grace wouldn't hear of it."

"How about Jonas?" asked Prescott at just the moment Jonas came in with a load of wood. "I brought Linton and Waters back with me and left John Ball at Nashaway. I think the four of us can herd the cattle. You can tell Grace it's only sixteen miles past the swamps and thick pines at Sudbury."

Twenty-year-old Jonas piped up. "I'll go."

Jonathan shot him a hard look and said, "Jonas has been looking for a reason to get out of Dedham."

Jonathan spared Prescott the ongoing argument about Jonas wanting to be a sailor. "This might be a time for him to see what it's like going out on his own." Jonathan took a draw on his pipe and blew a large smoke ring into the air.

"We'll be taking our cattle over the Indian trail that Oldham and Reverend Hooker used going to the Great River Valley," explained Prescott. Then he smiled at Jonas and said, "We must leave early in the morrow to prepare for the trip."

Massachusetts Military Company

Fighting broke out between the Narragansett and Mohegan tribes, both of whom had helped the colony in the past. Any disturbances with the Indians made settlers uneasy. Eleazur Lusher, chief military man in Dedham, decided to have eight training days for all eligible men, which meant Jonathan and all four of his sons. The training grounds had been extended two acres west to accommodate their growing male population.

As an early member of the Massachusetts Military Company, Lusher saw the benefit of advanced instruction in military discipline and tactics, especially for the younger men. Lusher asked the four young men he had recruited, including the Fisher brothers, to tell the others about the company.

The Fishers told the townsmen beguiling stories of green uniforms with red edging and the affiliation with the Ancient and Honorable Artillery Company in England. The townsmen were intrigued by extensive military weaponry—including modern equipment—that they would learn to use. The brothers celebrated the camaraderie of the special group's rigorous monthly training in Boston.

The last comment in the recruitment discussion caused a stir. Lusher announced that the motto of the Massachusetts Military Company was "*Acta Non Verba*." He waited for the men to recognize the Latin words. Then he translated, "Deeds, not words."

Immediately, George Fairbanks, Robert Crossman, and Anthony Fisher proudly stepped forward. After a short hesitation, George Bearstow joined his friends in the front line.

As Jonas rode home from herding cattle to Nashaway for Prescott, he turned southeast on the path the Natives always took to Wigwam Plain. He reached the gate of the Fairbanks dooryard as the snowfall intensified, but his mind went back to his first glimpse of Prescott's Nashaway. He saw himself atop his horse on Wattaquadock Hill, overlooking the fog-covered valley, with islands of pines pushing through a sea of boiling gray-white clouds. That reminded him of seeing the New World the first time when his sailor friend pointing out what appeared to be an island of trees in the mist. Once again, he felt a sense of belonging.

Jonas tied his horse to the post ring, anxious to tell his family about Nashaway where the Prescotts would move that spring. First, he called hello to Grande, who was barking down by the chicken yard.

Jonas opened the door carefully, holding it against the wind gusts. Grace stood up. Immediately her hand flew to her mouth. She stared as he closed the door. Jonas touched his mustache and beard, smiling. *Mother doesn't know me.*

Jonas brushed the snow off his hat and walked briskly over to his mother and reached out for a hug.

"Jonas!" exclaimed Grace. "You've gone thin. And all that hair. I hardly recognize you. Come, sit down, and eat."

Ready to regale the family with stories of his trip, he sat in his usual spot. Grace set a large trencher in front of him and ladled out extra pheasant stew. Jonas scooped the steaming stew into his mouth as if he hadn't eaten in days and beamed at his mother. "This is good. John Ball at Nashaway isn't much of a cook."

"You have not heard the news of Dedham, since you were away," Father started, wiping his mouth with the large square napkin that was tucked into his collar. "George and Robert Crossman were accepted into the prestigious Massachusetts Military Company."

Mother chimed in, "Your friend is ambitious. Crossman now owns a house and land, and he is now part of the military."

Jonas's news seemed to pale under their excitement about

George and Robert. Jonas barely raised his eyes and kept shoveling stew and tearing big chunks of bread with his teeth.

"George is going to need your help with the barrel business even more," said Jonathan. "He has training in Boston once a month. In a couple of months, you'll need to start working the fields."

Jonas glared at his food, dropped his spoon, threw his napkin on the table, and stomped upstairs with his bundle.

Martha Pidge

Mary and Grace pulled their skirts up between their legs from the back and tucked them into their skirt waists to keep their hems dry. The summer sun shimmered on the water of the swimming hole where Mary Elizabeth, now Mistress Metcalf, Jr., and Grace threshed rotted flax against the river rocks. They would soon be soaked through with sweat and flying water from beating the limp, reedy flax stalks against the rocks. Mary Elizabeth stood and arched her back, accentuating the small growing mound beneath her apron skirt. Grace heard the threshing stop and stood to wipe her own brow and check on Mary. "Is the baby kicking?"

"Aye, and I have news," said Mary Elizabeth. "Father Metcalf is going to wed again."

"That's wonderful. Who will he marry? I should have heard."

"She's from Rowley. Her husband died in '43 after a bad fall."

"Does she have children? Michael already has so many." Grace looked up to the sky, remembering Sarah laid to rest not long before.

"That's the problem," said Mary Elizabeth. "This woman, Mary Pidge, has ten of her own."

"Ten!" exclaimed Grace.

"The youngest is about four," Mary Elizabeth went on. "She's having trouble keeping them all. She tried to get uncles in Connecticut and Virginia to take the littlest one, but they declined." She paused and twisted herself far to the left and then to the right. "Mother, they have asked Michael and me to take her." Mary Elizabeth looked down and rubbed her belly. "I'm due in January. What if I have trouble delivering this baby? What if...?"

"We'll take care of you, Mary Elizabeth. I've delivered lots of babies." Grace returned to her work. She had worried relentlessly about her daughter's first birth but didn't want to worry Mary. "When are they to be married?"

"Banns are planned for an August marriage, and after the marriage, Goodwife Pidge will move to Dedham."

"Mother . . ." Mary Elizabeth paused so long that Grace stood up and looked at her. "Susan will marry soon and leave you. Why didn't you have more children after we came here? You were still young."

Grace looked away and didn't answer.

"Couldn't you use a young girl to help you, especially with your dairy and spinning?" Mary Elizabeth chuckled. "She could sit on Susan's cricket by the hearth and turn the spit."

Grace hesitated, then said, "Oh, Mary Elizabeth, this is not a small request. How old is she, again?"

"She'll soon be four."

"What's her name?"

"Martha, Martha Pidge," said Mary Elizabeth, still searching her mother's face. "I would help you with her while she's young, but we all did chores by the time we were five. She could help with my baby while Susan and I help you with other chores."

Grace hesitated. "This is something your father and I will have to discuss."

The Fairbanks house bustled with activity in December as they prepared for Martha to join their household.

"It's been a long time since we had a small child about the house," said Grace. "John's boy is still a babe in arms."

Susan held up a skirt and bodice she had made for Martha from some of her own older clothes, painstakingly stitching by the fire each evening.

"She'll look like a proper wee lady," said Grace.

On a chilly, gusty day, Martha accompanied Mary Elizabeth to the Fairbanks house, Martha carrying a ragged poppet by its hand. It looked as if the doll had belonged to each of her older sisters in turn. As Mary Elizabeth entered the door, Martha held to her skirt.

Grace remained at the hearth, cutting root vegetables into the pottage, but smiled warmly.

"Good morrow, Mary Elizabeth. Is this your little friend, Martha?"

Susan jumped up and started toward the door, but Grace put her arm out to stop her. Martha ducked behind Mary Elizabeth's skirts. Susan squatted to Martha's level several paces away. Holding up the much-tailored miniature ensemble, she said, "This is for you."

Martha looked up at Mary Elizabeth, who teased Martha's fingers from her skirt and directed them toward the new clothes. Martha inched forward until she could reach out for the skirt and bodice with her free hand, still holding her poppet in the other. Susan eased forward and held the brown skirt and a mustard-colored bodice up to Martha's front. Martha grabbed them with both arms, still holding the dangling doll.

"It's just for you," said Susan.

Martha twirled around, holding the new outfit.

Seventeen-year-old Junior burst through the door. Ignoring the women in the hall, he charged up the stairs.

Shortly after, Jonas came in from doing chores, his cheeks

rosy from the cold. "Look who we have here," he said, and he picked up Martha, new clothes, doll, and all and twirled her around until she giggled. When he put her down, he looked at her closely. "You must be about the same age as Lydia Prescott."

Nashaway

When Prescott rode up to the Fairbanks dooryard, he noticed Grace's herbs had started shooting up around the perimeter of the house, and Jonathan was chopping at one of the remaining stumps in the yard.

After a proper greeting. Prescott addressed the purpose of his visit. "Jonas was a big help moving the cattle out to Nashaway in '44."

Jonathan raised an eyebrow.

"Does he still do woodwork with you in the hall chamber?"

"Yes, but he helps George with his barrels too. I believe that boy will be a carpenter."

Six-year-old Martha ran past, and Traveler, Jonas's hound, bounded after her.

"What's your hurry?" called Jonathan.

"Gammar needs me," she called back as she disappeared in the door.

"Looks like she's settled in," said Prescott. "It's good of you to take her. I suppose your own won't be around for long, and this big house will be empty."

"Aye, John and Mary are both married, George is getting married this year, and Susan seems to be interested in our town drummer, Ralph Daye. That leaves Jonas and Junior." He paused. "We don't know about Jonas." Jonathan shook his head. "At his age, I was courting Grace. . . . Did you find ore in the hills?"

"We've looked no more since we sent samples to England. I think Winthrop Jr. was right. You must have a town settled before you try to mine or process metals. My hands are full getting people to settle in Nashaway to fulfill our grant covenant."

"You aren't the only one with problems. Have you heard? King Charles was handed over to Parliament after his capture."

Prescott restated his mission, showing no interest in a lengthy conversation about politics. "Lo, I need a carpenter in Nashaway. If we expect families to move there, we need someone to build houses and make furnishings. Would Jonas be interested late this fall when harvest is in?"

"You don't remember. When we first came to Massachusetts Bay, the colonial government banned us from moving outside the coastal towns. Now they say we are in great danger again, at least the inland towns—Concord, Sudbury, and Dedham. No one can leave these towns unless they get allowances from the magistrate or selectmen of their town. They didn't mention Nashaway, so I suppose that is why you haven't heard—you aren't a town yet." He smirked, then looked at Prescott to be sure he knew he was teasing. "Really, though, Prescott, I'm sure our selectmen will allow Jonas to go. Your biggest trouble might be with his brother, George, because Jonas is an invaluable help to him."

Jonathan put his arm around Prescott's shoulders, guiding him to the house. "Grace will fix you something to eat."

Grace welcomed Prescott with open arms and said, "Why didn't you bring Mary and the children?"

"There's much to do and no servants. Mary does the trading at the trucking house while I'm gone."

Grace shuddered at the thought.

"She's not too keen about dealing with the Natives," Prescott said, acknowledging the shudder, "but she said it's better than fording the Sudbury River after almost drowning last spring."

Grace pressed her lips together to keep from chiding

Prescott for taking Mary to the wilderness. She turned to tend to her fires.

"What else do you hear from England, Jonathan?"

"There is a big push in England to convert our Natives. It's as if we're in a race to reach them before the Papists do," said Jonathan. "Our minister, Mr. Allin, met with Mr. John Eliot, the Rowley minister, and Mr. Thomas Shepard of Cambridge—they are a committee to devise a plan about the Natives' civil and religious reform."

"What do they propose? I've heard of this in our area."

"They're planning their first real meeting with the Natives this fall. They recruited a young Native, Cockenoe. He was a captive of the Pequot War, then educated in Dorchester. He will help preach."

"So, when will they start?"

"Mr. John Eliot has made several attempts, but this meeting will be with Waban, a prominent man of the Massachusett Tribe," Jonathan explained. "Waban already sends his son, Thomas, to Dedham to attend school. His band wishes to learn about our English God, as they say, but the Sachem and Powwows of the bigger tribe won't allow the Christian teaching in their village. Reverend Eliot helped Waban's followers to move to a place near the Watertown mill, called Nonantum, and that's where they are having the meeting."

Prescott looked pensive. "So, the Nonantum meeting is what our Nashuag Natives are talking about. Some of them are planning to come. They said an Englishman will preach in their tongue."

"Reverend Eliot has earned the title Apostle to the Indians," said Jonathan. "I believe the first sermon is planned for October. How goes it with your doctor friend, Robert Childe? Is he still involved in the ironworks at Braintree?"

"He's back in England getting financial support for it. We

need young, smart, motivated men like him in the colony," said Prescott. "By the way, he believes that a man shouldn't be restricted from voting just because he hasn't joined the church."

"They are still pressing me hard on that," said Jonathan.

"Isn't that what you came for?" asked Prescott.

Jonathan sidestepped the question. "I'm surprised you've gotten this far without a minister. Spreading true religion is one of the main reasons for settling new plantations, according to our governor."

"We had a minister planned, Mr. Norcross, but he left for England before we settled Nashaway. There are so few families thus far that we can't afford a minister, let alone build a meetinghouse."

"They'll soon be sending Apostle Eliot out to preach to *you* instead of the Natives," Jonathan quipped. Governor Winthrop had already called the investors of Nashaway profane for not belonging to churches.

"I think the colony government is as interested in finding and processing ore as I am. Until we are ready for ores, Nashaway is just bait for the hostile Indians. A buffer for the Bay towns," said Prescott, not able to hold his tongue. He pinched the bridge of his nose. "If we don't get a minister soon, the colony threatens to close us down as a plantation and take all that we have worked for. That's why I need Jonas to help build, so people will come."

"We should give you one of our many ministers from Dedham." They both laughed.

"This conversation reminds me of our conversations in England," Prescott said. "Maybe we just traded troubles by crossing the ocean."

"Aye," said Jonathan. "It has changed from the king dictating my religion, to the colony government and the town minister dictating it. At least this is the practice I believe in."

Jonas rode up in a gallop, reining in sharply. "I hoped I'd get here before you left." he said to Prescott.

"You're the man I want to talk with," Prescott said.

"I'm always happy to see you. Are you going to Boston, as usual?"

"Aye, to talk to John Cowdall, the trader. He bought the trucking house and its land in Nashaway after King and Symonds died. I am negotiating to purchase both, since I'm already the trader."

"I'm going to Boston, too," Jonas said. "George has asked me to buy rings for the barrels. You mind if I ride with you? I'll also see Cousin Richard, who is building a tidal mill. Two of your men—Symonds and John Hill—were helping him start it."

"I'd enjoy the company," said Prescott, "and I can talk to you about coming to Nashaway."

Captain Thomas Cromwell 1646

Jonas entered the trader's shop in Boston as a particularly deep voice was saying, "Did you hear about the loot he brought in from those three Spanish ships?"

"Aye, but it's all for the Earl of Warwick," said another.

"Sure, but no one can bring in that much bounty and not be wealthy themselves when the trading is done," said a third.

"Have his sailors gotten into trouble here? I heard they were so distempered with drink at Plymouth that most of them were jailed."

"Aye, they could hardly keep them contained," said a gravel-voiced man. This was all fascinating to Jonas compared to the news in Dedham, and he pushed in closer.

"If he is so wealthy, why is he staying in a hovel with a man in the meanest part of town?" asked a well-dressed man.

"He's young and foolish—but twenty-nine-years old. He'll grow into his new wealth."

"He may not have his wealth for long," said the well-dressed man. "He may not even have his head."

"You haven't heard? They acquitted him at court today," said the deep-voiced man.

Jonas, forgetting his mission, joined in. "What's his name?"

"Captain Thomas Cromwell," said the well-dressed man, looking Jonas up and down.

"Can you tell me where to find this Captain Cromwell?" Getting directions, Jonas left immediately, without doing his business there.

After a few inquiries, he found the hovel they described. An older unkempt man opened the door cautiously at Jonas's knock. The man had long, stringy hair pulled back with a strip of leather, and his left hand held a knife barely visible behind his back. Jonas saw plates and silver stacked in the corner behind him.

"May I talk to Captain Cromwell?"

"Who asks?" growled the older man. Jonas could see a dark figure inside the hovel. That man had a groomed beard, mustache, and long hair and sat watching the exchange at a table set with two mugs and a deck of cards.

"He will not know me, but I'm Jonas Fairbanks. I came from West Yorkshire some time ago, but I'm now from Dedham. On my voyage, I became friends with a young sea hand named Thomas. I thought the captain might be that man—he's about the right age."

The man at the door looked back at the captain, who nodded, so the older man stepped aside and let Jonas enter.

"Who are you looking for?" The man at the table asked. "I'm Captain Cromwell."

Jonas remained standing and recounted the story of his family's voyage and the young sailor he befriended. He explained his desire to go to sea.

"I don't remember you. When was this? I came over the first time in 1637."

Jonas's shoulders slumped. "We came earlier." He turned to leave.

"Wait," said Cromwell. "I can surely tell you about going to sea as a young man." He sized up Jonas. "I guess you heard about my trial for killing one of my men."

"I heard you were acquitted—nothing else."

"Suffice it to say, that man died under my leadership as captain. If I hadn't fought him, he would have killed me or some of my men. I hit him with the hilt of his own sword. The blow to his head was tended, but he died of his own accord. And yes, I was acquitted and will return to the sea soon."

The captain watched Jonas's reaction, who did not recoil nor ask for details.

Cromwell relaxed and asked their host to bring an extra mug. He held out a hand to direct Jonas to the other stool at the table.

"Many think it strange that you stay in this part of Boston when you could stay in the best places in town," Jonas said.

"When I was a low sailor of mean estate, my host, a poor man"—he looked up at the old man— "took me in and entertained me when others would not. Now, when I can do good for him, I won't go elsewhere."

Jonas raised his mug to that. The others followed.

"Fairbanks, you said? Fairbanks, you have an interest in the sea, and I've lost a seaman. Would you like to sail out with me when I depart?"

Jonas stopped, his mug halfway to his mouth. He couldn't speak. The captain was not the type of depraved sailor his parents had warned him about. He was an honorable man, doing good to another. "When will you go?" he asked.

"In a couple of days. We will be out as long as it takes to

bring in another Spanish ship. You'd have to be ready to leave everything. Do you have a wife, children?

"No." Jonas failed to tell him about his father's promise to disinherit him if he became a sailor, let alone a buccaneer.

"Will you go?"

Jonas stared at him.

"You don't need to tell me now, but you must be on the ship by the time we sail. We can't wait for you. Go home and get your things in order." Captain Cromwell smiled and said, "I think we could be good friends, like the sea hand you met on your voyage." He drained his mug.

"Now, will you join us down at the commons? There are much prettier things than cows there for a man to enjoy."

Jonas stretched a sheepish grin and pushed his stool back abruptly. "I must go home to prepare to sail."

Caterpillars

How could Jonas tell his father he was going to sea with a buccaneer? At twenty-two he was expected to farm, build a house, and marry a nice Dedham girl, as his brothers had. But he did not want to farm or turn wood for spinning wheels. He did not want to marry just to have a wife. If he went with Captain Cromwell, he reasoned, he would not need his inheritance. His father had done well without much of one.

Riding toward Dedham, Jonas noticed fields of wheat and barley with bare spots. He rode closer to the crops and saw dark areas on the young stalks and blades. When he dismounted to investigate, he saw worms chewing at the edges of the blades. The infestation became more pronounced the closer he got to Dedham, the gnawing larva having stripped some of his own family's fields in just the days he had been gone.

Junior came running when Jonas rode up to the house. "Jonas, come quick!" he cried. "We're picking the 'pillars off George's field and we'll go to Michael and Mary's next. Where have you been? Even Mother and Martha are picking off caterpillars."

Jonas looked back toward Boston, knowing Captain Cromwell wouldn't wait. He was planning only to tell Mother he was leaving, but now his plans had changed.

"Jonathan," said Grace as the family walked home after lecture day, "what were Minister Allin and Elder Hunting talking with you about at noon break?" She patted Martha's head and the little girl ran ahead to where Jonas was strolling with Robert Crossman and pulled on Jonas's breeches leg to swoop her up onto his shoulders.

Jonathan nodded silently. Grace knew he was telling himself that this was how it should be—Jonas had known his duty to help save the crops. George walked with his new wife, Mary Adams, and Susan was among a group of older girls giggling at a distance behind them. He gave Grace's shoulders a squeeze.

"Mr. Allin told me about the service he will hold in October with John Eliot and Thomas Shepard—for Waban and his band."

Grace sensed Jonathan was evading the question. "So why was Elder Hunting talking with you, too? They both seemed so intent."

"Well, Grace," said Jonathan, "like you, they think I should join the church."

"You're a godly man, Jonathan, but even I don't understand you sometimes." Grace took his hand for a moment. "If you join the church, you will have more influence—you can vote in the colony affairs."

"I have my say in town affairs. That's enough. I'm a man of few words, but when I speak, I am heard."

"So, what did you tell them?"

"That I'll talk with them again this coming week and bring some questions."

"This is your decision, Jonathan. With your stubbornness, I can't hope to sway you. This is between you and the Lord." Grace dropped his hand.

The next Sunday, Jonathan was called to the minister and elder's table at the front of the church. "Our brother, Jonathan Fairbanks, would like to speak to the congregation," said Mr. Allin.

Jonathan broke into a short but eloquent speech declaring the workings of God in his heart and the true signs of faith and repentance in his soul—all that was required for acceptance. He spoke with such conviction and passion that a murmur enveloped the congregation when he finished. Jonathan returned immediately to his seat.

Time seemed to pause. Silence hung around him.

Mr. Allin took his position at the table. "Thank you, Brother Fairbanks." He nodded at Jonathan. "Now you must be accepted by this congregation."

Jonathan sat erect on his bench, his knee jumping as he faced forward. Grace, on the women's bench across the aisle, dabbed the corners of her eyes.

"Do you choose Jonathan Fairbanks to sit as a member among us?"

The whole congregation erupted in "Amen!"

When church was dismissed, Grace and Jonathan could barely get through the door as people welcomed and congratulated him. A few of his closer friends said, "It's about time."

Jonathan and Grace walked home with a lightness of step, a great burden lifted. He had been accepted by a Puritan town and church, given important jobs, and granted land. Why did his father treat him differently than he treated his half-brothers?

Meetinghouse

"Where is our schoolhouse?" asked Jonathan. The other men at the town meeting voiced their agreement. "I don't have sons to attend school, but I have a grandson that's six years old."

Fairbanks did not often speak up at general meetings, but on this day, he spoke with conviction. "We voted unanimously in 1642 to set aside land to provide money for a school. In '44 we voted for a free school and school rates to pay for it. There wasn't a kernel of corn in that hat. Dedham was well ahead of the General Court passing a law in '46 that towns had to have schools. But here it is,1648, and we have no schoolhouse. What is our school rate money being used for? Building an Indian village in our backyard?"

Henry Chickering crashed his gavel against the wooden table. "We *do* have a schoolmaster in town. The boys are learning at the meetinghouse."

Another voice piped up, "Holding school in the meetinghouse inhibits its use for other purposes."

Chickering repeated his attention-demanding blow of the gavel. "We've been busy with negotiations about the Indian village—there are many opinions, not only among us in town, but between Mr. Eliot as minister, the Natives, the General Court, and Dedham as a unified town."

"I say we get things started here before our boys have to go to school at an Indian village," announced another voice. "After all, we invited Indian boys to come to school here."

With that, all the proprietors voted that a schoolhouse should be built during the next year.

Jonathan stormed home after the meeting, finding Jonas in the house. With no preamble, he announced, "Jonas, since you have not settled, you have time to help our village build a school—when you are not helping George make barrels."

Jonas stood squarely facing his father. "But George just received the town's permission to fell trees in the commons. We'll be busier than ever. Why must I do what *you* tell me? I'm twenty-four years old. How much longer will I have to follow the paths you dictate?"

"But you haven't yet chosen a path of your own. As long as you live in this house, you shall help this family and this town."

Jonas silently glared at his father. "Were it not for saving your crops from the caterpillars, I'd be on a ship now with Captain Thomas Cromwell." Jonas yanked his cloak and hat off the peg and opened the door to leave.

Before he could close the door, Jonathan called to his back, "John Thurston is building the school. Go see him."

At a special meeting in Dedham, one of the proprietors spoke up from the rear of the meetinghouse. "The General Court and Mr. Eliot want to take some of our land only eleven miles away for the Indian village. I think we should build a watchtower on the schoolhouse."

"We needed one for watch and ward during the Pequot War," said another.

"But these are peaceful praying Indians, Waban's band." replied Minister Allin, one of the committee to help the Indians. "His son goes to school here, and we've always had other Natives scattered around the land, at Wigwam Pond, Purgatory Plain, and Wollomonopoag."

Another proprietor interjected, "The Court wants to take back land they granted *us* to make an Indian town. I thought the land was ours."

The town agreed to build a watchtower at the back of the new schoolhouse, and until then, watch would be kept at the church.

"Ralph Daye has beat the drum long enough for our warnings. Why not put a bell in the tower instead—to call to worship and alert us to danger?"

"Where do you suppose we could get a bell?" asked another.

George Fairbanks looked knowingly at Eleazur Lusher, prominent in the town, a selectman as well as the Second Lieutenant of the Massachusetts Military Company. Eleazur looked back at George, shaking his head with caution.

George looked around and noted that none of his Massachusetts Military companions seemed to make the connection between the bell and the stories they heard at the last Military Company training.

Lusher finally spoke up. "I might know where we can purchase a bell." A stir of interest swept around the room, but Lusher said no more and stared George into silence.

George ached to tell someone about the discussion at the military training. His mother longed for a bell like those at the churches in England.

Shortly after the meeting, George took Jonas with him to fell trees in the commons, saying, "This reminds me of the first time we took you out into the woods to make our canoe." George pointed out his mark on a cedar.

"I've changed a lot since then," said Jonas, and they both laughed as Jonas maneuvered opposite George and chopped a wedge out at the base.

"You have really helped grow my trade," said George.

"Don't plan on me staying, said Jonas. "This isn't what I want to do the rest of my life."

"I thought you gave up being a mariner."

"No, Father gave up on me being a mariner. I almost left on a ship in '46, but I couldn't go while our crops were in danger."

Jonas's axe came down extra hard on the tree for the next few bites. "I want to do something that will take me away from Dedham. Something with adventure."

A few minutes later, George lowered his voice and said, "Someone spoke of a buccaneer at the last Military Company training."

Jonas rolled his eyes at yet another story about the Military Company.

"A captain had just sailed into Boston with loot from a Spanish ship. He was young and had already brought loot in from several other Spanish ships about three years ago."

Jonas stopped chopping.

"Jonas," said George, nodding to his brother. "It's your turn. We must get this done by dark."

Reluctantly, Jonas resumed chopping as George continued. "This time he brought in six large bells, the kind you'd find in church towers, along with lots more wealth."

"So that's where you think the town can get a bell?" said Jonas. "What was the captain's name?"

"Captain Thomas Cromwell, but he's dead now," said George.

Jonas let his axe fall to his side and looked at George. "Dead?"

"Yes, he fell off his horse onto the hilt of his sword. The crossbar of the hilt stuck right into him. Serves him right. They said he killed a man with the hilt of a sword."

Jonas raised his axe and brought it down hard and left it stuck in the tree. "He was acquitted, George. He was acquitted." Jonas walked off.

George scratched his head where his hair was thinning. "Weren't we talking about a bell?"

Iron Rush

"Attention! Forward march. Left face. Halt. At ease. Fall out." It was blustery cold when the Military Company of

Massachusetts, under the decorated Captain Robert Sedgwick, sat down for a break in a well sheltered area of the Boston training fields. Sedgwick, a man of ambition and action, and a strong supporter of colony progress, had been a founder of the company. He was spending time with the Dedham military men, hoping to get to know them better.

"I'm surprised no one from Dedham has found ores around your village," he remarked, seemingly wanting a break from training talk. "Didn't your Goodman Abraham Shaw receive the first grant in the whole colony to search for coal and metal? Your town's only fifteen miles from Braintree, and we set up the colony's first ironworks there. They found plenty of bog iron."

Eleazur Lusher, the senior officer from Dedham, said, "You were one of the investors in Braintree, weren't you?"

"Aye, but we've found that Braintree doesn't have sufficient water flow to run an ironworks. The new manager, Richard Leader, is trying to salvage the forge, but he's moving the whole works to Lynn, on the Saugus River. There's plenty of water flow, ore, and trees there. Hammersmith, as it's called, will need lots of raw iron to smelt if the ironworks is to be successful."

The men of Dedham listened with interest, and when they rode back home, they discussed ore, mines, and ironworks. By April, Eleazur Lusher and Mr. Allin told the selectmen about their finds of bog ore around Dedham. Ten days later, Lt. Fisher and Sgt. Fisher reported a find on the north side of the Charles River.

Jonas joined Crossman on the meetinghouse steps on the Sabbath. "I've heard about the ore finds. Remember when we talked about Shaw's grant and how we would hunt for treasure some day? I think it's time."

"Well," Robert stammered, "I have a house and my own land to work now. I was just a boy with big dreams then. I don't have time now."

Jonas's ears burned, his eyes narrowed, and his fists clenched at his sides. His family was always chiding him because he had not settled, and now his best friend was calling him a boy with big dreams.

On a Sunday in early June, Jonas took his place next to Robert on the men's bench at the meetinghouse. As always, Mr. Allin started the morning by reading notices pegged to the meetinghouse doors.

After announcing a few banns of marriage, land sales, and women's activities, Mr. Allin looked closely at the next item on his list. He glanced in the direction of Robert and Jonas first and then toward Anthony Fisher. "It looks like Anthony Fisher won't let his relatives get ahead of him. He and Robert Crossman have announced finding metals above or westerly of the place where the Neponset River divides."

Jonas's mouth dropped open but snapped shut into a clenched jaw as Robert Crossman looked his way.

"I couldn't tell you," whispered Crossman out the side of his mouth, watching the tithing man. "Anthony made me promise to tell no one. Just like I promised I wouldn't tell where you thought Shaw's ore was."

The tithing man looked directly at Jonas and Robert, tapping his staff on the floor. The conversation was left until noon break.

"It's been over seven years since we talked about finding buried treasures and ores," began Crossman as soon as they could talk. We both work hard to earn money. We both pay country rates in Dedham this year.

"You spurned me but had time to search for ore with Anthony," snapped Jonas. "Don't you remember when we were building the gristmill, we talked of doing something together?"

"Jonas, this just happened. The Dedham men at the Military Company training talked with Captain Sedgwick about ores and ironworks, and everyone got excited. Anthony asked me to explore with him, and we found some. He has the money to make this thing work."

Jonas kicked hard at a clump of grass and glared at Crossman as Junior passed by with Debra Shepard. Jonas was painfully reminded that Junior was planning to post banns for an October wedding. Jonas would be the only one in his family not married, and that would give his parents more reason to pressure him. Now he had been betrayed by his best friend.

Natick

In early spring, Prescott carried furs and Indian trade goods over the cart path from Nashaway to Sudbury. From there, he would take the only beaten path to Dedham to see Jonathan. A band of about fifty Indians dressed in a jumble of Native and English dress and carrying large bundles were coming toward him on the path.

Prescott was puzzled. The women generally carried the woven reed mats and materials for making their wetus, traveling light, but today men were also carrying parcels, as well as heavy English tools. John took his horse off the path and watched as they passed, followed by Mr. John Eliot on horseback with additional burdens of supplies.

"Where do you go, Apostle Eliot? It looks like you are following your followers."

"You probably haven't heard. England has approved the Society for Propagation and Education of the Natives. They'll send money from England to provide for a praying town for them."

"You've already resettled Waban and his band twice. I thought I saw the Sachem in the group."

"Aye, not only do we need more land but a place they can plant in peace. We think we've found that here."

"Then the negotiations went through with Dedham? Fairbanks explained the land you will be settling is part of Dedham's original grant land." Prescott looked back at the receding procession.

"Well, I can't say it is part of *their* land. The Natives believe it still belongs to their forefathers. It appears we will have an agreement soon, though, and we are going to start settling now, just north of the Charles River at the west border of Dedham."

"I have rarely seen the men carry," said Prescott.

"Aye, we are teaching the Natives the English way, as well as our precious faith. The men are even learning to plant English grains with our tools. We need everyone working to settle, putting in crops for a fall harvest, and making a town large enough for others to come to our meetings or join us. I would like this to become a center where all Natives may pray and serve God."

"I must get on my way," said Prescott. "The winter trade goods must get to the wharf before the ships sail."

"When you see Fairbanks, have him relay to the teacher—a Mr. Wheelock—that we'll need Waban's son. I hear Thomas is good with numbers, so he'll do the reckoning of the books for our village." Mr. Eliot tipped his hat.

Before Prescott rode off, Eliot called back, "By the way, the Natives call their village Natick. Some say it means 'land of hills,' but my praying Indians say it means 'my land.'"

A few miles further on, Prescott heard the rustle of grasses and found Jonathan and Jonas in the rosemary field south of the Charles River, not far from where he had spoken to Mr. Eliot. Jonathan and Jonas laid their tools down when Prescott called to them.

"I just saw Eliot with a band of Natives," said Prescott,

when he'd ridden up to them. "So I guess Dedham is letting them settle the land northwest of here."

"I think Eliot is a bit ahead of himself," replied Jonathan. "The general opinion in Dedham is we agree with teaching and converting the Indians. That's even in the colony charter. We're sending men to view the land to be ceded and report to the town—but *then* we make the final decision."

"Oh yes, Eliot said he will need Waban's son, Thomas, to help with the books in Natick."

"Natick—they have already named it?" Jonathan looked in the direction of the planned village.

Prescott wiped the sweat from his brow and looked at Jonas. "It doesn't look like you can accompany me to Boston this time, Jonas . . ."

Jonas spiked his fork hard into the soil and eagerly asked, "Have you found ore in Nashaway? There's a lot of talk of the new ironworks on the Saugus River at Lynn. One of the men you know, Joseph Jenke, was granted an independent blacksmith shop there. In fact, three different groups have found ore right here in Dedham."

"Aye, Jenke helped us petition for a cart bridge over the Sudbury River, thinking we would start a foundry in Nashaway," said Prescott. "But we are too busy building a town to work ore. Dedham will only be supplying Saugus when they start bringing up the ore here. Hammersmith has a monopoly on Massachusetts ironworks and mines—discovered or undiscovered—for the next twenty-one years."

"Humph!" Jonas mumbled. "And Crossman thought it was so great to find ore here."

"Reverend Eliot and the General Court have asked me to build a new way out to the Great River Valley," said Prescott. "The men of Nashaway are busy settling, so the Natives are helping." He looked first at Jonathan, then Jonas.

"Jonas, would you come help again? Twenty-one years is a long time to wait for an ironworks at Dedham. By the way, Mary named our new baby boy Jonas, after you."

Jonas turned red.

PART IV

1650–1652

HAMMERSMITH 1650

Jonas sat on the men's Sabbath bench as Mr. Allin held up the first missive pinned on the meetinghouse door. A moment later Crossman pushed in beside him.

"Where've you been?" Jonas asked out the side of his mouth as the tithing man pounded his staff on the floor for order.

"We men who claimed ores in Dedham went to see Hammersmith. There was a fashionable tour with all sorts of gentlemen and ladies there. Hammersmith has eleven waterwheels!" Crossman bumped Jonas's shoulder with his. "I looked for John Elderkin but didn't see him."

Jonas scowled, knowing he had been left out again.

"I've got a job for us," whispered Crossman while the minister read the notices. Over the years, he and Jonas had gotten better at evading the tithing man's staff.

Jonas glared at Crossman, "You won't even search for mines with me."

"Too much to tell now. But I'm going to get us both out of Dedham." Crossman winked.

Jonas turned toward him but turned quickly back when the tithing man came shuffling and clicking his staff behind him. Jonas squirmed with anticipation like a boy, pulling on his earlobe and shuffling his feet until noon break.

The procession out of the meetinghouse was led by Mr. Allin and his wife, followed by the town dignitaries, then the congregation. It dragged on far too long.

Under a tree away from the noon break crowd, Jonas stood with Crossman, his head rocking from side to side in cadence with his sarcastic words, "What do you mean you're going to get us out of Dedham? You just told the selectmen you found iron. You're not going to leave now."

"But I am—I-I mean, we are," stammered Crossman, almost dancing to his words. "I must know how to get the ore out and what to do with it. By Gaw, Jonas, the ironworks are massive there, and the place is powerful, it's dirty, and maybe it's a bit coarse." He smirked and they both laughed.

Serious now, Crossman said, "They need help."

Jonas listened raptly, ignoring the others gathered to eat from the table by the meetinghouse.

"I talked to the carpenter at the forge, where the real work takes place," said Crossman. "He has seven waterwheels to oversee at the ironworks. There are a total of eleven to supply the whole operation. Remember William Osbourn in Braintree? We met him when we were hunting wolves there?"

Jonas nodded.

"He's running the whole place until a new manager takes over. He said they need help."

"What does that have to do with us? We don't know anything about working ore."

"We do know about working with wood and waterwheels, though," Crossman said, beaming. "There are things to do around the forge: carpentry, mechanics, even forge work itself. If we don't know how, we'll learn."

"Where would we stay?"

"There are small family houses at the site. Some single workers live with the families, but there are large buildings for other workers. The company owns some of the housing, so it's like their own little town called Hammersmith. They even have their own church, so to speak, so I guess that satisfies the people of Lynn. But not many of the men and women attend, and they can be a little rough."

"If my father would disown me for becoming a sailor, he won't be pleased with me going to this Hammersmith."

"I thought about that, so I asked. Mr. Osbourn says if we come, he'll put us up at his house, room and board. His place is about a mile from the works."

"The town sounds more interesting," said Jonas.

"That doesn't mean we can't visit," Robert said with a lop-sided grin under his mustache. You're going to get your hands dirty and maybe your reputation. Several of the workers have already been called to Essex County Court. It's not as stiff-backed there as at Dedham."

"What kind of money will we make?

"Better than we can make here," said Crossman. "Osbourn says we'll work hard—ten-hour days, every day. The ironworks pays well because they don't have to pay taxes. And we don't have to go to militia training while we work there."

Jonas hadn't taken his eyes off his old friend, and Crossman continued. "This is where the money is. Iron goods are costly from England. With fewer ships coming, prices are rising for the colony, and we will be the ones supplying New England. Rich people from England are the investors and believe in it, as do Governor Winthrop's son and that doctor, Mr. Childe."

"When do we go? Jonas asked with more enthusiasm. "I will be glad to tell George I'm not working for him any longer. I never wanted to be a cooper, anyway. But first, of course, I must help Father harvest."

"After harvest will be too late. They close down the operations when it freezes, because the traces can't carry water to the wheels. They won't open again until spring thaw."

Jonas kicked the dirt hard enough to dislodge a clump of

grass. "Sure," he growled. "That's when we'll be getting ready to plant. I'll never get away."

"Well, I'm going. Kingsbury and I tore up my indenture papers five years ago, and I can do what I please," said Crossman. "You wanted an adventure. You'll find one at Hammersmith. Those are hard-working, rough-living men and women. Everyone leaves them alone, because no one else can do the job they can."

In Sickness and in Death

In the recently added lean-to on the north side of the house, Grace placed her stamp perfectly at the center of a cheese wheel and tightened the press. She wanted her brand to reflect the care with which she made her cheese, which was valued in the society. Many ate her "white meat" during the winter to save their beef, pork, and poultry for special occasions.

A sound emanated from the front of the house. *There it is again.* Grace froze. *Someone's in there.*

Martha was ill with a high fever, and Grace had settled her in the parlor on the trundle, so she could tend to her easily. Grace stood still and listened again. She heard nothing. She peeked warily through the hall door, remembering the time Indians visited without announcement. "Jonas? Jonathan?"

No response. Grace crept into the hall, "Jonathan," she said with a sigh of relief.

Jonathan stood inside the front door staring at a folded paper with a wax seal. A small parcel lay at his feet. He hadn't taken off his hat.

"You're home already?" she said.

He looked up absently and then back at the paper.

"What have you brought from Boston?"

"A letter from England. I picked it up from Richard's tavern."

Grace bustled to his side, excited for a letter from the homeland.

Martha awoke and hobbled out of bed with stringy wet hair. Grace shooed her back to the trundle and tucked her in.

"Who—who's it from?" Grace stammered. Jonathan didn't answer. It felt like the time the messenger brought the note about Jonathan's father, and she worried.

"It came from James Platts of Sowerby. It's George's will." Jonathan looked up at Grace with a bewildered expression. What would his half-brother leave him?

"The Plattses are Mary Prescott's and my relatives," said Grace, who kept track of such things. "Mary was a Gawkroger Platts." She fetched Jonathan's spectacles from the parlor table and handed them to him in exchange for his hat. Then she stood by his side as he looked at the shipworn letter.

George Fairebanke   his
last Will &
      Testam t.
              For his louvinge Cusen Jonathan
               Fayrebancke in new Ingland,
                    these
                    Deliu r.

"Did you know he was ill?"

"Nay, we haven't corresponded. Maybe he succumbed to influenza. They had earthquakes in northern England. Influenza often follows."

"Does this mean you were named in his will?" Grace let her excitement seep into her voice.

"I don't know." Jonathan ran his hand over his bald head fringed with gray streaked black hair. "George didn't have any children." He looked at Grace with uncertainty.

"Would we go back home if you got land there?" Grace clasped her hands in front of her chest to keep from clapping them.

Jonathan walked into the parlor and sat in the ladder-back chair beside the table. Grace followed, standing behind him with her hands on his shoulders. Martha tossed in a fitful sleep.

"Why didn't you read it when you received it?"

"I wished to be in my own home." Jonathan's hands trembled as he carefully peeled the seal away from the paper with a knife.

"What does it say?" Grace peeked over his shoulder. Jonathan looked up at her, knowing she wouldn't be able to read all the words.

Jonathan scanned the names as Grace looked on. "I see Platts," she said. "Many Platts. No doubt some of my relatives and Mary's."

He paused with his finger on the paper. "And there is a Jonathan Fairbanks."

Jonathan squeezed Grace's left hand, holding the paper in his right, adjusting its distance from his eyes.

"Oh, Jonathan, what did he leave you? It's about time your family acknowledged you."

"This Jonathan Fairbanks is my cousin, curate of Luddenden, my Uncle George's son." The hand with the paper fell to his lap. He stared into the room. "It seems George lived with James Platt in Sowerby before he died."

"Does it talk of land?"

Jonathan read on, leaving a cold silence in the room. "Nay, he probably gave the land before writing the will, as my father did."

George had named no less than twenty people, including some of Jonathan's half-siblings. "He wrote not my name."

"Why, Jonathan? Why would they send you this will if you aren't named?" Delight drained from Grace's face.

"Maybe he wanted to let me know I still haven't been accepted by the family. He said he would have nothing for me if I left Thornton-in-Craven."

Grace squeezed Jonathan's shoulder and remembered the reading of Jonathan's father's will twenty-five years before. "We have our own family now, Jonathan, with lands and a fine house. You are the father you never had."

Martha coughed and coughed but didn't awaken.

Grace, disenchanted by the will, turned to tend her little helper. Martha had become like a daughter to her in the five years since she had come to stay. Grace looked at Jonathan, but he was far away in his thoughts. "Now our children are gone, she's the light of our world," said Grace. *I must spare her from this pestilence. One child in every family has been lost this year. She's all we have left.*

Jonathan placed the will on the table and rested an elbow upon it. His other hand covered his eyes.

Grace nodded toward the parcel by the door.

"Jonathan, what's in the package?"

"I don't know." He didn't look up.

Grace went to the package and brought it back to the table to open it with her sewing scissors. Inside was a glimmering brass sundial. "Oh, Jonathan, look!"

Jonathan looked up with little interest.

"The date is 1650, made in London," said Grace brightly. "The outer package is corrupted by seawater. All I can read is Fayerbank, Dedham. We'll accept this as a token from George," she said decisively.

"So it shall be," Jonathan mumbled with less enthusiasm. "I know when my work is done. I cease when there is no light nor life to support it. I don't need a sundial for that." Jonathan scowled, "My work is never done."

Martha woke with an uncontrollable cough, and Grace

hustled to fetch the tea of honey, peppermint, and thyme. Jonathan wallowed in painful memories a bit longer before he rose to touch Martha's small, flushed face.

Natick's Champion

Stout Reverend John Eliot, dressed in his pastoral gown with his thin mustache and line of beard from his lower lip to his chin, rode his stocky horse on the main lane in Dedham—the two a matched pair. Townsmen tipped their hats as he rode by.

Mr. Eliot passed Grace as she walked into town taking cheese to her customers. "Good morrow, Mr. Eliot," she said. "You're doing a fine thing, teaching the Natives about God."

"Thank you, Goody Fairbanks, I'm here to ask Mr. Allin and Lt. Fisher to view more land to the north. We hope to extend our little village."

Grace's lips firmed, and she bit them until he passed.

This was the first of many visits Mr. Eliot made to Dedham. Each time he requested Mr. Allin and other prestigious town representatives to accompany him to the place the Indians had settled. They passed Dedham's Rosemary Meadows on their way to the budding Natick Praying Village of the Massachusett Natives.

Mr. Eliot continually rubbed his left thigh as his horse plodded along. At the edge of the mission village, he said, "I'd like you, Mr. Allin, and you, Lt. Fisher, to help with potential bounds for the land we can expect from Dedham.

Mr. Allin pointed out a large building and looked at Mr. Eliot, who said, "Aye, that's the meetinghouse. The families will live in wetus for now. They go up faster, are less expensive and warmer in winter than are English houses. And the Natives will stay here year-round."

Mr. Allin and Lt. Fisher looked at each other in concern.

"You have started a couple of paths on the north side of the river," commented Lt. Fisher.

"They're calling one of them Eliot's path," the minister said, sitting taller in his saddle. The meetinghouse is central. Simple, but a fine two-story building. The hall downstairs is for the Sabbath, for meetings and for our planned school. The upstairs storage room is used for skins, trade goods, tools, and supplies. A corner room is for me when I come to preach." Eliot rubbed his left leg harder. "Riding in bad weather causes me considerable pain. The doctor calls it 'sciatica.'"

"I hope to gather larger numbers of praying Indians here. See that hill over there?" He pointed north. "We could use more land in that direction. We might need more land within your town, too."

Lt. Fisher gasped. "Our town has not yet set bounds for what we will cede."

"Mr. Allin supports our endeavor," said Mr. Eliot confidently, staring at Allin. "He was on my committee in '45, and I'm hoping you both will champion our plans before the townsmen."

"We'll let the townsmen know your thoughts," said Mr. Allin. "Many support your work with the Natives."

"But we cannot speak for the town," cautioned Lt. Fisher, glaring at Allin. "Mr. Allin and I must return. Good morrow to you."

As they rode out of earshot, Fisher said. "Looks like we need to get the men out here to set the bounds. Now."

On the Sabbath, Mr. Allin announced Mr. Eliot's proposal to the townsfolk as one of the meetinghouse door announcements.

"What about Dorchester, Sudbury, Watertown, and even Roxbury? What are they giving?" called someone in the congregation.

"Are we being compensated? The land was granted to us," announced another.

Eleazur Lusher responded. "We're appointing a committee to set the bounds that we'll relinquish."

Mr. Allin cleared his throat. "This is a lecture day, not a town meeting." But the rumble within the room did not stop.

Jonathan Fairbanks grumbled under his breath, "If this town is as slow at deciding this as it has been at everything else, this time it might cause trouble."

In late summer, Eliot wore a wide-brimmed hat against the glaring sun as he rode into Dedham and collected Mr. Allin and Eleazur Lusher to join him to visit Natick. Upon arrival, the men reined in sharply, gasping at the sight of stones piled on either side of the Charles River at the narrowest point.

Eliot beamed, saying, "See the fine footbridge the Natives are building over the Quinobequin? That's the Charles River to you, of course."

"Why a bridge to the south side?" asked Lusher. "Additional land will be ceded only north of the river."

"But the land south is already Native land. Sagamore Wompituk, whom you call Josias, claims the land is his. He's the son of Sachem Chickataubutt, who deeded the land to the Massachusetts Bay Colony in 1633, but Josias says the land was given to his mother by her father, Sachem Wompituk. It was not Chickataubutt's land to deed. Sagamore Josias, now of age, gladly gives the land south of the river to Natick."

Eliot pointed south of the river. "As soon as they finish the bridge, Natick will build a road on the south side and lay out lots with two big common fields and orchards."

"Dedham was granted the deed from the General Court," Lusher harshly objected, "and the land we're ceding is *only* north of the river."

"Josias's claim is stronger than yours," said Mr. Eliot.

Mr. Allin and Lusher looked at each other, and Lusher said, "We'll bring this up to the proprietors. Until then, you are improving Dedham land."

Richard Elice, Dedham's constable, rode northwest with Jonathan Fairbanks toward Sudbury from Medfield, the new town carved out of Dedham land along the southwestern Charles River.

Jonathan and the constable followed the Charles River as it bent eastward. As they approached Natick, the native men were working on the south side of the river in established lots. Elice and Fairbanks stopped to chat with Waban and his men. "Why have you set up houses and planted on the south side of the river?" asked Jonathan.

Another native replied, "Mr. Eliot says work here."

The constable looked at Waban and said, "The land that Dedham gave Natick was only on the north side of the river."

The other man replied nodding, "We better it. Mr. Eliot says yes."

Jonathan and the constable tipped their hats and moved on, noting there was now a full stockade around the main village. They kept their horses at a walk while leaving Natick, then spurred to a gallop to get back to town. "Dedham will be less willing to work with the Indians now," said Fairbanks in disgust. "How can we trust they won't keep taking land?"

Eleazur Lusher addressed the ad hoc town meeting that night. "We're a town built on peace and love. We've handled our problems without getting the courts involved. We should handle our differences with Mr. Eliot and the Natick Indians the same way."

"Lusher, you should write a peaceable letter from Dedham and request the Natick people to abstain from expanding onto the south side of the river," suggested Michael Metcalf Sr.

"Be sure to add that they must keep their traps out of our fenced areas," grumbled Jonathan as he twisted his left ankle around. As a woodreeve, I've stumbled onto them times aplenty. And remind them that by accepting the land north of the river, they quit claim on any land south of the river."

Ironworks 1651

The hush of deep winter snow covered Dedham in January. "I'm going to Hammersmith," Crossman told Jonas. "They've been in operation for about a year and a half now. Are you coming?"

"I thought you said they won't begin work until the water flows."

"They have eleven wheels and traces that carry water to them, and the winter freeze causes leaks. Those bellows are as big as you or me, and they must be tallowed, so they won't crack. There's enough to keep us both busy until spring.

Jonas kicked an icy clod of snow, sending it skittering across the frozen beaten path.

"By Gaw, Jonas, be a man. Have your own way. Come with me to Hammersmith."

"Maybe being a man is *not* walking away from your family when they need you," Jonas said, picking up another ball of icy snow and throwing it hard against a barn. The ball shattered, just like Jonas's dreams, and the exploding ice became sparkling crystals in the sunlight. *If only my broken plans could turn into something so beautiful.*

"I'm the last son at home," Jonas said. "If Father's current illness becomes as bad as Martha's did last year, he'll need all of us to open the fields to plant. It is like when I planned to go to sea and came home to the worms."

"I'm still going," said Crossman defiantly. "I hope you come before you become a sick old man."

Jonas picked up another clot of ice and threw it in Crossman's direction.

"What do you mean?" asked George. "I built this cooper business as a two-man operation when you came to work for me. You can't just leave."

"You built this for you. There was no partnership, no covenant. I am no more than a servant. You expanded it because I came to work for you."

"I depend on you, Jonas. What about fidelity, trust?"

"You could trust me when I was here, and I'm leaving now to learn a trade of my own. A trade worth more than barrels." Jonas threw a metal ring, clanging it onto a pile of other rings.

"What am I to do with the business I've built?" George waved his arm toward all the lumber, barrel stays, hoops, and tools. "I have covenants."

"I will stay until I open Father's ground. You, John, and Junior will take over when I'm gone. I suggest you find an apprentice. I'm not going to be your servant anymore."

"When did you start telling others what to do?"

Jonas walked out of George's shop without a backward glance. George threw a hammer into one of the nearly finished barrels.

The sun crossed the Charles River, casting its last glow over the ridges of the Dedham hills. The oxen team leaving the common plow field quickened their plodding pace as they hurried to the barn. Jonas and his hound, Traveler, followed—no reason to nip at the heels of the beasts.

Jonas, having risen before dawn, methodically finished his chores in the gathering shadows of darkness and wondered if he was more hungry or tired. *Tomorrow, I'll plant,* he decided. *One day closer to going to Hammersmith.*

When he entered the house, Mother sat by the hearth embroidering a pocket for Martha to tie about her waist to carry her knitting, handkerchief, and a few scriptures.

Martha ran to greet Jonas and Traveler, but then quickly returned to her duty at the hearth—to prepare a trencher with leftover pottage, cheese, and bread for him. Father looked up from the Bible, his shoulders slumped, his face pale.

"How does the field turn this spring? I'll come out with you on the morrow," said Father.

"Well," said Jonas, "we've worked that soil long enough that it accepts the plow nicely."

"A neighbor asked if you'll use our oxen to turn his field, too," said Father.

"But I was to plant tomorrow. I go to Hammersmith when I've finished our field—Crossman is already there."

"That is still your plan?" Jonathan spat out the words. "Will you live and work amongst the profane and coarse instead of here among our people?"

Jonas, hungry and tired, was in no mood to argue. "The crops will be laid by before I leave. Your other sons can help then."

"Aye, but they have farms and families. You are unmarried, have no farm, and have no trade of your own."

"Ironwork will be my trade." Jonas stood with his legs wide and his arms crossed over his chest.

"What about George? He needs your help with *his* business."

"I will not be a cooper, either. We have stockpiled timber for him. He'll have to do without me."

"Have you told him you're leaving?"

"Aye," said Jonas. "He can contact a company in England who will find an apprentice for him for the passage over."

"So, you are leaving the family?" Jonathan's piercing eyes burned into Jonas's.

"Nay, I'm not going to sea, I'm going to Lynn to start a trade and a life of my own choosing. I can be a part of the family without being a servant to it." No longer worrying about being hungry or tired, Jonas stomped up to the children's room in the parlor chamber.

The next morning, Jonas rose early, before anyone else, and grumbled while managing the oxen as they pulled through the heavy clods of the neighbor's portion of the common field next to the Fairbankses' allotment.

His mind wandered while he planted the crop dictated by the town—this year everyone would plant wheat. His thoughts jerked back to his work just as the oxen team veered off course. "Good, Bright and Bitty! Keep the rows straight."

His mind traveled to Hammersmith. He remembered the smell of molten iron at Prescott's forge when he turned the grinding wheel. He wondered what it would be like at Hammersmith, a big forge. Spying a rail down on the Fairbanks portion of the fence, Jonas flung his head back and shut his eyes with a sigh. "Another delay."

The fence mended, Jonas charged on, working harder and longer to get everything done.

Meeting his mother in the barn at dusk, he blurted, "When is Father going to be strong enough to help? This is his farm, and it'll be Brother John's next. I may not inherit anything, yet here I am, doing all the work."

"Jonas, you are a good son. Your father was not primogeniture either, so he inherited no lands in England. That's why we're here, so he can make a better life for his family. We all must work the land." Grace looked back at the house. "It appears your father's humours are getting worse."

"Prescott was in support of my working at the ironworks, Mother. He would be at Hammersmith now, if they hadn't opened Nashaway for the ores there. He told me to learn all I can, so we can build an ironworks in Nashaway when he gets the town settled."

Jonas didn't give his mother a chance to speak. "I didn't go to sea, but I am going to Lynn. Father cannot rule my life."

"You go on to Hammersmith, Jonas. You got the crops in, and the other boys can take over. But Jonas, remember—this is home." Grace turned away as her eyes welled.

A New Trade

Jonas boarded the shallop captained by Theophilus Bayley, who wore a canvas hat to protect him from the sun and rain. He was one of the boatmen for Hammersmith and regularly picked up iron bars from the ironworks and brought them to the warehouse at the mouth of the Saugus River, to be distributed to England and New England. The flat-bottom boat rode high and light without a load on the quiet Saugus River as the tide pushed the single-sailed vessel along. Further on, the water churned with life, and many Native fishermen were catching great numbers of cod. Ospreys circled overhead to collect their share of easy prey.

The cool spring breeze suddenly turned warmer, and a glow shimmered over the trees around the bend. Jonas's nose twitched as it had in the fetid hold of the ship from England. This time the smell was of rotten eggs, not of excrement and spew. A rhythmic pounding pulsed through the air, trees, and even the water. Jonas put his hands over his ears as the clang from the forge became louder.

"Better get used to it, son," said Theophilus. "It never stops.

Well, not until dark. Then again, it doesn't get dark. That giant dragon is our sun."

As they turned the bend, a roar greeted them as oily fumes and blue flames belched into the sky from the furnace. The shallop driver poled the boat in the shallows and said, "Once they waken that monster, it never slumbers for thirty weeks while the water runs, from June to November. It's hot as Hades around there. How those Scotsmen stand it, I have no idea."

"Scotsmen?" asked Jonas.

"They were brought over in the ship *Unity* in December. They're prisoners from the Dunbar War. They thought they could get Prince Charles II on the throne, but Cromwell and his roundheads drubbed them and marched at least five thousand captives to Durham with no food or water, as they tell it." Theophilus shook his head. "They were jailed at Durham in the Norman cathedral without much in the way of living or food. Then they were shipped. They were thin as sticks and sick as dogs when they arrived. Don't you worry, by the by—they feed workers well here."

"How many Scotsmen are here?"

"They say about a hundred and fifty came by ship," Theophilus continued, "but only sixty are here at Hammersmith. That's enough for me. They are barbarians just like the Indians."

"What happened to the rest of them?"

"They were sold off in Boston and down the coast."

Jonas pointed at a small dock and building dwarfed by the furnace and two other buildings. He was amazed at the immensity of the complex.

"That's the warehouse," Theophilus said, and handed Jonas a pole to help maneuver the shallop next to the dock. A graceful, finicky snowy egret high-stepped across a long, narrow pile of dark, pitted clots by the river. "That's the slag pile. It grows by the day."

As Theophilus pulled up to the dock, Jonas saw the Scotsmen walking across a natural raised bluff onto a wooden platform around the mouth of the furnace. They carried baskets of materials to pour down the dragon's throat like sacrifices to a deity. Jonas helped Theophilus tie the boat, while Theophilus explained, "They are bonded. When they serve their term, they're free to go. Not a bad alternative to starving in England. The company supplies their lodging, food, medicine, clothes, tobacco, and drink."

Jonas handed the pole back to Theophilus, who said, "Don't worry about feeding that monster. The Scots do that," he said. "They mostly do the unskilled labor."

What has Crossman gotten me into? Jonas thought.

"Lead your horse off the boat and help me load the iron from the shed," Theophilus ordered as if he directed the place.

Jonas looked down at his soiled riding clothes. His mother would have reprimanded him for working in these traveling clothes, but he would do the work at the ironworks now. He took Buck's reins near the bit to steady him as he led him off the rocking boat, then tied him to a ring on the building, took off his doublet, and followed Theophilus inside. Jonas picked up half as many iron bars as did the boatman. Even with the smaller load, Jonas staggered as he stepped onto the unsteady boat.

"Look there," said Theophilus, pointing toward the furnace barn. "They're dragging a pig to the forge."

Jonas stopped in his tracks and peered intently at the activity on the hill. "I don't see a pig. It looks like the dragon gave birth to a giant centipede."

Theophilus roared with laughter. "You *are* green! That piece of cast iron dragged behind the oxen is called a pig or sow. See the teats? It's about two hundred pounds. At the forge, they change it from cast iron to wrought iron. If you're man enough to stay, you'll find out about that soon enough."

Jonas lowered his head. He vowed to himself to say little and listen closely until he learned more about the ironworks.

A man came down the sloping ramp to the dock. "Hello, Theophilus. You have a new hand?"

"He came from Boston. He's good help for someone so green."

"Are you here for the tour?" the man asked Jonas, looking him up and down.

"I came to work in the forge with Robert Crossman. Do you know him?"

"Why aye, he's been staying with me. I'm John Diven, the potter. He's making a name for himself. Crossman seems to be holding his own with the workers. At least he can curse like the best or worst of them. They can be rather tough here, especially Pinnion, Perry, and Vinton. The company doesn't know what they'd do without them, and the town doesn't know what to do about them."

"Hurry, Goodman Fairbanks, let's get the boat loaded," called Theophilus, "I must be on my way before this iron bottoms it out when the tide recedes. Besides, I want to be out of here before the idle gawkers come down to ask a lot of foolish questions."

"I'll help you finish," said the potter. "They haven't yet broken the plug on the furnace to fill my molds." Diven winked at Jonas and said, "Theophilus exacts a steep price for passage up the Saugus River."

As Jonas carried his last load of iron, a group of smartly dressed ladies and gentlemen gingerly picked their way along the dirt path from the top of the bluff toward the mouth of the furnace. A well-dressed guide pointed out things along the way. They turned their heads to and fro like weathervanes in a fickle wind.

"Who are they? Inspectors, agents?" asked Jonas. He tried to wipe the black residue off his shirt but only smeared it.

"Those are the gawkers. They think this is the newest wonder of the world. Our iron is as good as any from England, and England's running out of trees for fuel—but see all of ours? We have everything we need—bog ore, wood for charcoal, water, and flux."

Jonas wanted to ask what flux was, but he did not want to risk asking another stupid question.

"This is where I leave you," said Theophilus. "If I don't go now, I won't be able to move until the next tide. Are you sure you want to stay?"

Jonas looked up at Hammersmith and back at the boatman with a determined nod.

"Help me untie," said Theophilus.

"Where will I find William Osbourn's place?" Jonas pointed across the creek and behind the blacksmith shop to the company town. "Over there?"

Diven laughed and said, "No, he lives in Lynn, in a big fine house. It's about a mile that way."

Before leaving the dock, Theophilus ordered Jonas to drop his bags and then tossed him guns, one by one, that had been covered by a canvas on the boat. Jonas caught the first one, putting it on the dock quickly to catch another. "Are they expecting an Indian uprising?" Jonas asked, cursing Crossman under his breath.

"No, my good man. These are the colony's damaged guns that are to be melted into reusable iron. You won't have to worry about guns here. All full-time workers are exempt from military training and duties. We have no trouble with the Indians—the two we have, Anthony and Thomas, cut wood."

He nodded farewell, leaving Jonas on the dock with the

guns as if he knew what to do with them. The boatman called, "If you plan to work here, we'll see a good deal of each other."

A New Life

Whispering, giggling women and stalwart men were making their way down the steep path, following their stocky, well-dressed guide to the base of the twenty-one-foot furnace.

Jonas trudged up the ramp in his soiled clothes and tied Buck to a heavy piece of wood in a grassy patch. He joined the group as they arrived at the furnace barn. His attention was drawn to a man wielding a triangular hoe with giant gloved hands. He was dressed in a shirt stained with sweat and soot and heavy leather breeches with thick woolen stockings. Jonas looked at his own shoes, thinking them quite flimsy compared to the sturdy boots the man wore.

The workman dragged his hoe to make a deep V-shaped trench in the sand, starting from a clay-plugged hole at the bottom of the furnace stack. When the large trench was completed, he pulled small trenches off either side.

He's making one of those sows with teats, Jonas thought.

The guide couldn't speak loudly enough for his followers, who had distanced themselves from the smelly, noisy process. Jonas inched forward until the guide warned him back.

So he went to inspect one of the various wooden and clay molds stacked along the wall. He examined the cast iron skillets and kettles strategically placed beside the buried molds to depict the purpose of each.

As Jonas studied the molds, a worker with a long poke pounded and broke the clay plug of the furnace. The already stifling heat in the barn became unbearable, and the visitors backed further down the ramp and turned away from the heat, the men dabbing at their faces with kerchiefs, the women fluttering their fans like young birds trying to fly.

Jonas, transfixed by the process, stood sweltering as he watched red shimmering liquid pour from the hole into the trench. *This is not a monster,* he thought. *This is a volcano, venting from its side.*

The fiery liquid filled the trench and its fingers, boiling as it cooled. The fumes above the boiling ore swirled with color like oil spilled into a puddle of water.

Jonas inched closer, his shirt already drenched in sweat. Several men presented their long-handled ladles to the sacred spout where the liquid continued to ooze. After they filled their ladles, they carried them unwieldy and heavy on their long shafts, to fill the clay molds. It was like an intricate dance. Each knew their precise steps. Jonas, coming dangerously near to the hot molten iron, was not welcome in the dance. One of the men shouted, "Out of the way!"

Jonas glanced back at the mesmerizing glowing hole, then hurried to catch the tour. He took off his doublet, then remembered the stains on his shirt and put it on again. When the visitors were several yards from the forge, Jonas noticed there were two giant waterwheels on each side of the building. *Why four?* He walked up the steep ramp towards another barn-like building that had only rows of small openings in the back wall to let in a little light. The two forges and chafery lit up the barn. The guide held out his arms, preventing the tour from entering, but all strained to see the huge hammer that pulsed inside as giant bellows fanned the coals. The forges roared and bristled in anger from being disturbed, and the women in the tour put their gloved hands over their ears and backed away from the noise and heat. The men held handkerchiefs to their noses and leaned toward their guide to hear.

At the door, Jonas leaned in as far as he could, where sparks flew almost within reach, and the smell of sulfur engulfed him.

"This is the walloon," the guide said. "We melt our iron

twice, unlike the older method. That sets us apart from other forges."

As the hammer pummeled the iron on the magnificent anvil, Jonas nodded with the rhythm. *If the furnace is the dragon,* he thought, *this is the beast's heart.* As the bellows expanded, Jonas unconsciously took deep breaths and exhaled as if to aid the bellows in fanning the charcoal. *This is my adventure. This is where I belong.*

The guide clanged two pieces of metal together, regaining Jonas's attention. "This is bar iron. It is our finished product. We send it to local smiths to work into tools, latches, and other iron instruments that require stronger iron. Some will go to the rolling and slitting mill that we will visit next."

At that moment, a young forge worker took a clay jug from the sill of the back opening. His finger in the ear of the jug, he raised the base atop his bent arm to take the spout to his mouth, all the time walking toward one of the forges.

A worker with a graying beard yelled out, "If you bring that closer, I'll swat you with these tongs!"

Jonas eyed the six-foot tongs that had just held glowing iron.

"If I've taught you anything, boy . . ." the tong man said, adding profanity. "If a *drop* of that gets next to this lot, it will explode, and we'll all have a black, fiery death."

More profanities followed. The guide hurried the tour to the next building, where Jonas waited his turn and peeked into the smaller room crowded with equipment. "We roll the iron bars into flat sheets," the guide said, "and cut them into smaller rods. Blacksmiths make the thin rods into nails."

Nails were hard to make and expensive.

"Where did you come from, young man?" the guide asked Jonas.

"I'm Jonas Fairbanks. I came here to work. I'm supposed to see Mr. William Osbourn."

"You're looking at him," said the stout man. "We'll talk after the tour. Now stand back. I have important men here that I'll be entertaining." He looked Jonas up and down. "I hope you brought clean clothes. You'll be joining me for supper at my house in Lynn."

"I will be pleased to, sir," Jonas answered, and stepped back to the rear of the tour group.

Osbourn mentioned a Joseph Jenke, a name Prescott had identified as someone who was interested in Nashaway.

"Jenke received the first machine patent in the colony in 1646 to make scythes, sawmill blades, and edging tools. He's been asked to make the die for the first coins to be minted in Boston. Although this is his private blacksmith shop, he supplies many of the iron parts that the ironworks needs."

One man ambled over to a pile of logs and asked, "Are you shipping these huge logs to England for masts?"

"Nay, those become shafts for our bellows, waterwheels, and hammer."

Oohs and aahs emanated from the group.

Jonas looked beyond the logs, behind the blacksmith shop, and over the creek into the town of Hammersmith. "Is that the company town?" he asked, pointing.

Osbourn scowled at him and announced, "We will now go to the manager's house for refreshment."

As they passed the warehouse, Osbourn explained how local investors were needed to supplement the original English investors.

Jonas slipped away from the tour and turned back to untie Buck, who shied as Jonas led him past the hammering at the forge. He collected his bundles from where he'd stored them at the dock and crossed the creek into Hammersmith, a town of small, thatched shanties. Halfway down a narrow alley between houses, Jonas heard a woman's voice shout, "Get ye hoom, you old hog, get ye hoom!" A haggard old woman came cowering out of the house, followed by a younger throwing stones. The older woman scuttled away.

An old man, sitting by his front door taking a pipe, looked up at Jonas. "Don't mind them. That's her mother-in-law." He laughed.

Jonas looked around. He saw no other men in the town, so he left to find Osbourn's house. Just outside the works, a well-worn path ran north, and he guessed this would lead to Mr. Osbourn's house in Lynn. After less than a mile, he found himself on the Boston Road at a tavern with a sign reading The Anchor. He ordered a much-needed ale and observed no one who appeared to be an ironworker among the townsfolk, much as it was in Dedham. He asked the self-important tavern keeper, Joseph Armitage, for directions to William Osbourn's house.

Jonas tied Buck outside the dooryard and washed his face and hands at the well. A manservant met him at the door and showed him to a well-appointed room with three small cots. After Jonas changed into a clean shirt and breeches, the servant led him into the dining area of the large house, where several men—including Crossman—sat at a well-laid table.

The rotund, rosy-cheeked Mr. Osbourn sat smiling at the head.

Crossman, his old friend, acknowledged him with only a nod before Jonas addressed the host. Another man with spectacles sitting with his back to Jonas turned briefly.

"Good even, Mr. Osbourn," said Jonas, as William Osbourn stood, and the other men followed.

"Welcome, Jonas, we've been expecting you. I'd like you to

meet Jonathan Coventry." As young Coventry bowed slightly, his spectacles slipped. "He's learning to clerk."

"And of course your friend, Robert Crossman." They nodded to one another.

The smartly dressed servant indicated another service he had set for Jonas next to Crossman. Jonas sat and looked at the fork in awe. He'd never used one.

"Did you have a good trip up the Saugus?" asked Osbourn.

"Aye. The boatman, Theophilus, was very informative."

"I hope not so much that you already plan to leave," Osbourn said with his eyes glinting.

"No, sir—this place is intriguing."

"I think you'll find it comfortable boarding here with your old friend and a new one. You may find Lynn to be like Dedham, but the works and Hammersmith are quite different. Most of the skilled workers come from abroad." He continued, "They bring their religion, morals, and customs with them. They don't always follow the Puritan model of conduct. They curse and drink more than we do." Osbourn winked as the servant poured more wine around the table. "Seems to be their nature, and no collection of rules or laws curtails them."

Jonas and Crossman shared an understanding smile.

"Your Dedham man, Abraham Shaw, was the first to be granted benefits of rights to minerals and mines in '37, I understand. And now, here in 1651, we have two men from Dedham to work in our forge." Osbourn slapped his knee.

The conversation remained congenial, and the wine flowed generously. Osbourn called his manservant for a quill, ink, and paper as they retired from the table. He looked at Jonas. "You must get suitable clothes for the forge. There are no gentlemen there, only hard workers. I'll see to it you get a proper leather apron and gloves. He looked at Jonas's shoes, then tried to hide a belch as he scribbled something on a scrap of paper. "Here are the names of the cordwainers in Lynn—Philip Kertland or Edmund Bridges. They make company work boots.

"Good morrow, my good man," Jonas called to the cobbler. "Mr. Osbourn sent me. I'll be working at the forge and need a pair of boots."

"Aye," I know exactly what you need. He measured one of Jonas's feet and went to a shelf of thick-leather, serviceable boots. He had the customary three sizes, each boot fitting either foot. The cobbler looked again at Jonas's feet and pulled down a pair, and Jonas reached in his pocket for money.

"I believe these are on the company. You are a bonded servant, are you not?"

"Nay, I'm hired. I'm living with Mr. Osbourn."

"Let me take this up with him," said the cordwainer.

Another shelf held only a few pairs of fine leather boots with turned-down cuffs. As Jonas examined the soft supple leather, the cordwainer said, "You have good taste. Those are fashioned after King Charles's boots. Well, not exactly. I'd be shut down for making boots the same as those of a king or prince. They're the most desirable footwear for a gentleman and come well over the knees for riding. The tops fold down for comfort while walking. Working at the ironworks, you'll soon earn enough to purchase a pair—if you are, as you say, a hired worker."

Jonas took one boot off the shelf and ran his hand respectfully over the smooth leather.

"You know why the king wears these 'great boots'?" asked the cordwainer. "King Charles had a gimp leg when he was young. The royals can't be seen having any defect. So, his parents commissioned a pair of high boots made to cover his brace. Then all the royals started wearing them to divert the attention from the prince. It became the fashion for those with money."

Jonas put the boots back on the shelf, looking at them longingly. "Good morrow, sir," he said, picking up his work boots and walking back out into the morning sunshine.

Initiation

Jonas climbed onto the company's ox-driven cart with Robert Crossman, who, as they rode, showed Jonas the huge smoldering moss-and-turf-covered hills of wood becoming charcoal. Anthony and Thomas, the Native woodcutters, were unloading another cart. The Scots, in charge of making charcoal, cautioned Jonas that if the pile of wood or the stored charcoal caught fire, the whole ironworks could go up in flames.

Several men seemed to be gigging fish and frogs near a swampy lake, but upon closer scrutiny, Jonas realized they were using picks and shovels to pull chunks of bog iron out of the swamp.

Crossman snapped the whip over the back of the ox, but she just turned her head to stare at the cart. "Nahant, where we get the gabbro for flux, is all the way to the coast. It's too far to visit now."

"Gabbro, flux—what's that?"

"Flux makes the bog ore release its iron. Since we don't have the lime that is used for flux in England, gabbro works as well.

"So, what's the slag that's building up along the river at the warehouse?" asked Jonas, remembering Theophilus's comment.

"You'll learn quickly. If not, you'll get a hard time from the men at the forge," Crossman said with a sneer at Jonas." Slag is the waste left after the iron is pulled out of the bog ore."

"Slag, gabbro, flux," Jonathan repeated. He was not going to be made fun of here. He had enough of that growing up with his brothers.

When they arrived at the furnace, Jonas said, "Yesterday,

a man said if a drop of water got in the molten iron it would explode. What about the furnace? It's an open hole. What if it rains?"

"Oh, that. You haven't been up there yet, have you?" Robert answered. "The maw is so hot that any amount of rain evaporates before it reaches the molten slurry inside."

At the bottom of the steep slope, Jonas recognized Mr. Osbourn managing the oxen dragging a sow from the furnace to the forge. Jonas looked at Robert in disbelief that such an important man would do this himself.

"I told you, Jonas," Robert said in answer to the unasked question. "Everyone does everything around here. You will get paid well for any extra work."

"Well enough to buy great boots?" Jonas looked at Robert.

"You saw those, too?"

Four whirring and splashing waterwheels welcomed Jonas to the forge. A rhythmic flapping and whoosh of the giant bellows sent blasts of air into the forge to produce intense heat and a steely blue flame. The giant hammer hit the iron with ringing thuds that warned away anyone who dared enter.

This time, Jonas was a part of the din, in the midst of flashing sparks, glowing metal, and the stench of sweat, dust, and sulfur. Bent bodies with long tongs dragged a fiery ball from the forge to the hammer. Robert pulled Jonas back from the hammering as sparks and an occasional stream of liquid fire erupted from the cavity in the mass, shooting above the workmen's heads.

"Who did you bring with you today, Crossman?" barked one of the finers remelting the cast iron. "When he showed up yesterday, he looked like a peacock, dressed so pretty." Jonas remembered the man's graying beard from the day before. "That's Quentin Pray up from the Braintree forge to help," said Crossman.

"Whose idea was it to let a gentleman work in the forge?" asked a gravelly voice Jonas had heard the day before.

Crossman looked back at the man and said, "By Gaw, Pinnion, this here's my friend, Jonas Fairbanks. Taught him everything he knows about carpentry."

"Oy, he'll never make it here, then," Pinnion roared, and the nine men in the forge stopped momentarily to laugh. All except the hammerman, who could not leave off positioning the iron bars under the huge hammer that continued to pound.

Crossman nodded to Jonas and then toward the hammerman. "John Francis is paid twice as much to work that 550-pound trip hammer, the most dangerous job at Hammersmith."

Jonas moved toward the hammer and into the sparks until Crossman caught him by the shirt. "You'll have so many holes in your clothes getting that close that your mother will think you've been sleeping with moths."

Another man roared with laughter and said, "Osbourn will get you a long apron that will at least protect your pants."

Bring that jug down and pass it around," called Pray. "We need to celebrate a new scullion to do our work."

The lanky young man who had taken the jug the day before went after the vessel on the windowsill and handed it first to the man at the chafery. John Francis was the name scratched into the hood over the blazing elevated hearth. Jonas was amazed the ten men could share the small jug. He watched as each took his turn, apparently in order of their prestige. Jonas received the jug last. He took a generous swig, then nearly doubled over trying not to spit it out.

Crossman clapped him on the back as he coughed.

"Lo, put him to work, Crossman," called one man. "Since he doesn't have his apron, let him drag the loop from the finery to the hammers. He can squeeze between the sparks."

Jonas didn't want to ask what a loop was.

Crossman took his own apron from a peg on the wall, sliding the neck strap over Jonas's head, then pulled the leather strings around to tie in front. He handed Jonas a pair of six-foot tongs. Pray pulled an overgenerous orange glowing glob from his finery onto the metal plates on the floor, and Crossman showed Jonas how to position the tongs to pull the loop to the men for manual hammering.

Everyone turned back to his work. Jonas, ready to show he could carry his weight, pulled on the heavy glob, which barely budged. He looked behind him to see everyone's eye fixed on him with stifled sniggers.

Crossman leaned in, saying softly to Jonas over the noise, "They do this to every new man. Don't be uppish, don't give an inch, and you'll do all right."

Red-faced with muscles grinding and bulging under his shirt, Jonas inched the glob to the closest manual hammer. The men seemed to settle back into their routine. Jonas stayed out of the way of the long-handled instruments and watched intently.

The day dragged on. Jonas looked outside for the sun to set, heralding the end of the day's work. But it was still as light as midday within the forge. His stomach growled and churned. He knew it was past suppertime. The fineries and chafery streamed a timeless glow from the ceramic ovens that remelted the iron as the smoke curled up the stacks into the sky.

As the last of the molten iron was drawn out of the finery and prepared for the chafery, the carpenter, Nicholas Pinnion, took an expensive-looking watch out from behind his apron. Jonas stared wide-eyed at the fine piece, more intricate than his own father's. The coarse man held it delicately in his burly fingers and flipped the case open.

"It's nigh ten of the clock," said Pinnion in his gravelly

voice. "I'm going home to be sure my goodwife, if there be such, doesn't have company with her tonight."

A muffled laugh circled the forty-foot building as the machinery groaned to a stop. The trace gates shut to the waterwheels, and the last man with a hammer finished his piece.

"See you in the morrow," Pinnion said with a smile as he clapped Jonas hard on his already sore shoulders.

Robert and Jonas arrived at the Osbourn home to find a small fire glowing in the hearth. The servant rose from his pallet by the hearth and filled two trenchers with the evening pottage that had dried in the kettle. Jonas ate with as much relish as if it had been his mother's Yorkshire pudding. Finishing, he stripped off his shirt as Robert led him to their room and, without taking down the bed rug, collapsed onto the cot and fell into a deep sleep.

When he awoke, someone was shaking his shoulders. He drew an arm back to throw a punch, but his muscles were so sore he couldn't have even fought the cock that crowed outside.

"You'd better clean up and look the part," warned Robert. "This is the day that'll make or break you."

Jonas remembered the second day he and his father had gone out to make canoes. He had to prove he was a man then, and now he had to show these men he was a forger. He wolfed down everything the servant set before him and used yesterday's bread to wipe his trencher clean. The servant nodded toward the firkins covered with cloths that held their midday meals.

Jonas headed for his horse, but Robert called out, "Leave him be. It's only a mile, and there's no place to keep him at the ironworks."

Back, hips, and leg muscles screaming, Jonas tried to keep pace with Robert, switching the firkin from hand to hand as his shoulders threatened mutiny. He did not know how he would get through the day.

Men were already stoking the fineries when they arrived at the forge. The gates from the traces to the waterwheels had been raised allowing the splashing and churning to begin. Soon the bellows and hammer joined the orchestra of sound Jonas hoped one day to love.

Pinnion met Jonas at the door, blocking his entrance. In his raspy voice he said, "I thought we told you to stay home, townsfolk."

Jonas hesitated. "You can't get along without me."

"Oy, let's see." Pinnion pointed at a new leather apron on the peg next to Crossman's. Someone had etched Jonas's name in the leather with a nail.

Jonas willed his arms to lift the leather strap over his head and tie the leather strings around his waist. His muscles objected, but no louder than his will to become a part of the forge. His will won out.

Jonas worked mostly with Pinnion and Crossman on carpentry, repairing working parts. But over and over he was told he had to know how to work all areas of the forge. The first lesson was safety, for they played with fire.

Jonas wiggled his toes safely inside the strong pair of new boots with thick soles. He had worn blisters on the way to the ironworks, even with his heavy stockings. He had thought he was strong, but when he saw the number of men it took to lift the sow of iron into the opening of the finery, he knew he would ache for a long time.

Voices called for more blast and faster hammer action, then warned of danger, creating a sound as rich and varied as the quick changes of light and color in the dusky forge. Jonas understood that he was among specialists, ten to twelve men, the men most highly skilled at the craft. But he would earn his place among them. Maintaining the working parts took a lot of attention, and he was up to it. The forge wouldn't work if the equipment didn't run.

The Company Town

After weeks at the forge, Jonas stretched his arms and legs carefully in the mornings to gauge their anger. New muscles were making themselves part of him, and he could sleep at night without feeling the pound of the hammer throbbing in his head nor dreaming of being engulfed in fire.

"Lo, Jonas, we've got an evening off together," called Robert, stretching in his own bed across the room. "Let's go to Hammersmith. They have a dice game going."

"Don't they get sent to court for idling?" Jonas asked, then felt ridiculous. No one could call these men of Hammersmith idlers, regardless of what his father would say about them.

After supper, Jonas and Robert passed the long Scots house on the way to Hammersmith.

"The Scots are a friendly, jovial sort, if you don't cross them," said Jonas. "At least the ones I can understand."

"Aye, they are hard workers," said Robert.

When they arrived at the works, men were still charging the blast furnace. They had opened the hole to let out the molten iron early that morning, and they would break the plug again soon. The two skirted around the furnace to avoid the heat. They hurried to pass the forge before anyone saw them and called for help.

"I hope Pinnion is in there preparing to train two Scotsmen for repairs," said Robert. "That will ease some of our carpentry and mechanics work."

At the forge, they heard the roar of a man's voice in a stream of cursing. "That's Quentin Pray, to be sure," said Robert. "He has come from Braintree to help again."

"Now I hope Pinnion isn't working tonight, or there could be real trouble—with Pray in that humour," said Jonas.

"Those two always quarrel, men well suited for work in a fiery forge."

"Thank goodness they are seldom together," said Jonas. Then came a gravelly voice raised in defiance of Pray. "It's Pinnion!" yelled Jonas as he ran for the forge door.

Both fineries were blazing. Several jugs from the back window were upset or smashed on the floor. The hammer pummeled an iron bar, charging the argument with menace.

Quentin Pray swung a long wooden handled ringer—still glowing—around the room, threatening Pinnion.

It was Pinnion's turn at evoking evil with foul language. "By God's blood"—the rest was lost in a mumble. Both were unsteady on their feet, swinging and poking their long tools at each other like absurd duelists. They had no idea they had an audience.

"Looks like they've drained our liquor allotment," said Crossman.

"Are we going to stop this?" asked Jonas as they stood and watched. "I've never heard anyone curse like Quentin. He's a real muckspout."

"No one escapes Quentin's mouth," said Robert. "He called his wife a jade and roundhead for telling him not to swear. He threatened to beat her with a stick as big as a bedpost. She avoided that, but he kicked her into a wall and threw a bowl of porridge at her, nearly breaking her arm. When they took him to court, he didn't mince words with the magistrates, either. He called them more devils than men— right there in court!"

"Seems strange they let him get away with that," said Jonas.

"Like they say, Quentin and Pinnion have made themselves so valuable that no one can afford to lock them up nor lock them out of the operation," said Robert.

Jonas and Robert watched the melee, and finally Jonas rolled up the sleeves of his only clean shirt.

"I'll take Quentin," said Robert. "I'm used to Kingsbury's mouth. You take Pinnion."

"But Pinnion's no better. He brags of being taken to Essex Quarterly Court for swearing and not attending church. His wife claims he killed five of his own children, some before they were born," said Jonas.

"Stay out of the way of that ringer!" yelled Robert.

Jonas ducked as something whooshed over his head. As Jonas and Robert got closer, Pray's ringer took purchase on Pinnion's brow, knocking him to the ground in a bloody daze. Jonas and Robert each caught one of Quentin Pray's arms and wrestled the ringer from his grasp.

A bigger audience had gathered outside making side bets by the time Jonas and Robert subdued the two men. They turned Quentin over to the men at the furnace barn—they pledged to keep him overnight on their pallets.

Jonas tended Pinnion's wound while Robert closed down the forges. Together they carried and dragged him to his house across the creek in Hammersmith. When they arrived, a man came out of the house hiking up his breeches.

"What happened to our night at Hammersmith?" asked Jonas.

"Lo, it's still light," said Robert. Looking back at the furnace, they chuckled.

"We don't have to worry about participating in a little dice game and drinking tonight," said Jonas with a laugh, looking at his soiled clothes that no one would notice.

"Nay, just another adventure in Hammersmith," said Robert, winking. "Enjoy yourself, good man. We're among a whole different people here, at least some of them. We are the least of their worries. Perhaps they can't do without us, either."

Dig My Grave

Ten-year-old Martha placed a cool cloth on Jonathan's forehead while Grace slept on the trundle bed in the parlor after ministering to him all night.

"Poor Father," Martha said, "I know how you feel. I didn't think I'd live last year."

Martha waited for Jonathan to grab the cloth from his brow and profess he wasn't ailing. She'd never seen him in bed during the day, for he always woke before dawn and went to bed long after she was tucked in upstairs.

Martha sang her own version of *Barbara Allen*:

Oh, Gammar, oh, Gammar, go dig my grave
Make it both long and narrow.
Sweet Father died of love for me
And I will die of sorrow.

"Open your eyes, Father! You can't die." Tears rolled out the corner of her eyes and down the sides of her nose until she licked them from the corners of her mouth.

"It's time for your infusion," Martha said as she lifted one of Jonathan's eyelids with her thumb, seeing only the white of his eye. She laid her head on his chest to listen as Grace had demonstrated. Jonathan's chest rose rhythmically but barely lifted her head. His breath was a wheeze like the last bit of air escaping from a bellows, with a gurgling like a small stream over a rocky bed.

"Wake up. I promised Gammar I'd give you this infusion."

Martha struggled to lift his head and prop it on the bunched pillow. She lifted the small, spouted vessel to Jonathan's lips and explained. "It's bitter yarrow. I hated it. But look at me—I'm better now." She pushed the spout between his lips, grating against his teeth, then tipped the spout, and carefully poured the amber liquid. It rolled out of the corner of his mouth and onto the pillow.

"I promised Gammar, Father. You must wake up!"

Martha left the limp man and inched to the trundle to see if Grace was awake. Grace's breath was quiet and easy. She looked so peaceful. Martha looked back at Jonathan, the cloth rag still on his head. She heard his faint wheezing across the room.

"Gammar, Gammar," she said quietly but urgently, "I can't wake Father."

Grace started, bolted upright, and looked both ways.

"I can't get him to take the infusion," whined Martha.

Grace heard the wheezing as she looked over at Jonathan. She patted Martha's hand. "That's all right, dear. I was about to get up."

Grace shrugged off the bed rug and went to Jonathan's side. "Martha, go to the hall and tend the kettles. It'll be just you and me today."

Sitting beside Jonathan on the bed, Grace took his hand in hers and removed the cloth from his forehead. She dipped it into cool vinegar water and started wiping his whole face. "Jonathan, you must wake for your infusion. Dr. Avery said we must administer it regularly." Grace shook Jonathan's shoulders. "Martha and I need you. We can't lose you."

Tears rolled down Grace's cheeks. She had never seen Jonathan so ill. "You haven't made your will," she said in distress. "That's important to you. Wake up. You can't leave us like this." Grace shook his shoulders again. This time Jonathan's feeble hand shook on its way to his forehead. He threw the cloth on the floor.

"Grace, you are still here. You turned into a small girl before."

"That was Martha."

Jonathan turned his head on the pillow to look around.

"She's in the hall. You must take this infusion while you're awake." Grace lifted Jonathan's head and poured small amounts into his mouth. This time he swallowed, seeming to awaken a bit.

"News comes," Grace said. "Michael Metcalf Sr. and old John Kingsbury are recovering. If they can get through this, so can you." She laid Jonathan's head on the pillow. "There are at least ten others that are sick. Both Henry Brock and his wife have it."

Jonathan seemed uninterested, but Grace talked and poured in trickles of the bitter liquid, trying to keep him awake to finish it.

"The chores, who's doing the chores?" Jonathan asked, as if he would rise to tend to them.

Grace smiled. *He is improving.*

"Jonas stayed home from the ironworks until the crops were in. John, George, and Junior are taking over the chores."

Jonathan closed his eyes and couldn't be roused again. Half the infusion was left in the vessel.

Jonathan's body shook, and though he was chilled, his forehead felt like it was on fire as he pulled the bed rug up. "I'm so cold," his voice rasped.

Grace hurried to him and lifted his hand. His fingertips were cold, but the bed was wet again from sweat. "Martha, go for Dr. Avery."

After the fire was settled, Martha came into the parlor to find Grace with her head lying on Jonathan's chest. She covered Grace with the bed rug from the trundle and ran out in the rain.

Grace woke briefly. Jonathan was talking nonsense, just like Sarah had before her soul left her. Grace pleaded, "Jonathan, stay with me." *Martha hurry.* Grace thought before falling asleep again.

When Martha found Dr. Avery, she brought him back to the house, nearly pulling him through the door. Grace was again lying with her head on Jonathan. Martha, her wet hair dripping onto the floor, bent over to catch her breath while Dr. Avery put his hand on Grace's shoulder.

"Jonathan!" cried Grace.

"Nay, Grace. It's Dr. Avery. Are you well? Martha fetched me. She thought you both were sick. Or worse."

Grace composed herself, sat up and pushed the hair off her forehead and tucked strands back under her cap as she looked at Jonathan. He was no longer restless; his forehead was dry. She put the back of her hand to her own forehead and then to his. "His fever has broken."

"He is very pale," said Dr. Avery. "He's been through a lot, but I think he has turned the corner."

Jonathan's eyes fluttered open for a moment. He pulled the corners of his mouth into a weak smile, then closed his eyes for another trip into the restless darkness of his illness.

The evening sun was growing dim when Jonathan woke again. "How long have I been out? I'm supposed to view the fences with Kingsbury, Bullard, and Hayward."

"They are all well. They took care of it," said Grace.

Jonathan pushed himself up onto his elbows and turned to his side as if to get up. "The crops. It's already spring. We must get them in."

"Jonas did it before going to the iron making place."

"He what? And left George without help and me without a steady hand?"

"George has a new apprentice from England. His name is James Fales."

"Where will that family stay? George doesn't have room."

"The man came over without his wife and son."

"Oh, Grace, right now I don't feel like I'll ever be able to farm again. Maybe I should make my will."

"You can make a will later. Don't be ridiculous—you are

only fifty-seven years old. Other men your age have had this illness, and none of them died.

Jonathan was not perspiring, but his arms shook as if they would not support his weight. Grace pulled his feet back onto the bed; Jonathan did not resist. He fell into a deep sleep.

Grace pushed Jonathan out the door to the town meeting in the fall. These gatherings were his least favorite responsibility in their society. Grace knew he needed to return to the life he had before his illness, though he and ten other older men in the community had been so severely stricken that they received pardons from country taxes.

Peter Woodward, one of the selectmen, was speaking when Jonathan crept in late. "We have tried through our letters and negotiations to get the Indians to stop planting on the south side of the river. It's time the Fishers represent us at the General Court to settle this."

The Fishers returned to Dedham after the October General Court session and stood before the proprietors. Sgt. Fisher addressed the meeting: "As expected, Mr. John Eliot appeared at court on behalf of the Natick praying village. Eliot told the court"—here Fisher read from the court document—"'God has cast them to begin Indian work within the bounds of the land granted to Dedham. Natick, seated on the edge of Dedham lands with other towns coming to their doors.' He requested, on the Natives' behalf, that the court ask the other towns bordering to yield land to Dedham, so Dedham will see fit to yield more land to the Natives."

Lt. Fisher added, "We reiterated Dedham's stance that we are giving land only north of the river."

"The Court approved Dedham's tender of two thousand acres for the Natick village," the sergeant went on, "and ordered

Dorchester, Roxbury, Watertown, Cambridge, Sudbury, and Dedham men to form a committee to seek more land for Natick."

"Another committee, another delay," grumbled Jonathan. Just sitting at the meeting had exhausted him.

Great Boots

Ice formed in the traces and closed down the ironworks in November. Crossman and Jonas sat at the breakfast table at Osbourn's house while the manservant brought bread, cheese, and a hearty pottage.

"Our big payday is coming," said Jonas. "I never expected to make this much money. I may not be making what Pinnion and Vinton do, but this is a lot more than I'd make in Dedham."

"What are you going to do with yours?" asked Crossman.

"Remember those great boots? I'm buying a pair."

"Aye, I fancied those, too, but I have to save my earnings," said Robert.

Jonas looked at him with narrowed eyes. Crossman said no more.

Osbourn went by the breakfast table as Jonas and Crossman finished. "You boys hear of the Sumptuary Law passed in October? You'd better rethink those great boots." He walked out the door.

"Have you seen a broadsheet on that Sumptuary Law?" asked Jonas.

"Nay, but we have no time to read a broadsheet, anyway." Crossman and Jonas looked at each other and shrugged.

More interested in what Crossman was holding back, Jonas asked, "Are you still planning to mine in Dedham without me?"

Robert's cheeks colored.

"What are you saving for? You have a house and land in Dedham already. What more do you need?"

Crossman looked away, composed himself, then looked back. "I'm marrying Sarah Kingsbury."

"What? When did this happen? You haven't even *been* in Dedham."

"We've been writing. We've had a fondness since I apprenticed for Kingsbury. She's old enough now, and I have that land and a small house. I can afford to take a wife."

"Will you come back next year, if you're married?" Jonas felt betrayed again.

"Aye, the money is too good. Sarah can stay in our house— she'll be near her parents. They'll look after her while I'm making money to give us a good start."

"And learning how to build our ironworks in Dedham," Jonas reminded him.

"Aye, learning to build an ironworks," said Crossman.

"I'm getting those great boots," Jonas declared. "I've earned them. This is hard work, and I don't need to save my money for a wife." He winked at Crossman.

Smoke curled from the chimneys into a cloud-dotted sky as Jonas tied Buck to a post ring of the dooryard and walked through the drifts to the big flat rock at the door. He peeked in as he slapped his hat against his leg and stamped his boots on the stone. "Anyone home?"

"Jonas!" squealed Martha, nearly tipping her spinning wheel as she rose to greet her brother.

"Jonas, you're home!" Grace throttled her own spinning wheel, and her heavy wool skirt caught on her legs as she hurried after Martha.

Jonas hung his hat on a peg. Before he could take off his boots, he picked up a giggling Martha and swung her around.

"You two." Grace stood with her hands on her hips. "That must stop. Martha is not a little girl anymore. She's ten and must act like a young lady." Grace looked down at Martha.

Her young helper covered her mouth to stop the giggles, but she continued to shake with glee.

"And you, Jonas, must treat her as one."

Jonas and Martha looked at each other with conspiratorial grins.

"Yes, Gammar," Martha nodded, straightening her skirts.

"Go to the lean-to and finish cleaning the pheasant for our next meal. I'll be out in a bit to work on it with you."

Grace saw that Jonas's boots were dripping on the floor and said, "Those are fancy boots, but they still have to come off when they're wet."

Jonas didn't comply quickly. He just looked at his mother. She didn't even recognize how very fine these great boots were. *Just as well. She would see them as prideful, not useful.* Instead of taking the boots off, Jonas gave his mother a big warm wintery hug.

Bells 1652

Clang, clang.

Grace stopped short with the small hearth shovel in her hand after settling the fires for the Sabbath. She had known for weeks it was coming. She listened again. *Clang, clang, clang.*

Grace grabbed Martha's hand and pulled her out the front door into the February cold where snow drifted against the fences. They stood on the great stone at the doorway where the snow had melted. Grace stretched her arms down to her sides with her palms forward and lifted her face to the sky. She let the metallic sound reverberate through her. Martha watched Grace and followed her example.

Martha loved the drums that called Dedham to Sabbath,

but now she stood with her mouth agape and twirled round as if to capture this new sound.

Grace imagined Susan standing beside her husband, Ralph Daye, with their two-year-old daughter in her arms. Ralph would be holding his mallets ready to beat the drum at the correct time, just in case the bell didn't toll.

Jonathan came up from the barn and silently took Grace's hand. She let the bells take her back to St. John the Baptist Church at Halifax where they were married thirty-four years before. She felt the joy of the church, markets, faires, and celebrations that elicited the ringing of the bells in England.

For a moment, fifty-four-year-old Grace felt the passage of time. A metallic shiver went through her as the bell tolled again. This bell rang out a new beginning for her family. It was time to leave the toils and fears of the past behind.

Jonathan looked down at Grace and said, "Some wanted the bell mounted in the new school's watchtower so the watch and ward could immediately warn of an attack."

"No!" Grace blurted, fending off the intrusion of his thought. "The bell belongs in the meetinghouse. It should ring us to church, meetings, and celebrate the progress of our town. I won't think about attacks. Listen, Jonathan, just listen."

Springtime

Grace pushed hard on the long pole of the sweep to bring a heavy bucket of water out of the well. The dogs ran to the fence and barked, staring down the lane. Prescott rode up to the dooryard, and Grace let go of the long pole suddenly, the sweep barely missing her head. She stumbled backward as the bucket splashed back into the water.

"I always know it's spring when you come to town to bring your winter trade to Boston," she said. "How do Mary and the children fare in the wilderness?"

"Mary's much happier now that we have nine families and ten new babies in Nashaway. They want to call the town Prescott, if the General Court allows. What do you think of that?" Prescott smiled and tied his horse, then opened the gate to the yard. "Where's Jonathan?"

"Upstairs finishing a gateleg table for me. He must get it done before planting time."

Prescott entered the door to the narrow, steep staircase that wound around the bricks of the chimney. He heard the whish, whish rhythm before he got to the top.

Jonathan was using a plane to smooth a tabletop in the hall chamber, unaware of Prescott's presence. He rubbed his hand along the smooth surface, then planed it again. He blew the curls away, passed his hand over the wood, and planed anew.

"I bet you wish your town grew as smoothly as you finish that wood."

Jonathan startled, but he smiled when he saw Prescott and put his tool down. "You're right. We are still rough on the edges, but Dedham is a fine place."

"Is one of those rough edges Natick?" asked Prescott.

"Aye. Eliot wants to bring more Natives from different areas. Why doesn't he settle them around *his* town at Roxbury? We've had challenges to all our borders, not just from the Natives. Newtowne, I guess it's called Cambridge now, claims some of our swampland. Dorchester, Watertown, and Providence have claimed some of our borderlands. Even Medfield, our own daughter town, argues with us over their boundaries."

"You have broken into a sweat," Prescott noted. "Are you that upset about the Indians?"

"Nay, nay, I'll be all right. Been a bit tired lately. Dedham has a plan to keep the Indians from moving further. We're building a herd house with a chimney and fencing in an area for our cattle and horses to graze. A herder will be there year-round. We're also going to make dividend grants for each Dedham proprietor, to improve our holdings."

"Why don't you take this to the General Court and let them settle the claim on the land?" Prescott asked.

"We have." Jonathan coughed, "First they sent another committee and now they tell us we must follow due process by going to County Court, the Court of Assistance, then the General Court, if it goes that far."

Mr. Eliot rolled up his sleeves. "Good morrow, Lt. Fisher," he said jovially from his work helping the Natives build their sawmill.

Fisher did not dismount to speak. "Dedham sent you peaceable requests to cease all work on this mill on the south side of the Charles River until you get approval from the town."

"Aye, but I know how we can satisfy your fine town. We will give Dedham £40 worth of boards. We expect to have them cut shortly." Mr. Eliot slapped sawdust from his hands.

"Your insistence upon continuing to improve the land and building the mill after requests to cease is causing much dissatisfaction. You have no clear claim to the land. We hoped to settle this without going to court." Lt. Fisher surveyed the mill. "However, I'll propose your plan to the town. Good morrow, Mr. Eliot." He wheeled his horse sharply and galloped toward Dedham.

The town meeting exploded with conversation. Someone shouted from the back of the room, "We *have* a sawmill. We don't need theirs." Eliot's proposal to compensate for the land with boards was denied.

The next day Lt. Fisher rode out to talk to Eliot again. "I must inform you that the town of Dedham won't accept the boards for the use of *our* land. If you are interested in having more than the two thousand acres we gave Natick, you must use some means to resolve the case within three months. At that time, Dedham will issue the proprietors dividends of the land south of the Charles."

Mr. Eliot waved an arm over the land. "We've already worked the land, fenced it, and planted orchards. If we're to leave this land, our work is for naught. We'd have to start all over again. Where would we go? Everything is already granted. If we go only north, some of the Natives would be at least two miles from the meetinghouse. That's not conducive to growing a church community, especially for those who have just accepted the faith."

Mr. Eliot's face and tone took on an air of confidence. "I shall do nothing but pray." Then he shrugged. "If Dedham makes use of the land, the Indians will accept it."

If he only prays, this could take longer than appealing the case to all three courts, thought Lt. Fisher.

Mr. Eliot did nothing to relieve the disagreement, except pray. Dedham laid out parcels of dividend land, and Jonathan drew his twenty-four-acre lot of land at his turn. His sons, John and Junior, received land adjoining his.

Problems erupted when the Dedham men had a chance to view their grants. Timothy Dwight, who had helped lay out the bounds of the Natick Village—then Edward Richards and Thomas Fuller—found their lots already claimed and improved by Natick residents. Shortly after, other Dedham men complained about Waban and other Natives claiming land that had been laid out to them.

Summons

A persistent knock disrupted the momentary quiet at William Osbourn's house in Lynn. The servant rushed to answer. He opened the door and bowed to the constable standing ready to enter. The official held his six-foot black staff with a brass knob.

"One moment, please," said the servant. "I'll call my master. You may wait here." The servant turned smartly and entered the parlor. "Mr. Osbourn," he said without expression, "it's the constable with papers."

Mr. Osbourn stood, taking his pipe from his mouth. He nodded at the three young men sitting with him and started for the door, but the constable stepped in with his staff and said, "I'm here to serve notice to Jonas Fairbanks."

Mr. Osbourn looked back and Jonas jerked his attention to the constable. He jumped to his feet. "Me? Did you say Jonas Fairbanks?"

"Aye, I have a warrant for your appearance at the Essex County Quarterly Court at Salem on the 25th day of the ninth month of the year 1652. There are penalties if you do not attend on this date."

Jonas snatched the summons out of the constable's hand and tore it open, ripping part of the writing.

Having satisfied his obligation, the constable nodded to Mr. Osbourn and left. Jonas's jaw firmed as he read. Pressure built behind his eyes. A vein in his neck bulged.

Sitting at a small desk in Dedham, Jonathan placed his quill in its holder and folded the paper, pressing his seal firmly into the wax. His mind raced. *He would send this by messenger to Jonas at Hammersmith. I'm only fifty-eight, but I feel like an old man. Where's my energy? Why has God stricken me so?* He had joined the church, worked hard, served the town. He provided for his family—land and a fine house. *Is that not pleasing to God?* Jonathan paused in his thoughts to take a draw from his pipe.

Ah, but Jonas. *Is it my fault that Jonas has gone astray?* Not married. Not settled into a respectable trade. He was working around profane men and women, even barbaric Scotsmen. The work might be respectable, but the men were not. *He should be around our godly folk.*

Mr. Osbourn's servant answered a polite knock at the door as his master and tenants finished their late evening meal. He brought the messenger's stack of folded and sealed papers and handed them to Osbourn, who settled his spectacles on his nose. He passed one to each man at his table, then shuffled through his own papers and stuck them in his interior doublet pocket.

Robert waved his in the air, saying, "It's from Sarah."

Coventry nodded and stowed his away for later.

Jonas looked at the address on his. "It's from Father. He doesn't write unless it's important."

The others, saving their missives until they were in private, stared at Jonas as he opened his.

Jonas, reading silently, looked up to find the others watching but continued to read to himself. Jonas smacked the letter down on the table. "He wants me to come home to help harvest." He glanced at the others around the table, hoping for support.

No one replied.

"He was sick last year. He's been weak since, but it's been over half a year. He still takes dividend grants, making more work for all of us."

The other men nodded.

Jonas's words came faster. "I'm not even sure I'll get an inheritance. Does that make me a slave? I'm the only son who has the will to go out on my own, but he doesn't want me here. He's trying to pull me back."

No reply came from Crossman nor Coventry.

"Ironworking is now my calling," Jonas said. "I'm making good money. I'm done with farming."

Everyone had cleaned their trenchers and were anxious to retreat to privacy to read their letters.

"Jonas," said Mr. Osbourn, "you had better go help your father. Things may not be what they seem here." The young men simultaneously turned their eyes to Osbourn, but he shared no more.

"Go home until your father can handle the rest of the harvest. Then come back. You should have time to finish the thirty weeks you signed for in your covenant."

Jonas stopped by the forge before boarding the afternoon shallop to Boston. Pinnion and Vinton grumbled as Jonas said his goodbyes and promised to return.

"By Gaw, you're abandoning your duties," said Pinnion. "You're leaving your work for everyone to pick up your slack."

Vinton added, "Wait 'til ye get back. We'll work ye so hard, ye'll wish ye never left. Haven't ye got any iron in yer spine?"

The other workers wished Jonas luck and bade him a quick return.

"There's no other place I'd rather be," said Jonas. If I don't have iron in my bones, that hammer has surely become my heartbeat, and the bellows my source of air. I'll have to return to live."

They all laughed and passed around the jug from the windowsill. This time, Jonas took his turn before the newcomers, letting out a hearty "Ahhh," then wiped his mouth on his sleeve. "That should last me until I return."

Martha heard a horse canter up and stop. She ran around the corner of the house to see who had come to visit. "It's Jonas!"

she squealed. She ran to him with her basket of early turnips and herbs, nearly tripping over roots of the stump that refused to relinquish its stronghold in the dooryard. "I didn't expect you until it got cold."

"Aye," said Jonas, and picked her up and tossed her into the air as he had when she was younger.

"You're strong." Martha grinned as he placed her lightly on the ground. The front door opened, and she straightened her apron and cap.

"Martha, go back to the garden. I must talk to Jonas," said Grace, without even greeting her son. Martha dropped her head and went back around the side of the house with her basket, but she looked back just as she rounded the corner and waved at Jonas.

Grace pulled Jonas into the house. "You don't have on those fancy boots."

"Nay."

"I heard about the ironworkers being called to court for pride and disregard for the law. For wearing silver trim, lace, tiffany hoods, and GREAT BOOTS."

"Mother, where do you get this information?"

"I have my ways." She crossed her arms over her chest.

Jonas quickly calculated it in his head: Crossman had been writing to Sarah, and that must be how the whole town knew about his boots.

"Jonas, this is a disgrace for the family." She snapped her kitchen towel down on her knee and glared at him. "No member of our family has been brought before a court. We are a decent family with morals."

"Well, if I stayed in Dedham all the time, I wouldn't be brought to court now, either. Dedham is lax on the Sumptuary Law, so when I wore my great boots here, I got compliments, and no one turned me in. Lynn is different. They watch the ironworkers the way Archbishop Laud watched the Puritan ministers. A lot of locals from other towns like Saugus and Salem have been called to court on similar accounts."

"Jonas," said Grace, "you know the folks at Dedham view you differently on account of your father. His worth earns him the right to wear the boots, and if you don't have the right on your own account, people around here know you as your father's son."

"I think Dedham is more lax on many laws," Jonas replied. "Remember when Dedham was fined by the General Court for not putting up stocks or a whipping post?"

"This town was made according to Governor Winthrop's ideals, to be a 'city on a hill as an example to all of the world.' Why, then, would Dedham need those nasty things?" Grace looked around to see if Martha had come in. "And watch your tongue around Martha," she said in a fierce whisper.

"I'll be worthy of buying great boots soon, working at Hammersmith instead of Dedham." Jonas jingled a few coins in his pocket. "Besides, I have been traveling so much between here and Lynn to help Father, I did not have time to see the broadsheet with the notice."

Grace glared at Jonas, and said, "Yet, being brought to court like those base men at the ironworks and even their wives—"

"Mother, those men can afford the clothes. We are paid well. Some may even be worth more than Father. There are just some local men there that want to make a point—they always go hardest on the folks from Hammersmith, and they think that's where I'm from."

"Why don't they know you are a Fairbanks from Dedham?"

"Because I don't choose to tell them. They are making assumptions about me based on those I am associated with at Hammersmith, just as they are making assumptions about the people I work with. Some may act a bit coarse, but the people of Hammersmith are hardworking, good people, and skilled at their trades." He pulled an impish half-smile. "We do have a few that tarnish the reputation of all. I've told you about them."

"What are you going to do about this, Jonas?"

"Why, Mother, I'm going to court."

"Be off with you, then," Grace said as she picked up her towel and snapped it at him.

Jonas turned on his heels to make a quick getaway out the back door. He paused just long enough to wave at Martha in the lean-to and give her a wink.

As Jonas opened the door, he found his father with his hand out toward the latch.

"Father!" Jonas blurted.

"Jonas," Jonathan said more quietly and looked his son up and down, then he ducked under the low door lintel as he entered the lean-to.

Just then a bell rang in the distance, and Grace stepped into the lean-to, smiling for the first time since Jonas arrived.

She beamed and said, "It reminds me of England. No more of those morose drums." Then she backed up into the house to let Jonathan through.

Jonathan asked Jonas, "When did you get back?"

"Just now, but it seems my reputation precedes me."

"That it has," Jonathan said with a furrowed brow."

Jonas followed his father back into the hall, where Jonathan put the gun he carried in the corner by the door. "Prescott wants you to come out and help him build a road."

"Who says I'm not going to Hammersmith next spring?"

Jonathan ignored his question and said, "You might want the latest news. Prescott came by the house and said Nashaway has twenty people now. The General Court has given West Town—that's what they're calling it—clearance to have their own selectmen. With town status, they must build a road to Sudbury. He needs extra hands . . . and it sure wouldn't hurt you or this family if you were gone a bit longer this winter, until the gossip mongers move past you and the great boots."

"Father, if little Prince Charles hadn't been born with a gimp leg and wore great boots to cover his brace, wearing them wouldn't have become an issue." Jonas's teeth clenched. "Why do they have the right to tell us how we can dress just because we aren't wealthy or prestigious? I have the money to buy the boots. I thought we came here for freedom."

"Jonas, that was religious freedom. We are still Englishmen under English rule."

"Doesn't look like we are free to pick our religion, either," Jonas said, and turned again to leave the house, pulling the heavy front door closed fast behind him.

Troubles

Jonas was welcomed back to Hammersmith by the smell of sulfur and the warmth of the giant belching furnace as the shallop glided between the riotous fall colors on the banks of the Saugus River. He listened for the muted thud of the massive hammer tolling his independence after finishing his part of his father's harvest. Theophilus was not chatty this trip as he navigated up the tidal waters.

"What?" Jonas had said at the morose expression on the man's face as he maneuvered the boat upstream. "You have nothing to say to me on my return?"

"Nay, it's not you. Things are changing," said Theophilus.

Jonas waited for him to continue, but sensed questions weren't welcomed.

As they glided into the dock and Jonas secured the flat-bottom boat, Crossman was carrying bar iron down to the warehouse.

"Welcome back, Jonas." Crossman called, his biceps bulging under the load.

"You're just the man I want to see," replied Jonas. "Did you write to Sarah about my going to court?"

"Nay. I might have said that several of the workers were going to court—all for foolish lace, silver, and tiffany hoods. I never mentioned your name. All I said was one man was going to court for wearing great boots." He didn't evert his eye contact. "Sarah says they looked fine at church."

"Lo, you got me into trouble, man. My parents are disgraced and are saying I must leave town over the winter to quell the gossip about going to court."

"You have little troubles," said Crossman, "if you compare them with what's going on here. The investors in England are unhappy with their returns, and the fault has fallen like the forge hammer on Gifford's shoulders. Henry and James Leonard—you know they're two of our best men in the forge—they and Ralph Russell have been invited to Taunton to help with a new ironworks there."

"I thought Hammersmith had a twenty-one-year monopoly on iron production," said Jonas.

"They do, but just in Massachusetts Bay, not in the other colonies."

Jonas took part of the load of bar iron from Crossman and started stacking it on the boat as Theophilus headed up the hill to see his friends.

"Are they going?" asked Jonas. "*I'm* not leaving. I belong here."

"I suppose we must finish our covenants, at least. And you are expected in court in November. You don't want any further trouble for not showing up."

"I calculated it, and I must work until the last week in December to get my time in. Maybe it'll be better next spring. I don't want to go back to farming or barrel making.

But the first thing I must consider is Essex County Quarterly Court."

"You're not alone. Pinnion and his wife must attend, as must Goodwife Jenke. That tavern keeper, the senior Armitage, has always been a troublemaker for us. He's a witness in their cases." Crossman mentioned several other witnesses.

"Aye," said Jonas. "Some of those witnesses are on my case, but not Armitage. He must know not to meddle with me."

"Do you have the ten shillings for the fine?"

"Aye, but I plan to tell the magistrates who I am and what service I have done for them. Besides, they're just padding their coffers. I haven't worn those boots here since the orders were published, or at least when *I* saw them."

Jonas, dressed in his church clothes and riding cloak, rode Buck to the Essex Quarterly Court in Salem before dawn, through a November snowstorm. His great boots sat useless at Mr. Osbourn's. He could have used them against the blustery weather, and the high tops would have prevented the saddle from chafing his legs.

Jonas felt trapped within the plaster walls and heavy woodwork of the unfamiliar courtroom. The session started early in the morning, but he knew he'd be there all day. The room throbbed with people waiting their turn or enjoying the pageantry of quarterly court. The magistrates sat at a large table in front of the room with wide-lace collars and broad hats with large feathers in the bands.

Jonas greeted Pinnion and Joseph Jenke, Jr., with their wives. Pinnion and his wife had been to court frequently for severe grievances made against them. *They might be recognized by the magistrates,* Jonas thought. *Maybe I should sit across the room.* But he chose to sit with his comrades anyway.

He scowled when he saw the tavern keeper. Joseph Armitage had brought many workers from Hammersmith and other towns to court, even after he himself served them strong drink.

"The Essex County Quarterly Court this 25th day of the ninth month of 1652 is now in session." The judge's gavel came down hard.

Jonas paid little attention to the first cases, until one of the witnesses for his own case was sworn in as clerk of the market for Lynn. His stomach twisted. The next case was a man fined for taking tobacco, contrary to the law. All of Hammersmith, including Jonas, could be called up for that. Hammersmith even bought the tobacco for their workers. *Eight more cases. Could this move any slower?*

Nicholas Pinnion and his wife and the wife of Joseph Jenke, Jr., were called to the table. Two men from Lynn with the same sumptuary charges were also called, but the Lynn men stood a significant distance from the Hammersmith people.

Then Joseph Armitage held the floor against several debtors, including both father and son Jenke. The day wore on, and it seemed Armitage was addressed in every other case.

Two young ladies were presented for violation of the sumptuary law, and each was pardoned because her family was worth over two hundred pounds. Jonas's father was worth more, but Jonas was determined to stand as a man on his own credentials, not in his father's shadow.

Jonas laughed with the rest of the court when a wife was presented for calling her husband a "gurley gutted divill." The case was discharged.

Jonas was still chuckling when he heard his name. Standing abruptly at the summons, he bumped the back of his knees on the bench, sending it screeching against the floor. He strode to the judges' table with his hat in his hands.

"Please state your name."

"Jonas Fairbanks of Dedham, Suffolk County." He stated it carefully to differentiate himself from the bond servants at Hammersmith.

"It says here that you are from the ironworks."

"I was contracted to work at Hammersmith twenty-six weeks last year and thirty weeks this year. I reside with Mr. William Osbourn, but I pay country rates at Dedham."

The judges looked at each other with raised brows.

"What say you about wearing great boots in disregard of the Colony Sumptuary Laws of October 14, 1651? Are you worth two hundred pounds?"

Though confident in his answers, Jonas felt a bead of sweat trickle down the side of his brow and another down his spine. "I bought the boots at a cobbler shop at Lynn before leaving the works late last fall to return to Dedham for the winter." He did not name the cordwainer, so as not to put him in danger, nor did he tell them he had worn the boots all winter at Dedham without a problem.

"Would you say this was after October?"

"Aye, your honor, but I hadn't seen any published orders stating I couldn't wear the fine boots." *Like a little prince with a gimp leg.*

The judges looked at one another. Whispers circled the vultures. The gavel cracked. Jonas flinched. "Your case has been discharged. It appears you didn't wear great boots after the law was published. You may take your seat, Goodman Fairbanks."

Jonas nodded and walked back up the aisle with a lighter step. As he made his way to his bench, the next case was called: a man who lived in the colony who had left his wife in England. He was ordered to go back to her or pay a fine. Jonas wondered about George's apprentice, James Fales. His wife and daughter were still in England. Would they run him out of Dedham, too? Jonas doubted it.

Christmas

Boughs of evergreen adorned the Osbourn house as the fire crackled with chestnuts on the twenty-third of December. Jonas and Crossman sat at the evening table with their host. This would be their last meal there for this season of ironworking. They'd leave in time to arrive at Dedham for the Christmas traditions.

Jonas sniffed the air. "I already smell the cinnamon figgy pudding that Mother has been preparing for days. Our family is big, but we still gather at Father's house. I need to get home before the Yule candle and Yule log are lit.

"Blessings be that we can still celebrate," said Jonathan Coventry, his spectacles sliding down on his nose. "England hasn't celebrated Christmas festivities since they banned them in '47."

"We can celebrate Christmas, but we can't wear great boots," teased Crossman as he looked Jonas's way. Jonas scowled back.

"I'd like to be around here for Christmas, I bet there's drinking, mumming, wassailing, and gambling in Hammersmith. There'll be none of that in Dedham, even though we can observe the holiday," said Jonas.

Mr. Osbourn placed his pewter mug on the table. His manservant came to refill it, but Osbourn dismissed him, giving him a task that took him away from the dining hall. Osbourn lowered his voice so only the men around the table could hear. "I have news," he said, looking at each of the men, assuring he had their full attention. "I will leave for Boston this winter. I'll not return next season."

"What? Why? What are we to do?" probed Jonas.

"Things aren't going well with the ironworks. The Company of Undertakers is forming a commission to oversee John Gifford's managerial work. Frankly, there are credit problems. I'm not sure how long they'll honor the payroll."

Jonas and Crossman looked at each other with wide eyes. Color drained from their faces.

"You'll be quite all right," Osbourn said. "I'll give each of you your wages as you leave." Mr. Osbourn took his last drink of strong ale. The young men followed suit. Jonas's mouth was dry and his mind was spinning.

"You will both find ample opportunities elsewhere. You have skills that few possess."

"What about the ironworks?" asked Jonas. "Who will keep it running?"

"Francis Perry has been helping to apprentice two Scotsmen in repairs. Not to say they can replace your fine work, but perhaps they can keep the place going."

"I suggest you lads find other employment. It may get rough around here. You have been here at the best of times—be glad of that. Thank you for coming when I needed you. Now I must send you on your way, so I can help my goodwife prepare for our Christmas Eve."

Mr. Osbourn rose. The three young men stood in respect. As they stood, still in shock, Osbourn shook each one's hand with fatherly sincerity. "I suggest you all have a good night's sleep and take the shallop out in the morrow, early. You don't want to be the ones to tell some of these men what is coming, nor do you want to be here when they find out."

"We can't even say farewell to our friends in the forge?" asked Jonas in a sulky tone. Osbourn barely shook his head.

Jonas was pelted by icy rain as he stood against Buck for warmth on the shallop. In Boston, people bustled about town in preparation for the holiday. Jonas and Crossman pulled the hoods of their capes up against the wind for their horseback ride to Dedham. They missed the heat of the giant furnace, their personal sun.

Jonas bade Robert farewell at his small house where Sarah, due with their first child in the spring, waited for him. It was almost dark when Jonas arrived home. There was a faint glow in the window, and Jonas wondered if he had missed the lighting of the Yuletide candle. New logs were stacked by the door for the Yuletide fire. The old Yule log must have already been taken in for good luck.

He put Buck in the barn, and his great boots crunched through the frozen grass and stiff snow to the back entrance of the lean-to. Jonas removed the boots before entering the hall door, so he would not interrupt the Christmas rituals.

The lit Yule candle sat in the middle of the table. The mazer bowl was there as well. Father took the first drink of wassail from it and handed it to John. George would take it next. Jonas hurried to his place to receive it after George. Junior would take his turn and then it would continue around the family until everyone, even the youngest, had taken a sip. It reminded Jonas of the jug he and the ironworkers had passed around at the forge. In its own way, it had bound them as a family there, and Jonas's heart mourned his loss.

Jonas attended the Dedham annual meeting with the rest of the Fairbanks men on January 6. A few days later, the selectmen held a meeting, asking Robert Crossman to attend.

The day after that meeting, Robert was taking Sarah to a distant neighbor's house when he met Jonas walking Dedham's main lane.

"Jonas," Crossman called, dismounting and leaving his wife on the horse. "Did you hear about the water mill at Wollomonopoag? The selectmen asked me to build it."

"When did this happen?"

"Yesterday. Remember our plans to bring mining to Dedham?" Crossman nearly puffed with pride. "This might be a start toward that. I want you to help me build the water mill. Your father is a woodreeve this year. That'll help us get the timber we need. I must give them my consent before next Lecture Day. What do you say?"

"I'm game," said Jonas, "as I sure don't want to help father make spinning wheels. We'd just fight." Crossman slapped him on the back.

As Crossman left, Jonas thought about this providence. Wollomonopoag was fifteen miles away, and they must build a place to stay while they worked there. *This gets me out of the house without leaving the area. I won't be running away from the Dedham gossips, either.*

On the Sabbath, Crossman pulled Jonas aside.

"Lo, Crossman," Jonas blurted. "When are we going to start setting up a place to live at Wollomonopoag?"

Crossman spoke quietly. "Jonas, I wanted you to be the first to know." He looked around to see if anyone else was listening. "Remember the Leonard brothers at the forge? I told you they were asked to go to Taunton and start an ironworks. Lo, they've just asked me to join them." Crossman searched Jonas's face for shared excitement.

Jonas stood blank-faced, listening.

"I'm going to tell the selectmen that I can't build their water mill," said Crossman.

Jonas looked up to the sky, trying to keep the disappointment from his face.

"I'll still be around for a while, but I'm leaving soon after Sarah has our baby. I'm sorry. I know I promised we'd work together on the mill, but I can't pass this up."

"Of course, you have much opportunity." Jonas kicked the toe of one boot with the heel of the other.

Arctic air reached the Massachusetts Bay Colony, and snow settled in drifts, climbing the lean-to of the Fairbanks house.

But the cold that Jonas felt was more from betrayal by his friend than from the weather.

Martha ran to greet him at the door as always, but Jonas didn't respond to her affections, so she turned back to her work.

Jonas looked at his mother and said, "I'm going to Nashaway to help Prescott build his road and house."

"You don't belong there, Jonas," Mother said. "Your father and I always planned to keep our children near us. That means in Dedham. Once you cross the Sudbury River, there are lots of Indians. I can't fathom how Prescott could take Mary and the children to that wilderness. But a wife like Mary will follow her husband anywhere."

"You came here with Father. Some wives stay in England. And we have Natives at Wigwam Pond that haven't given us any problems."

Grace scowled at Jonas.

Jonathan came down from the hall chamber, joining the conversation. "Nashaway is called West Town now. Let him help Prescott this winter. The Farrar brothers from West Yorkshire are going out there and James Draper has already signed their covenant. Ralph Houghton is going, too. Let him go, Grace. When the gossip settles about Crossman and the Wollomonopoag mill, your goodies will be looking for other fodder to chew. By the time Jonas returns to help plant in the spring, they'll forget all about the great boots."

PART V

1652–1668

BEGINNINGS AND ENDINGS

The Sudbury River was low in the winter. Jonas rode Buck over it on his way to West Town, contemplating his losses and abandoned dreams. He pushed himself high in the stirrups to see ahead—Prescott had warned that a weary traveler could get lost at night on the Indian trail leading from Boston to the Great River Valley. Traveler trailed at Buck's heels, then barked and chased a rabbit across the snow. When Jonas reined in and whistled for her, Traveler ran back and looked up expectantly at Jonas.

The trees created an ominous tunnel with their arms and fingers reaching out toward each other, obscuring the trail ahead. Jonas kept a vigil for sinister yellow eyes reflecting the moonlight sifting through the trees. *Wolves*, he thought with a shudder. They came in packs, and without Traveler, they could surround him without his knowing. *No one would ever find me, like young John Dwight in Wigwam Swamp.* Jonas shook his head to dispel the images.

At a tree where two paths diverged, Jonas dismounted and felt the bark for a scar indicating a Native village was near that welcomed travelers. Before mounting again, Jonas patted the saddle bag that held tobacco for a welcoming host. He thought he saw a flickering light through the dense trees, beckoning. He hoped it might be a place to find shelter from the teeth of the night.

A small brook burbled nearby. While Buck drank his fill,

Jonas thought. The Natives would rather welcome guests than have strangers ride into their village unannounced. He laughed to himself. With their keen intuition, they probably knew he was coming when he left the Bay Path.

Jonas was welcomed into a wetu, a domed woven hut with a central fire that vented through the top. He was offered a place to sleep on a platform covered by heavy furs. Jonas was comfortable sleeping with his siblings and travelers at ordinaries, but the experience of sleeping with the Native family, with their different ways, stole much of his slumber.

Before light, Jonas bade "Ta" to the squaw cooking at the central fire and handed her a parcel of tobacco. Buck's steps crunched over the frozen grass as they headed for the Bay Path again toward West Town. Jonas mounted the crest of the Wattaquadock Hills, where an ocean of fog with pine tree islands had greeted him on that earlier trip. Today, snow crystals made the fields glisten like jewels. Where there had been two small houses near the wading place and the night pasture, now there were more thatched roofs situated on either side of the Nashaway River.

Buck picked his way down the steep hill, sliding over loose rocks. Jonas examined more closely the soft shapes of the hand-hewn homes in the valley. He could still see smoke coming from the trucking house on the slope of George Hill—Prescott had sold the house he built earlier for Mary to Ralph Houghton, cousin to John Houghton of Medfield, the man Jonathan had commissioned to make a chest for Grace.

As he drew near the trucking house, Prescott's younger children ran barefoot onto the cold encrusted grass to greet Jonas. The girl in the lead had flaxen curls escaping her white cap. *Lydia. She'd be about eleven, a year older than our Martha.* Lydia held the hand of a small boy. *He must be Jonas.* The thought made Jonas blush.

Prescott's dog barked as Traveler playfully pounced at the older dog with her forepaws, then turned tail to start a game. The older dog, ignoring the challenge, continued to warn the family of a stranger.

Prescott called out as he came from the barn, "Glad you came, Jonas. Welcome to West Town." He spread his arms wide, inviting Jonas to take it all in. "Are you ready to clear a cartway back toward home?"

"After coming on the trail, I see why you need it," quipped Jonas.

"We built a house for John Rugg last year. He's from Sowerby but came through Watertown to West Town. You'll stay with him while you're here."

Jonas and Rugg were invited to eat at the Prescott house often, where Thomas Sawyer and his wife Marie, the oldest Prescott daughter, were always at the table. Rugg seemed interested in Martha, the second oldest, and sixteen-year-old Sarah, the third, was always placed near Jonas at the table.

It felt very much like they were trying to match him up, Jonas thought, and cringed.

The winter yielded to the sun as their road work continued. Small blades of green grass pushed past the golden matted thatch. Those journeying to the Great River Valley bringing mail from the coast enjoyed the improved way from Sudbury to West Town. One day a letter came for John Prescott.

My Dearest Friend,

I hope your road work and building went well this winter. I need Jonas at home to open the fields and plant. I gave my land at Medfield to George. He'll be building and moving his wife and seven children there soon . . .

Your Loving Friend Jonathan

Prescott shared the letter with Jonas, who grumbled, "The need for me to work must be greater than the embarrassment of gossip."

Understanding the great boot and court situation, Prescott consoled Jonas. "Your knowledge and industry from working at Hammersmith makes you an asset anywhere. Once we get this town settled, we'll consider an ironworks in West Town with the bog iron we found on our early expeditions."

"I'll look forward to that." Maybe Crossman wasn't the only one who would be working at a new ironworks.

New Merchant 1653

The rotund John Gaye called to Jonathan as he came out of the blacksmith shop.

"Lo, Fairbanks, do you know Richard Hartley who came into town? He's a merchant from Stansfield, West Yorkshire, not far from where you hailed. He's replacing Michael Powell as Dedham's merchant. Mr. Hartley is living in the small house James Draper owns."

Fairbanks stroked his chin. "There were many Hartleys in Sowerby. One witnessed my father's will and another the will of my late half-brother. The family had land dealings with them in Thornton-in-Craven."

"The word is that Hartley left his wife and daughter in England," Gaye said in an accusing tone.

"Aye, but that is not altogether unusual." Jonathan stopped himself before mentioning George's apprentice, James Fales.

"The magistrates of Essex Quarterly Court are sending men back to England or fining them for abandoning their families. Why don't you talk with Hartley about this? We don't want problems in Dedham."

Jonathan straightened his long cloak, removed his hat, and rapped the brass knocker on the door of the small house Draper built. Now there was a merchant's shield by the door.

A man of substantial build answered, standing erect and proud in his fine blouse and jerkin, though his ample girth stressed the closure. He held papers in his hand. "Welcome, good man," he said.

"Might you be Richard Hartley, merchant?" asked Jonathan. "From West Yorkshire?"

"Aye," said Hartley, "I have just come to this fair village."

"I want to welcome you as another West Yorkshireman and see if you know the Hartley's from Sowerby. I am Jonathan Fairbanks from that town."

"Do come in, Goodman Fairbanks." He led him into a well-appointed parlor in disarray.

The bed frame was grand and the linens fine, but the home lacked a woman's touch. A large crate sat in the middle of the room, and the floor was strewn with packing materials. Various pewter, brass, and even a few silver items lay on the floor, table, and fine chairs.

"What brings you to our town, Mr. Hartley?" Jonathan asked.

"I'm an agent for companies in England. They consign me products to sell in the colonies."

"Do you know James Draper? I believe this was his house," said Jonathan. "Do you plan to stay and open a business here?"

"Aye, and I have brought my first merchandise with me." Harley motioned towards the collection of items. "And what do you do, my friend?"

"Farm, as we all do, serve the village, often by surveying and supervising road constructions. I also work as a wood reeve. In winter, I make and repair spinning wheels."

"I've heard of your skills, indeed. I understand you know all who work in spinning and weaving in this area."

"I've been here from the start of the town. I believe I know everyone. As you will soon in your trade," said Jonathan.

"I fear I won't have that luxury. I travel to England for products and then peddle them around New England, often taking other items in trade. I have the threads of your spinners woven into cloth to sell here or in England. It's important for me to meet other traders and travel to where I can make the best connections and profits."

"Is that why you have not brought a wife?"

"Aye, my wife and daughter remain in Stansfield. The Drapers are from there, you know. I may ask him to weave some of your spun flax and wool to send to England. I'll see my wife and daughter on trips to the homeland. Be it known: my wife didn't want to come. And without her, I'll need an assistant to watch my business when I travel. Knowing everyone in town, could you introduce me to the most responsible, trustworthy man also skilled in words and numbers?"

"You don't have to look far for an educated man in Dedham. However, the best I can offer stands before you."

"I'd like nothing better than to work with a West Yorkshireman. We know the breed of our area, hardworking, frugal, and dependable. Would you consider the position?"

"Aye, I much prefer numbers and words to plants and animals, though I fear I'll still need to farm to keep my wife and my young ward, Martha."

Jonas rode home over the new Sudbury cart path. Dedham had recently finished their own cart path from Sudbury passing Natick, then past Dedham's herder house at Rosemary Meadow.

When Jonas arrived home and called out that he was there, he found his father discussing business with a large, finely dressed man in the parlor. "Jonas, I would like you to meet Mr. Richard Hartley," said Father.

Having heard Jonas's voice, Grace came from the hall and around the stairway, but she stopped when she saw the men engaged in discussion and retreated to the hall.

Jonas extended his hand, and Mr. Hartley rose, pulling his waistcoat down over his ample belly.

"It's nice to meet you, Jonas. Your father tells me you worked at Hammersmith. They produced fine iron—it's a shame the company is in such a row with the investors." Hartley waited, expecting Jonas to add information for him to peddle during his travels. "Did you know the manager, Gifford, was sent to jail?" Hartley paused again and raised his bushy eyebrows.

Jonas cringed, considering his father's opinion of the ironworks.

When Jonas didn't offer any information, Hartley continued. "The townsmen recommend your father as a well-respected, educated man. I have asked him to help me with my trade here."

"Trade?" asked Jonas, looking at his father. *He's taken on yet another task?*

"Yes, I need a good assistant here while I'm traveling. Dedham's a bit far from a port."

"It's good for Father to have a less strenuous job than farming after his bout of sickness a few years back," Jonas said. "I'm here to help him with the spring planting, but I won't always be around." Jonas looked steadily at his father.

Jonathan returned a piercing glower over his spectacles while reading the covenant that Hartley had brought.

Too late, Jonas realized his father didn't want his health or frailty discussed in front of this man. Jonas excused himself and rushed upstairs.

Lost at Home

Even though Jonas felt Crossman had betrayed him several times, he missed him and felt lost after his old friend left for Taunton to start the new ironworks.

Grace continued to needle him about marriage and paraded young ladies of Dedham at the Fairbanks house, but Jonas found fault with each one.

"How about John and Mary's girls? You met them this winter. Marie's married, but Martha, their second, would make a good wife."

"Mother, John Rugg had his eye on Martha all last winter. He's talking of marrying her, and I won't interfere."

"Well, what about Sarah? She's a bit younger, but there aren't many men out there. You could bring her to live in Dedham. I'm sure Mary would let her daughter leave that wild town for such a good marriage."

Knowing there was no stopping his mother, Jonas returned to his work.

Jonas sat next to George at the family Sabbath supper, and George asked, "Now that you're home, would you help build my new house?" He was building west of the Charles River by Medfield. It would be the only house west of the river and must be garrisoned. "There are already twenty to thirty lots granted on the east side, but across the river, we'll be vulnerable."

"That's a big job," replied Jonas, cautiously.

"I've found a place on a rise by Bogastowe Pond with a good view of the surroundings. The land yields copious rocks, and there's already a vacant two-story stone house down by the pond. I'm planning at least a stone foundation, and I'll need your true measurements to level and face the stones. I have nine other men in Medfield who will help, as well."

"I—" began Jonas.

"There are bachelors in Medfield you can stay with," George interrupted. "They even call it Bachelor's Row. You wouldn't have to live with Father."

"You know that appeals to me."

"Fine. We'll start as soon as you get his planting done." George wiped his mouth and pushed back from the table.

"Wait," snapped Jonas. "I'll help as a brother, not as a servant."

"You were never my servant," answered George indignantly.

"Maybe not to your thought."

Jonas was still smarting over the loss of Crossman when he met Richard Wheeler, one of the men helping George build. Wheeler was a good-looking, hard-working man with a wife and a growing family. He and Jonas made a team as they measured and shaped stones for the foundation. They also paired up during partner exercises on training days back in Dedham.

The General Court commissioned Rowley to give Dedham their Drake cannon, and on the next training day after its arrival, it was Jonas's turn to practice firing the Drake. He chose Wheeler to assist him. When they fired the cannon, the whole town heard the report.

That evening, Grace complained to Jonathan. "See, the General Court is giving us a Drake cannon. They know we're in greater danger having the Indians live so close. If there's trouble, you and our sons will have to fight."

"Grace," Jonathan said, putting his hand on her forearm, "as I've said many times before, the Natick Indians aren't threatening. We're just having land issues, not unlike those we've had with Watertown, Dorchester, Roxbury, and even Medfield. There's no cause for alarm."

Mill for West Town

Training days were always festive, but an extra air of jubilation surrounded West Town when Prescott congratulated the winners of the November exercises, presenting the overall winner with a red ribbon for his hat. The men jostled each other and joked as they headed to the sheltered area to enjoy ale and meat pies away from the brisk wind.

As the supper ended, John Wilder, a prominent man in West Town, stepped onto a stump and started, "Prescott Town—" he hesitated. "No, the General Court said our town has to be called West Town." He threw his hands in the air and said, "I just can't get used to that name."

After the laughter died down, he said, "We have voted to grant John Prescott, our founder, permission to erect a gristmill. I suppose it's only right that we grant him a mill, since we can't name the town for him." Everyone laughed again, and then John Wilder looked down with a serious stare at Prescott. "It must be operational by May."

The men cheered and dogs barked. "No more daylong trips to and from a mill." Wilder shouted.

"Or standing in long lines for grinding." called out another.

"Our plantation will be looked upon as a real town, with a mill," concluded Wilder.

Prescott prepared eighteen-year-old John Jr. to take charge of the farm when he left for Boston. The harvest was in, but there was plenty to do before the snow—Prescott was racing the weather. He needed more help to build the mill by May. Before he left, he promised Mary she would finally have a real house built near the mill instead of having to stay in the trucking house.

"You sold my first house before I could even live in it," Mary said skeptically. "And now we've lived in the trucking house for nine years."

"Work must begin on the mill first," Prescott said, "for we must set posts before the ground freezes. I must also order grinding stones and mill irons from England at once. The roads are no more than cart paths, and we must haul the heavy stones before spring brings the mud." Prescott shook his head at the urgency of all the tasks. "It must be done before the thaw, for then the crops must be planted."

He put his arms around Mary and said, "And, yes, we have to build you a house."

Prescott's first stop on the way to Boston to find a millwright was the Fairbanks house. He didn't have time to talk about the Natives, still a major topic in Dedham. After brief greetings, Prescott started in. "I was granted a gristmill and plan to build a house nearby for Mary this winter."

"Much to do in a short time," said Fairbanks.

"Aye, I came to hire someone who knows how to erect a water-driven gristmill. I want a good one." Prescott winked.

"You never want anything but the best, my good man," said Jonathan, smiling.

"As do you," Prescott retorted. He eyed Jonathan's fine house. Then he looked back at Jonathan and said, "Do you know any good millwrights?"

"We used John Elderkin of Lynn. He is quite busy up north. Last year, we offered a young man, Robert Crossman, a grant to build another mill here. Instead, he left for Taunton to set up an ironworks. Jonas has learned a lot about the ironworks, mills, and carpentry from men named Pinnion and Perry at Hammersmith. He knows more than I could teach him upstairs." Fairbanks's eyes shifted to the hall ceiling as he tamped his pipe. "I hear the man to build gristmills in the Bay is John Founell in Charlestown."

"I'm sure he'll need help. I also need to build a house." Prescott blew a smoke ring up the bricks of the hearth. "Mary has been patient." After another pause, he said, "Can you spare Jonas again this winter? He's a responsible man, works hard, and delivers good quality."

"Jonas may be happy to get out of the Bay again," said Jonathan, "He's never been satisfied here after Hammersmith, though gossip has quieted."

"No doubt, Jonas will be a man worth more than great boots in his lifetime," said Prescott, staring into the crackling fire.

"You may ask him," returned Fairbanks, relighting his pipe. "Jonas is at Medfield helping George build a garrison house."

Jonas, overjoyed to leave Dedham, packed a bag, tied Buck to the cart, lifted Traveler in, then climbed onto the cart seat with Prescott. "I'm treated as a man in Nashaway—uh, West Town—not as a son, younger brother, or servant," he said.

They headed toward John Founell's place in Charlestown. The millwright nodded and pulled on his right ear lobe as Prescott explained his need to erect the mill before spring thaw.

"What kind of help do you have in the wilderness?"

Prescott presented Jonas. "This man, Jonas Fairbanks, is a carpenter and has worked at Hammersmith on the waterwheels and in the forge." Prescott patted the handsome, well-built Jonas on the back, his solid stature suggesting his strength.

"The Fairbankses have one of the finest houses in Dedham," Founell said, looking at Jonas. "Hammersmith has seven waterwheels?"

Hat in hand, standing straight and tall, Jonas answered, "Eleven in all. I helped build my father's Dedham house and the Dedham gristmill, and I was at the forge in Hammersmith for two years."

"Everyone in the town will help, too," said Prescott.

"If you don't mind, I'll also use a man of my own," said Founell. "I have an indentured Scotsman I can bring. Will you have a Scotsman in your town?"

"Aye. We are a bit more tolerant of men than most, as long as they are of moral character."

"When would you need me to start?" asked Founell.

"I'll order grinding stones and irons now with your suggestions. Then we"—Prescott nodded at Jonas— "will prepare for you."

"Take Mordecai MacLeod with you. I'll give you a list of things to prepare. Mordecai knows what I need and how I like it done."

"We'll be happy to have him."

Founell shook both men's hands and went to summon the Scotsman.

Prescott snapped the reins over his stout horse, and the cart rumbled over the rough path leading west. Jonas bounced on the stiff bench, envying Mordecai's berth among the supplies.

Jonas had been curious about all men from the time he learned about the New World and the Natives in school in England. The seamen of the voyage and the men at Hammersmith represented many different cultures. Dedham was settled by families from all over England, and Jonas befriended various Natives who helped build the cartway as well as the two Natives and Scotsmen he had come to know at the ironworks. Mordecai's language was difficult to understand, but Jonas was intrigued enough to make an effort to untangle his Scottish brogue.

While Prescott tended the horse and cart, Jonas turned to Mordecai, who was nestled between two large sacks of flour, his arms draped across each. "Are you from the Battle of Dunbar come on the *Unity* to Hammersmith in '50?" Prescott had many times told of how he'd barely escaped being called to fight in England's war, and Jonas was fascinated with the details. The Scotsman had much to share once the topic was raised.

"Ye might know me cousin. In '50, after King Charles the First was beheaded, me lord pressed me into the fight for Scotland at Dunbar. We fought for young Prince Charles II to sit the throne, instead o'yer Oliver Cromwell. We lost many men with Captain Leslie and the ministers leading the battle.

"We had Cromwell's troops pinned against the sea, but the ministers wouldn't let us attack on the Sabbath. Cromwell flanked us then. A bloody battle it were. We ran, who weren't slain. Thousands captured, including me brother John and me."

And then what? thought Jonas, willing him to continue.

"We who could fight another day were marched twenty-eight miles to prison in God's house, at St. Nicholas Church at Durham. We starved on the march and in the church until they put a hundred-fifty of us on the *Unity* in the winter. They shipped us like cattle, but it wasn't much worse than in the church.

"We got to Charlestown in December. I don't know how me and John lived. They took him to the mines and me to Thomas Kemble, who sold me in Charlestown. I knew building, so Founell indentured me for his mills. Someday I hope to be free."

Jonas leaned back and reached his arm out to shake Mordecai's hand. "Many thanks for telling your tale," he said.

Telling the story sapped the energy from Mordecai. He

slumped onto one of the bags and slept. When they were entering West Town, Mordecai woke from a fitful doze and looked up at his two travel mates in hopes they could vouch for him in the community.

Twelve-year-old Lydia, quick and agile, ran out of the trucking house when her father drew the cart up. She drew her skirts up so she could run like a boy. Her white cap fell off revealing her blond curls and hung around her neck. She didn't seem to notice it as she greeted her father. Jonas knew his own mother would have come out of the house to scold Lydia for unladylike conduct, but Lydia seemed unconcerned as she warmly greeted both Jonas and Mordecai. She looked intently at Mordecai's red hair and giggled, "Someone set his head on fire."

Jonas was considered the specialist in preparing for the mill, even though Mordecai had worked with Founell and knew his plans. Jonas regarded Mordecai as an equal, as he had the Scotsmen at Hammersmith after they attained expertise in their work. He consulted Mordecai about Founell's preferences, and their friendship flourished.

On March 23, two days before the new year and only four months after Prescott was granted the right to build the mill, the first grain was ground. A great feast was held, with breads and pies made with finely ground flour from the mill. The whole town and the people of Sudbury would use the mill and turned out to celebrate.

Founell, Jonas, and Mordecai were lauded for their work during the festivities. The two from Charleston left.

"Jonas, why don't you stay in West Town?" said

Prescott. "You've become well-respected. This is a land of opportunity."

"Aye, but Rugg will soon turn me out of his house when he marries Martha," Jonas said, "I also need to help my father with planting."

"We've already assigned the first round of lots and are taking inventory of boundaries so we can grant the meadow lots. You could get in early on the grants. That's what your father wanted when he came to the colony."

"Aye, he did," said Jonas.

"We're talking about capping the town at thirty-five. We have room for only fifteen more, and we've discussed it—we'd like you to stay." Prescott studied Jonas's face. "You have talked of mines and foundries. We bought this land for the ores, you know, and we'll move on to that soon, I hope. Now is the time to buy land with your Hammersmith money to guarantee you receive further grants."

Prescott tried another angle. "There are plenty of eligible young ladies here, too."

Jonas felt sure Sarah, Prescott's third daughter, was one of ladies he meant. He did not want to be pressured into marriage, even in West Town. Henry Kerley Jr. tore his wedding banns with Elizabeth White, daughter of one of the wealthiest men in town. Jonas wondered if that marriage was contrived due to the lack of eligible men. It seemed all the girls were eyeing the new religious teacher, Mr. Rowlandson. He'd be the most prestigious man in town when he was ordained.

"I must return this year to help Father," he told Prescott. "Brother John is planning to get involved in the clay digs on Bearstow's property and may not be available to help. George is in Medfield now. I'll still have just enough time to stay and finish your house—Mother wouldn't forgive me if I didn't help with the new house for her best friend."

The Ledger 1654

Merchant Richard Hartley arrived at the Fairbanks house with his hat in hand.

"Come in, Richard," welcomed Jonathan.

"Ta," said Hartley as he entered, handing his hat and cloak to Grace.

Jonathan guided Hartley to the parlor where Grace had the master bed made and embroidered curtains drawn. She always prepared the parlor for unexpected guests.

"Have a seat by the hearth—it's still cool outside."

"I have some changes to our covenant, if you're agreeable," said Hartley.

"Pray tell. I'm quite satisfied with our arrangement, but I'd be happy to hear you out." Jonathan took a puff on his clay pipe.

"I'm moving to New London this spring. Reverend Blinman bids me to come. He's quite interested in trade and is well-connected. Young John Winthrop is there also. I have already acquired land on the southern Mill Cove where I plan to build a warehouse and wharf."

"This is Dedham's loss," said Jonathan, surprised and disappointed. "You've been good for this village."

"I'm not forsaking this place. I'm retaining my house and continuing trade here. Perhaps you'd agree to become more involved in my absence. I'll need someone to take in receipts and arrange for goods in exchange for trades."

"Why, I'd be honored."

"You are principled, and the men in town trust you, as do I. With you, it'll be handled well. Shall we make a covenant on it?" asked Hartley, bringing papers out of his front waistcoat pocket.

"We shall," Fairbanks said as he reached for his spectacles on the side table where the Bible lay open.

Court 1655

Elder Hunting addressed the Dedham townsmen. "We'll wait no longer for Mr. Eliot and the Praying Indians. No one responded to our peaceable letters to remove from our land south of the river. Lt. Joshua Fisher and Sgt. Daniel Fisher will petition the General Court on our behalf."

On May 23, five years after Eliot and the Natives started planting at Natick, the Fishers brought back the verdict from the General Court, and the lieutenant said, "Just as Captain Lusher said in 1650, the court required us to follow due process of the law and go to each level of the court to rectify this case."

Meanwhile, the General Court charged Major Humphrey Atherton, a prominent figure and magistrate in the colony, with ordering and governing the Natives in the Natick praying village. This appointment relieved the court of many of the cases it was hearing regarding the Indians.

Mr. Eliot approached the new counselor for Natick when they were both there. "As you know the law, Major Atherton, I'm asking for your help on the pressing problem of Natick's land." He explained that the Indians had been working the northwest land also claimed by Dedham since 1650. He listed the progress the Natives had made and presented their claim to the land based on Josias's line of inheritance from his mother, not his father, Chickataubutt, who deeded the land to the colony. "What is the best course for us to take?" Eliot asked. "Dedham is adamant that the south part of the land is theirs. The Natives have nowhere else to go."

"Aye, you have a problem," Atherton responded. "I've been called to take matters of contest between the Natives. But this case is far too complicated for a local court here at Natick. I see why you cannot settle. You both have arguments to your credit. I suggest you stay on the land you have improved and continue to work it until this can be taken before the courts."

Meetinghouse for Lancaster 1657

"The General Court is going to pull Lancaster's grant if we don't get a meetinghouse built," Prescott complained to Jonathan by the Fairbanks front gate on his regular spring trip to the Bay. "Oh, yes, and we are no longer West Town," he said with a tiresome sigh.

"Your village changed names as much as Dedham did," responded Jonathan.

Prescott continued, "Since John Tinker has taken over the trading in Lancaster, the town's business fills most of my days. Even with my sons and son-in-law handling much of the farming, blacksmithing, and millwork, I can't get things done. I need more help."

Jonathan recited the litany of obligations his married sons had.

Prescott nodded and looked at Jonas out of the corner of his eye. "I know it's near planting time, but all Lancaster wants Jonas to come to help build our meetinghouse."

Jonas fidgeted with a dried winter weed. *Father's stalling, trying to find a reason I can't go.*

Prescott patiently waited for Jonathan's answer.

"I suppose since my grandsons are old enough to help, we can do without Jonas for this planting."

Prescott turned to Jonas and said, "Would you come out again?" He took Jonas's shoulders in his hands and looked him straight in the eyes. "Since Hammersmith is in trouble, the General Court has granted permission for Lancaster to start an ironworks." Then he shook Jonas in delight.

"What?" Jonas said, wide-eyed. *At last, a real opportunity?* "Wait here, and I'll get my things."

After tying Buck to the back of Prescott's cart and telling Traveler to jump in, Jonas hugged his mother and Martha and tipped his hat to his father. Prescott snapped the reins over the rump of the horse. As they rode off, Prescott explained, "We'll go to Charlestown. Mordecai's indenture must expire soon. If not, maybe we can lease him from John Founell until it is over."

Jonas smiled. He'd be working with his friend, in a place he loved.

Once they'd found Mordecai free for the project, Prescott bought a horse in Charleston for him to ride to Lancaster along with Jonas while he finished business in Boston. Jonas and Mordecai waited for Founell to tear the indenture paper for Mordecai's official release.

Jonas urged his horse up the predawn dark of the hill, saying, "Mordecai, I want to show you something."

As they topped Wattaquadock Hills, Jonas motioned to stop. The rising sun kissed the valley, and Jonas didn't want to spoil the moment with words. "You missed this when we first came to build the gristmill because you were sleeping in the back of the wagon.

"It's like looking toward shore from the vast sea, don't you think?" Jonas continued, forgetting Mordecai was kept in the hold of the ship. "The mist rolls in waves as it covers the area between us and the great Wachusett Mountain. The islands of pines float on the mist."

Jonas lost himself within the immensity of it, the secrets and promises it held under its undulating surface, willing someone to challenge it. The sun flared Jonas's dream into a wakeful possibility. He had found something he'd been searching for.

Jonas delighted in the tranquil sensation of a calm sea vanishing into a green glow emanating from beneath the yellow blanket that covered the valley. There were signs of spring amongst the trees as amorous birds and squirrels called to one another.

As they rode on, Mordecai spied Prescott's garrisoned house near the gristmill. The waterwheel churned nonstop on the Nashaway River. He turned his horse and started down the hill, but before they reached the Prescott house, he reined in to let Jonas take the lead.

Prescott had told Jonas of the grief that had stricken his household, so Jonas prepared himself before Mary greeted them at the door. Still, it pained him to hear her recount details of the death of Martha and the twins. "They died within days of each other," she said, then pressed a finger against her lips, tears welling in her eyes. Jonas and Mordecai consoled Mary as well as they could before she sent them to John Rugg's house, where he was now alone.

"Rugg," Jonas called as he jumped off Buck before he fully stopped. They embraced while Mordecai settled the horses. When brawny Mordecai entered the house, he drew out the melancholy by bellowing, "Hullo! How ye doin'?" in his blustery Scottish brogue.

"Mary has asked us to supper when Prescott returns," Jonas said. "I suppose she'll have the Scotsman, too"—he winked at Mordecai. The Scot had been to the Prescotts' home many times while building the gristmill.

"I have seldom gone to the Prescott house since my Martha died," mumbled Rugg. "Even though our religion instructs us not to pine for the flesh, it hurts. But I will come while you are here."

"We'll feed yer good humours, Rugg," said Mordecai. "We shall all go."

Lydia sat on the cricket turning the roast over the fire. Jonas and Jonathan Prescott, eleven and sixteen years old, greeted the men. Jonas's namesake cried "Jonas!" and rushed to measure himself against the grown man.

Lydia, surprised, twirled around, leaving the roast dripping into the Yorkshire pudding, and ran to the door where the men gathered. Stopping short, she hesitated, then curtsied. She pushed the tendrils of golden curls away from her face with the back of her hand. "You came back!" she exclaimed.

Jonas stared, his mouth dry—words wouldn't come. *This can't be the small girl that was here five years ago. This is a young woman.* "Y-your father has asked me to help build the meetinghouse," said Jonas, and then he gathered himself to tease, "You will have to feed me again."

Lydia nodded, her cheeks turning a deeper pink.

Jonas's mind played the scene of the young girl who had hurried to him with her basket at dinnertime when the ladies fed the workmen those several years ago.

Sarah and Hannah greeted the men, too, and returned to setting the table board while tittering. "Old Mr. Kerley will be livid when he finds out the Scotsman has returned," said Hannah. Mary shushed them both.

After welcoming the guests, Mary's thoughts returned to the dinner. "Lydia, the roast," she reminded, and Lydia twirled around and rushed to turn the spit before the roast charred.

As a topic for dinner, Prescott started, "This Lancaster meetinghouse should have been built already, but after harvest the harsh winter delayed work. Every man in town will help at times," he promised, nodding to Jonas. "We'll build it on the natural knoll near the Old Settlers Burial Ground. Jonas, you'll be foreman. Rugg and Mordecai will direct teams of men. This meetinghouse will be the Lord's means to save our town."

The men worked from sunup until dusk, and the women cooked tirelessly for the workers. The young girls and ladies carried baskets or firkins covered with clothes to the worksite. Sarah, the oldest unmarried Prescott daughter, took her basket to her brothers when they weren't helping their father. Hannah took her basket to John Rugg. Two of the Prescott girls shared the handle of a basket for Mordecai, except when Lidia Lewis, Lydia Prescott's good friend, took her own basket to him. That only happened when Mr. Lewis, the wealthiest man in town, was not working on the meetinghouse. Lidia couldn't show her fondness by bringing her basket to Mordecai in front of her father.

Lydia Prescott constantly sought out Jonas to proffer her basket, as she had when he helped build the gristmill. He teased her as he did his little sister, and Lydia enjoyed the attention. Jonas began expecting her. He laughed when she tried to hurry discreetly with the awkward load, vying to reach him first.

Jonas noticed that Lydia always had energy and enthusiasm, unlike the girls of Dedham, who were reserved and proper. The food Lydia brought was good, too. She always included one of his favorites, like fresh strawberries and cream. Jonas marveled how Lydia had seemed so young when he had last seen her. Now she looked like a young woman, but she had retained her playfulness.

Mordecai drew Jonas aside one evening when it was too dark to work. "Jonas, before we go to Rugg's house, I want to talk with ye."

"You sound serious." Jonas punched him in his bulky arm. "What ails you?"

"Nothing's amiss, yet," said Mordecai. "Ye know these townspeople. Do ye think they would have me settle amongst them?"

"Mordecai, after all you've done for them, how could they turn you away? I, too, am considering settling here. I would like you as my neighbor."

"Aye, but some will not."

"Prescott likes you, and he's the father of this town. Talk to him."

Mordecai scratched the unruly reddish scruff on his chin. "By the way," he said, "I've been watching ye and the little Prescott daughter."

"What do you mean, watching us?" Jonas bristled. "She brings my dinner to the building site."

"Aye, but Lydia brings her basket just to ye."

"Well, isn't Lidia *Lewis* about her age and bringing hers to you?"

"Aye, but I be several years younger than ye." He pushed Jonas on the shoulder. My Lidia tells me the Prescott girl talks about ye all the time."

"It's nothing. I'm just friends with her family."

"That little Prescott girl is fond of ye, I say," said Mordecai, in the straightforward Scottish manner.

Jonas felt the nape of his neck grow warm. He whistled at some birds.

"By Gaw, everyone can see it," Mordecai said with a laugh. "Ye watch yerself. There are two older Prescott girls before her, even if John Rugg *is* sniffin' after Hannah."

Private Exchanges 1658

As spring bloomed, Lydia skipped like a child across the meadow lit with tiny white flowers and yellow buttercups. Jonas watched her swinging her basket gently and kicking her skirts through the grasses and blossoms. It was as if the petals came alive with each step, taking wing as yellow butterflies fluttered into the air around her, coming to rest on Lydia's white cap and sleeves. Instead of brushing them away, she stopped, brought her arm up before her, and seemed to talk to them.

As Lydia neared him, Jonas turned back to his work but

turned his head toward her again just in time to see her bright smile as she caught his eye.

Lydia held the basket up with both hands. "I made this for you, myself," she beamed.

He climbed down the ladder and took the handle of the basket. "Thank you. Would you like to join me? Judging from the weight of the basket, I'm sure there is enough for both of us."

Lydia nodded and watched expectantly as he peeked under a corner of the cloth.

Jonas sniffed. "It's an apple tart—my favorite." He winked.

Jonas carried the basket to a giant elm tree away from the other workers and the women who had brought meals to them. He spread the cloth and motioned for Lydia to sit, then perused the basket further. "All of my favorites."

Lydia glowed and said, "I've listened to what you like. Mother says this isn't a proper meal, but since I prepared it myself, she allowed me to bring it."

Jonas noticed a strand of golden hair falling over Lydia's forehead from under her white cap. With one finger, he brushed it off her brow as easily as he would have for his little sister. Immediately, he realized what he had done. Lydia turned her head away and giggled quietly. Jonas's neck and ears burned, but he did not apologize.

As they finished the repast, Lydia gathered the wooden bowls, clay pots, and cloths into her basket. Jonas lifted the basket, and she smiled as he took her small, soft hand in his rough, strong one to help her up.

As she turned to go, Jonas sneaked a finger gently into the bottom edge of her cap. As she started to walk away, the cap came off, revealing the fine golden halo of curls he had longed to see.

Lydia didn't look back. She grabbed her dangling cap,

then let it bob on her back as she laughed and ran through the meadow. Further away, she looked back once with a broad smile and disappeared in a fluttering yellow cloud above the meadow.

Noontime together became a ritual. Jonas and Lydia established the huge tree as their place. The elm was old and grand with faultless shape. Every day, Lydia spread a meal on a cloth, and Jonas came to her as soon as he got to a stopping point.

"I bet this is the largest elm tree in all New England," he said.

"Really?" marveled Lydia. "I left Watertown when I was four and have been nowhere, except to Dedham for your sisters' and brothers' weddings."

The tree had a hole in its knot, at a height Lydia could just reach. The hole was deep enough to conceal small notes or gifts. As Lydia was leaving that day, she told Jonas to look in the hole after he finished work.

Jonas returned to work as he saw the other men moving toward the partially finished meetinghouse. Lydia lingered until Jonas was on the other side of the building before slipping something into the hole.

"You go on. I'll catch up," said Jonas, as he and Mordecai passed the elm at the end of the day. "I forgot something." When Mordecai was far enough up the path, Jonas tried to peer into the dark hole in the tree. He pushed his big hand through the knot and drew out something woven of straw. A heart.

That night at Rugg's hearth, as the other men smoked their pipes, Jonas took out his knife and a piece of wood he had picked up on his way home. The next day at dawn on his way to work, he paused at the elm tree as Rugg and Mordecai walked on, finishing their conversation. Jonas admired his own whittling. He had carved a dog, just like Traveler, and placed it in the hole.

About noon, Jonas found excuses to work on the elm side of the meetinghouse, waiting for Lydia and her basket. She spread her cloth and put her basket under the tree as usual, then she stood on tiptoe and reached into the knot of the tree. She giggled with surprise as she retrieved the little whittled hound and held it to her heart.

Without a word, each time one of them checked the elm tree, they found something special. Once Lydia left a small rounded reddish stone with a natural black crystal cross. When Jonas found it, she told him why it was so special.

"When we first moved here, we lived by the brook at the trucking house on George Hill. My sisters wouldn't go, but John Junior and I went to the creek and walked over the stones, listening to the brook babble over the rocks. One day, I found this stone that had been tumbled smooth." She took it from him and ran her finger over the crystal. "There are many on George Hill, but most are rough. Father sent some back to England early on, to see what they might be. The Nashaway men were told the rocks meant ores might be found in this area, maybe gold or silver." This one is shiny and shows the black cross. That's why I give it to you."

Jonas stuck it in his pocket and rubbed it on his way back and forth each day.

Another time, Jonas whittled a whistle for Lydia. She always tried to mimic the birdcalls when she was with him.

"You should hear the Indians whistle birdcalls; you can't tell them from the birds themselves," said Lydia in amazement. "Mother won't let me whistle." She rocked her head from side to side mocking her mother. "'Whistling girls and cackling hens always come to some bad ends.' I want to talk with the birds."

On the side of the tree, Jonas carved their initials. He remembered how his older brothers, allowed to have knives on the ship, carved their names in the wood of their bunking space. This was far more satisfying than carving his name on a ship.

The delicate green of spring took on the deeper hue of summer. The meetinghouse was almost finished. Jonas hesitated one day as he left a folded note in the hole of the tree. Lydia searched the elm knot while they were together. Jonas's face, neck, and ears burned as she drew the paper out.

Jonas grabbed the paper before Lydia could open it and held it high. "This is for later. When you're alone."

Lydia, quick and agile, jumped, snatched the paper, and ran a short distance. She knew Jonas wouldn't follow. He'd draw the attention of the other men.

Lydia read the poem in a whisper.

"When winter's days are past and gone
May pleasant calms appear,
I know sometimes in ashes deep
Sleep hidden coals of fire,
With these few lines
You will a question find,
Sweet is the answer, mark it well,
Friend, farewell, farewell."

A cloud covered the sun and stirred a sudden wind that threatened rain. "Jonas?" Lydia asked, her face contorting with emotion. "What does this mean? Are you leaving? Are you going back to Hammersmith?" She collapsed to the ground with the message in her lap. "I know the meetinghouse is near done, but Father is planning an ironworks and a sawmill. I want—*we* want you to stay."

"Lydia, you must know your mother and father have encouraged me toward Sarah. Even Hannah is older than you. But in this poem, you will find my real feelings. You will understand why I must leave." Jonas folded the paper, pressed it into her palm and cupped his hands over hers until the paper disappeared. "Don't read this again until you are alone, then show it to no one. If you cannot figure it out, read only the first words of each line."

Then Jonas rose to his feet and held his hat to his heart. "I'm leaving for Dedham. I'll only return if I can offer you more than a poem."

Challenges of Love

Before leaving Lancaster, Jonas surveyed the parcel of land next to Prescott's trucking house. George Adams, an early investor in Nashaway, had defaulted on his covenant and his land had reverted back to the town. It was a long, gentle slope running from a meadow up the face of George Hill to a large rock near the top. The ground would be easy to till in the meadow, but there was some clearing to do on the hill. Jonas would do whatever was necessary to marry Lydia, the Prescott daughter he loved. With the money from working for his brother, for the forge at Hammersmith, and for Prescott here at Lancaster, he could buy the Adams land.

Mordecai had received land a distance north of the main town. Jonas went there to bid him and Rugg goodbye as they built Mordecai a small house. Then he urged Buck through the slush of late spring rains with Traveler at Buck's heels.

When he reached Natick, instead of turning to Dedham, Jonas turned south along the Charles River toward Medfield. He'd talk with Richard Wheeler before returning to Lancaster. As he rode, he mused. *My good friends have lost wives recently and suddenly. Rugg lost Martha and the twins at the same time.*

321

Wheeler lost his wife and two of his children on the same day as well. Having a wife involved too much hurt. The silence of the ride did not quiet his mind. *Who am I to deceive myself? If this works, even God ordains this marriage.*

Jonas knocked at Richard Wheeler's door, and his friend called,"Come in." from inside the house. Richard's hands were tangled in his young daughter's braids as his son played with the butt of his gun near the door. Jonas picked up the little boy and carried him to where Richard was struggling.

"It appears you could use some help," said Jonas, still holding the squirming toddler.

"The town ladies help me with the children while I do chores and work the fields, but then I must repay by helping their husbands. By the time I return home, we all fall asleep, usually in my bed. We start all over at the crack of dawn the next morning. I wasn't meant to be a housewife."

"I think I can help you."

Richard offered up the ends of the braid. Jonas laughed. "Not like that."

Finally, Richard twisted the hair and curled it on top of his daughter's head. He smashed her slightly dingy cap on top of it. "Maybe Goodwife Fales can deal with this."

"Is George's former apprentice in Medfield now?"

"Aye, but how are you going to help *me*?" Richard took his young son from Jonas, who had wrinkled his nose and held the boy at a distance. Richard went to a basket of laundry Jonas knew must have been done by neighboring women.

"If I can find you a wife in Lancaster, would you be willing to move?"

"I would like to know who the woman is. Is she kind to children?" Richard put the boy on the table board to change

322

him. "How well do you know her? Is there good land out there for me?"

"She is Sarah Prescott."

"The Prescotts. You talk about them frequently. Why aren't *you* marrying her?" Richard raised his eyebrows.

"I'm going to marry her younger sister."

"Then there is something wrong with this Sarah. How old is she?"

"She is a fine young lady who has helped raise her younger siblings and her sister's children, too."

Richard stared at Jonas as if he were leaving something out.

"She's twenty-one years old," Jonas said and hesitated. "I'm in love with her youngest sister."

"And how old is *she*?"

"Seventeen."

"She's Martha's age!" Wheeler glared at Jonas and threw the dirty linen out the back door into a pail of water.

"I know. I didn't even know I was falling in love. But I think she knew it all along."

"By Gaw, Fairbanks. You think I can bail you out of this one?"

"If Sarah is betrothed first and the other sister marries the man she fancies, the youngest will be free to marry."

"So, what's your design?"

"Your children can stay with Mother and Martha while you and I go to Lancaster before it's time to plant. You can meet Sarah there. I think you'll really like her." Jonas paused. He knew this was a lot to take in. "You and I could live in the same town. I'm sure Prescott will help you find land there. He and his wife, Mary, want to keep their daughters close."

"I would fancy getting away for a few days if your mother and Martha are willing to take my three a while."

Jonas went home to fulfill his duties on the farm, more

concerned with sowing a relationship between Sarah and Richard than with planting his father's field. As soon as he washed the Dedham soil from his hands, he returned to Lancaster with Wheeler. He was also returning to Lydia, hoping Richard and Sarah would be suited for each other.

They topped the Wattaquadock Hills and looked over the valley, with no fog over the rivers this day. As Wheeler took in the English parklike valley dotted with lakes, Jonas exclaimed, "Even royalty would want to build their country houses among these trees and lakes." The blue sky contained mounds of billowing clouds that were reflected in the two ribbons of the lazy rivers below.

Jonas pointed at George Hill, the old trucking house, and the brook. That was his marker for what would be his land, the area that lay just southwest of it. "There's plenty of land for you, too."

"I hope Sarah is as pretty as this land," Richard said, and smiled sheepishly.

Jonas hurried them on to Prescott's to meet Sarah. The family welcomed Wheeler, but Sarah kept her distance. As Grace had brought young ladies to meet with Jonas, Sarah's father had brought every eligible suitor to their door, and Sarah was wary of having to deal with another one. But before long, she was intrigued by their lively conversation and joined in.

Shortly thereafter that evening, Rugg came to the door, bringing Mary some early produce from his garden.

"Since I eat supper with you often, I hope you can use this," said Rugg, staring hard at Wheeler, wondering if he were another suitor for the Prescott girls. "Who's the stranger?"

"This is Richard Wheeler," said Jonas. "I told you about him." Rugg relaxed as he looked in Hannah's direction.

Wheeler had to return to his children and farm, but by the time he left, he and Sarah had agreed that a marriage was in both their interests, and Richard was pleased. There weren't many single women in Medfield that would marry Richard with his three children, for there was an abundance of single men on Bachelor's Row.

Sarah and Wheeler agreed to post banns of marriage when Richard had laid by his crops at Medfield and returned to Lancaster to prepare a place for Sarah and the children. Jonas, knowing Sarah Prescott had a suitable match and that John Rugg had his eye on Hannah, cherished the thought that, at last, Lydia would be free to marry.

Wheeler and Jonas returned to Dedham to make preparations. Jonas needed to build a house quickly for Lydia and himself, so it couldn't be a garrison house—Mordecai and the Prescotts would help. When Wheeler came to Lancaster, they would garrison his house using the knowledge they gained building George's fortified house in Medfield. Jonas wanted to find land close to his for Wheeler.

Jonas looked forward to telling his mother he was marrying her best friend's daughter.

As much as it delighted Grace, she couldn't help but remark, "But Jonas, she is so young."

"Lo, Mother, we are in love. She's a better match than you could make for me here. She's not like Dedham girls—she grew up in the wilderness."

In early May, Jonas returned to Lancaster to find a garden patch already on his property with corn, peas, squash and herbs planted. Lydia and her brothers and father had opened it for him. He felt quite welcomed.

Jonas surveyed the land with satisfaction, but then suddenly, an uneasy motivation engulfed him. He was responsible for someone besides himself. He'd have to get in a late crop beyond the garden.

It was dusk when he got to the Prescott house. Sarah was the only one who didn't greet him. Busying herself, she barely looked in his direction. When the evening meal was finished, Jonas asked, "John, Mary, may I ask Lydia to walk with me?"

Jonas and Lydia walked far enough from the dimly lit house to become shadows in the starlit night. Jonas took Lydia's hand and pulled her close. "I want to marry you right away."

Lydia hugged him so tight, he didn't need an answer.

"We'll post banns now. Then all we need to do is find someone to marry us," Jonas explained. "I already asked Mr. Rowlandson, but he doesn't have a colony license to perform a marriage."

"What about Mr. Tinker?" asked Lydia.

"The man who bought your father's trucking house?"

"Aye. Father said he acted as a lawyer and magistrate in Boston before he came here. Oh, Jonas, we could be married in Lancaster, not another town."

"Could your father talk with Mr. Tinker?"

Lydia nodded and crooned, "Since you built the meetinghouse, do you think we might be married *there*?" She looked up into his dark eyes as they held hands.

"That would be an honor, but the meetinghouse hasn't been used for any town function yet. I don't want to wait until it's been inaugurated to get married."

They ran hand in hand to the house with their plan. Slightly breathless from the run and the idea of marriage, they announced their engagement and asked Prescott about the meetinghouse.

"It's only right, Jonas. You did the most to build the place. The town has no plans for it until our June first selectmen's meeting. You and Lydia should be married there."

"We want to be married in Lancaster." Lydia pleaded, "If we bring someone from Sudbury or Marlborough, they will claim the marriage for their town."

Prescott smiled toward his daughter. "I will ask Mr. Tinker if he could perform the marriage."

Mr. John Tinker regretted that he didn't have a license to perform the ceremony. Though he was eligible, it was late to petition for the privilege. Jonas and Lydia might have to wait or have their marriage registered in another town as had all the young couples of Lancaster before them.

Message

Now sixty-eight years old and feeling it keenly, Jonathan came in from the fields one evening as the sun blinked its last light over the Dedham hills. "Grace, I'm an old man. My bones talk of hard work, harsh winters, and scalding summers. Until Jonas left, I didn't realize how much I relied on him."

"Aren't John's sons helping?"

"Aye, but there are only two, and they're young. It takes both to make up the work of Jonas—he knew just what to do."

"That's good," said Grace. "He'll need to know what to do to open his own farm in Lancaster. Sit down and read this—a messenger brought it from New London." She waved a folded paper in the air. He saw it had a red wax seal, with a raised heart within a box.

"It's Richard Hartley's seal," Jonathan said. "I wonder when he's coming back." He carefully slipped a knife under the wax. He read parts aloud to Grace.

"'Dear and Loving Friend,' he begins." Jonathan read a moment in silence, then added, "He says that Minister Blinman… You know the New London minister that came by here? I think he stayed for dinner?"

Grace nodded.

"Mr. Blinman informed Hartley about the business I've

done for him. Hartley says he must stay in New London for the present. He's asking me to use his ten pounds to buy cloth and send it to New London with Amos Richardson, the merchant tailor from Groton. If that's too much trouble, he wants me to keep the ten pounds until next spring and turn it to a profit for him."

"He is very trusting, Jonathan."

"Aye, and he wants me to collect the debts owed him by several men in Dedham, pay what he owes, and keep the rest in hand until we meet."

"Sounds like you are the merchant here until next spring," said Grace.

"It doesn't sound like Hartley plans to return. Of course, he does have a warehouse and wharf at New London for all his shipping." Jonathan paused, then said, "You'll like this, Grace. He's giving us his bedstead from his Dedham house." He looked up at Grace as she beamed. "And a hoe for seeing after his business."

"His bedstead. That's a fine gift. He values you highly."

Weddings

On May 26, 1658, Mr. Tinker rushed to the Prescott house and held up the paper the family had anxiously awaited.

Tinker read the document ceremoniously. "It is ordered that Mr. John Tinker shall & is hereby empowered to marry . . . Jonas Fairbanks & Lydia Prescott . . . who are published according to lawe." The order included other couples in the town, but none before Jonas and Lydia. "I had no idea how busy I'd become until the town found out I was getting this permit," he said as he chuckled.

"Oh, Father," Lydia said, "we must get married soon if we are to inaugurate the meetinghouse. We have only four more days."

"You can't be married on the Sabbath," said Prescott

"And I must notify my family," Jonas said with a smile. "Mother will demand to come."

"Of course, they must be here," Prescott replied. "Send a note by the messenger that brought Tinker's approval. He's still at the tavern."

About a week after Grace gave Richard Hartley's message to Jonathan, Grace's face lit up as she handed him another letter.

Jonathan looked at the paper and shifted his eyes to Grace. "The seal's missing." Martha giggled in the background.

Grace grabbed the message and waved it in the air. "Jonas and Lydia are getting married."

"Aye, finally." Jonathan peered at Grace with caution. "You will go, will you not?"

Grace hesitated, but then she said resolutely, "The Sudbury River that almost killed Mary and her children won't keep me from the wedding of my son who is marrying my best friend's daughter. But Jonathan, we have no time to plan. They are having the wedding as soon as we arrive, before June 1. We must go now."

Early the next morning, with white knuckles Grace held onto the side of the cart and took a deep breath as they started over Sudbury Bridge. The river churned only a few feet below the bridge because of the spring thaw. She peered into the dark boiling water where her best friend and her children almost drowned thirteen years before.

The three Fairbankses arrived with Richard Wheeler at Lancaster that evening, the night before the whole town would attend the wedding. Martha excitedly inspected the preparations for her *brother's* nuptials—there would be plenty of fine cakes and rum.

Richard Wheeler stood by Sarah during the ceremony and celebration as she looked longingly at Jonas and Lydia. Sarah put her hand in Richard's. They would have their own house built by August, so he and his children could come to Lancaster.

John Rugg, not so recently widowed now, stood next to Hannah, and everyone knew his fondness for her.

Mordecai had come into town from his farm in northern Lancaster. No one celebrated Jonas's marriage more than he. After all, he'd revealed to Jonas that Lydia had feelings for him. The Scotsman stood close to Rugg and took in the English customs, but after some rum, Mordecai entertained the whole town with stories, songs, and dance.

The Fairbanks family bumped over the rutted cart path on their way home. Jonathan turned to sixteen-year-old Martha in the back. "You are the only young one not married now," he said.

"Not for long," said Martha. Both Jonathan and Grace quickly looked back to see her grinning so big that the jostling might break her teeth. "Benjamin Bullard is building a house next to George's in Medfield," she explained. She paused and looked from one to the other. "That house is for me."

Grace gasped.

"Don't worry, Gammar, we'll court for a year and get married early next April. Benjamin can put in a crop, and I can put in a garden."

"I'm not worried, dear," said Grace. "I'm happy you found a worthy husband, and that you'll live next to George and Mary."

"But what about the chores and dairy?" Jonathan asked Grace.

"Not to worry. John's Sarah is thirteen now and much help. We'll make do. We no longer need a big garden nor to preserve as much food. And our girls always come home to help me."

"I will, too," added Martha.

"Another wedding," mumbled Jonathan to the horse as he snapped the reins over its rump.

Shy but excited, Lydia prepared herself for her wedding night. Her older sisters were little help. Marie had ten years' worth of children to mind, and the others were not married yet and could not advise her. Lydia remembered how happy Martha had been when she'd married John Rugg. The sadness of losing her and the twins lived in a dark corner of Lydia's mind.

Lydia had long looked forward to this day, with joy and with trepidation. It was a time in a woman's life that young girls whispered about in secret. The elderly ladies in town patted Lydia's shoulder and shared their sage advice: "Keep him happy, Lydia."

Hannah asked Lydia if she wanted help preparing her linens and shift for the wedding night. Lydia was happy to have Hannah help sew the new dusky blue dress she would wear when standing before Mr. Tinker in the ceremony. But she feared taking Hannah's offer of additional help would bring bad luck—she needed to prepare her own apparel for the marriage bed.

Jonas waited in the hall, thinking of how, earlier that week, they had tied the rope knots of the bed that would hold them and their marriage together every night. Their short, formal courting had not given them an opportunity to bundle as other couples did—fully clothed and with a chaperone. As he waited, he imagined her slipping out of her wedding clothes and welcoming him to their bed.

"You may come in, my husband," Lydia said, then giggled.

Jonas peeked around the corner from the hall, took off all

but his long shirt, and climbed in beside her, under the light sheet in the early summer heat. He was careful not to rush upon Lydia but let his fingers trace the delicate embroidery at the top of her nuptial shift.

As Jonas's body quieted, he took his wife in his arms and smoothed back the treasure of curls he had so longed to touch. It was like letting gold fall between his fingers. He peered into Lydia's swimming eyes and pulled back slightly. "Are you all right? Did I do something wrong?"

"I'm tender, but not broken," she whispered. "This was so new to me. I hope soon, as we become one again, I can bring to you the passion you bring to me." She paused, and Jonas wiped a tear rolling down her soft, flushed cheek with his thumb.

"I hope we have a baby," she whispered.

Goodbyes 1659

Jonathan and Grace held their capes around themselves and pulled hoods and hats on as they rode through the incessant spring rain. The muddy path sucked at the wheels of the cart, threatening to mire it. The church bell pealed to call the congregation to the wedding of Benjamin Bullard and Martha Pidge.

Grace whispered, "You look splendid" to her daughter Susan, in her eighth month of pregnancy, as they entered the meetinghouse. Susan and Ralph Daye's ten-year-old daughter carried two-year-old Ralph, as he did not fit well over Susan's protruding belly. The Dayes found their reserved bench for their whole family, including their other two children, ages six and five, who followed their parents.

Grace proudly looked over at Jonathan and took his arm to get his attention. "More grandchildren," she said. "Our family fills most of the meetinghouse. It's good they added the upper galleries in time for the wedding."

The ceremony was simple, and George and Mary entertained the guests at their house afterwards. Martha and Benjamin would spend their first night together in their own house next door.

"Won't you be lonely out here away from Dedham?" Grace asked Martha, who had been with her since she was four, the only child at home most of that time. Grace doted on her.

"No," said Martha as she gave Grace a loving hug. "I have Benjamin, George and Mary, and all their children. Benjamin and I hope to have a family soon ourselves."

Grace felt alone amongst all the people enjoying the wedding fare. Her own home suddenly seemed too big to return to for just the two of them. While she was lost in her thoughts, a young boy pushed through skirts and breeches in the crowd to hug Grace around the knees. She ruffled his hair and whispered as she looked into his eyes, "We'll fill the house with you grandchildren every time we can gather you together."

A few days later, Jonathan came in from chores and propped his long gun by the door. "Grace?" he called. No answer. He hadn't seen her in the garden, the chicken yard, nor the barn. "Martha?" His voice seemed to echo off the wooden walls as he remembered his mistake. Since Martha had gotten married, the house was too quiet.

Grace bustled through the door with a basket of quilt pieces. "You're home," she said, setting down her basket, and taking off her cape.

"Is supper ready?" asked Jonathan.

"I've been at a quilting bee all day. We're making a quilt for Susan's next baby."

"Martha's not here to warm it up, either," grumbled Jonathan, looking around as if he had lost something.

"No, it's just you and me."

"I don't think I like that."

"You do like grandchildren, don't you? Susan is about to give you another."

"Harrumph," Jonathan gave Grace a tight squeeze. "In the forty-two years we've been married, we've had children in the house for forty-one."

"Don't worry—the children and grandchildren all live close, except Jonas. Christmas will fill this big house you built."

In the steamy heat of a July night, Jonathan and Grace slept with their lightest bed clothes over them. Grace was restless. As darkness cooled the earth, an urgent knock startled her, and Grace pulled the bed rug up to her chin. Jonathan roused, too, pulled his breeches on, not tucking in his shirt, and reached for his gun by the door before opening it.

Ralph Daye stood there disheveled and panting. "Grace," he called, looking past Jonathan.

Grace sat up, letting the bed linen fall. "It's coming finally?" From her calculations, Susan should have had this baby a couple of weeks ago.

"She needs you now."

"I have a bag packed. I can be ready quickly."

Ralph went into the hall to give Grace privacy, pacing as Jonathan, seasoned by the births of his children and grandchildren over the decades, offered him ale, cider, beer, and even rum.

Ralph shook his head and paced.

"I'm ready," announced Grace. "Take me to her, then bring the children here and stay with Jonathan until I call for you. Notify the women nearest your house to come to help with Susan."

A few minutes later, Grace bustled into the Daye house

and found Susan during a strong contraction, her face flushed and twisted grotesquely. Between contractions, Susan whined, "Mother, this came on so quickly."

"Yes, they often do when you've had five."

Grace lost Susan's attention to another contraction as two neighbor women joined them. Grace had presided over many births and methodically pulled the sheets up to check Susan's progress. She found the sheet under her daughter wet and tinged with black.

The other women gasped behind their hands and stepped back. Grace kept her concern concealed from Susan and checked for the baby's head. "The head is coming first," Grace said with a sigh of relief. The head surged against Susan's soft tissues as another contraction convulsed her.

Grace remained calm, hoping Susan had been too occupied by the contraction to notice the other women's reactions. "Now Susan, the baby is big, and you will tear more this time, but it has to come now."

Grace was stern but gentle. She slathered butter on Susan's flesh around the baby's head to protect Susan as much as possible from the tearing pressure. The next contraction produced the baby's bluish face, and the next revealed one shoulder. Grace put her finger in the baby's armpit and gently pulled the infant downward. "One more push, Susan. Make it a good one."

The tear was already long, and the baby slid out without more help. It was bluish and covered in black stickiness. Grace's eyes swam with tears as she struggled to keep her voice steady.

Grace quickly handed the baby boy to one of the women waiting with a clean cloth. The new quilt lay on the dresser.

"Turn him upside down and rub him vigorously while I deliver the afterbirth."

The baby was blue, quiet, listless, and covered in black stickiness, streaked with blood. The woman shook and slapped the baby to get him to breathe. Ultimately, she covered the perfect baby boy, head to toe, in cotton cloth.

Susan, exhausted, didn't notice the bustle of activity around the baby in the back of the room.

"She's bleeding," Grace said quietly to the woman who left the infant and was standing next to her with a wooden bowl for the afterbirth. Goody Daye, Susan's mother-in-law, handed Grace clean cloths as tears streamed down her cheeks.

"Susan," Grace called. "Susan!" Grace called louder. "Open your eyes."

"Mother, I'm seasick. I want off this boat."

Grace motioned for Goody Daye to put pressure on the gaping wound where the big baby had made his way out of his tiny mother.

Grace went to Susan's head. With bloody-black streaked fingers, she brushed the matted hair back from Susan's face. "I'm sorry, Susan," she whispered. "I'm sorry."

On the next Sabbath, Mr. Allin officially announced to the congregation the death of Susan Fairbanks Daye and her stillborn baby boy. No one was surprised, for nearly the whole town had joined the procession to the cemetery several days earlier.

Grace had lost grandchildren before, but never one of her own daughters. Try as she might, as her faith demanded, she couldn't relegate Susan's body to the earth without sadness. The hole that they opened to receive Susan and her baby was no larger than the tear made in Grace's heart.

At church, Grace heard little of what Mr. Allin said after he mentioned Susan's name. He did mention the drought that had come after the torrential rains of spring. Grace's heart was drying up, too, after a torrent of tears.

Then the minister declared a ban on Christmas. The meetinghouse rumbled as Grace's head swirled into a fury. She popped off the bench in the middle of the announcement, full of anger and bewilderment. Realizing suddenly where she was, she dropped down and held a handkerchief to her face. Christmas had been a special time for Susan. She loved the evergreen boughs, the Yule log, and the Yule candle more than just about anyone. How could the wassailers and mummers ruin it?

Grace envisioned the mazer bowl in its special spot in the parlor. They had used it for all special family occasions. It had held water to baptize her grandchildren and had come to represent their family as a unit. *WE WILL pass the mazer bowl to unite the family at Christmas,* she promised herself.

Mediation and Court 1660–1661

Mr. Allin pleaded for the town to give him and the church one more chance to rectify the dispute between Dedham and the Natives. Mr. Allin and Mr. John Eliot, pastor of the Church of Roxbury and Apostle to the Indians, had presented the land issue to selected clergy in hopes that they could solve the problem without going to court.

The clerics closed their session by saying, "We doubt that anyone will own error in this occasion, but we hope they will acknowledge it. We hope there will be forbearance and forgiveness of one another with loving communication for the future, as is called for in the book of Colossians, 3:12:13."

The meetinghouse bell rang out on an ordinary weekday in October, and men looked up from their fieldwork to count the rings and rhythm to assure it was not an alarm. They were being called, again, to a special meeting of all proprietors.

"I'll bet it's about the Natick Indians again." called John, as he forked dry hay onto the cart.

"How are we to get our work done?" asked Junior.

"Come on boys," said Jonathan, circling his arm as he walked toward the meetinghouse.

The sons brushed grass off their clothes and joined the others.

Edward Richards, the selectman in charge, knew he had to get other business out of the way before bringing up the real issue. Richards announced the recently laid boundaries of Dedham's newest town, Wrentham, formally called Wollomonopoag. He asked the men not moving to that area to sell their Wrentham meadows to those residing there, to encourage families to settle this new town south of Dedham.

Then Richards announced, "It's been nine months since the lots south of the river near Natick were granted to our proprietors. There's been no resolution to the dispute over the land allotted to Dedham proprietors yet claimed and improved by Natick men. We will act as a society, paying all court costs in this matter. We will go to court."

After ten years of stalled negotiations of ownership between Dedham and Natick land, both sides gave extensive testimonies at the Suffolk County Court. Time passed slowly for the men awaiting the verdict.

On January 2, the County Court magistrates sat before both parties, presiding at their table in their black clothes, lace collars, and broad feathered hats. People from many communities gathered in the gallery to hear the decision.

The jury foreman rose and said simply, "The jury has found for the plaintiffs, Dedham."

A rustle spread through the courtroom.

"Upon hearing the testimonies of both parties, only such lands that are free from former grants and have not been taken up by others, by order of this court." A barely audible sigh emanated from the Dedham contingency visibly relaxing on the floor and in the gallery.

But a foreboding murmur emanated from the magistrates' table as their heads formed a tight circle. Then the gavel reported against the wooden block and a magistrate rose to speak. "The magistrates refuse the verdict, and the case will go to the Court of Assistance on October 21 of this year."

Once again, the Dedham men sat behind Lt. Fisher, Sgt. Fisher, and Eleazur Lusher on one side of the chambers of the Court of Assistance. Mr. Eliot sat in his pastor's vestments with various Natives from Natick on the other side. The testimonies were repeated before this jury, and the courtroom rumbled as they waited for this panel's verdict.

The room fell silent as the jury returned after a lengthy deliberation. The spokesman for the panel was recognized by the magistrates. "Your honors," he said, "the jury finds for the plaintiffs, Dedham, in land and in cost of the court proceedings."

The head magistrate took the paper from the juror and nodded for him to sit. The papers were shared amongst the magistrates, who conversed in a low drone. The head magistrate looked up, plied the gavel and announced, "The magistrates request the jurors to leave to deliberate again."

The men of Dedham glanced at each other uneasily. How could this be happening?

Time drew on, and the jury again filed to their seats. The head juror held up a paper and addressed the magistrates. "Your honors, after further deliberation, some of the jurors dissented from the previous verdict."

A rumble filled the courtroom until the head magistrate cracked his gavel twice on the elevated table. "This case is adjourned until the next Court of Assistance on the 12th of May, 1662."

Discord filled the stately room, Eleazur Lusher bitterly complaining to the Dedham group. "That means we can't present our case to the General Court this spring; the papers for our case will be tied up in the Court of Assistance. Our case *needs* to be decided. It's been too long."

The Dedham men filed out of the courtroom, solemn and disgusted. When they got outside the building, Lusher stopped as many as he could. "I have a plan," he said. "When you get back to Dedham, tell whoever you see to attend a special session at the meetinghouse as soon as the bell rings."

Petition 1662

Lusher drew up a petition to present to the General Court and summoned the townsmen with the bell. Jonathan, John, and Junior Fairbanks entered the meetinghouse together because their grant land south of the Charles River was affected by this struggle.

Lusher stood before the proprietors and explained the process of trying to help bring education and religion to the Natives near Dedham for the past eleven years. Now it had ended in a dispute over the land. "This petition requests the General Court to release the papers of all previous testimonies and proceedings that were being held by the Court of Assistance. The General Courts must have these when they sit this spring to hear our case. If we miss that session of the high court, we will have to wait another six months."

"What are the chances this will work?" asked a young voice.

"If we don't try, there's no way it can," said Jonathan Fairbanks, invoking his role as a founder.

"Each month that passes, the Natives improve more of our land," said another.

"Where are they to go, if the General Court sides with Dedham?" asked another voice.

"I don't know," said Lusher. "What I do know is we gave them free and clear two thousand acres and more. There were only fifty-one Indians to begin with and now there are sixty. We asked for no return for that land. We all support the education and conversion efforts, but if we allow them to move further and further south, none of our land is safe. They haven't abided by the bounds we set, so let the court set the bounds once and for all. At least we should get recompense for any additional land we cede to them."

Lusher placed the petition on the table facing the proprietors. He pushed the inkwell and pen towards them. "All we ask here is for our papers to be transferred to the General Court for a final decision on our land dispute," he said.

Jonathan and Michael Metcalf, Sr., signed just after the selectmen. When it was John Fairbanks's turn, he took the quill and set down his own name.

Junior was next in line, and Jonathan noted that men he'd known for many years were as well: James Fales, George's former apprentice, and Ralph Daye, poor Susan's widower.

Jonathan's sons rejoined him as the rest of the forty-seven men signed. "We want this case to be decided for Dedham, but more than anything, I think every man wants this whole thing to be over. We will support whatever the General Court decides. It is in God's hands," said Jonathan.

More Loss

Grace's flax-spinning wheel hummed until she heard a knock at the door and opened it to a stranger. In his hand was a missive with a red seal, a heart inside a square. Grace recognized the seal as Richard Hartley's and held out her hand for it.

"I must hand this directly to Jonathan Fairbanks. Could you take me to him?" asked the stranger.

"Aye, he's in the barn."

Grace and the messenger walked silently along the path. Grace couldn't help glancing back at the ominous folded paper.

Jonathan pitched another fork of hay out of the loft to the whinnying horses and kicked more hay into the back of the loft, preparing to fill it with the summer harvest.

"Jonathan," called Grace, "there's a messenger."

"Aye, a minute," Jonathan said, and climbed down the wooden ladder slowly while bits of dried grass fell from his clothes to the floor.

"You look like a scarecrow," said Grace as she brushed at more grass.

"Good morrow, my good man," said Jonathan. "What can I do for you that my wife couldn't handle?" Then he saw the red sealed message in the stranger's hand and reached for it.

The stranger held it away.

"It's my sad duty to inform you that Richard Hartley has died in New London on August 7," said the messenger, then handed Jonathan the paper.

"But…" Jonathan hesitated.

"His death was unexpected. His will was written August 5. He was attended by a midwife as he passed."

"Aye, his wife and daughter are in England, I believe," said Jonathan, looking over at Grace.

"I'll take my leave, Goodman Fairbanks," said the man. "My service is done."

Jonathan held the message in his hand and looked at the seal while Grace walked the stranger to the house and gave him a coin from Jonathan's pouch, bidding him "Ta."

Jonathan was at the house by the time the stranger rode off.

He sat in the hall in his work clothes. He didn't even take off his work shoes.

Grace brought his spectacles to the table as he broke the seal and looked over the message.

"Grace, Hartley had no sons. He says he is leaving his property to his wife and daughter. If she chooses not to come to New England, the house-lot, warehouse and wharf are to be sold in her name. I am supposed to close out his accounts here and make sure his wife and daughter receive them."

Jonathan's eyes swam as he looked up at Grace. "We are fortunate to have our sons and daughters. They will always take care of you."

General Court May 1663

It was tedious waiting for the General Court's call to reveal whether the Dedham vs. Natick case would be heard. Any time Constable Elice passed in town, everyone's eyes followed him.

Dedham men bailed out of the land dividends they had received in the disputed area. Most came to the selectmen suggesting specific lands in recompense.

During a February snowstorm, Constable Elice knocked on Eleazur Lusher's door, holding a paper in his gloved hand. "You have been summoned to General Court on the seventh day of May of the year, 1663, for the case to be heard between the plaintiffs, the town of Dedham, and the defendants, the town of Natick.

Lusher sent the notice to Mr. Allin to announce before the sermon on the next Sabbath.

"Huzzah, Huzzah, Huzzah!" the congregation cheered.

Grace leaned over to Mary Elizabeth and said, "You'd think they'd won the case, but they are just happy to finally get to General Court for a firm decision."

Many attended court in Boston to hear the final verdict on Dedham's years of discontent. Tension grew for the Dedham representatives; the exhaustion of their testimonies and years of emotional expenditure weighed heavily. The presence of their fellow townsmen in the gallery buoyed them as they waited for the magistrates.

The officials in their fine dark clothes returned to the room in a single file with decisive, determined steps. They called representatives of the plaintiffs and defendants to come before them. These men stood, anticipating the gravity of this decision.

The head magistrate pronounced the verdict:

For a final issue of the controversy between the town of Dedhame & some particular inhabitants of the said town & the Indians at Natick, the Court, having considered the pleas & evidences presented by both parties, and finding that although the legal right of Dedham thereto cannot in justice be denied, yet such have been the encouragement of the Indians in their improvements thereof, the which, added to their native right, which cannot, in strict justice, be utterly extinct, do therefore order, that the Indians be not dispossessed of such lands as they at present are possessed of there, but that the same, with convenient accommodation for wood, & timber, & high-wayes thereto, be set out & bounded . . . and that the damages thereby sustained by Dedham, together with the charges expended in suit about the same, be also considered & determined . . . , & such allowance made them out of Natick lands or others yet lying in common as they shall judge equal, & appoint, making report to this Court the matter of charge, that so the Court may determine where to lay the same or any part thereof.

Then the man sat down again, and the men in the gallery whispered amongst themselves.

"See, the General Court agrees the land is ours," said John Fairbanks to his brother.

"Aye, but they also say it belongs to the Indians," said Junior.

"In the end," said Jonathan, "the Indians will keep all the land they improved. But finally, we'll get just compensation for the land that we gave and the additional we are ceding, along with the expense of the court cases."

"What do you think, Father?" asked John, leaning past his brother to talk directly to Jonathan.

"I think we need to start looking for land that hasn't already been granted to others. The Indians couldn't find any nearby for themselves. We also need to know how much we will be compensated."

Finally, the General Court set the bounds between Dedham and Natick. The committee found sixty Natives living on 4000 acres of improved land that included land north and south of the Charles River.

The committee further proposed that the town of Dedham be given five hundred pounds sterling, to be paid by the Country at one hundred pounds per annum, or four thousand acres out of the common lands of the Country for land ceded. Later, on May 27, it was determined that Dedham should have eight thousand acres of land in compensation, and Dedham was responsible for finding land not previously granted.

When the proprietors met, someone voiced their greatest concern: "There's no farmable land close that hasn't been granted, or the Natives would have taken it. Where are we to find the eight thousand acres the court has granted us?"

"Maybe we should take the one hundred pounds sterling each year that the General Court offered as an option," called another voice.

"But good land, once it's improved, yields more than that, and it would be up to each proprietor to earn the gains. How would we divide the money, anyway?" countered Lusher. "Fairbanks, your son Jonas is in Lancaster with your friend John Prescott, correct?"

"Aye."

"There's newly opened land there. Might they know of eight thousand acres that we could take as our compensation grant?"

"Jonas and Prescott laid out 640 acres of Colony land just southwest of Lancaster for Captain Richard Davenport for his public service in 1658," said Jonathan. "It's good land." He tapped his son's shoulder and said, "John here could ride to Lancaster and talk with Jonas and Prescott about land availability."

"We'll send Lt. Fisher with him," said John Dwight.

Ah, to have land near my wayward son would be a blessing, thought Jonathan. "John, you and Lt. Fisher get right on that before the land is taken by others.

Elder John Hunting, the presiding selectman of the next Dedham meeting, started by saying, "John Fairbanks and Lt. Fisher, we're sorry your expedition to Lancaster wasn't fruitful." He shuffled through some papers and said, "However, we have information about a tract of land about seventy miles away, north of Hadley in the Great River Valley."

A general restlessness and low murmurs blanketed the crowd. Seventy miles was a long way.

Hunting continued. "Captain John Pynchon, a land trader, found this land abandoned by the Pocumtuck People, who were preyed heavily upon by the Mohawks."

"Considering we haven't found another place worth accepting, I think it wise we look at it," said Peter Woodward.

"Do it soon," called Dr. Avery, "before other grantees enter upon it."

"Lt. Fisher will lead a committee to look at the land." instructed Elder Hunting. "Will you join him, John?

"Nay," said John Fairbanks. "The Fairbankses have just received our land in Wrentham. I'll stay and settle that."

I'll get more grant land seventy miles away, thought Jonathan Fairbanks. About a mile for every year of his life. He was in no hurry to farm there.

Changing Troubles 1665

Jonathan stayed with his cousin Richard Fairbanks on a trip to Boston. His cousin asked, "So, what do you think of King Charles II after two years of reign?"

"We've had so many boundary problems in Dedham, I haven't kept abreast of happenings in England. Jonas did say Joseph Jenke of Hammersmith made the die cast for a new colony coin. I don't suppose the king was fond of that."

"Aye, did he add that they put a pine tree on the coin instead of the king's image, and they are melting the English coins to make the colony coins?"

Jonathan looked wide-eyed at Richard. "The king is not happy, I'm sure."

"Aye, and the king's Navigation Acts seem a bit harsh," said Richard. "We should be able to trade with anyone, but we must have our goods stop in England, so they can tax us. It takes longer for me to get supplies."

"Agreed," said Jonathan.

"Things are getting more intense," said Richard. "King Charles II is mandating we follow English laws regardless of whether they align with our religious principles or not. He's sending commissioners to reaffirm our loyalty and make sure we comply. The king is trying to revoke the charter and consolidate all the colonies."

Richard looked up to see Elizabeth beckoning him to help with other customers.

"Excuse me. I hope to exchange some ale and wine for some pine tree coins." Richard smiled as he left.

Jonathan returned to Dedham to share Richard's information with the selectmen.

"Look at it this way," the chairman said. "The English government gave a charter to the governors of the Massachusetts Bay Colony to manage on our own. Now they want to take back our right to self-govern. Do you see similarities of the Massachusetts government giving us our Dedham land and telling us to give it back to the Indians?"

"But we have settled our differences with the Natick village. It's time to support our colony government," said Fairbanks.

"We could prepare a petition of support and present it personally to the General Court when we officially receive our Pocumtuck grant," said Eleazur Lusher.

"Can you get the petition written in time?" asked another.

"I'll have to gather all the facts. We must get enough men to sign it before we appear in court."

When the Dedham proprietors learned of the difficulty their colony government was having with England, they were eager to sign a petition of support. Jonathan proudly signed his signature as one of the sixty-nine proprietors who did so.

Omens 1668

Jonathan trod from the barn in the gathering cold of a March evening, pulling his collar tighter and searching the sky for signs of a storm. A chill enveloped him as a blazing ball followed by a long tail split the sky. Jonathan shuddered. *A comet—an omen? Have I become too complacent?* He continued to see the comet over several weeks but didn't tell Grace.

Nothing happened. A comet of that magnitude portended a disaster in the future, but over time, Jonathan forgot about it.

That May was the hottest Jonathan remembered. Bugs teemed around the barn, and he slapped at mosquitoes. One day toward the end of the month, after he completed his chores, Jonathan groaned as he pushed open their heavy front door. He had to jerk his hand away from his flank, before Grace could see him supporting it.

"Have you hurt your back, old man?" questioned Grace.

"Nay, the fields have been sown for some time and evening chores were light."

"Then you are just an old man," she teased. "I shall get you a staff."

"Bah—I keep up with the young men," said Jonathan. "Maybe not my grandsons . . ."

"Sit," commanded Grace. "I'll put your supper on."

Jonathan pushed his trencher away before finishing his meal. He rubbed his temples and held the back of his neck.

Grace put the back of her hand on her own forehead and then to his. "You're warm, even for a hot evening. You must wash and go to bed. I'll prepare an infusion."

"You worry so about me, Grace, because you don't have little ones to care for now." Jonathan went outside and pulled the bucket up with the well sweep. He poured a bit of water into a hollowed stone to wash himself. He sat on the edge of the well bracing himself with both hands, then swatting black buzzing insects as they swarmed around the water.

When Jonathan returned to the house, he didn't complain about Grace telling him to get into bed even before the kitchen hearth fire was stifled. Grace stayed up to finish her embroidery by the remains of the lamplight, then climbed into bed, hugging her edge. Jonathan's heat radiated. *If you'd only do that in the winter,* she thought.

Grace woke before Jonathan and prepared his breakfast before she met their granddaughter Sarah at the barn to milk the cows. The girl carried the pails to the lean-to using a shoulder yoke, then quickly straightened her clothing. "I must go, Gammar. I promised Mother I'd help her as soon as I finished here."

Grace hugged Sarah and went into the hall, where Jonathan's breakfast remained on the table. She crept around the hearth to the parlor to find Jonathan had thrown his bed linens off. Grace whispered his name, and Jonathan opened his eyes.

Grace gasped as her hands flew to her mouth. The deep yellow eyes of a swamp wolf stared at her.

"You're ill. You are very ill," she said. "I'll get Dr. Avery."

Jonathan opened his mouth to speak, and a bilious yellow geyser erupted from his mouth. Grace looked around fretfully. She could not leave Jonathan to go for help. She hung a white cloth outside the door, hoping a passerby would come to their rescue.

Vinegar for the fever. Milk thistle or burdock and turmeric for the yellow. Oh, this is too much like '51. "Stay with me, Jonathan," she pleaded.

Grace changed sheets, coaxed infusions down his throat, and drew fresh water from the well, mixing it with vinegar to cool his brow. Time passed slowly. She glanced regularly at the door and watched the sunrays pass the noon mark on their floor. She was not willing to step out to check their cherished brass sundial.

Grace started with hope when she heard a faint rapping at the door. She raced to open it—had her prayers been answered?

Eleven-year-old Hannah, John's youngest daughter, held up a small basket, "Mother said to bring these to you, Gammar."

"Oh darling, ta," said Grace, who took her granddaughter's shoulders and looked into her eyes. "Can you do something very important?"

Hannah's eyes grew wide.

"Run up the path to Dr. Avery's,"—Grace pointed north. "Tell the doctor to come *fast*."

Hannah tried to look past her into the house, but Grace took the basket and shooed Hannah with her hand, shutting the door.

Dr. Avery came with vials and herbs, but he had little more to offer than Grace had. "He's very ill, Grace. Is he still sane?"

"Yes, but it's difficult to wake him."

"Call for Thomas Metcalf to draw up his will, he knows the words to use. Jonathan would want that. I'll stay as a witness."

With her heart in her throat, Grace ran to Thomas Metcalf's home, but he couldn't be contacted until late evening. Grace returned and encouraged Dr. Avery to go home until morning, then bring Thomas. "Perhaps Jonathan will sleep tonight and have more reserve in the morrow," she said.

On the third day of June, Jonathan's fever broke a bit during the night. He ceased his violent vomiting, but his skin had turned the color of a pumpkin. He stirred and seemed to awaken while Grace changed his bedclothes. He knew his friends were coming.

Dr. Avery and Thomas Metcalf arrived early, and Thomas started right in. "Are you sound of mind? This is your last testament," recited Thomas Metcalf.

"I've thought about this a long time," said Jonathan. "Be

sure you have plenty of ink." Jonathan's dry, cracked lips broke into a weak smile.

Death looming, Jonathan ordered his life and death in detail. "Please don't divulge the contents until I'm gone. Eleazur Lusher and Peter Woodward know that John will be the executor. I wish them to oversee and assist him."

"We have it down, Jonathan. I hope we don't need to verify it in court for a very long time," said Thomas.

Jonathan slid down on the pillows as Metcalf and Avery left. His eyes wouldn't open, even to take Grace's infusion.

Jonathan recovered, but he never recovered his full strength. He relied on his local sons to run the farm. To give his life purpose, he read, prayed, and carried milk from the barn for Grace when Sarah was not about. He helped the boys with light evening chores.

The early morning sun baked the earth into cracked clay. Grace and Jonathan walked up from the barn after milking. The pails Jonathan carried swayed irregularly. Grace reached to take one, thinking the weight was too great for him.

"Two buckets help me balance, Grace," Jonathan protested.

A deep rumble emanated from the earth's throat, and the path shuddered under them. The pails swayed erratically, sloshing the milk. Grace grabbed for a pail but instead caught Jonathan's arm to steady herself. They stopped, using all their will to stand. The ground rolled in waves. The shutters banged against the house. The tops of the trees waved like warning flags on poles.

Everything went still and quiet. Jonathan and Grace looked around. All was intact, except the milk that covered the path and their shoes.

Grace looked at Jonathan, searching for an answer to the unasked questions: *What have we done? Why is God so angry?*

Jonathan remained silent, then he told Grace about the comet. He put both nearly empty buckets in one hand and took Grace's hand in the other. The trembling no longer came from the earth but from their souls.

Jonathan and Grace's lives drifted into a routine. Jonathan, seventy-three, spent more time around the house, for he became too tired to walk any great distance. Grace, seventy-one, continued to have the children's families to dinner one Sabbath a month. Her daughter, daughters-in-law, and Martha brought food. The daughters picked and preserved the harvest, and Grace helped. She brought enough home for Jonathan and herself for winter.

Jonas seldom stopped and never stayed long at the house when he went to Boston for supplies. He feigned that he was too busy farming and providing for Lydia and their four children in Lancaster.

Fall blazed with color where a few trees remained or had started to grow again on the balding Dedham hills. Jonathan and Grace found these autumn evenings more pleasant spent on a bench outside where they listened to the crickets chirp. The sun lingered over the top of the Dedham hills to the west, and Jonathan and Grace watched the show of colors as it disappeared behind the elevation. Just as the sun began to slip behind the hills, a spear of light shot across the sky, heading directly for the center of the sun. It seemed as if it pierced the sun just as it slipped out of sight. The air chilled around them as evening darkened.

"I hope the sun rises on the morrow," said Grace, grabbing Jonathan's hand, dragging him inside. "We've had so many omens."

Grace rushed to the shelf on the north hall wall and lifted the lacquered jug with the Michaelmas daisies. *The daisies are a sign of something coming to an end.* Grace trembled putting her other hand under the jug to secure it. *Yet the daisies are protectors from darkness and evil.* She looked up to the heavens.

Cold and snow set in early, before the leaves fell from the trees. Big limbs thunderously crashed to the ground from the weight of the snow, and Jonathan pulled on his cloak to move branches away from the house. Grace tugged at the collar of his cloak to stop him at the door. "They can lie there until spring."

On December 6, Jonathan did not get out of bed.

"Are you all right? Should I call for Dr. Avery?" Grace reached for her scarf and cape.

"No, Grace," Jonathan said. He put up his hand and waited until Grace returned to his bedside and took it in hers. "You should call for the children."

The Summons

Dark clouds hung over another harsh December day. The early snow had gone, but a sharp north wind blew hard over the bare trees. Jonas and his eight-year-old son, Joshua, were in the barn for morning chores. Lydia carried a pail of milk to the house, her cloak gaping over her swollen belly.

Outside in the dooryard, Lydia was surprised to see Junior rein in his horse and hop down to help her with the pail. Lydia wrapped her arms around him the best she could with her protruding belly and called back to the barn, "We have a visitor."

In the house, Marie, their oldest daughter, stirred the pottage, her skirts hanging dangerously near the embers of the fire. Five-year-old Grace turned a rabbit on a spit.

Junior sat for breakfast as Jonas kicked his boots on the

stone step at the door to release the straw and muck of the barn. The door opened with a blast of cold. Jonas entered followed by Joshua who pushed the door hard to close it against winter's assault.

Before removing his cloak, Jonas strode over to embrace his brother.

"What brings you here? Is Father all right?"

"No," said Junior, and Jonas glanced at Lydia. "He declines daily," Junior went on, "in spite of Mother's and Dr. Avery's remedies."

"What can I do? I'm so far away." Jonas hung his coat on a peg. *I'm far away in many respects.* "I have a family and a farm to run with only an eight-year-old son to help." Jonas nodded toward Joshua.

"There's nothing to do, Jonas. Father just wants to talk with each of his children before he dies."

"Our talks never go well. Father's chosen a bad time to summon me. The crops are in but must be stored. Lydia can't make a trip in her condition." They both looked at Lydia. "I can't leave her."

"Father wants you to come," said Junior.

"He has never favored my life choices. He wrote his will six months ago." Jonas waved his hand dismissively. "Whatever he's decided, Father won't change now. You, John, and George already have his land." Jonas ran his fingers over his head. "I bought my own land here. I'm not coming back."

"I can only do the bidding. Father may not be alive when I return. This may be your last chance."

"Don't make any promises to Mother," said Jonas.

Lydia lay in bed next to Jonas with the bed drapes closed around them. She looked at her husband, who was staring at the canopy. "You must go. You and your father have differences, but he's still your father. He's been nothing but kind and supportive since we married."

"You didn't hear him when he threatened to disown me when I wanted to go to sea. Or when I went to the ironworks."

"You were following your own dreams and beliefs. They differed from his."

"Then he sent me here to Lancaster after I was called to court for wearing great boots. He said I was a disgrace to the family. He didn't want to hear my side, nor did he care when I was totally acquitted." Jonas continued to stare at the canopy of the bed.

"You said you came to Lancaster to get out of Dedham and not be judged by the townspeople. Weren't you as eager to help my father settle the wilderness as your father was to found Dedham?"

"Yes, I was anxious to get away," said Jonas, still not looking at Lydia.

"Then you should go to your father."

Jonas placed his hand on Lydia's bulge, and the baby kicked hard. "You may have another son soon," she said. "As a father, you may learn to see things differently."

Death's Door

Jonas hesitated on the doorstone, wondering why he had come. Then he knocked on the door of his childhood home, remembering when he used to just walk in.

Mary Elizabeth opened the door, wiping her hands on her apron tail. "Jonas!"

"Where's Mother?" asked Jonas, looking past Mary.

Mary Elizabeth tilted her head toward the parlor, taking Jonas's hat and cloak as he shrugged them off. He walked over and put his cold hand on his mother's shoulder as she sat by the bed. Numbed, Grace didn't acknowledge it. Jonathan lay motionless.

After a moment, Grace looked up with tears streaming down her cheeks, then stood and hugged Jonas with her head deep in his shoulder. She moved away and motioned for him to sit in her place.

Mary Elizabeth pulled the window drapes tighter. She had covered all the pictures and mirrors to retain her father's soul a bit longer. Patting her father's hand, she left.

"Jonathan." Grace leaned over, put her hand on his and raised her voice. "Jonathan, Jonas is here. Jonas has come home."

Jonathan's eyes flickered. He pushed himself to his elbows but crumpled back onto the bed.

"Lie there, Father," said Jonas, "You wanted to see me?"

"Aye, son." Jonathan's shaking hand took Jonas's. His grasp was weak, but he seemed to gain energy from the connection. Jonathan coughed and cleared his throat. "I tried, but I didn't get to my father's bedside." He paused as if to muster more energy.

"I know—you told me."

"He left me no land. He left land to my half-brothers. I received only a young daughter's portion." Another pause. Jonathan closed his eyes, and they remained closed. "I will never know why he treated me so, but it has followed me through my whole life."

Jonas swallowed hard but couldn't speak around the lump in his throat. Grace stood by the wall, her hands over her mouth. Her eyes welled.

Jonathan took another long raspy breath and opened his eyes, seeking Jonas's attention. "I have not always approved of your life decisions."

Jonas nodded silently; his jaw firmed.

"I will be giving you no land."

Jonas sat back but didn't release his father's cold hand. Silence hung between them.

"You reflected a part of me. The part that didn't conform." Jonathan gasped. "I followed my religious principles and hopes to provide better for my family—at great risk."

Jonas put his other hand on his father's and bent closer, so he could hear his father's fading voice.

"I feared your choices for your future as I feared mine. You had the courage to explore your own path." Jonathan swallowed. "That both frightened me and made me proud." He closed his eyes again, his hand relaxed in Jonas's. He remained silent a long time.

His rheumy eyes flickered. "A family should always stay together. You always wanted to leave. Will you stay now?" Jonathan's voice became hoarse and labored.

"I never left. I'm here now, Father."

"You will always be a part of this family."

Grace moved to the bedside. Jonas rose to give his mother the chair, but she sat on the bedside, placing her hand on Jonathan's cheek. Jonathan, with shaking arms, reached up to Grace's shoulders and pulled her onto his chest. He put his hand on her head.

"We always promised to keep our family together." His words came out in little more than a sigh.

"A family is made to last forever," whispered Grace for both of them.

EPILOGUE

Like Jonathan Fairbanks, Jonas received no land in his father's will. After providing for Grace's comfort for the remainder of her life, Jonathan left all his children with a substantial inheritance. His house, land, and town privileges went to John, as a primogeniture. George and Jonathan Jr. received land and other items before their father's death, totaling fourteen pounds. Jonas received no land but received fourteen pounds, equivalent to the inheritance of the other sons. Uncommon for the time, Jonathan gave his daughter, Mary, the same fourteen pounds as he had given her brothers, plus a valuable gift of a suit of clothes. Susan, preceding her father in death, left behind five children and her husband, Ralph Daye. They were given smaller amounts. Sarah, Jonathan's granddaughter, inherited a cow.

Grace died in 1673 and Mary in 1674, at which time the colony alerted towns to prepare for war because of colonial and Native unrest. The sons lived to participate in the deadliest per capita and most costly war of this nation, King Philip's War.

Cast of Other Characters

All people named in this book lived in the 1600s, except two, the young sailor and farmer Parker of Watertown. The actual individuals are depicted in historical literature in their general locations and roles at that time. Their descriptions, thoughts, words, actions and relationship with the Fairbanks and Prescott families are fictitious.

England

King James (reign 1603–1625)   King Charles I (reign 1625–1649)
Oliver Cromwell (leader 1653–1658)   King Charles II (reign 1660–1685)
Archbishop George Abbot (1611–1633)
Archbishop William Laud (1633–1640)

John Fairbanks Family of England

Only wives and children represented in this book are noted

Margaret Symmes	Isabella Staincliffe	Ellen Parker
1. John	1. Susan	1. Anna
2. George	2. Jonathan	2. Michael
Other children		3. Marie
		4. Jeremy
		5. Susan
		6. Abigail

Massachusetts Bay Colony

Mr. Francis Higginson (arr. 1629)
John Winthrop Sr. Governor of MBC (arr. 1630)
Sir Richard Saltonstall (Watertown-1630)
Samuel Cole (First Boston innkeeper-1630)
John Coggan (First Boston trader-1633/34)
John Cowdall (Boston/Nashaway trader-abt. 1643)
Captain Thomas Cromwell (Buccaneer for Earl of Warwick, d. 1649)

Religious Dissidents

Roger Williams (Providence, RI-1636)
Anne Hutchison (Portsmouth, RI-1637)
John Wheelwright (New Hampshire 1637/38)

Watertown

John Vahan (bachelor with house-1633)
Timothy Hawkins (John Vahan's friend)
Captain Thomas Cakebread
Robert Feke
John Oldham (Watertown trader)
Oldham's Nephews: John and Thomas
George Munnings (Watertown Tavern-1634)

Concord (Musketaquid)

Samuel Willard (trader, military leader, founder-1635)
Matthew Mitchell (Yorkshire trader-1635)

Yorkshiremen

Abraham and Bridget Shaw   George and William Bearstow
Reverend Richard Denton   James Draper (weaver)
Michael Matthews (merchant) Richard Hartley (merchant)
Farrar Brothers

Dedham (Tiot)

George and William Bearstow (from Halifax Parish)
Richard Crossman (Hammersmith with Jonas Fairbanks)
James Draper (associated with Richard Hartley)
John and Hannah Dwight (sponsored Jonathan Fairbanks)
Son, John Dwight (lost in Wigwam Swamp)
Thomas Fisher (built first meetinghouse)
Goodwife Genery (lady in church)
Goodwife Hinsdale (lady in church)
Richard Hartley (English merchant-Dedham/New London)
Ezekiel Holliman (Dedham/Providence)
Ralph (Lancaster) and John Houghton (Dedham/Medfield,
made Fairbanks Chest)
Edward Kemp (blacksmith)
John Roper and son (possibly built Fairbanks House)
Joseph Kingsbury (carpenter/mechanic)
Abraham and Bridget Shaw (West Yorkshire/Watertown/Dedham)
Richard Wheeler (Dedham/Medfield/ Lancaster)

Churchmen
Mr. John Allin
Elder John Hunting

Doctors
Henry Deengains
William Avery

Constable
Richard Elice

Millwrights
Abraham Shaw
John Elderkin (Lynn/
Dedham)
Nathanial Whiting

First Militia of Dedham
Daniel Morse, Sgt. of Arms
Abraham Shaw (clerk)
Captain Thomas Cakebread

Teachers
Ralph Wheelock
Michael Metcalf Sr.

Massachusetts Military Company
Captain Robert Sedgewick
Captain Eleazur Lusher (1638)
Anthony Fisher (1644)
George Fairbanks (1644)
Robert Crossman (1644)

George Bearstow (1644)
Lt. Joshua Fisher (1640)
Captain Daniel Fisher (1640)
Richard Fairbank (1654)

Various Dedham Selectmen 1669–1668

Edward Alleyn (clerk)
John Kingsbury
Eleazur Lusher (clerk)
John Dwight
John Hayward
Samuel Morse (first clerk)
Michael Metcalf, Sr.
Henry Chickering
Peter Woodward
Michael Powell (merchant)
Timothy Dwight
Joseph Kingsbury

Henry Phillips
Anthony Fisher
Edward Richards
Joshua Fisher
Daniel Fisher
John Gaye
John Hunting
Richard Everett
Henry Wright
Ralph Daye
William Avery

Indigenous People
Tribes
Massachusett-Nipmuck
Narragansett-Sachem Miantonomo
Neponsett
Nipmuck (John Speen and Thomas Speen)
Pequot-Sagamore John
Powhatan-Pocahontas, Amonute – Matoaka
Mohawk-west
Montauk-Cockenoe
Mohegan-Sachem Uncas
Pocumtuck
Ponkapoag

First Praying Village – Natick
Chickataubutt (Neponsett)
Grandson Josias
Sachem John of Mystic
Sachem Wompituk of Tiot
Waban-Waanton/Mistwaben of the Massachusetts
Thomas or Weegramomenet (son of Wab)

Englishmen and Organizations Assisting Indigenous
England's Society for Propagating the Gospel in New England
Committee for Education and Civilization of the Indians 1646
MBC Committee: Mr. John Eliot, Mr. Thomas Shepard,
Mr. John Allin (Dedham)
Mr. John Eliot (apostle to the Indians)
Daniel Gookin (First Governmental Superintendent of
Praying Indians 1656–1686)
Major Humphrey Atherton (First Superintendent of Indian
Affairs 1658, Natick)

Hammersmith Ironworks

Promoters
John Winthrop Jr.
Dr. Robert Childes
Captain Sedgwick of the Massachusetts Military Co.

Managers
Richard Leader
William Osbourn
John Gifford

Blacksmiths
Joseph Jenke and Joseph Jenke Jr.

Workers
Francis Perry (carpenter)
Roger Tyler (furnace)
John Diven (potter)
Theophilus Bayley (boatman)

Forgers
John Turner
John Vinton
John Francis
Quentin Prey (and carpenter)
Henry and James Leonard
Ralph Russell
Nicholas Pinnion
Jonas Fairbanks (and carpenter)
Robert Crossman (and carpenter)
Ralph Russell

Natives
Thomas and Anthony (woodmen)

Scotsmen
From the Battle of Dunbar to the Massachusetts Bay Colony

Tavern Keeper
Joseph Armitage Sr.

Charlestown
John Founell (millwright)
Mordecai MacLeod (indentured Scotsman)

Lancaster
John Ball (prepared Nashaway)
Richard Linton (prepared Nashaway)
Lawrence Waters (prepared Nashaway)
John Kerley Sr. (early settler)
John Kerley Jr. and Elizabeth White (tore banns for marriage)
Lidia Lewis (friend of Lydia Prescott and Mordecai MacLeod)
John Rugg (husband of both Martha and Hannah Prescott)
John Tinker (trader and magistrate)
Joseph Rowlandson (religious leader)

Named Fictional Characters
Thomas – young sailor on voyage
Farmer Parker – boatman up Charles River to Watertown

AUTHOR'S NOTE

Made to Last Forever is written as a story. When I started researching the family a lifetime ago, I only wanted the facts. *Don't tell me if it's not a fact.* Over time, I learned that few wanted in depth fact driven knowledge of history, they want the story. Rudyard Kipling said, "If history were taught in the form of stories, it would never be forgotten." This story connects facts and actual events through theories and intuition.

The original Fairbanks House, the oldest frame house still standing in North America, is essentially unchanged from its beginning in 1637. The Fairbanks House is now a museum operated by the Fairbanks Family of America, Inc., and is a National Landmark and symbol of the family legacy, Dedham history, the Massachusetts Bay Colony (MBC), and the nation's heritage. Unlike the elite, military, clerics or those who kept detailed records, the Fairbankses represent the humble common people that made up the fabric of this country and whose accomplishments continue to shape our nation.

This book was started during COVID, which was eerily like the 1625 plague in England. John Fairbanks, the English father of Jonathan Fairbanks, died during the height of the plague. His will was preserved, giving us a possible glimpse into the relationship between the father and son.

The ship manifest is lost or destroyed like 50 percent of all ship manifests of the 1600s. The account of the voyage is modeled after ship journals of others. A nine-year-old boy such as Jonas was surely fascinated by the trip. His young sea hand friend, Thomas, is one of the few named fictional characters. Thomas provides Jonas's possible connection with Captain Thomas Cromwell, the buccaneer, whose own story is true. We don't know any actual relationship between Capt. Cromwell and

Jonas. Dedham did receive one of the bells Cromwell brought into Boston. Nothing comes to fruition in the Fairbanks story that is not supported by fact. Jonas did not go to sea.

The first record we have of Jonathan in the MBC is March 23, 1636/37 when he was unanimously accepted as a proprietor into Dedham. However, he was the first man to receive a lot in the second round of Dedham grants which probably puts him in MBC before that time. Jonathan's relationship to Richard Fairbanks is not known. We know Richard Fairbanks and his wife came to Boston in 1633 according to church records.

Jonas' involvement in Hammersmith is documented on the "Ironworks Papers" found at the Baker Library at Harvard Business School, Harvard University. Jonas's court case and those of other ironworkers are found in the records of the Essex County Court.

The Fairbankses and Prescotts were likely friends; both emigrated from Sowerby, West Yorkshire, England. The occasions for Jonas going to Lancaster, though unknown, are based on real Lancaster events. Many historians relate that Jonas went to Lancaster, Massachusetts, to help "found" that town. Building the meetinghouse was one of those occasions. Jonas was allowed to marry Lydia Prescott as the first event held in the new meetinghouse and the first wedding registered in Lancaster.

The father-son relationship of Jonathan and Jonas is also unknown. Jonas appears to differ from his brothers. He is the only son who strayed from the Dedham area or worked in a less than Puritan environment. Jonathan is documented as very ill in 1651 and wrote his will in June 1668. The omens preceding Jonathan's death are documented events in New England history. He died in December that same year. Jonathan's will indicates a resolved relationship with Jonas, if there were difficulties in earlier years.

All named characters, except two, are real persons who

Jonathan and his family might have known. Much information for this book was found in T*he Early Records of the Town of Dedham, Massachusetts*, both volumes 3 and 4 by Don Gleason Hill, et al. The information about the indigenous came mostly from volume 4 and Rev. John Eliot and Superintendent Daniel Gookin's accounts. John Fairbanks of England and George Fairbanks of England were found in more current issues of the *New England Genealogical and Historical Society Journal* as is the letter to Jonathan from Richard Hartley. The poem in Jonas and Lydia's courtship is a 1600s poem found in the *Journal of American Folklore* in an1948 issue. We can always strive to get closer to the actual story through our continued shared research.

Almost all people in America that descend from a Fairbanks are descendants of Jonathan and Grace Fairbanks, the first immigrants. The living descendants number in the tens of thousands. The present-day Fairbanks family is still cohesive through the Fairbanks Family in America, Inc. They preserve the 1637 family house for the family, Dedham, and the nation. They welcome extended family and members from across the nation to a yearly national reunion and open the home to the public during the summers. All who are interested in our nation's history and growth may also become members of the organization of the Fairbanks Family in America, Inc.

To book a tour of the historic Fairbanks House or donate to help preserve and restore the house, go to www.Fairbankshouse.org. To find this author go to www.FairbanksHistory.com.

ACKNOWLEDGMENTS

Made to Last Forever results from a collaboration of amazing individuals. Heartfelt gratitude to all those who helped bring this story to life. The book gains meaning when its words touch readers. By reading, sharing and reviewing this book, you become part of this "book's family."

My parents, Lloyd J. Fairbanks and Betty (Schweizer) Fairbanks, taught me the ethics of hard work and dedication.

The Fairbanks House, Fairbanks Family in America, Inc. played a vital role. Betina Blood, past president and board of directors member; Stuart Christie, docent and historian; and Kathleen Milster, visitor coordinator, all encouraged me and pre-read the manuscript to assure the facts align with those of the Fairbanks House. Thank you to Johanna McBrien, the Dedham Museum & Archive executive director, and Heather Lennon, the Lancaster Historical Society president, for their valuable resources.

In England, Ruth Fairbanks and James Landberg, the Howard family, David Glover of the Halifax Antiquarian Society, Bob Abel of the Earby Historical Society, West Yorkshire Archives Service, and relatives Christine Butterworth and Barbara Perkins all helped enrich the historical context.

Thanks to Saugus Iron Works NPS, and papers at the Baker Library at Harvard Business School for insights into the family and national industrial history.

My writing journey was guided by the Gulf Coast Writer's Association, Hurricane Critique Group, the Historical Novel Society, Jill Dawson of Gold Dust Mentoring, and editors Lori Swick, Cindy Marsch, and Reyne Shleifer.

To my family: John, my husband, and Shawnee Korff, my sister—thank you for your unwavering support. Macy, my daughter, championed my creativity. Aaron, my son, and Evan Williams were my tech heroes. Allison Stabile, you were my reader model. To my blog followers at Fairbankshistory.com— you kept me motivated.

A special thanks to early readers: Connie Twiss, Twila Williams, Barbara Taylor, Janette Paull, and Linda Patti.

Thank you to all readers—you give this book purpose. Please spread this bit of fascinating history with others. With heartfelt gratitude.

ABOUT THE AUTHOR

 **Sharmin Fairbanks McKenny** grew up on a traditional family farm and flew an airplane before she drove a car. After graduating with honors and a master's degree in nursing, Sharmin cared for early kidney transplant, burn, critical, and trauma patients and was a pioneering civilian emergency helicopter flight nurse.

Ms. McKenny visited all lands of her ancestors in England and the USA, including the 1637 Fairbanks House in Dedham, Massachusetts. She is a board member and acting historian of the Fairbanks Family of America, Inc.

Sharmin and her husband, John, live in Florida. They have two adult children, Aaron and Macy, and a granddog. Sharmin enjoys reading, writing, golf, travel, her Orphan Orchid Program, historical research, and blogging at Fairbankshistory. com

BOOK CLUB DISCUSSIONS

Thank you for coming on this journey into the past to a foreign land, to a wilderness being settled and into a family with the same trials and triumphs as many of our own. Please leave your personal review of this book on Amazon and GoodReads. You will find more questions and Book Club Party Ideas for this book at FairbanksHistory.com/book-club-discussion. You can contact this author at FairbanksHistory.com to ask questions or plan a book club author appearance or Zoom call.

Questions for Made to Last Forever

1. Can you relate to any of the main characters? Do you know people who remind you of one of the main characters?

2. Have you or someone you know moved to a new country or region to settle in very different conditions or in a different culture? How did you/they deal with it?

3. Does age effect how we think or act? Are innate, environmental or learned traits stronger? Did Jonas and Lydia differ from their siblings because of their nature or their environmental influences?

4. Does birth order effect the dynamics of a family? Are you an only child, firstborn, middle child, or baby of the family? Are expectations, tasks, responsibilities today the same as they were in the past? Why did they practice primogeniture: the first son receiving the land, house, town benefits? Was it fair? Does this happen today?

5. The Puritans left England because they couldn't practice religion in the way the believed was right. In the New World, the Puritans banished anyone who didn't practice as they did. Was this right? Do we form groups around religions, beliefs, or cultural differences? Do different groups treat others differently? How does today's world "banish" or deal with people they think are different?

6. This book identifies events in history that seems to repeat itself. How was COVID like the Plague of 1625? Name other events that have repeated themselves. By understanding history, do we respond differently to an event that appears to be repeating itself?

7. Omens and superstitions were a way of life for Puritans. God's pleasure or wrath was often cited as the cause for good or bad occurrences. There were many days of thanksgiving and days of humiliation. The Michaelmas daisies on the black jug, earthquakes, and comets were also omens. Do we have omens and superstitions today? Can you name some sports figures who wear special clothes during games or perform special rituals before an event?

8. Jonas wanted to make his own life decisions. Why were his parents so against them? Was Jonas leaving the family by following his own ambitions? Did you follow your parents' plans for you?

9. What might have happened if Jonas didn't return to his father's deathbed? Is this history repeating itself? Is it important to connect with family members before their death?

Family

Exploring your family history helps you to know who you are, where you came from, why you think or behave as you do, and how your family shaped the world you live in. Knowing your family history can strengthen your identity and give you a feeling of belonging. It can also spark a greater interest in the past, especially when you realize your family lived through and participated in historical events. Understanding their values, struggles and their accomplishments can inspire your personal growth and pride. Their history helps maintain stories, traditions, recipes, and rituals that keep a family connected. Family isn't always defined by blood. It includes those who care for you, act in your best interest, and are there for you when you need them.

Use these last pages to write your family lineage.